IONA CARROLL

FAMILIAR

YET FAR

*To Mike and Andy
with best wishes
from Iona Carroll*

The Story of OISIN KELLY

Mauve
Square
Publishing

First Published 2015 by Mauve Square Publishing
www.mauvesquare.com

A catalogue entry of this publication is available from the British Library.

www.ionacarroll.co.uk

Cover artwork copyright © Kit Foster
www.kitfosterdesign.com

Cover photographs by © Noela Mattiazzi

Windmill illustrations by © I.E.McGregor

ISBN: 978-1-909411-39-5

Typeset in Georgia

ACKNOWLEDGEMENTS

This novel has been a journey for me and I would like to thank the following for their encouragement and support.

Marie and John Livingstone.

For the cover photograph and support, a very special thanks to my friend of many years, Noela Mattiazzi.

I would like to mention my appreciation to fellow writer and friend, Oliver Eade for his encouragement and belief in me as a writer.

Pearl Glasheen on the Downs.

To the many people I have met along the way. Nothing exists in isolation and what I have observed has benefitted me in the writing of this novel.

Thanks to the editorial work done by Mauve Publishing and for their continual support of my writing.

And finally to my husband, Iain, as always.

For my daughter

Isla McGregor

Courage comes from love for others

GLOSSARY OF AUSTRALIAN WORDS AND EXPRESSIONS

Amber fluid	Beer
Arv, Avro	Afternoon
Barbie	Barbeque
Barney	Fight, scruffle
Bonzer	Great, ripper
Buckley's chance or Buckley's	No chance
Bugger all	Very little
Buggered	Exhausted
Buggered if I know	I have no idea
Bullamanka	Imaginary place way beyond the black stump
Bundy	Bundaberg. Bundy is the usual term for rum which is produced here.
Bushed	Exhausted
Chook/s	Poultry, hens
Crows fly backwards	Outback
Dole bludger	Person who lives on benefits and avoids paid work unjustifiably
Drongo	Idiot
Ekka	Brisbane Agricultural Show
Fair dinkum	True, genuine
Fit as a Mallee bull	Very fit and strong
Game as Ned Kelly	Courageous. Ned Kelly was an infamous bushranger
Gone troppo	Escaped to a state of tropical madness

Hard yakka	Hard work
Hooroo	Goodbye
Kangaroos loose in the top paddock	Someone whose not very intelligent
Mad as a meat axe	Angry
Mouth like the bottom of a cocky's cage	Dry, usually after a drinking bout. Cocky (Cockatoo)
Nasho	National Serviceman
Old Queenslander	Traditional weatherboard house built on stilts in Queensland
Pavlova	A famous dessert made with fresh fruit, meringues and cream
Pom, Pommie	Englishman/woman
Rellies	Relatives
She'll be apples	It's OK
Stone the crows	Exclamation, good grief.
Strewth	Exclamation
Stubby	A 375 ml beer bottle
Tucker	Food, a meal
Unit	Flat, apartment
Up at sparrow's fart	Early rising, dawn
Ute	Utility truck, pickup
What d'ya reckon?	What do you think?
Woopwoop (1)	Back of beyond, isolated place
Woopwoop (2)	Call of the barking owl
Yabber	Talk incessantly

KILGOOLGA 1857

An argument had taken place at the top paddock near where the rough ground gave way to a dry bed gully. The gully, a river in the good times, was dust now except for damp spots beneath the stones. No rain had fallen there for six months. It was here that Heinrich Seefeldt argued with Jamie Paterson about the line of a boundary fence. When Heinrich returned home in the late afternoon, there was blood on his shirt and revenge in his heart.

In Kilgoolga, Heinrich was famous for his quick temper. It was a fact that his enemies outnumbered his friends. Those friends who were of a forgiving nature attributed the young German's often violent nature to the circumstances of his life. He was single, living an isolated existence with his Pastor Uncle Albert. Everyone in Kilgoolga agreed that the elderly pastor was a severe and God-fearing man who spoke no English at all and he would have to be difficult to live with. Heinrich's enemies, on the other hand, would hear none of it. In their view, the German was nothing but an ill-mannered bully and to give excuses for his often violent temperament was tantamount to exonerating a rather unpleasant young man from taking responsibility for his anti-social behaviour. Everyone knew that Heinrich would not listen to another's opinion if it differed from his own. Once he had stormed out of the

1

Kilgoolga hotel in a fury. He had argued about the price paid for some of his sheep and refusing to listen to anyone, had thrown a chair across the room and overturned a table. So the generous and the not so generous were in agreement that it was best not to get into an argument with young Heinrich Seefeldt especially after he had drunk a few too many beers. It seemed that the only person Heinrich would take any notice of was his older sister, Lotte, two years his senior and married to Cyril Bradshaw. But even Lotte could not pacify the young hothead when the temper was on him.

Nor did Heinrich see eye to eye with his brother-in-law, the Englishman, Cyril Bradshaw. Lotte had married well and the Bradshaws owned property as far as the eye could see. Heinrich's two thousand acre holding was on poorer land. Toil was virtue enough and possession of the land, a God-given right, Heinrich thought enviously as he surveyed his brother-in-law's vast property. On the other hand, Cyril Bradshaw did not hold much store with Heinrich's opinions for the Englishman was the son of an aristocratic Lord. Cyril viewed his place in the universe as a divine right and he considered Heinrich a lesser mortal who was, after all, nothing but a poor German immigrant. However, the truth was stranger still. Cyril Bradshaw, although he was the son of an English Lord, happened to be the result of a rather messy encounter between the self-indulgent younger brother of His Lordship and a dairymaid from the village. This fact Cyril carefully kept to himself and the real story of his parentage was not uncovered until after his death at the age of eighty-four.

Cyril Bradshaw, it transpired, had been given a small annual stipend and, at the age of twenty, sent packing to the Colonies along with all the other miscreants and malcontents and those respectable citizens, all hoping to make a fortune so far from decent civilisation. This was Lord Bradshaw's method of putting out of sight his younger brother's unfortunate bastard son, a solution that Cyril's

2

father was totally in agreement with for he was now a respectable married man himself with an equally respectful and dull wife of his own class. However, the boy would not be able to lay claims of any sort on the stately home and everything that went with it. The only stipulation for such generosity on the part of Lord Bradshaw was that Cyril could never return to England and, if he did by some miracle manage to make enough money to do so, he would not be welcomed by any of his father's family or by any of their descendants. However, should Cyril apply himself, Lord Bradshaw said and he added with all the condescending attitude that had been bred into his class for generations, then Cyril might indeed prosper on the other side of the earth. Of Cyril's mother, the unfortunate dairymaid, nothing was mentioned and she was to die prematurely, a week after her son set foot in the Colony of New South Wales.

A few weeks after his arrival in Sydney Town, Cyril met a pastoralist who was busy making a name for himself in the new colony and as luck would have it, he took rather a liking to the young man. This pastoralist had managed to acquire a considerable property west of the Blue Mountains and he saw Cyril's potential. Having befriended the young man and liked what he saw, the next logical step was to employ Cyril to work on his vast acreage. Here Cyril gained the knowledge needed to deal with the livestock and the crops, a necessary requirement to have in this new land which was so different in every way from the green pastures of England. The ambitious Cyril developed and grew more confident. In a very short time he was able to gain the trust of the pastoralist to such an extent that more and more responsibility, which included the management of the men, was assigned to him. Now Cyril spoke with authority and was put in charge of both freemen and convicts. He was a hard task master but he had a way of getting what he wanted done. He received a measure of loyalty from his men but not much liking. After three years the young man who had been so ruthlessly expelled from the land of his birth had aspirations to become a gentleman pastoralist himself. It was time now for him to look around this new world and make a name for himself in it. This was the way that Cyril hoped to put the bitter expulsion he had felt from Lord Bradshaw's treatment of him out of his mind forever. Other white settlers to this alien country often suffered a sometimes painful transition that living in the far flung part of the British Empire caused. Depression, melancholy and despair were visited upon many a poor soul but young Cyril was one of those fortunate people who saw potential in the new land. He very quickly realised that the blue green grasslands of his new home would bring a prosperity never dreamed of back in the Old Country. He accepted that the isolation and hardship was a challenge for him but after all, there was no way back. Over the years, he was to recall the injustice of it all and perhaps he did retain a degree of bitterness towards the privileged Lord Bradshaw and all he stood for, but he kept these thoughts to himself. He remained a private man to the end of his days and rarely spoke of his early life. In the far flung colony he was to become a very rich man and, if at times he perhaps would have liked to return to England and flaunt his new wealth and influence, he never did.

So, in the summer of 1841 Cyril Bradshaw, acting on the advice and influence of his benefactor, borrowed money from a London bank, hired a farm manager, O'Leary and his wife, a stockman, four ticket of leave men and headed north. Their journey took six months. They camped under the stars. Pushing the plodding bullocks ever onward they navigated the swollen rivers and the high mountain crossings. They travelled at the pace of the bullocks and day after weary day they made their way north. Food and water became scare half way and they often had to walk and ride through the night to the next watering hole. Sometimes there were dray tracks left by other pioneering folk; often they pushed their way forward without any knowledge of where they were. And all the time the guns were at the ready in case they met a tribe of hostile blacks. A few properties they came upon were deserted and they rested there glad of a respite and grateful for the shelter. But the ghosts of the men and women who had tried to make a living in the wilderness unsettled them and they moved on. The wilderness – the lonely, nameless wilderness – and the endless plains they travelled on held the hushed secrets of the bush and these lay hidden to their eyes. This was a land to conquer not to understand and young Cyril was the patriarchal white man leading his small team into the unknown.

Finally, the land they had come for was there and it stretched to the horizon as far as the eye could see. The little band set to work. They felled the trees and fenced the land. They lived in two bark humpies. Cyril and three of his men travelled once again across the mountain range to Brisbane Town to buy cattle and sheep. One of his men got into a drunken brawl and was left to die outside the hotel's door. Cyril hired three more tough men and returned to his homestead. Four years later he had survived drought and flood, falling prices, failed crops and the loneliness. In the early days they had come close to starvation. Once they were without flour and down to three bags of sugar. That year they survived on pigweed, a few sparse vegetables they had somehow managed to cultivate and two of the starving beasts they slaughtered. Cyril Bradshaw, with the help of his little band of workers, had become a rich man despite his earlier disappointments and now, with land that he could call his own, he was someone who carried respect and authority in the town named Kilgoolga. Lord Bradshaw and all the Bradshaws back in England would never have believed it possible. Now it was time for the young gentleman squatter to find a wife.

He didn't have to look far. Lotte Seefeldt and her brother, Heinrich together with their Pastor Uncle Albert had taken up a two thousand acre holding on the boundary of the Bradshaw property. When Cyril first caught sight of the young German woman he decided there and then, that this was the wife for him. The Seefeldts were hard-working and frugal. Cyril admired this. Lotte looked the land in the face and never relented. She looked at Cyril and felt the same. It was to be a marriage of their time. Love did not come into the equation. They were married in the small Lutheran Church by Pastor Albert on a hot summer's day. Heinrich whispered the German vows to Cyril and Cyril answered rigidly in English. Then he kissed his bride. The next day, all were once again at work.

Heinrich, left to run his farm himself, set to work too and with a determination now that his sister had left to live in the big homestead, two hours ride away. Ambition burned in Heinrich but there was envy there as well and this, combined with his quick temper, was to be his undoing. His anger was directed not to his brother-in-law or to his sister but to his neighbour, the Scottish farmer, Jamie Paterson who had recently taken up land bordering the Seefeldt boundary fence. Jamie was as greedy for land as Heinrich. There was bound to be a clash.

It took three years for the hostility that both men felt for each other to come to the surface. First it started as a verbal altercation at the boundary fence and then one dreadful day, something far, far worse.

Heinrich pulled on the reins of his black stallion and, slipping from the saddle, called out for his sister, Lotte.

6

When she heard his cry, she left her work at the dairy house and ran outside into the bright sunlight. She had just started turning the butter churn. Her brother stood before her. And he trembled.

"Jamie Paterson is dead." He spoke in German. His eyes told it all.

"You young fool."

No need for the 'how' or the 'why' that would come later. Now there was urgency.

"Saddle my pony," she ordered. "Bring two shovels. Say nothing."

Back into the dark, cool homestead she ran to fill a saddlebag with water and German biscuits newly baked that morning. Instructions to her children:

"You collect the eggs. You weed the vegetable garden."

She scooped her sleeping baby from the cradle and gave instructions in broken English to Mrs O'Leary:

"Herr Heinrich and I, we need to ride. We return at sunset."

Mr Bradshaw away for three weeks in Brisbane, buying more sheep and he would not return for two months, thank God.

Then she swung her body into the saddle, no side saddle nonsense for Lotte Bradshaw and she tucked her thick black serge skirt around the saddle and tied her baby Rachael to her chest with a silken cord. On her head she wore her cabbage tree palm hat for the sun was already burning and there was much to do.

Brother and sister rode in silence for they could ride all day and still be on Bradshaw land, half the size of Wales before the boundary fence. They rode for an hour over the dry yellow plain until they reached the gully at the top paddock. Kangaroos fled from them, alarmed by the sound of horses' hooves on the dry soil and they heard the sound of a curlew. At the river bank Heinrich, astride his horse stared down at the body of Jamie Paterson but he didn't say a word. The heat rose from the ground. Here was a place of death and not a breath of air. The silence was a tomb.

Jamie Paterson lay face down on the ground with a wound the size of a cricket ball on his right temple. Black flies had already gathered and swarmed and settled on the dried blood but Jamie Paterson looked quite peaceful, lying there as if he were sleeping. Baby Rachael started to cry. Lotte lifted the baby into her arms and unbuttoned her blouse. The hot sun rose high in the midday sky. There was no time to lose.

"GRABE!" (Dig) It was a command.

Heinrich stared down at the body at his feet. He did not know what to do. He was helpless in front of his sister.

"GRABE!"

Then Heinrich dug. The ground was softer near where Jamie Paterson lay at the gully bed. Heinrich was strong. He lifted the heavy stones as if they were pebbles. The soil was damp there and he could dig. Lotte lay her baby to sleep under the shade of a wide spread acacia tree, its bright leaves gave shade. She took the second shovel and dug. Brother and sister did not speak until the hole was deep enough.

"JETZT ESSEN WIR!!" (Now we eat)

The German words sounded harsh on the still, silent plain.

After eating, they rested on the river bank away from the hole and the dead man. Neither spoke. The only sound came from the black flies that descended onto their food and circled around their heads. It was as if there was nothing else in the world but the cloudless sky above them and the loneliness of their thoughts which quietened everything. But Lotte knew what to do next. Together, brother and sister pulled the clothes from the body of Jamie Paterson and removed his leather boots so that he lay naked before them, growing more rigid as the day wore on. Then Lotte took a

8

broken spear, a black fella's spear that she had brought with her from the homestead and had carefully pinned beneath her skirts as she rode. Handing the weapon to Heinrich she said, and her voice was as cold as the frost of a winter's morning:

"STAB HIM NOW! THERE, IN THE CHEST! DO IT NOW! DO IT NOW BEFORE HE IS STIFF!"

But Heinrich stood, unable to move. Then Lotte held the spear high above her head and pierced the white flesh of Jamie Paterson. Drove the sharp point deeper and deeper through his chest until the deed was done.

On the river bank beneath the acacia tree, baby Rachael let out a cry.

"We take the spear and we end it... NOW!!"

Then Heinrich could move and he obeyed his sister. Together they clasped the spear and pulled it free. They turned the naked body of Jamie Paterson so they could not see his face and pushed the body into the grave they had made for him. Heinrich shovelled the brown soil of the river bed over him and placed the heavy stones on top while his sister looked on, her baby at her breast.

They buried Jamie Paterson's boots and his clothes a mile from the gully and the tired horses took them home. Above them black clouds gathered high in the afternoon sky. In a few weeks' time there would be a river where the gully was now. At the homestead Lotte carefully washed the blood from the black fella's spear and returned it to the shed where it had been before.

Heinrich was broken. He took his sister's hands in his while his eyes begged for mercy. Lotte's blue eyes looked into her brother's brown ones. She whispered in German:

"Gott weird dein richter sein." (God will be your judge)

She turned away. She had saved her beloved brother from the hangman's noose but now her children needed her.

CHAPTER ONE

The young man sitting by himself sat in such a way that his fellow travellers were reluctant to start up a conversation with him. In fact, he had spent all the time staring out the train window, so deep in thought that it seemed to those around him that here was someone who was best left alone. Someone, who by his very posture and sad expression had no desire to engage in banalities with strangers and, after glancing at the young man, people concluded quite rightly that to intrude on his privacy would not be welcomed. So the young man sat in silence.

Occasionally he would take an envelope from his pocket and examine the contents of it. And close his eyes. He had already been on the train for eight hours. He viewed the landscape as dreary and the monotonous trees tired him. Once or twice when the train stopped at stations – some with unpronounceable names – he left the compartment and walked up and down the platform and hoped that the exercise would help ease the tedium of the journey. The strong smell of the eucalyptus at these stations filled his lungs. He had never in his life experienced anything like this and he wasn't sure whether he liked it or not. It was almost as if he had suddenly arrived on a different planet. He had made a hasty decision to come halfway across the world to this distant country and it was his hope that the very remoteness of the land around him would neatly sever any ties he had had with his past life. The second time he left the train he decided it wasn't worth the effort and the best option was to remain on board until the end of his journey, a journey that never seemed to want to end but just to go on and on, tediously.

The conductor had been curious when he checked the young man's ticket.

"You've a journey ahead of ya, mate," he said jovially. "Ya don't look as if ya are from round here?"

The young man frowned.

"Just been in your country three weeks."

"Welcome to God's own country then, mate. Is that an Irish accent…?"

The young man didn't answer. He had no wish to be drawn into a conversation as to his nationality or the reasons for him being where he was at this particular moment in time so he just nodded and hoped that would be enough. It was and the conductor moved on calling out for more tickets to stamp. *Aye, I'm an Irishman right enough*, the young man thought to himself, *from Ballybeg, and here I am so far from where I belong - but where do I belong now?*

The compartment had emptied at the last station leaving just a group of about twenty young soldiers and four young girls. The soldiers were in good spirits and spent the time drinking beer and playing cards. Good natured, they all looked fit and healthy and flirted with the girls when they pushed their way along the narrow passageway between the rows of seats. The soldiers were on their way north to re-join their regiment. This was not a country torn apart by war. This was a peaceful land and although their fathers and grandfathers had fought in lands so far away, no wars had ever been fought on this nation's soil and the only blood spilled here had been by pale skinned invaders who had no need to declare war. But these young men would soon be called upon to fight again as their fathers had done, in a war not of their making, in a jungle in a foreign land and against an enemy that the politicians told them to kill. The young men did not know that this was about to happen and were cheery and enjoying the long train journey. They hadn't bothered the young Irishman and he sat quietly at the back of the compartment trying to make sense of where he was and what he was doing and why he was sitting in a train that never seemed to be going to reach its destination but just went on and on and on... ?

The cold wind whipped up from the Forth and funnelled through to Princes Street so that people had to scurry along the wet pavements in silent, endless waves and all of them seemed to be intent on finding shelter as soon as they could. Oisin Kelly pulled his coat collar higher around his neck and pushed his way through the crowd. He had lived in Edinburgh for three years and discovered quite surprisingly, that he rather enjoyed the city life. Living here was such a contrast to his home back in the West of Ireland, in Ballybeg. In Ballybeg everyone knew everyone else and there was no place to be yourself. *Just do what is expected of you*, thought the young Oisin, now twenty-six. He had a brother back there, Declan, he would tell people and a spoilt younger sister named Mary but he was careful not to mention his elder brother, Frankie, the priest. At least Oisin thought his brother was still a priest; nothing had been heard of Father Frankie for years. But people in the city weren't too bothered either way and Oisin rather liked that. Gave him a feeling of anonymity that wouldn't happen back home: 'Oh, you're Mad Mick's nephew' or 'that English girl, she's you're mother.' That was what you were back there, put in a pigeon hole. Well, if he'd stayed in Ballybeg, that's what it would have been but he'd got out, thanks to his 'Mad Uncle Mick' who wasn't perhaps as mad as they all thought, God rest his soul. If Mick hadn't instructed his young nephew to, 'take the box and all its contents to Silvio Luchetta', Oisin would have, no doubt, stayed in Ballybeg like the rest of them. But he'd come to Edinburgh, met Silvio Luchetta and his family, decided he rather liked the city and stayed. *All the mysteries are solved now and Mick is at peace at last, thanks be to God*, he thought and he quickened his pace.

Life in the city suited him just fine. Back in Ballybeg, all people talked about was everyone else for there wasn't much else to occupy them except the weather and the seasons. Oisin, walking faster, neatly avoided a large black umbrella which was positioned in such a way that it almost stabbed his eye out. In Ballybeg your life was mapped out. *That's what happened to Mick,* Oisin thought, *and if he was different, so what? Maybe he wasn't mad after all, just different.* And with that thought the young Irishman's spirits lifted despite the weather and the crowds. Because not only did he find living in the city liberating, he was now deliciously, madly, hopelessly and totally in love! And he was in love with the craziest, zaniest, most wonderful girl in the entire world and Oisin Kelly from Ballybeg, West of Ireland had decided to ask her to marry him. He headed for the Mound and the wind wasn't quite so overpowering there and further on to Cecy Stanworth's flat where it wasn't half as cold. Oisin felt his heart beating faster as he anticipated being in the arms of this exciting young woman. Cecy was like no one whom Oisin had ever met before or ever likely to meet again. There are some people who radiate a kind of magic around them and draw you into their web almost without you being aware that this is happening to you. At least, that's what Oisin thought had happened to him when he first noticed Cecy. His first irrational instinct had been to run from her and so avoid anything further. But life sometimes pushes us forward, despite our fears, and forces us down a different path from one we could ever have imagined. And this is what Cecy Stanworth did to the young Irishman from Ballybeg.

He met her at a party. One of those parties where the air is grey with too much smoke and the only food available seems to be somewhere else; where the music is too loud and the company too dull; where youthful couples draped around themselves and people sat in tight groups passing a joint around and saving the world in the process; where the cheap wine was drunk with no thought to the taste or the consequence. This was the sort of party where perceptions and opinions were heard by the more vocal while others listened and tried to make some sense out of what was being said, hoping when their turn came, they could at the very least say something interesting. It was into this mêlée that Oisin found himself and it was here that he first noticed Cecy. She was sitting cross legged on the floor beside a bearded long-haired, youth of about twenty who seemed to be intent on being heard, for Oisin, on the other side of the room, could almost make out what he was saying. The girl seemed totally bored with the young man's enthusiastic ramblings. She appeared unable to move away from him. She sat, expressionless and composed with her eyes fixed ahead of her, not looking at her companion at all but focussed instead on the large macramé wall hanging on the wall opposite, just where Oisin had positioned himself in order to avoid falling over a boy and a girl who were entangled together on the floor. It was the girl's hair that Oisin noticed first. In the dull light of the smoke-filled room he could just make out that the colour was auburn, to her shoulders and held from falling into her eyes by the largest hairpin he had ever seen. Two huge golden circular earrings dangled from her ears. Here was someone who loved to

14

adorn herself with a variety of jewellery, he decided, for her wrists held bangles and green and red beads hung from around her neck.

The moment he noticed the hairpin was the moment the girl noticed him. She gave him a mischievous half smile. He returned her smile with a cheeky grin. Then he winked. This seemed to amuse her and she winked back at him. At that point he pondered on what to do and whether this was the moment to withdraw for he felt a little unsure of his next move. Someone handed him a bottle of warm beer. He wondered if that was the hostess because he wasn't too sure of who was who? *This was city life*, he thought. He had been invited to the party by a friend who hadn't arrived and so he had stayed, looking around at everyone but not taking part in any of the conversation. He seemed as much alone in the group as the girl who had winked at him.

Oisin was beginning to feel the effects of the warm beer and he decided it was time to unpin himself from the wall and go in search of some food. To do this he had first to get past the couple in front of him. The two of them were now fondling each other in such a manner that suggested they should soon find somewhere more private and Oisin had to take a giant stride over them in order to move from the wall. Neither of them noticed. He negotiated himself to the hall and away from the crowded room. It was quieter there except for a girl speaking on the phone. She kept repeating, 'I told you not to... I told you not to... 'and Oisin noticed that her eyes were full of tears. He could only wonder. There was a light at the end of the hall and he judged that this must be the kitchen and perhaps some food might be available there. He was surprised when he entered the room to find only five people there. A girl about his own age was perched on a high stool trying unsuccessfully to strum a guitar. No one spoke. It was one of those high ceiling Edinburgh flats where the pulley for the washing hung somewhat precariously above the kitchen table. A girl's black bra was positioned on the pulley line and Oisin observed it was rather on the large size but it was the sight below that the young Irishman had not expected to see. The light in the kitchen was a welcome relief from the candle light and incense burning of the front living room. Sitting there on the table, Buddha-like and naked to the waist was a girl with short black cropped hair; expressionless and silent. In front of her a youth with a mass of thick red curly hair and an equally fiery red beard was intent on painting the petals of a white rose around the nipple of her left breast. His artwork was almost complete as he had already carefully positioned a dragon on her right side. The dragon's head covered her right breast and a tongue of red fire spread towards the white rose. *It was actually a work of art*, thought Oisin, somewhat embarrassed. No one spoke and Oisin wasn't sure of his next move. Should he stare at the sight on the kitchen table or beat a hasty retreat? However, no one, including the girl being painted or the artist seemed in the least fazed by the newcomer. In fact, Oisin was invisible in the room and he could have remained staring all night till dawn if he hadn't noticed a pizza on the worktop near to the sink. He headed for it. When his hunger was satisfied, he decided it was about time to leave the party. He hadn't spoken a word to anyone all night. As he rummaged through the pile of coats at the door he became aware of a girl standing in the hall. It was the same girl who had winked at him; the one with the huge hairpin and the bored expression. She spoke,

"Let's get outta here!"

Oisin, somewhat unsteady on his feet, looked up to see where the voice was coming from and when he realised that this was indeed the girl, he grinned.

"You're on," he said.

Outside, it was cool and the air was crisp. The girl took Oisin's hand. When they reached the end of the street, she stopped and, without warning and without uttering a sound, she kissed him full on the lips, a long, lingering kiss. He was surprised that this had happened so suddenly. He felt the urgency in her body and he responded, delighting in the unexpected moment and half-drunk now from beer and passion. Above, the sky lightened as the dawn of a new day emerged. But below on the pavement, under the street light, Oisin and the girl, their lips locked together and with the urgency of desire throbbing through both their bodies, were totally and completely unaware of anything and anyone as the night gave way to day.

"I'm Cecy," she said when they met again a few days later, "well, Cecilia, actually but I've always been Cecy and guess that's what I'll be for always. What's your name?"

"Oisin."

"Why, that's some name, ain't it now?" And she giggled.

"Oisin Kelly," Oisin replied solemnly, "from Ballybeg, in the West of Ireland."

"And I'm Cecilia Mary Angela Stanworth from upstate New York. Now we have been formally introduced!"

"I've never met anyone from upstate New York."

"And I've never met anyone from Ballybeg in the West of Ireland!"

"Well, here we are," Oisin grinned, "the two of us in Edinburgh, Scotland. What happens now?"

"Sex happens now," said Cecilia Mary Angela Stanworth from upstate New York.

It began with an almost animal urgency and the quiet young man from the West of Ireland was completely and utterly overcome for he had never in his wildest imaginings

17

expected that his body would respond in the way it did and with such excitement. He felt he no longer had any control over his body and all he could think of was being with Cecy and there was nothing else in the world for him but the release of his desires. What followed then were the wild, crazy moments of pure joy. All these intense moments mixed together into the sort of wonderful experience of total sexual and emotional happiness that perhaps only happens once in a lifetime to a very fortunate few. This is what it felt like for Oisin with Cecy Stanworth for they couldn't get enough of each other. All this sexual joy and anticipation was great fun and so great a fun, Oisin decided, that he wondered how he had lived for so long without it and Cecy was good at it. She had been around a bit more than he had, he knew this, but she never mentioned any past lovers and he never enquired for some secrets are best kept hidden, he figured. They tumbled into bed at any opportunity and once they spent a whole day there. Emerging from her flat hours later, they were like drunks weaving their way along the street. People they passed smiled and a man winked at Oisin, at least Oisin thought it was a wink, and he grinned back. He felt he had become part of the human race at last and his newly awakened sexuality was visible to all. It was no wonder that strangers winked at him in the street.

Cecy proved to be a bewildering mixture of contradictions for Oisin. One moment her spontaneity often led to some outrageous behaviour; the next instance she turned conservative. She even seemed shy sometimes. Her changing moods delighted and intrigued him at the same time. His emotions when he was with her were all at sea but very soon after they met, he couldn't imagine his life without her. *This was what life should be,* he thought. And now he couldn't think of living without Cecy. Pictured their long life together, passionate and exciting until they grew too old – an unimaginable thought – but then they would still have each other. Comfortable, knowing each other's moods and thoughts like some of the old couples he knew. His future lay before him, planned, secure and with no surprises. *Some might think it dull to stay with one woman but they wouldn't know,* thought Oisin. *They wouldn't know what that one woman could do for a man.* Cecy Stanworth brought more happiness into his life than he could ever have imagined possible; bucketful's and bucketful's of happiness; a bottomless pit filled to the top with all this happiness. He relaxed and grew comfortable in his nakedness when he was with her. And she had no inhibitions it seemed and would delight in wandering around her small flat without a stitch of clothing on and tease the shy Oisin. He loved to watch her and they would lie together for what seemed hours exploring each other's bodies, making love and learning to love. There was to be no greater pleasure for Oisin than when he was in the arms of his beloved Cecy. He loved her. His had become an enviable life.

He learned a little about her as the months went by. Cecy had come to Edinburgh as an international student to study English Literature at the University. Her plan had been to use this year to further her career as a teacher back in the States. She didn't speak much of her family in upstate New York. Oisin gathered from her brief comments that her father owned a hardware store and her mother was an elementary schoolteacher in the same small town. She had brothers but she never spoke about them except one, her favourite. He was a soldier and she lived in dread that he would be sent to Vietnam. She hated American foreign policy with a vengeance. Oisin spent hours in her bed studying the Ban the Bomb poster fastened to the wall in front of him. Other times Cecy would talk passionately about the American dream. Patriotism, it seemed to him, ran deep within her and she would not hear anyone who was not an American, say things against her native land. It was as if she loathed the sin but loved the sinner. It was another aspect of her contradictory character and Oisin learned to keep quiet when she spoke about America. After all, he reasoned she had an opinion, a belief and a passionate hope for a better, safer world and that was stimulating enough for the young Irishman from Ballybeg who had never been to America and knew nothing of either the dream or the reality.

Cecy shared a flat with two other young American girls, both students. They were rather shadowy figures and Oisin rarely met them. One of the girls was from Kansas and Oisin felt rather intimidated when he was with her. She drawled and the young Irishman had difficulty understanding her and he was certain she harboured resentment towards him. Their conversations were brief. It occurred to Oisin that the girl from Kansas disapproved of his relationship with Cecy and that she was both judgemental and jealous of the situation. However, Cecy appeared unmoved and told Oisin not to worry. If, by any chance Oisin and the young Kansas girl found themselves alone in the kitchen or the living room, one or the other would beat a hasty retreat in order not to have to make polite conversation. To tell the truth Oisin didn't have a clue what to say to the Kansas girl as she only spoke when spoken to and then it was usually just a monosyllabic mumble. She was a devout Baptist and he was unsure whether he was quite ready to face judgement from her vengeful God for his sexual acts with Cecy before any marriage tie had bound him and Cecy together. This fact was not wasted on Cecy. She had lived for a few years in New York and there amongst the artists and the intellectuals, she had discovered a new and exciting world quite removed from her somewhat sheltered childhood. That, to her mind, made all the difference. She considered herself liberated and had nothing much to say to her Kansas flatmate either. The two girls rarely spoke to each other and existed together as ships that pass in the night. Neither girl expected they would ever see each other again when their time in the Scottish capital had ended. Cecy's other flatmate was an American as well, a long legged blonde beauty from California who moaned continuously about the damp, wet weather and longed for home. It appeared to Oisin that the three American girls had been flung together because of their nationality and that was their only common bond. When he visited Cecy, they spent most of the time in her bedroom. Here they were safe from both the prying eyes and the mutterings of disapproval.

Cecy lived in organised chaos for her room resembled herself in so many details. Clothes and books were flung together throughout the room so that no spot was empty. Indeed, if there ever was an empty space, it was quickly filled and mostly by books. The books took on the appearance of high rise tower blocks and they climbed one on top of the other into every available space and were forever in danger of collapsing. When they did happen to fall, Cecy would leave them on the floor for days, walking over them as if they weren't even there. She didn't seem to notice. Oisin was rather a tidy man and he often found it difficult finding somewhere to sit. Even the bed was a resting place for all manner of things from hair brushes to pens to lipsticks. She was forever losing a valuable piece of jewellery. Her vast collections of earrings were constantly being parted from each other to be found later under a book or on the floor or hiding in a corner somewhere. Once discovered, Cecy would squeal with delight at the reunion of her earrings and vow to keep them together from then on. But it never seemed to happen and the whole scenario would occur over and over. Oisin, in love, thought all the feminine items scattered around an adorable part of his beloved and he figured that what she lacked in tidiness she more than made up for in spontaneity and fun. *After all*, he thought, *what's clutter if not interesting*? And he recalled the chaos of the Protestant minister and his wife back home in Ballybeg. They lived with their possessions entrapping them but they were two of the most interesting people in the whole of Ballybeg. Cecy, too, fitted into that wonderful category in Oisin's head and he forgave her unreservedly. *Too many people make too many judgements*, he thought, *and after all, we are all together in this wonderful mixture of humanity*. With that thought in mind, he smiled. Cecy and her chaotic bedroom had become their love nest and was part of that wonderful mix and so was he.

Oisin's life had taken on a sense of security and he believed that this would be him to the end of his days, content in his work with wee Willie and deeply in love with his beloved Cecy. He would be quite happy to stay in Edinburgh or if Cecy wanted to, live in upstate New York, a place that had taken on a whiff of mystery for him. He would go anywhere, he reasoned as long as he could be with his Cecy. He did not think it was possible that anything or anyone could take away his happiness. He would work hard and the two of them would raise a family. He thought there could be no greater thing in the whole world than the joy of having someone by his side, to share his world, to listen to him when he was sad and to laugh with him when he was happy.

She wanted him to take her to Ireland. She pleaded with him but it was here that she encountered a barrier for Oisin had no desire whatsoever to return to Ireland. He wanted to keep this wonderful woman all to himself because he feared what would happen between them if he were to introduce her to his mother. How would his mother react and what would she make of this American girl who had no religion whatsoever to guide her and one whom he was sure his mother would view as totally immoral? His mother's Catholic faith had remained steadfast throughout her entire life. Oisin was certain that there would be an almighty clash between the two women. He had visions of Cecy plunging naked into the cold Atlantic Ocean along the strand from the family home at An Teach Ban and someone telling his mother. And then there would be no end to it and Oisin would once again feel the outsider in his own family because his loyalty would remain with his American lover. No, it would not happen. He would not allow it to happen. Cecy was his and no one should come between them. No one. Best that he keep Cecy and his mother apart for as long as possible.

"We could go for a trip up the Highlands instead," he suggested one day when Cecy was insisting on Ireland, "or maybe... to Italy, to Bologna. I have friends there. Silvio Luchetta and his sister, Signora Rosa Cavellessi... well, they're more than friends I guess... they're sort of family now?"

She pouted.

"Who are they? You haven't talked about them! It must be exciting to have Italian friends... family even. When can I meet them?" She was annoyed. "If we don't go to Italy to meet this so-called family, give me one good reason why we can't we go to Ireland then? Have you secrets there you don't want to share... a wife perhaps?"

"Don't be ridiculous! It's just... well, it's sort of boring, ye know. Lovely country and I missed it at first but now, I wouldn't know. I'm happy here in Scotland with you."

"Well, I still don't know why you don't want to take me but... the Highlands or Italy? Will we toss a coin to decide?"

It was a relief to him that she had given up on Ireland. He laughed and said, "Why not?"

And the Highlands won. They packed into Oisin's dark blue Mini and headed north. They pitched their tent beside the still waters of lochs and fought off the midges and felt the soft rain on their faces. The high mountains were achingly beautiful and when the sun shone through the grey clouds to their high peaks, Oisin's poet's soul awoke and a wonderful sense of tranquillity engulfed him. How he longed to put into words what he felt. It was the same feeling that can come to many people who are amongst Nature's wild places; those remote and majestic places that remain hidden from so many eyes. Those who venture there become mystics and experience such a profound awareness that many return time and time again, just for that wonderful feeling of peace. Never before had Oisin Kelly experienced anything like it. He recalled that sometimes when he looked out over the sea at Ballybeg, he had been humbled by the still, silent beauty that was there in the west. Here, beside Cecy, that beauty seemed somehow lesser than before. In awe of Nature's wonders and deeply in love, the young man looked around at what surrounded him. He was with a beautiful woman and they were together in a beautiful place; it was no surprise that here he felt so free and free from all the restraints and the disappointments of the past. He believed at that point in time and with his beautiful Cecy by his side that his life was just beginning and everything that had gone before was merely a preparation for his new and exciting life.

Cecy astounded him at every turn. He never knew what mischief she would do next. She teased him and loved him. He relaxed and laughed more than he felt he ever had done in his entire life. In a way, he had glimpsed heaven. This is how he felt it must be, if indeed it was there because he had begun to have serious doubts about his faith. Cecy had seen to that. A confirmed atheist, her philosophy was to live life to the full every day for you never knew what life had in store for you and the thought of finding out after you die, was something she could not, would not, believe in. Why wait for heaven? It was here already! And when she said all this, she whispered into his ear that she was ready for love. He collapsed into her arms and loved her for maybe she was right. Why wait for some invisible God to give you that sublime glimpse of heaven? And if it was the God of his childhood, he was doomed already to go to that other place. He began to think that Cecy's idea of heaven was the more probable one and definitely the idea of living life to the full and enjoying each day just had to make some sense after all for Oisin had made the discovery that sex was just so much fun and sex with Cecy was the best fun of all. How could a loving God not want his human creations to enjoy their bodies in such a beautiful and exciting way?

For Oisin the days just got better and the nights more intense. When it wasn't raining, they cooked their meals on the primus stove and huddled together inside the tent. They bought fish and chips when the weather changed and Cecy fed him chips, making him open his mouth wide and teasing him as he did so. Her suggestive actions brought on the laughter and the lovemaking. She read poetry to him and the words rolled off her tongue with her delightful drawl. She was thoughtful when she discussed the poems. This is what she had come to Edinburgh to do after all. She was a student and she needed to study. The romantic poets were her favourites. Oisin listened and learned and wondered if there wasn't anything she didn't know. When she explained to him what the poet was trying to say, he decided that her thoughts were wiser than any priest. *Father Byrne had never explained the mysteries of life to me with such clarity,* he thought, remembering his young life in Ballybeg. And the days slipped by. Something magical seemed to happen every moment. If only every one of these magical moments could be captured and stored for ever in some divine sort of casket, Oisin fantasised. It seemed to him that every new discovery that he made when he was with Cecy brought about more love and he loved this American woman from upstate New York with all his heart and every fibre of his being. The feeling was of such intensity that he never wanted to leave her or to see her go. She had turned into a goddess, a very human one, but a goddess, nevertheless.

Their adventures continued. One night they camped on a football pitch on the Isle of Skye and were asked to leave by an officious local man with a thick accent that they didn't understand. Undeterred, they bought a bottle of whisky and headed to a hill. Here under a sky full of stars and a full moon, yellow and bright, they got deliriously drunk and fell into the tent to sleep it off till dawn. Emerging in the morning, they found that they had camped in a farmer's field and the inquisitive cows surrounding them had trampled over the tent pegs and made deep hoof marks in the muddy soil. The clear night had given way to a miserable wet day and they were glad to leave. Cecy was quiet all that day. It was the only time in the Highlands that they were a little less at ease with each other. But the next day, she was her old self again and Oisin, ever mindful of his lover, was even more solicitous. It seemed that their relationship was becoming secure and happier as the days went by and any differences of opinion between them would be easily resolved. In fact, the slight tiffs they had led inevitably to the bed and more love making. Sometimes Oisin thought the arguments were worth it. He teased her and she loved it. She had a way of tickling him in all the right places. How could he not have fallen so deeply in love with her?

But that had been months ago and now Oisin was ready to ask Cecy Stanworth from upstate New York to marry him. The wind had eased a little and Oisin's pace quickened as he got closer to her flat. A neat privet hedge on both sides of a short narrow path led to the door of Cecy's flat. This privet hedge was once the cause of Oisin's confusion as there were only two flats with hedges anywhere along the street. All the other buildings were devoid of any greenery of any kind. In fact, they were all rather bleak and even bleaker inside for the dull ochre walls and a wrought iron staircase which curled upwards and upwards did not invite much in the way of optimism. Oisin was always glad to get to the top floor where Cecy and her flatmates lived. All the buildings looked the same and once, soon after they had first met, Oisin had got confused and ended up knocking on the wrong door. The door had opened to reveal a rather sullen old man who told him to be gone and to leave him in peace. After that, Oisin took more attention and was careful not to make the same mistake again. He recalled how Cecy had laughed when he told her the story and teased him, running her fingers through his black curly hair and telling him to be aware of what door he knocked on because there just might be a ravishing, available and sexy young student lurking there next time? It was no wonder that Oisin was so very much in love.

He pushed open the heavy front door and climbed the steps. Cecy was expecting him. His heart beat faster as he climbed. As he climbed he rehearsed what he was to say to her. There was no doubt in his mind that she felt the same as he did and he anticipated no problems with his marriage proposal. Hadn't Cecy murmured in his ear the other day how much she liked him and how interesting she thought he was? *No one had ever thought he was interesting before*, Oisin thought, but maybe with Cecy he was developing into something approaching that state, at least he hoped he was. At the top of the stairs, he stood for a few moments to straighten his tie and run a comb through his curly black hair. He had grown a beard and this too got a few desultory flicks. He was nervous but excited as well. He knocked on the door of Cecy's flat.

She was there in front of him, his beautiful Cecy. Then she pecked him on the cheek and playfully tickled his beard as she always did when she wanted to tease him. He took her in his arms, then kissed her on her lips while his tongue made discoveries that he knew would lead to the bedroom. She seemed so very happy to see him and Oisin thought what a fortunate man he was to have someone so beautiful to love and how beautiful she was. He placed both his hands on each side of her face and looked into her clear blue eyes.

"Oh, Cecy," he murmured, "how lovely ye are."

"Aw, you big softie, come on here. Give me your coat. You look frozen. What have you been doing to yourself?"

"Been walking up from Princes Street. It's perishin' out there. Is anyone in?" and Oisin looked towards the closed bedroom doors of the two flatmates.

Cecy laughed.

"I'm all alone, ma dear. Come on, let's have a cup of cawfee..."she drawled. He loved the way she said 'coffee'. "I've got a lot to tell you," she said.

"Such as?"

"Wait and see."

"I've got something to say too," and Oisin drew in a deep breath.

Cecy frowned but said nothing. He wondered why but he said nothing.

They drank their coffee in silence and ate some hastily prepared cheese and mustard sandwiches. The bread was stale but it didn't matter one bit. *This is how life should be*, thought Oisin. The simple pleasures, the joy of being with someone you love and knowing they love you and he smiled at the thought of so much love. Cecy seemed to have captured his mood for she no longer frowned. She smiled and stroked his hand in a familiar way, saying softly,

"You're a good man, Oisin Kelly."

"Ye bring out the good in me," he replied.

"Oh, ma dear, it's you who are good, not me."

When they finished eating they went into her bedroom, to make love and to love. Afterwards, Oisin knew that this was the moment he had to ask her to marry him. He must make all this love legal because he could not imagine of a life without her. Life without his beautiful Cecy would be devoid of any meaning. They lay side by side, holding each other, looking into each other's eyes.

"Marry me, Cecy."

He expected her to do something outrageous, to throw her arms around him, to announce that they should go right this very minute and find someone to marry them; tomorrow, next week, whenever. This is what he thought would happen but instead she rolled away from him and, with her back to him, got up from the bed, folded her silk dressing gown around her naked body and pulled the cord tightly around her waist. This was the orange and red silk gown with the grey Chinese dragon on the back which was so much part of her. Oisin loved to see her wearing it. Sometimes she would come to the door and Oisin knew that there was nothing underneath the gown but her naked body. Always the gown was there in her room, flung over a chair or on the floor, the silk dressing gown and Cecy. It seemed an age before she turned around to look at him again. She had lit a cigarette and she blew the smoke upwards towards the ceiling before she spoke.

"I thought you knew..."

"Knew what?"

"I'm engaged... to Chuck... "

She looked away from him and her eyes followed the smoke as it curled around her. Outside the winter night was cold but in the room there was a strange stillness, the stillness of a dream. Oisin, naked under the covers, felt as if he had had the air taken out of his body so great was the shock of her words. She had destroyed with those few short words, his plans of a moment before. He stammered,

"I don't understand... who in the name of God is Chuck?"

Still she refused to look at him. When she finally spoke, it was a whisper,

"A guy back home in upstate New York. I've known him since High School. It's all arranged. We're to be married when I return in the summer..."

"Do ye love him?"

"What is love?" She shrugged.

"Ah... ye *don't* love him!"

"I didn't say that."

"You mean, I was nothin' to ye?"

"I didn't say that either."

"Well, why are ye marrying him then?"

"Because it's for the best. The right thing to do."

Now Oisin was angry. He threw the covers back and pulled on his trousers but his hands were shaking as he zipped up his fly. This couldn't be happening to him. *Maybe I hadn't done the proposal bit right*, he thought. *Maybe I should have brought flowers or taken her out for a meal or got down on my bended knee, who knows with women?* But there was this Chuck. Who the hell is Chuck, this boy back home? And he wanted to kill this person whom he had not known existed just ten minutes before. He tried again.

"You mean all this..." and he motioned towards the bed with its ruffled sheets and the memory of love, "all this... meant nothin' to ye? I was just a game to ye. Mother of God, how could ye do all this knowin' all the time that there was a lad called Chuck back home for ye, waitin' for ye?"

Cecy wouldn't answer him. She extinguished her cigarette into the large glass ashtray on her desk and as she did, turned her back to him so that Oisin was just left staring once again at the Chinese dragon. It was a kind of dismissal.

"Do ye want me to go now?"

She didn't reply but shrugged her shoulders again. Oisin couldn't bear the silence in the room. Outside he could hear the noise of cars and people's voices but in this room the two of them were trapped like actors on a stage. They were actors uttering sorrowful and unrelated words from a sort of badly written play that didn't seem to have any

30

meaning or any purpose. But they weren't actors in some cruel drama and there was no audience, they were two people who had been very much in love, just a few moments before. He had to try just one more time, maybe it was some sort of crazy joke she was playing on him. Any minute she would laugh and tell him it was her way of teasing him to see how much he cared. She would kiss him and then laugh and once again he would hear that wonderful laughter he loved so much and everything would be as it had been.

"Cecy...? Tell me it's not true," he pleaded.

Finally she looked into his eyes. She did not speak, nor did she acknowledge him, or smile or frown. She stood rigid as a statue, an Aphrodite clothed in an orange silken gown, and Oisin knew then that it wasn't a dream. This was real. There was nothing he could do or say which would have changed her mind. She had become a stranger to him now. Just a few hours before, she had been his life. He fumbled for his coat and scarf and got ready to leave.

Like a blind man he stumbled to the door, past the privet hedge to the outside and into the dark Edinburgh night. The wind blew a fine rain over the pavement and in front of him; the cobbled street glistened like a thousand diamonds in the night light. But Oisin was unaware of everything and everyone around him. He walked with his head down and avoided any eye contact. He was no longer the cheery young Irishman who would speak to anyone he met. The cold winter's rain wet his hair and droplets of freezing water ran down his face to his neck but he didn't care. He walked rapidly but he didn't know in which direction he was heading, for in his trance like state, he was divorced from the everyday world around him. In his mind all he could see was an image of Cecy's back with her auburn hair and the orange silken gown with its grey Chinese dragon. He stepped off the pavement and a car had to swerve to miss him. He heard the driver swear but he didn't care. He wondered what it would be like to die.

31

Three hours later he fell onto his bed and lay, looking up at the ceiling. This was the bed where love had been. He remembered how the bed springs had squeaked in sublime time with their movements and, as their passion increased, the springs creaked louder and louder. It was on this bed that Cecy had first taught him how to love.

Finally, he closed his eyes and slept. It was Friday night. The next day he had planned that he and Cecy would go to the jeweller in the High Street and buy the engagement ring. He had spoken to the jeweller a week ago and a time had been arranged. He knew that Cecy, even with all her modern thinking, would love a diamond ring and he had been saving for it for weeks. Jewellery was something she adored and it would have been special. He would have made it so. After the purchase of the ring, he had made up his mind to take her to the posh restaurant off Princes Street that they had peered into so many times. They had studied the menu with such longing and promised themselves that one day, one very special day, they would blow all their combined savings on just one meal.

"Kilgoolga. Wake up now mate!"

The conductor placed his hand on the young man's shoulder. The train slowed as the station came into view and the young man woke suddenly and stared sleepily out the window.

"Best not miss it... easy to miss... not much here, hey? Bit different from Ireland, isn't it, mate?"

The conductor was a rather jovial sort most of the time and he grinned. He found it intriguing that a young man not much older than his own son, could be on a train bound for a dump of a place like Kilgoolga and that this young bloke had come all the way around the world from Ireland to here. The conductor had never been to Ireland but he knew all about it as his grandfather hailed from Tipperary and he was a little annoyed that this young bloke with the black beard hadn't wanted to talk about it. *That's what they're like these days*, he thought, *long-haired louts and dole bludgers most of them.* His own son wasn't in the least like that; he'd got himself a good job on the railways too and a nice girl as well. But the conductor thought that it would have been good to hear stories about the Irish from this young fella. Would have broken the journey a bit. He'd found out the bloke's name though after he told him about his grandfather in Tipperary. Thought he might know of the family but the young fella had just said something about being from the west and Tipperary was nowhere near where he had been born. Anyhow he said his name was Kelly, Oisin Kelly and he didn't know any Kellys in Tipperary and that's all, the bloke said. This compartment had nobody else of interest but for the soldiers and a few girls and they didn't want to talk. The conductor had rather hoped this young Irishman would have at least spoken a bit more but no; he just sat huddled up after those few words and non-communicative. *Well, you never know with folk*, he thought, *been doing this job long enough and there's always some weirdo's about.*

CHAPTER TWO

When Oisin Kelly stepped onto the platform at Kilgoolga Railway Station his first thought was that he had stepped back into another age and he must have somehow been transported through a time tunnel whilst he had slept on the train. Kilgoolga Station was empty of all life. Completely. Above the sky was bright, bright blue without a cloud in sight. He shivered slightly. He had thought Australia should be hot all the time but it was quite chilly in the early September afternoon and he was glad that he had slipped on a pullover a few hours before. He was stiff and tired after the long journey. The station was tidy but then there didn't seem to be anything around to make it untidy. He had got used to seeing the outback railway stations with their neat weatherboard buildings all painted the same dull yellow colour and with the name of the station in black lettering on a white board. So he was definitely at a place called Kilgoolga, in the back of nowhere. He stood on the gravel platform and wondered what to do next.

The train line stretched down the centre of the town or what appeared to be the town because across from the station, he could see a line of eucalyptus trees. Their straggly white barks and pointed leaves were becoming more familiar to him. Behind the trees he could see some shops. At the back of the station he noted there was a street of brightly coloured timber framed houses on stilts and all with their galvanised iron roofs of silver, red or green. He could just make them out through the two large acacia trees at the back of the station. There wasn't a soul in sight either way. Suddenly the peace was broken by a flock of pink and grey parrots. The birds appeared out of nowhere and disappeared across the sky just as quickly as they had arrived. Their screeching broke the stillness for just a few seconds and then it was quiet again. Oisin had found the journey incredibly long and boring as well but he half wished now that he was back on the train, just travelling. He decided that he would have even welcomed listening to the garrulous conductor but the train had only waited at Kilgoolga about ten minutes or thereabouts. No one but Oisin had got off and then the train was gone, snaking along the straight track towards the flat horizon.

It is a strange feeling to be alone in an unknown place; a place that is familiar in many ways but so alien in others. Oisin had never thought of himself as an adventurer and he would have quite happily, if his circumstances had not changed so dramatically, remained where he had been back in Edinburgh with Cecy and never ventured any further. He didn't want to think of Cecy. If he began to think of Cecy... no, it didn't bear thinking of. She was his past. Here he was now in this place called Kilgoolga. He hauled his heavy backpack towards a bench and sat there in front of the Stationmaster's Office. He wondered where the stationmaster was for there was still no evidence anywhere of human presence, just a sign on a closed door.

Oisin sighed and his sigh was the only sound on the empty platform. Kilgoolga and the Outback. Oisin had first heard about the Outback from Mrs Ryan back in Ballybeg. The Outback was a mysterious and intriguing place according to Mrs Ryan who could tell a good story as she happily recounted her brother Gerard's many adventures out there so far from anywhere. Her brother had made good in that remote place and the doctor's wife was very proud of Gerard. He had, after all made his fortune there and become a Mayor of the unpronounceable town as well! She liked to boast about it especially when a rare letter arrived from Gerard. Ballybeg people wondered if perhaps her brother wasn't quite as fond of Mrs Ryan as she was of him but that was another matter. That was conjecture and no one could match Gerard according to Mrs Ryan. Hadn't he arrived in Australia with just a suitcase and look what he had achieved in such a short time? For all these reasons, the Outback and Gerard had taken up a romantic place in Oisin's head all those years ago but he had never expected to see the place and looking around at it now, he wondered what Mrs Ryan would say about it? She was, after all, rather grand and somewhat pretentious and he smiled at the memory of that woman from his childhood.

A series of events had taken place in Oisin's life a few weeks previously. Some people may have called them coincidence and others might have viewed them as being more fatalistic but this was a philosophical argument and Oisin, being part of these events, could only accept that they had happened and here he was now in Kilgoolga. He had arrived in Sydney, tired from the long plane journey and, not knowing quite what he was doing, he booked into a Youth Hostel in the centre of the city for a few days. His plan had been to get his bearings and then decide what to do next. He had enough money saved to tide him over for a few weeks but he would have to get work after that. The only thought in Oisin's head was to put distance between his old life in Edinburgh and so get as far as he could away from there. He couldn't think of anything further away than Australia. The hurt and disappointment of Cecy haunted him and he found it hard to stop thinking of her and what their life together might have been. He was wounded. Although rationally he knew he would have to heal, given time this would have to happen for that was life, but he couldn't let the memory of

36

Cecy go no matter how hard he tried. So he had become a rather sad young man and because of this, all the new sights and sounds of the beautiful harbour and its surroundings were viewed rather negatively from his perspective of despondency. Until one day at the Hostel a young German called Wolfgang started to talk to him.

"This is a strange country," the German said after they had made the usual short civilities. "I just return from staying with distant relatives of my mother and I tell you, life is different in the country. Australia is a long way from home, I think?"

The German took a bite of one of a bundle of cherries that he was eating his way through. He carefully placed the seed beside the uneaten ones and continued.

"I travel on the train for twenty hours. Can you imagine? It is so vast this country so unlike Europe. I am called Wolfgang and your name is...?"

"Oisin Kelly from Ireland."

"Ah," replied the German and he looked pleased. "I have been to Ireland. I like the Irish. A lot of people come here from Ireland... Germany too," he added and put another cherry into his mouth.

"My aunt and uncle live near a small town... they are farmers... I work with them for the summer... so different. It was good. They still speak a little German and were happy to see someone from their homeland, I think. But yes, you must leave the city to see this country. I am not fond of cities, even Sydney, it has a beautiful harbour but too many people, I think. That is why I like Ireland... not so crowded!"

He finished eating the cherries and wrapped the seeds into a tissue.

Oisin was rather surprised by the young German's remarks. He had never thought much about cities. Living in Edinburgh had been different from life in Ballybeg, that was for sure, but he had got used to it and after he had met Cecy, he would have stayed in a city all his life. But now?

"Have you seen much of Sydney?" remarked Wolfgang as he got up to leave.

"No."

"Perhaps you would like to accompany me across the harbour... to Manly? I have just two more days and then I return to Germany to the university."

Oisin hesitated. He wasn't sure but Wolgang seemed a nice sort of fellow and it would be good to have a companion. He smiled.

"I would like that," he said.

"That is good. We will go tomorrow then." Wolfgang held out his hand.

Oisin took the German's hand. Wolfgang was so formal but an interesting person, Oisin decided. Yes, it would be good to cross the harbour and see something of this beautiful city and perhaps hear more of the country too.

The next morning after breakfast the two young men made their way to Circular Quay to board the ferry to Manly. The day was already hot and Oisin was glad that he had brought sunglasses and a wide brimmed straw hat. Wolfgang was in high spirits.

"This is good," he said when they were safely on the ferry. As they passed the Opera House with its white shimmering sail like features all under construction, he remarked,

"This is a wonderful building. It has cost a lot of money but later, when people see it built, they will say, 'What a marvellous thing this is. How fortunate we are to live in Sydney and have such a place.' But people have no vision when something is just beginning. That is what I think."

Oisin thought of this. *Perhaps Wolfgang is right. People never think beyond their immediate situation. I thought Cecy would be with me forever and look what happened. Maybe I should have had a different vision and she would still be there? Who knows?*

"You look sad, my friend."

"Just thinking. Aye, you're right. Should be a building to be proud of and it'll be a wonderful sight when it's all finished."

Then the ferry turned to head into the middle of the harbour, past Fort Denison and all the inlets and coves. The two men were silent each with their own thoughts.

"I am pleased I was able to come to this country," Wolfgang said, "perhaps in time you will think the same. Have you plans?"

"Not really."

"Then you must travel to see my aunt and uncle. It will give you time to see the country and they are kind people. I think they did not want me to leave. They said to me to stay... to work with them but my plan is to be a doctor... and I must go home to Germany to study. Maybe, I will visit them again, we never know in life. I would like to give you their address and maybe you could write to them and to say, I am well and I am a friend to you. That will be enough!"

It was as if the German had flung a rope to Oisin to rescue him from drowning. He still suffered. He had loved Cecy. Adrift, perhaps this invitation was what he needed. Then he might be able to move on somehow but it still seemed an impossible task.

So his first thought was, *Why not?* And then he replied in a quiet voice,

"That's good of ye. Aye, I'd like that... I don't really have any plans. Yes, give me their address please. That's kind of ye."

The next morning Wolfgang was ready to leave. He handed Oisin an envelope. Inside, on a piece of yellow lined paper Wolfgang had written his own address in Germany as well as the address of his uncle and aunt. His handwriting was neat, precise, just like the man. *He will make a good doctor*, thought Oisin as he held the envelope and read the names.

"I have written to my aunt and uncle," said Wolfgang. "They will welcome you."

"Thank ye, Wolfgang. I have been thinking about it. I might just take ye up on this. It would give me a chance to see a bit more of the place."

"For me it was a journey that I will never forget. The country... how do you say this in English? The country will, I think, captivate you because it is like nowhere else."

"I'd no idea I would ever come to Australia," replied Oisin. "I think because it's very remote from what we call 'civilisation', it has a sort of mystery but then, so many Irish came here. Nearly everyone has a relative or a friend somewhere. Everyone knows someone."

"Ah, I know what you mean but I think being here will change you and especially out there in the remote part of the world where my aunt and uncle have their home. I, too, was not sure about Australia but we have to take a chance sometimes, do we not? I think sometimes the people we meet and the people we no longer see are all a necessary part of our life journey. Ah, I am not expressing myself very well but I am glad to have met you, if only for a short time, Oisin. If you return to Ireland, perhaps you will be able to visit me in Germany some time?"

Wolfgang picked up his backpack and shook it into place on his back. He was a tall thin man and the backpack looked heavy but he had been travelling for weeks. He had seen a lot of the country, from the Far North and the Barrier Reef to Melbourne. Now was the time to go home and for his adventures to become a memory. The best time he had had was with his aunt and uncle and he was pleased that he was able to help the Irishman.

"I wait to hear from my aunt and uncle that you have enjoyed meeting them," he paused, "and by the way, it *is* a long train journey! It does not seem as if it has an end! But then, all of a sudden, when you do not think you can look any longer at the flat land or see another dry blade of grass, there is Kilgoolga!"

That was the first time Oisin had ever heard the word 'Kilgoolga'. It sounded exotic. He smiled.

"Aye, Wolfgang. I will go. Ye make it sound interesting. I've made up my mind! I think that I want to get out of the city too." He held out his hand to the German. "Thank you... and I hope we meet again..."

All that had happened a few weeks ago and Oisin was indeed in the exotic place called Kilgoolga which didn't look at all exotic now but instead a little frightening and daunting. *Aye, daunting was the right word*, he thought. He decided that his best course of action was to head over the railway line to the shops beyond the eucalyptus. He thought they were ironbarks but the trees here were so different, he wasn't too certain. As he stepped over the railway line, he heard a movement behind him but when he looked around, there was no one to be seen. Kilgoolga, it seemed was completely devoid of any sign of habitation, human or otherwise. It was about to get dark too and the red sun, visible all day in the cloudless sky, was starting its rapid descent beyond the flat horizon in the west. Soon everything would be black and even more silent if that was at all possible. Oisin could not see any evidence of any lights anywhere. Looking back to the railway station and beyond, even the houses appeared to be unlit. He heard that noise again. This time he was sure he saw a shadowy figure but in the half light of the dusk, he wasn't certain. He stood still but there was no sound.

The town of Kilgoolga was completely dark as he walked over the railway tracks to the barbed wire fence which served as a boundary between the shops and the railway. His backpack was heavy and, as he climbed over the wire, his trouser leg got caught and he had to pull the fabric off the barb. A small fragment of cloth remained on the wire. There were no street lights to guide him and only the paper thin moon, a tiny sliver of silver above, gave light. Oisin, tired, hungry and disoriented began to feel slightly anxious. His feet crunched the leaves underneath the line of ironbark trees which separated the railway line from the shops. The sweet smell of the eucalyptus filled his nostrils. *How distinct a perfume it was and how strange a place to be*, he thought. Behind him he heard a slight noise again and turning quickly, he was certain that he saw a figure with a wide brimmed hat behind one of the trees. He could feel his heart beating in his chest and in a kind of panic, he told himself to take a grip. He began to wonder if he was imagining things and that the long train journey and the fear of the unknown were combining to slightly change his perception of what was reality and what was not. Two large black shapes on silent wings swept above him and disappeared as swiftly as they had appeared. They were gone like visions of another world and melted into the night. As if their mysterious shapes were a forerunner of the next moment, the street lights flickered on so that Oisin could now see what was in front of him. He was relieved that perhaps there was more to Kilgoolga than he had first thought.

The shops in front of him were so different from the buildings of his childhood. In Ballybeg, they were packed together, side by side, stone buildings with centuries of memory, but here was space enough for many more and there was no long memory of human habitation in this place. He had a sudden unconnected thought about the first people who had wandered here and probably set up a temporary camp under the trees and then disappeared once more into the silent bush and left no trace. But the white settlers had stayed put. In front of him the awnings, horizontal to the shop windows displayed the names of the shops. He crossed over the road to the café and walked under the awnings noting as he did, the names of a butcher, the bank, the real estate agent, a draper, a barber and a hairdresser, a newsagent and at the end of the long street he could just make out what looked like a Post Office. At the edge of the railway line, he could see a garage with petrol pumps in front of it and a few cars. Smaller trees had been planted in front of some of the shops to give shelter. Their masses of red flowers would give shade and beauty. A few cars parked diagonally with their bonnets to the footpath were the only indication that perhaps there might be some human habitation here after all. But still there was no sign of life. At the other end of the long flat street, visible now thanks to the street lights, Oisin could make out a building which appeared to have some movement because he heard a voice shouting and another voice replying. He walked towards the sound, crossing over another road to a small park. Three acacia trees gave shelter to picnic tables and it was this small oasis which separated the building from the rest of the line of shops. It was on its own because the shops had ended beyond the park. Ahead was just the flat landscape of this empty land. Oisin paused as he took in the sight of this welcome building.

He stood in front of 'Kilgoolga Arms Hotel', its name proudly written in large white lettering on the red galvanised iron roof. A veranda led into the hotel and Oisin, apprehensive now but knowing that at least he might find someone here to guide him, entered the bar. A small black and tan dog of mixed parentage was fast asleep at the entrance and Oisin had to step over the creature. The dog opened a sleepy eye and gave a perfunctory wag of its tail before closing its eyes again.

Although Oisin had heard voices, he was surprised when he entered the bar to find just two men there, perched on stools and staring into their glasses of cold beer. Behind the counter a woman of about forty was busy reading a book. No one looked up when Oisin entered the room and no one spoke. He carefully eased his backpack onto the floor and slid onto the high stool at the other end of the bar. Now he had time to take in his surroundings. The bar consisted of a wooden counter with a large mirror behind it. In front of the mirror the various bottles of spirits were arranged in a neat row as were the pumps for the beer positioned ever so conveniently at the counter just in front of the two men. It was a small room as public bars go. Five wooden tables with wooden chairs at each were arranged in no order along the wall at the back of the room. Above these tables three white fly speckled overhead fans oscillated slowly and ineffectively. Oisin was surprised to see a large black and white photograph on the wall opposite the bar above two of the tables. The photograph showed a main street with a bullock dray loaded high with bales. *It was probably a view of Kilgoolga,* he thought, *in pioneering days.* Two portraits on either side – one of a stern man with long grey whiskers and the other of an equally stern woman with a white bonnet decorated the wall. *Why don't our Victorian ancestors ever smile?* thought Oisin wryly. He was hungry and his feet hurt although he hadn't walked very far. Tired from the long journey, he just wanted to eat and go to sleep. Tomorrow he would be able to work out what to do. He cleared his throat to make a sound. The two men kept staring into their glasses. The woman at the bar looked up and put down her book. With a quick movement she had her hand on the pump and filled a glass with the pale brown liquid but she wasn't looking at Oisin but rather at the man who had entered the bar.

"How's it goin', Charlie?" she asked.

A short man slid onto the bar stool alongside Oisin. He was joined by the black and tan dog that had followed him into the bar. The dog was busy scratching its neck with its back foot. No one spoke. The short man coughed. It was a dry sort of cough from too many cigarettes and too many bar stools. He didn't look at Oisin but took the glass from the woman and drank quickly. His face, a face browned from years under the hot sun, told a thousand stories for here was a man who had toiled. The deep furrows on his brow and around his eyes were evidence of that hard life. He took off his hat and laid it on the counter beside his glass. At that moment Oisin suddenly recognised the figure for wasn't it the shape that he had imagined behind him when he left the railway?

"Give us a refill, Bella love," the man said for he had emptied his glass with a few gulps.

He drank the next glass almost as quickly as he had the first and he lit a cigarette. It was then that he noticed Oisin.

"How's it goin', mate?" he asked.

Oisin, who up to that point had been wondering what he should do next and hadn't expected to be spoken to, was caught unawares. The woman at the bar now looked in Oisin's direction and she frowned.

"Haven't seen you in here before," she said. It sounded like an accusation.

"I've just got off the train," he muttered.

The woman shrugged. It was of no consequence to her although you didn't see many strangers in Kilgoolga and this one was a strange one, she reckoned.

"What can I get you?"

"I'll have a beer." It seemed to be the safest option. Everyone drank beer here.

The beer was cold and refreshing. Oisin swallowed half the glass of liquid in one gulp. He was thirsty. Now the woman stared at the stranger in the bar with a little more interest. She was a short woman and good at her job. She'd worked at the Kilgoolga Arms ever since she left school and knew all the locals. She decided it was time to find out a bit more about this young man with the black beard and long black curly hair.

"You look as if you've come some distance, mate?" the woman asked.

"Aye. Been on the train about twenty hours... from Sydney."

"Never been to Sydney meself. They say it's a great town..." she replied.

The short man sitting on the bar stool next to Oisin laughed.

"Ya couldn't handle Sydney, Bella love...wild men down there... them city blokes be too much for a nice country girl like you!" He winked at her and she grinned back at him.

He pushed his empty glass with his hand. It was an indication to Bella that he would like a refill. Bella, the barmaid obliged.

"There's enough wild men up here, Charlie!" She laughed. She had a cheery sort of laugh and everyone joined in, even Oisin. The ice was broken.

"I'm awful famished," he said. "Is there anywhere I can get something to eat... and I need a bed for the night?"

"Not much in Kilgoolga," Bella frowned. "Are you Irish?"

"Aye."

"Well, then... an Irishman ! Didn't think you was a Pom! Well... we'll have to see what we can do for you, won't we, boys? Any of youse got any suggestions to help this young man?"

Now everyone stared at Oisin. He was beginning to feel decidedly uncomfortable. A moment before he thought he was getting somewhere and now the atmosphere seemed to have changed but he didn't know why.

46

"There's Maudie," said Charlie.

"Oh, he can't go there... what about Louis?" said Bella dismissively.

"Too right, Bella love. Old Louis's been gettin' the leg over Maudie lately, Charlie. She's got no time for a guest, mate. Got her work cut out keepin' our resident Frenchman satisfied!!"

It was the other man at the end of the bar who spoke, the one wearing the blue shirt with the cut out sleeves and the face that looked as if it had been in the sun for far too long and who hadn't shaved in a week. Bella nodded.

"Lefty's right, Charlie. That's why we haven't seen Louis in here for a month. Thought ya knew all about it, Charlie," said Bella.

"Strewth, I clean forgot all 'bout Maudie and Louis. Must be gettin' old. The memory's goin'!"

Charlie winked at Oisin in a familiar sort of way. Oisin, who didn't know what was going on, just wanted something to eat and to put his head down and sleep.

"We can all see ya missin' him, Bella. Parlez vous," said the man who was called Lefty.

"Well, Louis's a gentleman... not like youse lot... knows how to treat a woman... "

"Whoo... hoo. Looks like our Bella can't resist the charms of our Froggie!"

The other sunburned man in the bar piped up. He looked a bit like Lefty only he was bald and wore glasses. Up till that moment, he hadn't spoken a word. Everyone laughed except Bella. She frowned.

"Oh, shut up all of youse! I'm tryin' to think... "

It was all getting a bit too much for Oisin. He was beginning to think he would have to find somewhere else to go because he didn't have a clue who they were talking about. He stood up to leave. His sudden movement surprised Bella.

"Take no notice of them blokes. They haven't got a brain between them, have ya, boys? I've just had a thought though, young man," she said confidentially to Oisin. She looked pleased. "How 'bout if I rustle you up some bacon and eggs and you could stay here? We've a small room at the back. Pretty basic but can't think of anywhere else in Kilgoolga... the Commercial has rooms but it's closed at present 'cause of the fire... our room might just do you for a night or two? What da ya reckon?"

Oisin, at that moment would have agreed to anything. Maybe they weren't such an odd lot, after all. He smiled.

"That sounds OK," he said. He suddenly remembered the address Wolfgang had given him in Sydney, the reason for his journey to this place.

"I've an address of some people in Kilgoolga," he said. He took the envelope from his trouser pocket and read out the names, " 'Hans and Hilda Seefeldt.' Do any of ye know them?"

He could have thrown a grenade into the room. The man with the cut out sleeves called Lefty got up to leave. He was over six feet tall and, as he stopped in front of Oisin, he spoke to him:

"We know them. We don't speak about them much round here, mate... "

Lefty had a tattoo of 'Mother' drawn on his upper arm. He was so tall that was all that Oisin could see. He wondered why he was called Lefty. He had hands the size of dinner plates. Maybe it was something to do with his left hook. Those hands would have been deadly in a fist fight.

"Yeah," said Charlie, "them Seefelds have always been a weird mob."

"They keep themselves to themselves. That's about right, ain't it?" Bella nodded.

Lefty grinned.

48

"Wouldn't fancy goin' anywhere near them, would ya, Bella?" he said.

"No way, Lefty," she replied, "but we don't want to frighten this young man, do we now? He's come all this way from Ireland after all," she laughed again. "Yeah, too bloody right. Hans and Hilda Seefeldt. We sure as hell *know* them!"

CHAPTER THREE

Hilda Seefeldt didn't often think about Germany. In fact, it was only occasionally when she remembered her grandmother's stories that thoughts came into her head of her ancestral home. Hilda had liked her grandmother. Her grandmother could speak German and used to sing Hilda to sleep with a lullaby. She could still remember the words and sometimes when she felt lonely, she would hum them to herself. Somehow the German words gave comfort.

Guten Abend, gute Nacht,
mit Rosen bedacht,
mit Näglein besteckt,
schlupf' unter die Deck!
Morgen früh, wenn Gott will,
wirst du wieder geweckt.

Guten Abend, gute Nacht,
von Englein bewacht,
die zeigen im Traum
des Christkindleins Baum.
Schlaf nun selig und süß,
schau im Traum 's Paradies.

But that was a long time ago. Once Hilda had asked her brother had he remembered that lullaby but Hans just dismissed the suggestion as if he didn't want to return to childhood memories. Hilda remembered she had felt sad then but that was Hans. He had his reasons, she supposed. After all, they had only been children when their grandmother had died. She was buried in the Seefeldt plot a quarter of a mile from the homestead and sleeping peacefully, Hilda imagined, amongst her brothers and sisters and her mother and father. Hilda wondered if she would lie there herself too when the time came but she wasn't sure she would like to be near her brother, Hans or whether they would both be buried in the Kilgoolga Cemetery now and away from all those relatives. After all, these family plots were a thing of the past these days. Either way, being beside Hans didn't really appeal to her. She had had a lifetime of living with him, maybe a rest from him in eternity would be preferable but she didn't want to think of that and it was rather irreligious to even have these thoughts. So Hilda lived out her days and tried not to think of what might have been and what was to come.

It was hard work on the Wiesental station but it was their home and she and Hans had their duties, all decided by Hans for both to obey, at least that was what Hilda thought. Not that her brother was a bad man, just uncompromising in his thinking. Least that's what most people thought when they discussed Hans. It would be fine to be like Hans where everything was black and white and routine was the order of the day. *He had been so different when they were young*, Hilda thought. There were always people around then. Hilda remembered the cheery squads of shearers who arrived and went away again. Back then it was all fun and hard work, for didn't the shearers eat? Why, she and her mother and old Aggie would be baking and preparing meals all day. She had enjoyed those times. But then times got hard and it was all political and she didn't understand too much about it but something to do with Britain joining Europe and not wanting Australian wool as much and Hans and her father had to sell the sheep. Well, all of the sheep had to go because you couldn't make a living anymore when there were no markets for your wool and everything changed after that. It had been a horrible time. For there was hardly any money left and the bank refused to extend the overdraft and the worst thing of all, both their parents died that same year. Hans said they might have to sell some of the land but no one would buy it, except perhaps their neighbours, the Bradshaws but even they might be struggling. And Hans hated the thought of the Bradshaws owning any of his land and the person he hated more than anyone else in that particular family was the high and mighty Eleanor. He lived in fear that Eleanor would take his land for he had hated Eleanor Bradshaw all his life. He tried to put a Christian face on it but there was something about the woman that he didn't trust. He thought she was avaricious and conniving. Others might be taken in by her but he knew what she wanted and no way would she get it. He thought he would put a bullet in his head if Eleanor made any effort to buy him out. 'No,' he said to Hilda, 'there is only one thing to do and that is to trust in the Lord and make ends meet. The Lord will provide. No more speculating and spending what we do not have. This is our land and we have worked hard here and we will not sell it. Eleanor Bradshaw will never own Wiesental station. Never. Remember, Hilda, the stories we were told as children about Pastor Albert and Heinrich, they were the pioneers and they left their legacy for us and we must trust that the Lord will reward us for our endeavours, just as those far distant ancestors of ours were blessed. They were brave men and women and they never flinched when adverse times came and there are many of those times for this is a harsh land and sometimes an unforgiving one. The Seefeldts have always trusted in the Lord to provide for them in the good times and the hard times will pass and there is no reason that this is going to change. We must pray and our prayers will be answered.' So every Sunday Hans and Hilda drove to the Lutheran Church twenty miles away and prayed as never before throughout that terrible time. And the Lord did provide for the rains came and they grew sorghum which had a market and bought an Aberdeen Angus bull and twenty cows for him and they learned how to care for them although Hans never forgot his sheep. The black cattle sold and the money began to trickle in again, slowly as the small herd increased. So in every way, they had enough to be content and their needs were simple, just like Pastor Albert and Heinrich's frugal lives were all those years ago. But even if Hans prayed and believed in its power there was something that he could never forgive and that was England. He saw betrayal. Hilda thought it was all because their ancestors came from Germany and it was different for them somehow. Hans would hear nothing of that. 'They talk of the Mother Country like children do', he told her,' and expect it to look after them. Britain no longer wants our wool but we will survive as our German ancestors did, thanks to Almighty God but we are neither German nor British, we are Australians and proud of it,' he said and nothing Hilda could say would change his opinion. His ideas were as rigid as stone sometimes and there was nothing to be gained if Hilda tried to reason with him. She sighed because Hans always had a way of making sense about these matters and making her seem foolish and maybe this time there was some truth in what he said.

Hilda remembered when the war came and the Mother Country was fighting the Fatherland and how she had overheard her mother and father talking. We will be interned, she thought she heard her father say but she was just eighteen and wasn't quite sure what 'interned' meant. In the end, they remained on the station for the farm work was part of the war effort and Kilgoolga was a long way from anywhere, anyway. Except that the local men were joining the Army and Jack joined up too. And Hilda had loved Jack. Why, they were engaged to be married and even though Hans disapproved, it didn't matter because her mother liked Jack. Neither of them wanted Jack to go off to fight but this is what men do, her mother had said, even though neither woman knew quite what it was all about. Europe was a long way away from Wiesental station, Kilgoolga. But no, Jack wanted to go. He looked so handsome with his slouched hat and polished boots. I'll be back, love, he had told her but he didn't come back. Killed in action at Tobruk. Hilda often wondered if it had been a bullet from a distant relative that had killed her sweetheart but decided it was fanciful to even think such thoughts. How could it be possible? She remembered when Jack's mother told her the news as if it was yesterday and how she had cried. How she had fled in tears to her German grandmother's grave and there, beside the granite stone, she had knelt in prayer and tried to understand. You'll find someone else, her mother told her a little while later; Jack would have wanted it. But Hilda never stopped loving her Jack and there was never anyone else. Grief is sometimes hard to put to rest and Hilda would not let her sadness go. Every night before she fell asleep, she murmured a little prayer to Jack, knowing when she woke in the morning she would be alone.

Hans would have been horrified had he even guessed his sister's thoughts for Hans's view on life was a simple one based on Holy Scripture. Every evening after their meal, brother and sister read from the Bible and Hans said a prayer. For Hans, all was God's will and God was at the top of a hierarchical tower and His presence was everywhere. Beside God was Jesus then below were their rulers; then men; women and last of all, obeying their parents, came the children. It all seemed so simple to Hans. Your reward for your faith came in Heaven and could never be expected to be achieved on earth. If you obeyed God as written in the Holy Scriptures, you were certain of a place but if you disobeyed, you were destined for a far less salubrious place. The only thing that troubled Hans sometimes was the bit about obeying your rulers because Hans didn't much like the politicians whom he assumed counted as his rulers for hadn't the politicians caused the price of wool to drop and almost brought them to face starvation? God's hand in the weather could be forgiven because this land had always been a harsh one. There were the droughts that went on forever when the ground lay bare and the cracks appeared in the soil while day after day, everyone longed for the rain and prayed for the rain too. And then when hope had threatened to turn to despair, everyone's prayers were answered. But the rains often brought floods that washed the top soil away and made life difficult for weeks. This was a difficult land and a cruel one sometimes but Hans would not have wanted to live anywhere else, given a choice. For wasn't it all part of God's will that he should be here and he would die here too in God's good time?

But for Hilda the land was different. Sometimes, when she had a precious moment to herself, she looked at the flat landscape and it was as if a longing for another life would come over her. She wondered then what it would be like to see green pastures and fat cows and cobbled streets with their picture book houses. Wiesental station and Kilgoolga was all she ever knew. She expected to die here, like Hans but it would have been wonderful to see another world, that magical world from her childhood memories that her grandmother told her about. But her grandmother's memories were from another older generation now gone and memories are impressions that aren't always true. *But it was strange how you remembered things*, thought Hilda and how the German words her grandmother had taught her seemed so real to her sometimes. That was why it had been so, so good to meet young Wolfgang. He had spoken German to her and she had been able to reply, hesitantly at first but her confidence grew as she pronounced the words. It seemed that they came from a familiar part of her very being and amazed her how effortless it was to speak them. Wolfgang encouraged her too. He said she spoke the words as if she were a native. How they had laughed together, though, when she stumbled over some of those words.

Tante Hilda, he always addressed her in this way after he had got to know her. *Tante Hilda.*

It surprised her too how it felt to be called 'Aunt'. She had longed to be a mother but that hope had died with Jack all those years ago and now here was this young stranger making her feel as if she could be. Strange really because she and Hans weren't even sure where Wolfgang fitted into the family. It was all so distant but then when they looked at the old German Bible that Pastor Albert had brought with him to Australia and the three of them studied the names, almost unreadable and fading, that they discovered that Wolfgang was indeed descended from a very distant cousin on their mother's side of the family. And at that news, Hilda hugged young Wolfgang and even Hans had managed a smile and shook the young man's hand. Then Wolfgang told them he had tracked their names down in Germany and hoped he hadn't imposed on their hospitality?

"Not at all," replied Hans and he insisted on opening a bottle of fine wine from white grapes grown on the Rhine, just to celebrate the occasion. That had been a wonderful evening.

And so Wolfgang settled happily for two months with Hans and Hilda and was never a cause for concern to either of them. In fact, he brought a glimmer of joy into their lives that they hadn't thought possible.

"If only he could stay," Hilda sighed.

"Well, you know he can't," her brother snapped. Some of Hilda's ideas were nonsense. "He told me he has to go back to Germany to study. He's going to be a doctor, you know."

"I know," and Hilda sighed again. "You're right, Hans... as always."

And that was the end of the matter. Wolfgang stayed and helped as much as he could but his fine hands and thin physique made the heavy physical work difficult for him. Hans grumbled but Hilda said nothing. Wolfgang could do no wrong in her eyes. But they were both grateful for the company and were sad when the young German had to say goodbye. His departure left a lonely little gap in their lives. Soon, however, the days returned to the inevitability of duty and routine and the brother and sister did not speak to each other of Wolfgang until one day when they received a letter postmarked from Sydney.

Wolfgang's letter was brief and written in his precise way. He wrote in English but added a few words in German at the end of his letter. He thanked Hans and Hilda for their hospitality and hoped they would keep in touch with him after his return to Germany.

Tante Hilda
Danke fűr deine gastlichkeit...
(Aunt Hilda
Thank you for your hospitality...)

Hilda liked that. She made a mental note to keep in contact and perhaps to write in German if she could? Wolfgang said in his letter that he had a friend from Ireland who might visit them sometime and this young man would be able to help them both as he was good with his hands. He had worked as a joiner in Edinburgh and grew up on a farm in the West of Ireland. When Hilda showed Hans the letter, he didn't say much. Just nodded his head and passed the letter back to his sister.

"Don't know why a young bloke would want to come to visit us... Kilgoolga isn't exactly on the beaten track! These young ones get some fanciful ideas... suppose Wolfgang was OK. I don't know about this one though. No doubt you'll want to spoil him if he does make it here."

57

But Hilda wasn't deterred by Hans. Not in the slightest. *I hope this young Irish fellow does get here,* she thought, *whatever Hans says. It would be so good to have someone else to talk to!*

Oisin was woken by the raucous call of the kookaburra outside his window. The bird began slowly, almost as if it was warming up its motor, and then the shrill cackle interrupted the early morning silence. Oisin stirred and looked at the small clock on his bedside table. It was seven o'clock in the morning and he felt sleepy and very much alone. Bella had been true to her word and had cooked him up a feast of bacon, eggs, three sausages and four slices of thick white bread which he had washed down with cups of strong black tea. She was curious about this young Irish bloke but a certain reserve held her tongue and so she talked about Kilgoolga and the drought – no rain for two years, the farmers are suffering, we all are - and the fire at the Commercial. The latter had been the talk of the town for weeks. The general opinion was that the owner had put a match to the hotel himself for insurance purposes because everyone knew the place wasn't doing very well. Ever since that wife of his had run off with the grain merchant, well, you wouldn't wonder, now would you? Eddie, the owner was always a funny chap, went to school with him, you know and he was odd even then. Never joined in. And as he got older, the odder he got, you know. Just because he inherited the hotel from his father, didn't mean he'd make a go of it. And he didn't. Wasn't cut out to be a publican, you know. No wonder his wife left him although why she latched on to that grain merchant, well, that's anyone's guess? Desperate, she must have been to get out of the place. Wasn't from Kilgoolga, you know, further out, Longreach way and Bella laughed thinking about it all. Been the most exciting thing that had happened in Kilgoolga for years and everyone had an opinion. Then the fire sort of brought the stories to life again. Seemed suspicious that the fire started six months to the day after Eddie's wife left him, wouldn't you think? Oisin had thought that Australians didn't say much but Bella was proving him wrong as each story led onto to another one until finally, she stopped in mid-sentence to say, somewhat abruptly,

"Well, we'd better get you to bed before it's time to get up!"

And Oisin, somewhat relieved, was finally ushered into the small room at the back of the bar which Bella had mentioned hours before. Here he was to spend his first night in the outback town of Kilgoolga and wake in the morning to a bright day with the sun already a hot yellow ball in the eastern sky.

Bella was nowhere to be seen and Oisin thought his best course of action was to explore the place a bit and find out how he could best get to Hans and Hilda Seefeldt. He had been a bit taken aback when he had mentioned their names the previous night in the bar because he had thought that Wolfgang was a decent sort of fellow and any relation of his, would have been decent too. It was all a bit of a mystery. However, Oisin decided that he had best stick to his original plan because after all he didn't really have much of a plan anyway! At least if he could find the place – Wiesental station – he might be able to get some work out there because there didn't seem to be much around in Kilgoolga. He stepped out into the bright sunlight to find that there was more to Kilgoolga in the daylight than had been evident the night before for the town was already awake and people were moving around. Now there were cars parked in the main street where last night there had been spaces. A tractor with a trailer full of bales of hay had stopped in the middle of the road. The driver of the tractor appeared to be having a lengthy conversation with another man who had got out of his utility truck to speak to him. The conversation seemed amiable and other vehicles swerved around the two stationary vehicles. Some of the drivers tooted and waved to the two men. Oisin crossed over the road and walked under the awnings once again. It was all so different from the night before.

People looked at him as he walked past them but no one acknowledged him. It occurred to him that he was virtually invisible and he could pass by without any of them making a comment. He noticed the name on one of the shop windows – *Louis Bercault Drapery. That surely must be the amorous Frenchman,* he thought*, there can't be too many Frenchmen around here.* It was intriguing that an unknown Frenchman had made his way to this part of the world but then Oisin himself had found his way here. What a contrasting thought! The shop door was open. The interior of the shop was dark against the glare from outside and Oisin could just make out a wooden counter. Behind the counter were rows and rows of drawers and arranged opposite in neat groups stood rolls of fabrics of different sizes. This was all Oisin could see except for a mannequin dressed in a blue silk gown. It was positioned dramatically in the shop window behind the wooden sign that advertised the owner. Thoughtfully, Oisin continued his walk past the shops.

He passed a café. The brightly painted sign advertised the fact that this was the ABC CAFÉ and it looked to be clean inside. He thought he would have something to eat there after he explored a bit more of the town. A few doors from the café and at the end of the street, on the corner, stood the sad remains of the Commercial Hotel. It looked as if it would require a lot of money to bring it back to what was probably once a rather grand wooden building.

Oisin had taken about twenty minutes to walk from The Kilgoolga Arms to the Commercial and all the time, he had felt many eyes on him but they weren't friendly eyes. As he walked, he became aware that he was being studied in a curious manner, noted by everyone but not spoken to, and he wondered if he had been known to any of them, would it have been different. At least, he hoped it would have been but at the present moment with so many eyes now focussed on his back, he wasn't too sure. It was with some relief that he finally arrived at the end of the shops and sat down on a wooden bench in front of the War Memorial. From here he could see the garage, the train crossing and beyond this, on the other side of the line, the wooden houses with their galvanised iron red roofs. It was already hot and Oisin was glad to sit down in the shade of an overhanging acacia. The ground was dry and the grass burnt brown. Cracks had formed in the soil. Around the granite War Memorial, a flower garden tended no doubt in the good times and allowed to bloom then, now grew nothing but rose bushes. The bushes had not been pruned and they looked uncared for, forgotten.

Oisin studied the War Memorial. He had a keen sense of observation and noted that the soldier, his head bowed and his two hands leaning on the butt of the rifle had his slouched hat somewhat unevenly placed on his head. It looked as if the sculptor wasn't too sure how to carve the hat or perhaps he had been in a hurry to finish the work.

IN MEMORY OF THE FALLEN FROM KILGOOLGA
AND DISTRICT
THE GREAT WAR
1914 – 1918

And underneath, six names from that conflict. The Empire had demanded sacrifice and this country had willingly sent its sons to die on foreign soil so far from home.

Then the World War Two fallen, more names – twenty in total – carved on the plinth below. From such a small community and so far from this country town, Oisin mused. Alone on the bench and so far from his home too, he felt a sudden sense of empathy for these lads, many of them younger than himself. Who were they, these unknown soldiers who had died so far away? What thoughts? What fears? What hopes had they? All that was left of them were names carved on a stone in the place where they were born and where they most likely had expected to live to an old age. Did any of them think of Kilgoolga as they lay dying on those foreign fields? Or was it all a great adventure, a means of escaping from the town of their birth? Perhaps the sense of mate ship so talked about in this country had held the boys together? When finally the reality of what was happening to them began to sink in was it their mates they thought of at the final moment? Or did they remember their mothers and the girls they left back home? Perhaps it was the pain and the blood and the fear of dying for these lads so far from home. Now there was another war and sacrifices would have to be made again. More young Australian boys would die in a foreign land and he thought of the soldiers on the train to Kilgoolga. They were laughing and joking then. Would they still be joking in the jungles of Vietnam? Oisin had seen the headlines in the papers and the call to arms. Conscription to be introduced, the papers said. No one consulted. Governments make the laws. Oisin sighed and he looked once again at the names and wondered if he would meet any of their descendants in this place? He took a mental note of some of them – Cpl F.J. Paterson, Pte L.D. George, Lt. P. Bradshaw, Pte T.M. Anderson. *No Seefeldts there*, he thought*, but then they were German after all.* Hilda and Hans Seefeldt were the only names he knew in Kilgoolga. He would have to meet them soon. He wondered what they were like. Wolfgang had said they were old but he seemed to like them. *Guess it's worth a try and someone* *must know how I can get to meet them*, he thought, *but certainly everyone acted a bit strange when the name, Seefeldt was mentioned at the Kilgoolga Arms*. He decided to head back towards the town and see if he could try to find someone to help him. It was then that a spiral of dust caught his eye.

He had never seen anything like it before. The swirl of dust moved in a tight ball, gathering dry leaves and grass into it. It grew larger as it progressed along the dry park. No other sign of wind was evident and this ball of fast moving air had appeared as if by magic. It sped past Oisin as he sat on the wooden bench and sucked in more blades of dry grass at the War Memorial. He watched as the spiral moved further away towards the main road and the garage and then it disappeared from sight as it crossed the railway line. He slouched backwards and rested his head on the back rail of the bench. The swirl of dry grass and leaves had appeared for a few seconds, then it had gone and everything was still again. Just as quickly, Cecy came into his mind. He lay on top of her and he could have sworn he felt her breathe. His body moved and to his horror he was experiencing an erection. He gripped the arm of the bench and closed his eyes. There was no one about. Cecy was there. He felt every movement of her body. It was as if he had become possessed by her at that exact moment. He hadn't thought of her for a day or two, ever since he had arrived in Kilgoolga, but he had never before felt such intensity of desire. And then just as the dust swirl had appeared from nowhere and vanished as quickly, Cecy left him. He opened his eyes and he was still in the same place near the War Memorial. The names appeared once more in front of him and everything was as it had been a few minutes before. When he got up from the bench, his legs were shaking.

CHAPTER FOUR

"G'day, Paddy... how's it goin', mate?"

Oisin heard the voice and recognised the face. It was Charlie from last night at the Kilgoolga Arms. The short man with the large hat and the black and tan dog, the one who looked as if he had been through too many summers and seen too much of life. This was the same man that Oisin thought had followed him in the half dark of the night before as he crossed over the railway line. Whoever he was, it was a welcome sound because no one else had paid any attention to Oisin as he walked back along the main street to the shops. Charlie was leaning on the side of a red utility truck. The truck looked the worse for wear for the whole of the tailgate was smashed inwards and one of the rear lights was nowhere to be seen. Oisin recognised the hat first and then the man. Charlie looked better in the daylight. He had shaved and his blue eyes had just a trace of merriment in them as he studied the young Irishman in front of him.

"Been thinkin'," he said and he pulled some strands of tobacco from a plastic packet. He rolled the tobacco into the thin paper, lit the cigarette and started to puff away just like Oisin's Uncle Mick had done, way back in Ballybeg. The cigarette hung onto his bottom lip and seemed to balance there by some miracle because when Charlie spoke, the cigarette bobbed up and down in time with the movement of his mouth.

"Been thinkin'," he continued. Oisin waited and waited. Charlie took another puff and the cigarette went back to its preferred position.

"Had a word with Bella this mornin'. She's a bit worried about you, ya know."

This surprised Oisin. Bella hadn't seemed to be very interested in him the previous night. She had fed him but talked about herself. She hadn't even asked what her guest was doing in Kilgoolga. It was all very confusing for Oisin who began to wonder what Charlie was thinking about and why the little man had suddenly taken such an interest in him. Charlie scratched his head and then he drawled,

"Bella and me got talkin'. 'What's this young Irish fella doin'?' she says to me. Well, Bella's like that...she's a bloody mother hen sometimes but she means well. Must have taken a likin' to you and that's a bloody good thing. Bella's a rough diamond but her heart's in the right place, mate. Remember that."

Charlie took a few seconds to get all those words out. *He's got the great Australian drawl*, thought Oisin somewhat amused. It was the first time he had really noticed the slow speech patterns of the Australians, and out in the bush, they spoke even more slowly than they did in Sydney where people rushed around all the time. Nothing happens very fast around here. He wondered where the conversation was heading next. He was also feeling hungry and had planned to go to the ABC Café for a meal but here he was, caught in the main street by Charlie who didn't seem to want to go away. *Still, he's at least talking to me*, thought Oisin. *No one else is.* He coughed slightly and then he said,

"I'm planning to go and visit Hans and Hilda Seefeldt. I thought they might be able to get me some work. I met a lad in Sydney who told me about them... said he would write to them."

65

It sounded plausible enough. Wolfgang had said he would write and Oisin thought the German looked like someone who would keep his word. Hopefully, Hans and Hilda Seefeldt would have the letter by now.

Charlie nodded his head. He spat a strand of tobacco onto the footpath and rubbed it with his boot.

"Well, that's what me and Bella have been talkin' about, mate. Thought we might be able to help."

Oisin looked puzzled. This was the last thing he had expected. The whole town of Kilgoolga had seemed unfriendly and just a little frightening.

"Well," Charlie continued. His thoughts appeared to have caught up with his tongue at last, "I've got to take a load of stuff out to the Bradshaws tomorra. Could take you out to the Seefeldts then... if you like?"

This all seemed to be a great idea for Oisin. His spirits lifted and he grinned.

"That's good of you," he said. "I was wonderin' how I'd get there. No idea where anything is."

"Seefeldt's place about eighty ks away. Bradshaws further along the road. Bradshaws own everything 'round here."

"Where will I meet you?"

"I'll find ya, mate. No probs."

Clambering into Charlie's battered up old ute was an experience in itself for Oisin. First of all, he had to find somewhere for his backpack.

"Chuck it in the back," said Charlie good naturedly.

There was a rather large generator, a metal container and tool box taking up most of the space available and the backpack looked rather small jammed between these items. A bale of hay secured by some twine filled the remaining space and on top of this, sat Charlie's black and tan dog. He wagged his tail when he saw Oisin.

"C'mon, Digger. In the front!" and at his master's command the dog leapt to the ground and then onto the driver's seat.

Oisin climbed into the ute and sat down too, next to the dog. The front of the ute was an untidy mess and there was a hole about the size of a football in the floor at Oisin's feet. It looked as if the vehicle might break down at any moment because it took Charlie about ten minutes to persuade it to start but once that was accomplished they set off at a respectable speed. To say there was any great need for Charlie to concentrate on his driving would have been an understatement because the road out of Kilgoolga just stretched in a straight line to the horizon. The empty landscape and the noise of the engine made conversation difficult. Charlie wasn't one for much talking and no words passed between the two men until they came to a fork in the road. They had been travelling for about an hour before Charlie spoke.

"Time for smoko, mate," he said.

He turned the engine off and pushed the door of the ute, giving it a kick with his right foot to open it. Digger leapt out followed by a rather disoriented Oisin. This was the first time that the young Irishman had experienced the enormity of the Australian bush. Charlie had parked the ute under a small misshapen coolibah tree. Rough shredded red-brown ribbons of bark at the base gave way to a smooth grey sheen further up the trunk. The coolibah's thick leathery leaves provided some shade underneath. The tree was a survivor. It grew beside a dry watercourse and its roots must have somehow found nutrients in the dusty soil because it was the only tree in sight. On the far side of the gully about five scrawny wallabies were attempting to drink from what little water there was still flowing. On hearing the noise of the truck and the sight of men and dog, the creatures took off and in a few seconds were gone.

"Poor buggers," remarked Charlie as he gave Oisin a cup of thick black tea in an enamel mug. "No rain for two years. But it's comin'. Feel it in me bones. Ma missus says I'm a rain god."

Charlie handed him two slices of thick white bread with a generous portion of ham between them. Oisin was hungry and grateful for the food. He was surprised however. He hadn't expected to hear that Charlie had a wife. He thought that the little man had to be a confirmed bachelor.

"Me missus's a great cook, Paddy. 'Here,' she says to me. 'Take some chocolate cake too, I'm sure that young Irish bloke'll be hungry'. Likes to feed everyone up, does me missus. Doesn't look like she's had much success with me, what da ya reckon?"

He patted his stomach. Charlie was as thin as the proverbial rake and Oisin grinned.

"I'm Oisin, by the way," he said. "Oisin Kelly."

He thought it was about time that he introduced himself properly to this rather cheerful little man. He was getting tired of the constant 'Paddy'. Although Charlie was a man of few words Oisin was beginning to like him.

"Stone the crows! That's some name. I thought all Paddies were Paddy!" Charlie was in the middle of finishing off the massive piece of chocolate cake.

How da ya say it?" he asked through a mouthful of cake.

"Ohsheen."

"Ohsheen. Well, well. Ohsheen Kelly. There's a family of Kellys out Milberra way. Any relation of yours, da ya reckon?"

"Doubt it, mate." Oisin shook his head. And then he laughed. He hadn't laughed for weeks.

His remark seemed to amuse Charlie and he grinned exposing his two front teeth. His teeth, spaced apart, appeared custom built to hold his cigarette.

"Well, mate. We'd best get goin'. Now, see here... " and he pointed to the left of the coolibah tree, "that's the road to the Bradshaws. All this, on both sides is their land. If we go along here to the right, we'll get to Seefeldts place and the Patersons are further along from them out Milberra way... but it's mostly Bradshaws. But you'll find out soon enough who's who and who isn't! Me, I've got bugger all 'cept what ya see in front of ya... and me dawg. Can't forget me old dawg! Got a house in town for me and the missus an' that's our lot."

"I'll take ya along to the Seefeldts now," he continued. "No worries. Her Ladyship can wait!"

"Her Ladyship?"

"Yeah... Lady Eleanor... don't get me started on the Bradshaws, mate! Could write a book 'bout them, if I could write, that is!" He laughed again.

It was now that Oisin thought he would find out what Charlie did for a living.

"Oh, me... I fix things. If it's got a motor and a few bits of wire, I'll fix it! Can't do much else... but I can fix things and the Bradshaws are always shoutin'. Farmers, hey?"

The rest of the journey passed in silence. Digger positioned his head on Oisin's knee and shut his eyes. It was reassuring somehow to feel the warmth of the little dog's body. He had found the road from Kilgoolga monotonous and the landscape had hardly changed for miles. At the fork in the road, the bitumen road ended. Now they travelled on a gravel track and Charlie had to drive more carefully in order to avoid the many bumps and potholes. There was a boundary fence on either side of the road. The grey wooden posts with strands of rusty barbed wire strung between them suggested a barrier and now instead of the flat landscape, hills appeared in the distance. Charlie changed into a lower gear in order to drive up a slight incline and then he stopped the truck at the top. The view was different from this vantage point.

"Seefeldt's place's about two miles from here," he pointed towards two iron gates. "I can't go no further, mate. He keeps everything bolted down... you'll have to walk from here. There's a track down the hill... you'll see it... the homestead's in the valley... ya can't miss it. Bit run down sort of place is Wiesental but them Seefeldts 'ave been here for generations. Ya'll find out."

Oisin got out of the battered up old utility truck and retrieved his backpack. He felt he was leaving the security of the ute for the uncertainty of the outside world.

"Thanks, Charlie," he said and the two men shook hands.

"No worries, Oisin, mate." The unlit cigarette dangled precariously from the little man's mouth as he spoke. "Watch out... Hans's a weird bugger sometimes. He's been known to throw a wobbly or two... best not to get on the wrong side of him...he gets mad as a meat-axe sometimes, mate. See ya round..."

And with that, Charlie persuaded the ute to do a U-turn on the uneven gravel surface, waved cheerfully and drove off in the direction they had come, leaving a trail of dust and exhaust fumes behind him.

The iron gates were indeed bolted down. Chains and padlocks secured the two rusty gates together. A wooden board was attached to the middle wire of one of the gates and on it was written in large black letters: WIESENTAL. Beside the other gate stood a forty-four gallon drum turned sideways and nailed down onto four wooden posts. The front of the drum had been cut in half and the name SEEFELDT was painted in black on the front of it. *At least I'm at the right place*, thought Oisin. He was feeling a little unsure of his next move. There was not a movement of wind or any sound of life about him. Wispy white clouds had now appeared in the sky. There was nothing for it but to climb over the gate and head for the homestead as it appeared that this was indeed the address that had been given to him by Wolfgang. The silence of the Australian bush, the sight and smells of the gums all around him and the loneliness of his situation was causing the young Irishman from Ballybeg to question his whole reasons for coming to this place. If Cecy Stanworth from upstate New York had suddenly appeared in front of him, he might just have been tempted to strangle her!

He hauled his backpack onto his back and started to walk along the road. It was more of a rough track devoid of the dry grass and it led downwards towards a small creek. Here, there was a small flow of water with some green grass growing at either side. It was the first greenery Oisin had seen for miles. He paused to get his bearings. It looked easy enough to cross the creek and he did so, stepping carefully from one rock to another. He noticed some black cattle in the distance corralled behind the wire fences; the barbed wire fences that seemed to be everywhere. He walked on towards them, following the rough track. It was a track for vehicles and Oisin decided that at least there must be something or someone to have made this possible. Above, the wispy clouds had been replaced by heavier cumulus ones and the air had grown slightly cooler. *Maybe Charlie was right*, Oisin thought, *rain might be on the way*. He hoped he could get to the homestead before the rain started because if there hadn't been any rain for two years, when it came, it would most probably be a deluge. At that thought, he quickened his pace. The track led up another slight hill and when he reached the top, he paused. He could see the homestead in the distance now and a skeleton-like iron windmill with two galvanised iron water tanks in the front of it. He opened another iron gate which didn't have a padlock to secure it, just a thin wire tied around the post and then, as he was about to shut the gate, he heard a sound like a gunshot overhead. He saw a scattering of black crows high above but he couldn't see anyone around. Nervous now, he slowed down.

He was closer to the windmill and he noticed its sails were beginning to turn slowly as the wind picked up. The two ridged water tanks sat precariously on top of wooden posts and a pipe led down from one of them to a water trough which must have been for the animals. That was the last sight Oisin saw because the next moment he was flat on his stomach with his heavy backpack pinning him to the ground. He heard the zing of the bullet a few metres from the top of his head and he dropped to the ground instinctively. The next moment when he opened his eyes he was looking into the double barrel of a 12 bore.

He slowly raised his head. He saw brown leather boots and faded blue denim jeans. He dared not look further. He could feel his heart pumping as if it was about to burst. He had broken the fall with his hands and in so doing, had cut his left hand on a small upturned rock. There were small drops of blood on the rock. The safety catch of the gun clicked above his head. He could see the finger on the trigger. He thought he was about to be shot. When he tried to say something, no words came out. *This is it,* he thought. *This is it...*

"WHAT ARE YA DOIN' ON MY LAND?"

He felt the cold steel of the barrel on his right shoulder.

"GET UP!"

Oisin slowly raised his head and eased himself onto his knees. He was trembling all over. He tried to stand up but the barrel was now so close to his face he could feel the cold metal on his cheek. Still, he couldn't speak. He had never been so frightened in all his life.

"MOVE!!"

The sound of the words brought Oisin to his knees and at last he was able to look into the face of the man who held the gun. It was not a friendly face.

"I'm looking... for Hans Seefeldt...," he stammered. He couldn't think of anything else to say.

"You're lookin' at him."

The gun and the hand withdrew and the barrel was broken. Oisin straightened himself and shook his backpack into a more comfortable position on his back.

"I ... I was given your name... in Sydney... " he mumbled. He was unsure of his words and they didn't seem to come out of his mouth the right way. It felt as if he had left his body and was looking down on the scene from above and his words were not coming from any part of him. At any moment, he would find himself somewhere else, far away. His hands still trembled. They wouldn't stop. It was surreal and all the while Hans Seefeldt just kept staring at him, an uncomfortable stare and it made Oisin even more nervous.

"A relation of yours... called Wolfgang... he gave me your name... said ye might have some work for me."

Oisin stumbled over his words. He wished he could remember Wolfgang's surname but his mind was a blank. The two men stared at each other. Hans Seefeldt was over six feet tall. He was a giant beside the smaller Oisin who hadn't inherited his father's height. The two men were like two wild dogs eyeing each other, working out each other's weaknesses. Then Hans said,

"Ah... Wolfgang... I remember him. Didn't expect to see anyone wanderin' round here today..."

The words dangled in the still air.

"Better come along then."

And with those words, Hans turned and walked at a fast pace towards the homestead. Oisin followed behind. At times the young Irishman had to trot to keep up. Hans looked neither left nor right but strode purposely ahead, his gun balanced on his right shoulder.

The Seefeldt wooden homestead with its faded red galvanised roof was typical of others and larger than some. Built in the valley, the building was further sheltered from the weather by two quite large paperbarks which grew at the back and would have given some shade in the summer. Wooden stumps elevated the house by about a metre or so. This allowed the warm air to rise and thus provide relief during the hot weather. A little way from the homestead, Oisin noticed a high fence which housed a motley crew of hens and a few metres behind the hen run was an open barn with a Land Rover and a tractor parked beside it. There was no sign of human habitation and the whole place looked as if it belonged to another era. A blue and grey cattle dog, chained to a post in front of the house, barked furiously as the two men approached. Hans muttered something to the dog and then kicked the unfortunate creature with his right foot which caused the dog to yelp and slink back towards the post, its tail between his legs.

Hans led Oisin up six wooden steps, onto the open veranda and into the kitchen. He didn't speak but carefully placed the shotgun on the rack in the corner of the room. The kitchen was obviously the centre of the house. The main focus of the room was a pine table with eight chairs neatly arranged around it. On one of the chairs a large ginger cat was asleep. Hans carefully picked up the cat in his arms and sat down, stroking the cat as he did so. The cat opened a sleepy eye and started to purr. As Hans ran his hand gently along the cat's body, the purring got louder. This was the only sound in the room. Uncertain as to what to do, Oisin stood at the end of table and looked around the room. His left hand still bled from the fall and he shoved it into his trouser pocket so as not to draw attention to it.

As he stood there his nervousness increased. He didn't want to look too closely at Hans. All Oisin could hear was the purring of the cat and the ticking of the clock on the wall above the window. Hans appeared to be lost in his own thoughts for he kept his head down all the time. His whole attention seemed to be on the cat. Oisin cleared his throat to make a sound and hoped that this would cause Hans to say something for in actual fact he wasn't sure what to do next or what to say to this strange man. Finally, Hans looked up and said,

"Wolfgang wasn't much use. What can you do?"

"Oh... I'm OK with a hammer and nail ... used to farmin' too... my parents had a farm in the West of Ireland... bit different from here... more rain... " Oisin tried to make a joke but Hans did not smile. Instead, he just stared and Oisin felt his face redden.

"Wolfgang thought I might be able to do a bit of work 'round the place for ye ... but maybe not... ?"

He was beginning to think the whole idea of coming out to the west and even to this country was the wrong one and his only hope might be to get as far away from the Seefeldt station and Kilgoolga as it was possible to be. He began to plan how he would be able to leave this place. Hans suddenly spoke.

"Might have some work. See what you can do tomorra. If ya shape up, I'll pay you fifty dollars per week and board. That's if ya can do a bit more 'round the place than Wolfgang. Useless bugger he was."

The cat and the purring got even louder. Oisin had to make a quick decision but he was uncertain of what to say. He would soon need money but to stay in this hostile and strange situation? He looked at the clock on the wall. It was half past four in the afternoon and it would soon be dark. He had nowhere else to go.

"That'd be OK," he muttered and immediately wished he hadn't been so hasty but then, what was the alternative? Wolfgang hadn't seemed bothered about his aunt and uncle, just said they were old, so maybe it might be alright, just for a day or two until he could work out what to do?

75

"That's sorted then. My sister Hilda'll be in soon and we can eat. She'll tell ya where everything is."

With those words, Hans stood up. The ginger cat jumped off his knee and ran to the door and Hans followed it slowly, leaving Oisin to take stock of his new situation.

Hilda Seefeldt was surprised to see a strange young man sitting on a chair in her kitchen. She had been collecting eggs and had carried them back to the house, arranging them carefully into her apron so as not to drop them. Both her hands held the corners of the apron and when she saw the young man, she let go of the apron and three of the eggs fell to the floor with a plop.

"Oh... clumsy me! What will Hans say?"

Hilda did not wait for either a reply or an introduction. Instead she placed the remaining eggs into a bowl on the worktop counter and kneeling on the floor in front of Oisin, she quickly cleaned up the broken eggs. She did not look at the young man but kept glancing at the open door to the outside as if she was expecting Hans to appear at any second and comment on the situation.

Hilda Seefeldt was a stout woman and tidy. She was always particular in her appearance and kept her grey hair plaited and tied up in a bun. Years under the hot sun had burnt her face dark brown; her forehead was lined and her skin leathery but she was still an attractive woman in her own way. Every morning she dressed carefully and always wore a cotton dress and an apron which she tied tightly around her waist. On Sundays when she and Hans went to church, she replaced the apron with her 'best dress' and would never go out the door without the straw hat on her

76

head and her mother's amethyst broach pinned carefully onto the top left side of her dress. On Friday, every fortnight, she and Hans would drive to Kilgoolga to do the shopping and on those days, she wore the same weekday dress minus the apron. But now the apron was wet from the broken eggs and she had to take it off in front of this young man with the blue eyes and black hair and beard. She was so flustered that she started to chatter. The young man with the sad blue eyes stood up. He looked unsure of what to do and didn't like to interrupt for he had no idea what this odd little woman was talking about. In fact, had Hilda been able to read his mind she would have discovered that the young man had begun to think he had arrived in a hidden world, a dangerous world too and although the gun was now safely on the rack at the back of the kitchen, the possibility of it being used again was very worrying for him.

"I'm Oisin Kelly. Can I help ye at all?" he asked gently.

Hilda, now busy at the stove, shook her head. Her head shook furiously as if she definitely did not need any help but then she remembered her manners and replied:

"That's an unusual name," she said. "Oisin. I've never heard that name before. You're not from round here, are you? Let me guess? That's a Scottish accent… no, I bet you're Irish!"

"I'm Irish."

"Oh."

There was a slight pause and then Hilda held out her hand.

"I'm Hilda Seefeldt… have you met my brother, Hans?" She giggled like a young girl.

"Aye. We've met."

Oisin and Hilda shook hands and then they smiled at each other.

About half an hour later, Hans came back into the kitchen followed by the large ginger cat. He didn't say a word but sat down on the chair at the head of the table. Hilda carried three plates to the table. The plates were piled high with beef stew, cabbage and mashed potatoes. Three glasses with tap water completed the picture.

"Sit down, young man," Hans pointed to the empty chair.

"His name is Oisin, Hans," said Hilda.

"Well, sit down then, Oisin and we'll eat," replied Hans.

Hans had tidied himself up and he seemed to be more civil. Both Hans and Hilda bowed their heads and Oisin did the same.

"Lord," Hans spoke, "we thank you for this meal and the goodness of the land that has provided it. We give thanks to you, O merciful God for all the bounties that we have. We are sinners indeed and call upon you for salvation and for mercy. We are unworthy of this life and pray that with each breath of our bodies, we grow closer to you and to the Day of Judgement for it as certain as the day will dawn, it is coming and Satan will be wrought asunder. His power will end and you will once again reign over us all. You have brought to this table, another sinner, a stranger from far away. Grant that he will prove to be a willing servant and work hard as we go about our daily chores, all the while aware of your dominion over us and all that is on this land. Grant that this woman, my sister, Hilda stays loyal to her duties and will provide us with meals such as this one which is now before us. The food on this table will help to sustain us in our daily life as we grow ever closer to you and your divine mercy. We thank you, Lord."

Thinking the prayer showed no signs of ending, Oisin quickly opened his eyes. He hadn't said or heard a prayer like this since his childhood days in Ballybeg. Father O'Malley was prone to long winded prayers then and Oisin had often been restless. The same feelings came into his head but he thought better of it, and quickly closed his eyes again. He had no wish to offend his hosts. As strange as the two of them were, the food looked delicious.

As abruptly as he had started to speak, Hans ended the prayer with a quick 'Amen'. No other words passed until Hilda started up once again:

"We haven't had a guest since Wolfgang was here... remember Wolfgang, Hans? He was such a nice boy, wasn't he ?" and she smiled at Oisin. It was a confidential type of smile and meant for just him.

"I'm a friend of Wolfgang's... "

"Oh, hear that, Hans? Isn't that a wonderful coincidence? Don't you think?"

"I believe the Lord has brought Wolfgang's friend to us, Hilda."

"I know, Hans. It'll be good to have some help again though, won't it?" she said.

"Well, we'll see," replied Hans dismissively.

Oisin said nothing. He glanced at the clock on the wall to check the time and wondered what would happen next.

After their meal, Oisin helped Hilda tidy up. At the end of the large kitchen were lounge chairs and Hans sat in one of them. He stared into the distance and didn't speak until everything was done.

"Hilda, it's time for our Bible reading," he said to his sister when she sat down beside him.

She rose obediently from her chair and took a large leather bound volume of the Bible from the oak desk which sat next to the gun rack. She handed the book to Hans and sat down again. She indicated that Oisin should sit down near her, on one of the kitchen chairs. Hans opened the Bible and read from the Old Testament – Exodus 22,

If a man seduces a virgin who is not pledged to be married and sleeps with her, he must pay the bride-price...

Hans had pale blue eyes and when he paused slightly, Oisin thought of Cecy and he bit his lip. *Help,* he thought.

Hans closed the Bible and shut his eyes. Outside, Oisin was aware of a strange call. It sounded like the barking of a dog but then again, it didn't seem real. Dog-like but not so. Woop! Woop! And silence. Then woop, woop again. Someone had talked of the Barking Owl and he contemplated if that was the noise he was hearing. The noise stopped and the only sound that broke the silence was the ticking of the clock on the wall. He wondered whether he should make any comment about the Bible reading and then thought better of it. Hans stood up. He seemed even taller than he had been before. He filled up the space at the end of the kitchen.

"Up at sparrow's fart round here, young man... " and Hans, noticing Oisin's puzzled expression, added, "that's six o'clock on the dot for you! We'll have breakfast first, then there's some fencin' to be done at the far away paddock. Have ya done any fencin' work before?"

"No, sir but I can learn," replied Oisin, nervously.

"Well, we'll see how ya go then. Have ya any strong boots?"

Hans looked at Oisin's brown leather shoes. They were not suitable for any heavy work.

"No sir."

"Well, think we've a pair of strong boots which would fit ya. We'll sort that out in the mornin'. Good night then," said Hans and he nodded to Oisin and Hilda.

Oisin got clumsily to his feet and was about to reply but Hans was already moving away towards another door which led into a hall. Oisin sat down again and looked at Hilda. She smiled.

"I'll make up Wolfgang's bed for you, Oisin," she said. "You should be comfortable there... he always said he slept well in it..."

CHAPTER FIVE

The morning dawned clear and bright and Oisin, mindful of Hans, was ready to get to work and he rose at six. He felt better after his sleep although he had been disturbed in the early morning by strange scratching sounds on the galvanised iron roof. That had been the possums, Hilda assured him and nothing to worry about although they could be a nuisance, she added, especially if they got into the house. They had been known to randomly nibble apples and cause a bit of a mess. 'Best to make sure all the doors were shut tight,' she said. Hans did not add anything to the conversation and ate his breakfast without making any comments.

The two men went out into the yard. The tractor was ready with a post hole digger attached to the back of it. Hans motioned to Oisin that he should load a pile of fence posts and barbed wire into the utility truck. Oisin hadn't noticed the ute which was parked at the back of the barn. Here, a variety of old farm machinery lay abandoned and rusting away in the sun. It appeared that Hans owned a lot of machinery. Some of it was still in use because there was a trailer, plough and a baler housed in the barn. He was relatively self-sufficient. *But this would have to be*, thought Oisin as he loaded post after post into the truck, *given the nature of the land and the sparse population.* For it occurred to the young man from the West of Ireland that it had to be a lonely existence out here and that help might not be close by if needed. Anyway, Hans would probably not ask for any assistance either. He would most certainly prefer to work on his own. Oisin remained wary of this man for although Hilda seemed kind, her brother showed no such benevolence. When Hans read from the Bible the previous night, Oisin had felt rather uneasy and he hoped that nothing would be asked of him concerning his religious faith which had all but disappeared since his meeting Cecy.

"Can you drive?" Hans spoke abruptly.

"Aye."

"Follow me, then. You can drive the ute and I'll take the tractor."

Without uttering another word, Hans started the engine and a puff of black exhaust fumes rose in the air. Hans and the tractor drove off without waiting for Oisin.

It was a bumpy ride over the dry grass. Oisin's attempt to avoid the stones and the larger rocks was unsuccessful and he had no alternative but to drive over some of them. At each gate, he leapt out of the ute to open the gate. Some gates were harder to open than others. Hans stared straight ahead as he drove the tractor through. One paddock held about twenty black cattle. They were flighty and trotted away when they spotted the vehicles coming towards them. The two men finally got to the place where the fence was to be erected. Oisin noted that Hans had already done a lot of the planning and some of the work. Three or four strainer posts were dug into the ground and a pile of smaller posts lay in a heap near where he parked the ute. The posts had been cut from the iron bark gums and split in half. This in itself would have been hard work and Oisin wondered how Hans had managed without any assistance? He had noticed an old saw bench and circular saw in an open shed behind the barn and guessed that was where the cutting would have been done. But the whole idea of one man looking after all this land was a mystery to Oisin. This was a different world of never ending plains and broken dreams, Oisin concluded as he hauled the posts out of the ute and onto the brown soil. Not a word passed between the two men. The only sounds Oisin heard were from black crows far up in the sky. A flash of noisy cockatiels appeared briefly out of nowhere and disappeared just as quickly to the line of gums. Here they sheltered for a moment and then they were off again; their wings a mass of grey bodies against the blue sky. Human voices were an intrusion into this vast space and only Nature could make its own noise here. The sun rose higher in the sky and the heat increased. Oisin began to sweat and he took off his shirt. His left hand still hurt from the stone and the fall of yesterday but he didn't slacken. He positioned the posts into the ground and wielded the heavy sledge hammer with a strength he didn't think he had. The previous day he wouldn't have believed it possible that he could work like this but the land and the heat brought out a kind of mystical determination into his very being. He worked on.

It looked like the line of the fence had been marked out. Hans spoke once to say that a fence must be straight and there is no excuse ever to have a crooked line for a well laid out fence was a work of art, a barrier and a statement as well. He used the tractor to dig the holes for the smaller posts. These were spaced about ten feet apart and Oisin hammered them into the dry ground. It was hard work. When the posts stood upright, the brown clumps of soil were packed down around them. The proposed fence stretched about a hundred metres and the object appeared to be to join this up with another fence, further along. This second fence would allow the cattle to graze on fresher pasture. Once this was done, the four strands of barbed wire would be strung between them using a fence strainer. 'The two wires in between were the most important,' Hans said. There was a lot of work still to be done and it was imperative that

84

the fence be in place before the rains came for it looked as if the drought was about to break. A spiral of dark blue clouds with a heavy underbelly of black had appeared in the eastern sky and the sun that had just a few hours before been a lonely yellow ball was now covered with cloud. The two men worked on without stopping.

At twelve o'clock Hilda arrived. She had driven the Land Rover through the open paddocks and came with an enormous lunch of sandwiches, chocolate cake and Anzac biscuits. The biscuits were delicious and Oisin ate three. Hilda was pleased for she liked to cook and Hans never complimented her, ever. Hilda and Oisin sat side by side on a tartan rug that she had laid on the ground. They were in the shade of the Land Rover but Hans withdrew and took his sandwiches and tea to the tractor where he remained until Hilda got ready to leave. She had brought the blue and grey cattle dog with her and the dog ran around madly at first but then settled beside the front wheel of the tractor to be near to Hans. When he finished eating, Hans took the canvas water bag which was strapped onto the bull bar of the ute and poured the water from it into a dish which he gave to the dog. The dog drank noisily splashing some of the water onto the ground where it dried up almost immediately. Hans took the dish and stroked the dog on the head. He passed the canvas bag to Oisin. The water was cool and Oisin drank. He was careful not to spill any for he was becoming more aware as the days passed how precious water was in this dry and parched country.

Four hours later, work stopped. The black clouds looked even more promising but nothing had happened. There were occasional roars of thunder and lightning streaks but no rain. It was as if the heavens were playing a game and tempting the land below with promises that might not be kept. But the air was cooler now and perhaps it wouldn't be all that long before the clouds would release their bounty. *But it wasn't to be today,* thought Oisin. His limbs ached and he was sunburnt but he was pleased with what he had done. The line posts were in position. Another two days would see them all in place and then the barbed wire could be strung between them. It would be a straight fence and perhaps a work of art for those who knew.

That evening Hans prayed at the table once again and thanked the Lord for the fence and hoped that the rains would soon come but not before the fence was completed. After the meal, the three of them sat on their allotted chairs and Hans read from the Bible. He opened the book at a random page and read whatever words were on that page so that there was not a continuation from the reading of the day before. Hans was sure that what he read would prove to be inspirational for that day and the Lord spoke to him through these words so it was important to read from them every day. This is what he told Hilda and Oisin. Today's reading was from the Book of Isaiah and spoke of the Helper of Israel. Oisin closed his eyes. He almost nodded off to sleep and would have done so but for a sudden crash of thunder which rocked the walls of the kitchen and was so loud that Hans had to stop reading. It looked as if the drought might be breaking after all.

But the rain didn't come. Every late afternoon while Hans and Oisin toiled building the fence, thick black clouds appeared in the sky followed by rumbles of thunder and occasional flashes of lightning, but no raindrops fell. A week passed. Every night Oisin listened to Hans read from the Bible and every night he fell into bed, glad to lie down but sometimes unable to sleep. His mind went over and over the events of the day, replaying all that had happened. His muscles ached for the work was hard and constant. But every day, he felt his body growing stronger. It was as if all this demanding physical work which required no thinking but just pure brute force was what was needed in his life at this particular moment and, as strange as it was in the isolated world of Hans and Hilda Seefeldt, living here was a welcome relief from all that had gone before. The memory of Cecy still remained. It was a wound that would not heal easily and it showed no signs of disappearing. Sometimes, out of nowhere, he would think of her and stop what he was doing for just a second or two as if in this way he could capture a moment's memory of her because he knew in his heart that he would never forget her, no longer how long he lived. Then the precious moment would pass and he could return to whatever he was doing. Sadder for the memory.

He began to admire the stamina of Hans, a man who must have been well into his seventies, for his employer hardly stopped all day and laboured from the moment of rising in the morning to the time for going to bed. He observed that the lives of Hans and Hilda were determined by an unending and exacting routine and although Hilda was kind, Hans hardly spoke at all except to issue an order or to read out aloud from the Bible. Oisin's few attempts to talk to Hans invariably ended in silence and so the two men spent their days working side by side but not able to reach any sort of connection at all. It was a strange existence for the young man from Ballybeg but in his present state of mind, he found it preferable that he didn't have to try and be friendly or to spend time making much conversation apart from the usual comments about the weather or the day's work plan. Hans always had the day's work mapped out when they sat down for breakfast and the weather was a source of constant observation for both Hilda and Hans as the drought showed no signs of ending and every day seemed hotter than the previous one.

However, on Sunday morning Hans did speak to him. No work was done on this day for this was the Lord's Day, said Hans and Oisin would accompany Hilda and himself to the church. Wolfgang had joined them every Sunday in prayer and after all, Oisin was Wolfgang's friend. There could be no argument. If Oisin was to live with them under their roof and receive their hospitality, it was necessary for him to observe the holy day. This was their custom and going to church had been observed by the family since the days of Pastor Albert and Hans spoke a little about Pastor Albert and what an inspiration that saintly man had been for the generations of Seefeldts who had come after him. Oisin was slightly taken aback by the uncompromising nature of the statement and try as he could, he couldn't think of anything to say which would have released him from going along with the two of them. In fact, to refuse might have unforeseen repercussions and he remembered the gun shot and the look in Hans's pale blue eyes. What would his Catholic mother have made of all this he wondered as he tied his green woven wool tie and smoothed his unruly black hair? But Annie was a long way away and not likely to know that her third son was about to enter a Protestant church and a German one at that! So Oisin tried to sound enthusiastic and said of course he would go with them and thanked them. It seemed to him to be the safest option.

The Lutheran Church was built on a hill and about twenty miles from the homestead. The building was compact and constructed of weatherboard timber. The outside walls were painted yellow with the familiar iron roof, this time painted silver. The building appeared to be well looked after although both the fence and the small gate, which were set at a distance from the church, needed some repair. The small iron gate was open and Hans, Hilda and Oisin were joined by other members of the congregation. No one spoke as they climbed the hill and, apart from a nod to Hilda from a rather large bosomed woman whose straw hat almost obliterated her face, the people appeared to be as silent as the land. When Oisin entered the church, he was surprised to see that there were only about fifteen people in the congregation; most of them were elderly although a man and a woman sat in the front pew with two children aged about ten or so. The children were fidgeting and the woman appeared somewhat embarrassed and kept telling them to stop. Oisin sat down beside Hans and Hilda and looked around. His thoughts turned to Ballybeg and the Mass and then to the Protestant minister and his wife who had livened up Ballybeg. He hadn't attended Mass after he met Cecy and although sometimes he had moments of guilt which usually came after receiving a letter from his mother, he hadn't actually been too bothered about it all, then or now. Cecy was a determined atheist and Oisin sort of went along with her so he felt a bit of a fraud being in this place of worship surrounded by strangers. The service turned out to be not too dissimilar to what he was used to and he sang the hymns and bowed his head and listened to the sermon given by a thin faced pastor who spoke with not much conviction for he kept clearing his throat and coughing. Of more interest to Oisin was the behaviour of Hans whose demeanour and expression was one boarding on fanaticism for the man kept his head bowed for far longer than anyone else and after the service had ended remained in the pew with his eyes shut tight while everyone else trooped out the door to greet the pale faced pastor. Hilda spoke to a few elderly women and introduced one or two of them to Oisin. They looked at him curiously but didn't enquire as to why or how he happened to be with the Seefeldts. The pastor shook Oisin's hand. He had a wet and weak handshake but he managed a thin smile.

"It's good to see a young face at our Divine Service," he said and nodded his head almost as if he wanted to convince himself that his congregation was growing because of this new 'young face'. "You're in good hands with the Seefeldts... " and he attempted a rather disappointing smile.

"Oisin comes from Ireland." This from Hilda.

"My... my. Whatever made you come to Kilgoolga?"

The pastor was puzzled. He said anyone making such a long journey had to have a fairly good reason for doing so and he wondered what it could possibly be. Oisin was about to answer as best he could but he was prevented from doing so by the arrival of Hans who commanded the pastor's attention. Hans stepped in front of Oisin and faced the pastor. He was angry and seeing the state he was in, both Hilda and Oisin withdrew to a safe distance and stood side by side away from the pastor and the rest of the congregation. Neither spoke nor could they make out what Hans was saying.

Hans appeared agitated. He pointed his finger at the pastor and shook his head. Just as the whole situation seemed to be getting out of control, a thin woman wearing a floral cotton dress and white straw hat came out of the church and stood next to the pastor. She successfully positioned herself between the pastor and Hans so that Hans had to step back a little.

"That's the pastor's wife... Madge," whispered Hilda confidentially.

Hans shook his head and then, with what seemed to be a violent movement, shook his fist at the pastor and strode towards the gate. He brushed past an elderly man who was leaning on his stick talking to another equally elderly man who was also leaning on a stick. Both men had to step back because Hans had no intention of stopping. As he reached the small iron gate, Hilda took hold of Oisin's arm and said in a frightened voice:

"Hurry... hurry... he's in one of his moods... we must stop him before he gets to the Land Rover!"

Hilda broke into a run down the hill. As she reached the gate, she tripped slightly on a clump of dry earth and it was only that Oisin was so close by and able to catch hold of her arm that she didn't fall. She was too agitated to say anything because Hans was already in the Land Rover and had started the engine. With a mighty movement for a woman of her age and height, she leapt from the gate to the door of the Land Rover and pulled the door open. She and Oisin climbed in beside Hans who barely noticed them as he thrust the vehicle into first, crunching the gears as it did, and drove off at speed down the gravel track without looking to the left or right. Two miles along the track they came to a T junction and Hans braked suddenly. The sudden and unexpected movement threw both Oisin and Hilda towards the dashboard. They looked at each other in surprise and then before they had a chance to say anything, both had to grab hold of the seat as Hans veered dangerously to the left. Oisin noticed the road sign in front of him for Hans had very nearly hit it: KILGOOLGA 90 km and MILBERRA 40 km. *The country's going metric,* he thought *but most people are still thinking in miles*. It was one of those weird and irrelevant thoughts that come into a person's head which has nothing to do with the circumstance which they find themselves in at that particular moment. Hans drove the rest of the way to the homestead. Oisin converted the figure back into miles and clung to the seat as if he thought that his life was about to end. Hilda, next to her brother, sat rigid and silent but once, as they careered around the one and only corner of the road with the speedo reaching 80 kilometres per hour and the old Land Rover spluttering in protest, she patted Oisin's knee, ever so slightly as if to reassure him. He didn't say a word.

When they reached the iron gates of the homestead with its two padlocks and chains, Hans put on the brakes again and a plume of dust rose around the vehicle. Hilda handed Oisin the keys to the padlocks and he stepped out. His legs were shaking. He opened the gate and Hans drove through the opening but instead of stopping, he kept on

91

going leaving a very bewildered Oisin to walk the two miles to the homestead.

The heat of the day grew more intense and night fall brought little relief. The dark clouds gathered once more and were full of the promised rain but still none came. The land lay as parched and as dry as it had been for months. Lying in his bed, tossing and turning and unable to sleep, Oisin went over the events of the day and the whole bizarre experience of living here with Hans and Hilda Seefeldt. He had no idea what had caused Hans to behave in such a way at the church and on the drive back. Afterwards, Hans remained taciturn and only spoke a few perfunctory words to Hilda and Oisin. Withdrawing abruptly after the midday meal, he had disappeared and didn't reappear again till night fall when he once again read from the Bible and prayed out aloud before retiring early, muttering words under his breath that neither Hilda nor Oisin could hear.

Alone in his bed, Oisin could hear the rustle of the possums on the roof above his head and a noisy lone mosquito intent on extracting food from his naked body. He lay naked on the sheet for it was too hot for bed clothes. Most mornings his bed was a pile of crumbled sheets and sometimes he only managed a few precious hours sleep. The windows of the homestead were all encased with a fine wire mesh to keep out the myriad of biting and annoying insects that made life in the outback such a misery but there were always a few, like this annoying mosquito that managed to get though. He tried to focus his mind on something else, a trick he had learned at school when the lessons had been boring and the something else was preferable to Latin or Mathematics. But it didn't seem to work tonight and the bothersome mosquito buzzed above his head, unseen and unable to be caught. He wondered what he could do about living here. It had been difficult for him in the beginning working with Hans. What a revelation then to discover that he enjoyed the physical work of building the fence and the other farm work. At night, lying in bed after the day's work, his arm and leg muscles had throbbed as if they were about to remove themselves from his body while his white Irish skin burned so much under the hot sun that it had taken weeks to change to a light brown. Hilda had been so kind then. She gave him a bottle of coconut oil to rub over his burnt body and gradually his skin hardened and he felt himself growing physically stronger. In fact, he had surprised himself at how quickly he learned what was required of him. But Hans was an enigma, and even potentially a dangerous one, unpredictable at times and to stay around here for too long might cause problems. He really couldn't think of a way out. Wiesental had become a cocoon for him and as uncertain as his future felt, he had settled into a dreamlike type of routine, locked together with Hans and Hilda. No one knew where he was. He was totally alone in this vast space of emptiness. If he disappeared tonight, no one would know what to do about contacting his family back in Ireland. Oisin Kelly had more or less disappeared off the planet. That's how it was. Many other souls had met the same fate in this lonely land. He shut his eyes and tried to get to sleep.

A thunderclap woke him about two o'clock in the morning. It was so loud and so close that he sat up in the bed with fright. Through the wire mesh of the open window, he could see the flashes of yellow and white streaks in the dark night sky. Then everything went still. Ominously still. And he heard drops of rain on the iron roof above his head. Droplets at first and then they multiplied and grew more intense until that was the only sound that could be heard. The thunder rolled overhead like some wild beast released at last and finally allowed to roam free and the rain; that wonderful, wonderful rain fell, as if created by an unseen magician onto the dry and parched earth below. Oisin lay back onto the bed. The air was cool at last. He lay and listened as the rain thundered onto the iron roof - a thousand drummers beating overhead. He closed his eyes. Despite the din above, he smiled before he drifted off to sleep. He had only been in this country a short while but he knew what the rains meant to everything and everyone.

The next morning Oisin was surprised to see Hans in the kitchen and standing at the fuel stove with a spatula in his hand. He was frying eggs and whistling. Oisin had never seen Hans showing any interest in domestic matters. 'That's women's work,' he had said and now here he was, animated and cheerful, cooking breakfast while Hilda bustled around setting the table.

"G'day, young fella. Sleep well? Drought's broken at last," Hans said cheerfully. Even his speech sounded different.

It was all rather strange and his behaviour, rather than putting Oisin at ease, achieved just the opposite. *The other Hans was more preferable*, thought Oisin, *this one's a bit unsettling. Rather have Hilda making breakfast.* He sat down. Hilda smiled confidentially at him. She poured him a cup of tea out of a brown china teapot. Oisin took the matching jug and added some milk. All the time, Hans whistled away and then he carried a plate with two eggs and three rashers of bacon to the table and set the plate down in front of Oisin. Other similar plates followed all delivered to the table by an elated Hans. Hilda poured herself and her brother a cup of tea. She, too, seemed to be slightly amused by Hans's uncharacteristic behaviour but she didn't say anything about it.

Outside, the rain was deafening on the iron roof. The corrugated iron tanks would soon be overflowing and the land would change from brown to green. Hans bowed his head and prayed out aloud:

"Dear Lord," he began, "we thank you for the food we're about to eat. We thank you most humbly for the breaking of the drought and the rains that have come at last and will save us all... " he paused. Oisin thought that the

94

prayer had finished and was about to start eating but Hans began again:

"Dear Lord... I beseech you to speak into the ears and the heart of Pastor Ernst and admonish him for yesterday he neglected to ask for rain at the Divine Service."

Hans opened his eyes. They were bright and alert. He took a bite of the slightly burned toast and looking at Hilda, not Oisin, said to her in a conspiratorial whisper:

"There you have it, Hilda. Can't ya see? Our pastor has no faith. I prayed for rain and rain came but he neglected his duties. He should have said a prayer to end the drought. That's what he should have done, Hilda. We have to remain vigilant, don't we?"

A week later the rain eased and blue sky appeared once again. The change in the land was biblical. Instead of the dry brown landscape, a green covering appeared. Water courses were full once more and all sorts of noisy flocks of parrots flew to drink from them. The black cattle, all but flesh on bones before the rains, gained weight as day by day, the grasses grew. Oisin, intrigued and delighted by the change, discovered that his spirits lifted a little too. The rains brought more than green grass and Oisin was able to talk to Hilda. In fact, he started to enjoy talking to her. He intrigued her with his stories of life in Ballybeg, where the land was always green and he even spoke of Edinburgh, that grey capital of Scotland where the green grass also grew and where he had found love. But he didn't mention that love but spoke of familiar things – the Castle, Princes Street, the Royal Mile, the Scottish people and even to amuse her, the savoury pleasure that was the haggis. All these stories to tell

95

and Hilda listened and enjoyed them for she wished she could see all those places Oisin spoke about and meet different people.

One morning, a few days after the rains had stopped; Hans sat at his desk in the corner of the kitchen. He wrote a cheque to 'Oisin Kelly' and the amount payable was for Two Hundred Dollars. Hans even managed a slight smile as he handed over the note.

"Think you need a day off, young fella," he announced, much to Oisin's surprise. "Take the Land Rover and go into town. I need some extra supplementary feed from Osborne's. Put it on my account."

With that almost friendly gesture, he took the Land Rover keys and the keys to the gate at the front paddock from the hooks above his desk and handed both sets to the surprised Oisin.

To say that Oisin was delighted with this unexpected release was an understatement. He let out a whoop of pure delight when he got into the Land Rover. This was freedom and, with money in his pocket and a day away from Wiesental with all its restrictions and uncertainties, he almost felt that he was regaining something of his old character. He whistled as he drove along the gravel track up to the padlocked gate. It was as if the rain was magic dust and had settled on the ground for all about was green of different hues. What had been a dry desert when he first arrived over a month ago was now so transformed that he could have been in a different world. He drove carefully along the gravel road until he reached the bitumen and then he put his foot down. The old Land Rover spluttered but it kept on going and he arrived in Kilgoolga in a fraction of the time that Charlie had taken a few weeks before. And he discovered a different sort of town. He hadn't even known that Kilgoolga had a river! What he had thought was just a dry gully with a wooden bridge that served no purpose was now a fully flowing river which snaked along the outskirts of the town. He noticed solitary heron fishing by the bank. With its long legs and large body it was a statue intent on spearing its prey and oblivious to everything around. Oisin drove over the bridge and into the town. He parked the vehicle, bonnet into the curb, beside one of the large red flowering trees that grew in the main street.

A few weeks ago Kilgoolga had been almost deserted and its inhabitants, distant and wary. Now the place was alive. The first person he met was Charlie, who called out in a friendly way,

"Hey... Oisin, mate... how ya goin'?"

He took hold of Oisin's hand firmly and then with all the fervour of a long lost relation, he started,

"Been wonderin' how things are goin' for ya out there with that old bugger? Think sometimes he's got a screw loose... what do ya think? Thank Christ the farmers 'ave all stopped their whingin' with this rain. Mebbe old Hans has as well to give ya a day awf. I've been talkin' to Bella about ya. She said what ya need is some mates ya own age. There's Lefty's son, Hefty, saw him comin' out of the Bank awhile back, he's around here somewhere... "

Charlie had been a man of a few words before. Now it looked as if he wasn't going to stop! *Maybe the rain changes them all as well. Makes them suddenly start spouting,* and Oisin grinned at the thought. His wicked sense of humour had been dormant for quite a while and he had even wondered if he would ever really laugh again. Never find anyone to laugh with after Cecy but here was this little man with the beaten up old face that looked as if it had seen many wars and who now seemed to want to be friends with him and even find some mates his own age. Before Oisin could reply, Charlie suddenly let out a yell:

"Hey, Hefty, mate... how's it goin'? Got a mate here I'd like ya ta meet... comes all the way from the Shamrock Isle!"

A young man about Oisin's age lumbered over and stood beside Charlie who now resembled a dwarf for the stranger was well over six foot tall and looked almost the same width. He had shoulders and arms on him that could have lifted both Charlie and Oisin up and quite easily flung them across the road. He was the son of the man Oisin had met that first night at the Kilgoolga Arms. He certainly did look a lot like his father, Lefty, for the son too had a tattoo on his right upper arm, not of 'Mother' but of a young woman, half naked who moved suggestively when Hefty flexed his giant muscles. Like his father, Hefty had brown eyes and a mass of dark brown curly hair. He had a few days stubble growth on his chin. He stared at Oisin as if he had never seen anyone like him before and then he grinned. Unlike his father, the son had a full set of teeth.

"G'day mate... any mate of Charlie's a mate o' mine. Jeez, Charlie, I've got a mouth like a cocky's cage after last night! Need the hair of the dog. How's about a glass of the amber fluid? The tried and tested cure, hey, mate?" Hefty grinned at Oisin who managed a grin too. He knew what Hefty meant but he could only imagine what a cockatoo's cage might be like."

"Too early for me, mate," said Charlie. "Bella's not open yet... don't know where ya'll get any at this time o' day. Talkin' of the local waterin' holes, have ya heard what's hapenin' to the Commercial?"

"Haven't heard a word, mate. Been talkin' to Matt, he thought the Bradshaws might be interested in buyin' it... that sure as hell sounds about their style!"

"Bloody hell. Is there nothin' that lot don't own round here?" exclaimed Charlie and he shook his head.

All these names puzzled Oisin. He'd heard of the Bradshaws before but he was yet to meet any of them. Hefty scratched his head and nodded.

"Guess when ya got the dollars, ya can buy anythin'," he replied and then he changed the subject.

"You Irish?" he said to Oisin.

"Aye."

"How'd ya get to this dump?"

"Well... it's a long story... "

"Usually is!" interrupted Charlie philosophically and he put a match to his 'roll your own'. "This young bloke's out at the Seefeldts, Hefty... Hans's been workin' the bloody backside awf 'im!"

Everyone laughed.

"Bloody hell, mate," exclaimed Hefty. "Don't envy ya out there with that old Bible basher!!"

Oisin grinned. He was beginning to warm to Hefty.

"He's given me a day off, so he has," he said. "Even let me drive the Land Rover. By the way, he told me to pick up some feed from Osborne's store... where are they?"

"Over the railway line. Turn first right... can't miss them, mate," replied Hefty and he shook his head. "Bloody oath, can't imagine what it's like for ya out there with that old weirdo? Guess Hilda's OK though, don't ya reckon hey, Charlie?"

"Yeah, you're not wrong there, mate. Funny setup though, Hefty... ya' gotta think that."

"Not disagreein' with ya , mate. Well, best be goin'... hey, what's ya name?" he asked Oisin.

"He's got some name, Hefty," said Charlie. "What's it again? Oisin Kelly... I kept callin' him 'Paddy' but he got the wind up with that, didn't ya mate?"

"Oisin Kelly. Strewth, that's sure some name ya got there, mate. Good on ya."

Before Oisin could reply, Hefty gave him a playful punch on the arm which nearly flattened him.

"We'll catch up, Oisin,... is that how ya say it? Hooroo."

With a grin, Hefty wandered off but he didn't get very far. He was soon talking to another man who appeared to be as brown and as worn as Charlie was. Hefty was obviously well known and a bit of a character in Kilgoolga. Oisin didn't know whether it was the fact that he had been standing under the awning with Charlie that people seemed more friendly to him because just about every person who passed them by said 'G'day' and a few stopped to enquire 'how things were going'? The last time Oisin had walked past the shops he had been aware of glances but not one person acknowledged him then but now, this had changed. From out of nowhere, he had somehow become recognisable. He suddenly was 'the young Irish bloke out at Seefeldts... ', and 'a mate of Charlie George', for that was Charlie's full name. Oisin had finally been introduced to the little man.

"Charlie George, that's ma name," Charlie had told him and winked. "Plenty of Georges 'round here, mate but we don't always see eye for eye! But we'll all see ya right, ya know, every one of us! Just say to ma rellies: 'Charlie's a mate o' mine!' an' that'll do the trick! "

It seemed a good idea and Oisin grinned. He was beginning to feel a bit better in this outback town with its strange inhabitants and upside down seasons. Christmas was approaching. There were Santas in the shop windows and snow scenes complete with tinsel. But in Kilgoolga after the rains, the heat increased daily and snow was an alien concept indeed. However, despite all this Oisin was growing stronger and browner under the hot yellow sun and beginning to think less of home and faraway snowy scenes. He wondered what Christmas would be like with Hilda and Hans.

The morning was fast approaching midday and Oisin thought it was about time he made a move but Charlie had other ideas. With an explanation that his missus was out working, he insisted that he should shout his new mate a pie and chips at the ABC Café and, with a 'You've got to try some real Aussie tucker', Oisin found himself in a fairly large room with about ten tables and matching chairs. Most of the tables were occupied but Charlie found one free at the back

100

and sat down. Nearly everybody seemed to know Charlie and a number of remarks were made to him about the whereabouts of his missus to which Charlie responded with equally good humour. The tables were all covered with thick green and white check plastic tablecloths, functional and clean. The whole place had an air of good humour and conviviality and Oisin felt safe amongst these strangers. He started to relax and when the waitress, who was about his own age, brought them pie, chips and mushy peas with a pot of tea to follow, he even managed to flirt a little with her. She was intrigued to see a young man, obviously a stranger in the café. Not many young men arrived in Kilgoolga and she had never met an Irishman before.

"Like the way you talk," she said and gave him a suggestive wink.

"Like the way *you* talk too!" replied Oisin with a grin.

"Cheeky bugger, aren't you?" smirked the waitress.

It was then that Charlie stepped into the conversation and, in the manner of an all knowing sage, explained to the waitress how he had met this young fella at the Kilgoolga Arms a month ago and how he had taken him out to the Seefeldts and well, you know what that old bugger Hans is like and it's about time this young fella met some people his own age because we all know what it must be like out there with Hans and Hilda. The waitress listened attentively but all the time she kept looking at Oisin and when Charlie finally stopped talking, she said:

"We could go out to Milberra. There's a disco on next week... not much doin' in Kilgoolga these days," and she grinned again at Oisin. "Milberra's where all the action is!"

Oisin thought about it. Thought about what it would be like. Thought whether it was a good idea? Thought again. And then he took a sip of his tea and thought once more.

"That sounds OK by me," he replied and the waitress smiled at him. She turned her back on the two men and balancing the empty tray on her hip, she went over to serve another customer. Both Oisin and Charlie stared appreciatively at the tight black mini skirt and the long brown legs that seemed to take forever to get to that skirt!

CHAPTER SIX

Milberra was a desolate sort of place. The rail line didn't go there and the only way in was by a gravel road track, dusty in the drought and a quagmire in the wet. It was hardly a town and more a hamlet. Population: 50 or thereabouts. The sign to the town told it all for the letter 'B' was target practice for the youth of the district. No sooner had a new sign been erected than the offending letter disappeared. In the end the authorities just gave up and the sign, riddled with bullet holes, just read Mil erra! After all, who would want to go to Milberra anyway? A general store with a petrol pump, half a dozen houses and a road which was a straight line without a single turn and ended as a track at Kinleven, the name the squatter Paterson had given to their property as a reminder of his Scottish Highland home. Milberra was on the Kinleven Road. Five miles along that track a brightly painted forest green weatherboard building with a galvanised iron red roof and a wide veranda stood in isolation on the flat plain land. Twenty miles further along from here the rather unusual wooden gates of the Paterson property was a reminder to all of ownership of land. After that, nothing for a hundred miles or so but bush.

The building twenty miles from Kinleven had begun life as the first homestead of the Patersons and it still sat on Paterson land. As the Patersons grew more prosperous they acquired more land and at the turn of the century, the original dwelling was deemed too small for the status they now felt they had in Milberra and District and so a larger, grander place was erected twenty miles further along the road. The original homestead remained empty for many years and gradually fell into disrepair. In 1948 an unlikely young couple from Brisbane had come across the forlorn-looking building standing in the middle of nowhere and in a moment of madness decided to see about buying it. The possibility of renovating the old property was a romantic notion for the two of them and after negotiations with the Patersons, a deal was struck much to the surprise and delight of the Patersons who had expected their original property would just to fall into disrepair and become an embarrassing eyesore. Indeed, the Patersons had viewed it as a tangible reminder of how far they had come in a hundred years or so. After the sale of the property, they spoke of their old homestead with an affection they had never had for it before and repeated to all and sundry how fortunate they were to have got rid of it - even if it had gone for a song! The new owners, full of energy and optimism, transformed the old building into a hotel and named it *The Drover's Rest*. No family were more surprised than the Patersons and no one in Milberra expected the venture to succeed. Everyone was wrong. Twenty years or so later *The Drover's Rest* had become *The Drovers* and it was the place that the youth of the Kilgoolga and District descended upon once a month. The daughter of the original owners was young and inspirational and she had inherited her parents risk taking skills. It was she who shrewdly transformed the monthly Saturday night into 'Disco' night. On these nights, the takings from *The Drovers* were more than the combined income for the rest of the month. Her parents sat back and applauded their daughter's ingenuity while the Patersons, now annoyed at their decision to sell all those years ago, viewed the whole place with envy and even at times, regretted leaving the home of their ancestors.

On 'Disco' night, all manner of vehicles and youth arrived at *The Drovers*. Some drove up in beat-up utes and others in their Holden cars with engines revving so noisily that the sound could be heard half a mile away. Distance was no object. It was perfectly acceptable to drive a hundred miles along the straight roads and at a high speeds to get to *The Drovers*. All expected to stay till the morning for the Disco went on most of the night. No such restriction as Licencing Laws applied at *The Drovers* for it was a well-known fact that the young police sergeant from Kilgoolga had himself met his future wife there and was quite happy to turn a blind eye to any afterhours drinking. Like the gathering of herds of sexually aroused beasts, *The Drovers* had become the mating ground of the human young. Many tales were told of lost virginity and nights of passion; nights they may or may not have remembered. The morning after the 'Disco', abandoned cars, sleeping individuals and items of clothing were scattered for miles along the track. It was not unusual to spy bras of various sizes and colours tied onto the fence posts in the manner of trophies. Some of these female garments would remain blowing in the breeze for months, even years later. Quite definitely, there was no place for miles around that could rival *The Drovers*.

All Claire Paterson's friends, and there were just a few of them, thought she was prim, that she had always been prim. Even her mother agreed with this. She had given birth to a prim neat little baby who never caused her any trouble. And as Claire grew to womanhood, she retained that air of

105

somewhat prudish demeanour which meant that people found her difficult and, on many an occasion, her mother wished that Claire might do just something a little out of the ordinary sometimes. Nothing outlandish or illegal, just do something that could be remarked upon by others in a jovial sort of way and then Claire would not be thought of as quite so odd. As a child, and her mother sighed when she thought about it, the boys would be rowdy and dirty but Claire, their only sister, never even liked to get her feet wet. If only she had been a bit more adventuresome, even naughty. But no, Claire was prim. Family and friends agreed. And the primness was leading to self-righteous behaviour which her mother feared was driving any potential suitors even further away. For what man would be comfortable with a girl who didn't like to get her feet wet or even allow dirt onto her hands without rushing to wash it off immediately?

So it was a surprise that Claire had agreed to accompany her friend, Janet to the Saturday night monthly event at *The Drovers*. After all, the Disco was held just a few miles down the road from her parent's home at Kinleven. She could get away early, Janet assured her friend, if it all got a bit rowdy. Perhaps it was curiosity that made Claire agree to tag along with her more extroverted friend or was it just that she had become tired of her three brothers relentless teasing? Despite their parent's mutterings about the lost opportunity all those years ago, her three brothers had no such qualms about going to *The Drovers*. In fact, the only way her three younger brothers would have missed a 'Disco' night was if the road had flooded and even then, they would have elected to try to get through the water with the help of a tractor. They always returned to Kinleven with stories that irked their big sister. Their tales of drunkenness and hints of sexual conquests that even the thought of made Claire furious. She would tell them to stop their nonsense and that they deserved everything they got, sore heads and all. What a surprise then that Claire, the prim young woman who dressed ever so demurely and who had never been heard to utter even the remotest of a profanity, agreed to go along to the Saturday night Disco where everything she disapproved was known to occur.

It was best to arrive at *The Drovers* later than earlier for if you arrived early, you just sat around if you were a girl, waiting, and if you were a boy, you hadn't had time enough to get yourself sufficiently inebriated to approach the girls with anything like the chance of success. The best time for both sexes was about nine o'clock. By then it was dark and enough people around to make the mingling, the drinking and the dancing more exciting. By ten o'clock both sexes would expect to have made contact in some form or other because by then the band played louder and louder and the noise successfully drowned out any attempt at speech. Contact started with the primitive gyrating dance movements and would end hopefully, hours later with movements of an altogether different kind. By then the band would have put away their instruments and they themselves collapsed into various places around the room. At *The Drovers* the music only ended when the exhausted band called 'Stop'. After that all the lights dimmed even more and the greatest pianist in the Kilgoolga District, Tommy George sat down at the piano to play slow soothing tunes until the early hours. When the bar eventually closed and the last of the shattered, drunken youth made their way outside into the early morning air, the roosters were already competing amongst themselves in the chook hut at the back of *The Drovers*. In the thin air, their triumphant shrill crowing extracting some revenge from the human noise of the night before.

When Claire and her friend Janet arrived at *The Drovers* there were already quite a number of young people milling around outside. Parking the car was difficult as the car park was already full and Claire had to park along the side of the road and the two girls walked the five hundred metres or so to the hotel. Janet, tottering along in her high heels, almost fell into a pothole and had to grab hold of Claire's arm to steady herself. 'Bugger', she muttered under her breath. Claire frowned but didn't say anything. She was too intent on taking in the scene in front of her to comment for *The Drovers* was lit up like the Queen Mary. Above in the dark sky, a thousand million bright stars twinkled down onto the scene below. *The Drovers,* the names lit by red and blue fluorescent tubes standing about three foot high, shone above the entrance to the hotel while dozens of other equally bright lights lit up the outside of the building. A wide veranda stretched round three sides of the hotel and served as a beer garden. It was lit well by fluorescent lights. Hundreds of tiny moths and insects were drawn to the lights and many of them fell down onto the tables below and often into the jugs and glasses of beer. Twenty or so silver metal tables with matching metal chairs took up most of the space on the veranda. At the table to the entrance of the hotel about four young men were slouched, laughing and joking. All held brown bottles of beer and it looked as if they had been drinking for quite a while because the small table was covered with empties. A fifth boy had perched somewhat precariously on the railings and he also held a stubby in his hand and a cigarette in the other.

"Hey, Miss Paterson," he called as Claire and Janet passed by, "been havin' a bit of trouble with ma multiplication... what about givin' me a hand?"

His voice slurred slightly as he pronounced 'multiplication'. He recognised Claire from the Kilgoolga High School. The rest of his mates giggled. Claire felt a red flush on her neck deepen but she looked straight ahead.

"I'm havin' trouble with ma square roots... " This was from another boy, a pimply-faced character with a mass of red hair and freckles. Everyone laughed except Claire and Janet.

"Ignore them," hissed Janet into Claire's ear but Claire's warm flush had already gone from her neck to her cheek. And Claire was having none of it. She turned and glared at the boys. Hers was an icy gaze of pure disdain mixed with a good deal of disapproval. She gave her most withering look to the boy perched on the railings. Then she raised her head in a defiant gesture and strode majestically into the hall of the hotel followed by Janet.

"Stuck up bitch," one of them said as she passed by but Claire didn't say a word.

The Drovers Disco took place in a specially designed room at the back of the hotel. The Public Bar was conveniently to the right whilst the Ladies' Lounge with its discreet opening from the hall was situated on the left. The Ladies' Lounge also served as a dining room if there were any occasions when there were paying guests for breakfast. This rarely happened. So it was a rather forlorn small room compared to other larger rooms in the hotel. A wooden staircase led up to the second floor. This is where the owners lived and this part of the hotel was strictly out of bounds. At the bottom of the stairs they had tied a rope between the two posts with a large notice which read PRIVATE.

There was a queue to get into the Disco room and the three guitarists gyrated madly on the stage while the drummer at the back of them pounded away on the drums with equally as much mad abandon. The sound was so intense that from now on, talking became difficult. Claire and Janet were anxious to find a seat. Tables and chairs, similar to the ones on the veranda, lined up along both sides of the room so that the area for dancing was fairly small. This was a cunning tactic used by the owners to encourage more money to be spent at the bar. The overriding plan of most of the young people of both sexes was to grab a seat at one of the tables, survey the scene from a more comfortable position and then attract a partner willing to get onto the dance floor. The musicians played almost without a break

109

for hours. They were considered the best band in the Kilgoolga District and were much in demand. Most of the boys spilled out around the bar at the corner while the girls headed for the tables. Claire and Janet spied a vacant table along the wall near to the stage. One of Claire's brothers, Tony was sitting at a nearby table with his fiancé. Claire avoided them deliberately but her eyes searched the room for her other two brothers. One of them, Geoff, was at the bar with a glass of beer in his hand. He winked at Claire as she passed by. She was still feeling slightly annoyed after her encounter with the boys on the veranda and so she ignored him as well. No sooner had the girls sat down than they were joined by Kanga. He plonked himself down next to Janet. He obviously had his sights set on her for the night but in the interests of keeping in with Janet, he enquired quite politely if the girls would like a drink. Both girls asked for a Bundy rum and coke. Kanga, so named because as a toddler, he would hop rather than walk, duly obliged with the drinks and then set about flirting with Janet. In the meantime, Claire sat, sipping her drink and feeling decidedly awkward. She still couldn't see her youngest brother, Harry anywhere.

Two hours later, Claire still drank from her one glass. She had been asked to dance only once and hadn't enjoyed the experience. The floor was so crowded with couples that speaking and dancing was difficult. She just moved her hips and legs in an unimaginative way and was glad when she could excuse herself and head back to the safety of the table. By now, Janet and Kanga were well into possible passion and both seemed oblivious to what was going on around them. The two of them performed such energetic moves on the dance floor than when they returned to the table both of them were sweating and in need of more drink. Kanga bought more and more rum and cokes for Janet and, as the night wore on both of them got more and more drunk and more and more amorous. They kissed and cuddled and purred into each other's ears until Claire felt like shaking them apart, telling them to stop. She was relieved, when about eleven o'clock, her brother, Geoff joined them. He was hand in hand with the waitress from the ABC Café in Kilgoolga. Claire disapproved. Geoff sat down and the waitress sat on his knee. She put her arm around his neck and Geoff stroked her thigh. She had on a red and green tartan mini skirt and Geoff's hand edged ever closer under the hem. The strap of her black bra was visible because two of the buttons of her white blouse had come undone. She giggled.

"Stop it, Geoff..." And she kissed him on his neck.

"Have you seen Harry?" asked Claire to her brother, ignoring the waitress.

"Can't say I have... he's probably scored tonight... that's why!" He grinned at his sister. He enjoyed teasing her. Both he and the waitress went back to what they were doing and so Claire sat, sober and prim, ignored by everyone.

The number of boys standing around the bar had thinned a little and it was then that Claire noticed the stranger, standing beside Hefty and Matt. She thought he distanced himself somewhat from the other two boys and that intrigued her for that was how she, too, was feeling at that moment. He looked so small besides Hefty, almost comical. He had curly black hair and a black beard. She was intrigued.

"Who's that guy over there, Janet? Next to Hefty... the one with the black beard... " She thought her friend was the best bet to ask although Janet seemed to be even more under the weather by now. Both Janet and Kanga looked in the direction of the bar.

"Oh... that's that Irish bloke," answered Kanga. It surprised Claire that Kanga knew anything. As thick as two planks, she had often thought.

The waitress lifted her head from Geoff's shoulder and looked around too.

"Oh, him... " she said, "he's been into the café... think he works out at the Seefeldt's place.

The waitress was surprised. She hadn't imagined that Geoff's sister would be interested in a man.

"Fancy him, do you, Claire?" she sniggered.

Claire glared at the waitress. She disliked her even more and wished that her brother would stop fondling the girl. She felt the warmth of the red flush on her neck. She didn't answer the waitress. Instead, she tightened her lips into that thin prim line that had become the trademark of disapproval for her. She reached into her handbag and located the car keys.

"I'm going now," she said, not looking at the waitress but at Janet.

Janet shook her head and looked at her friend through a half drunken haze.

"I'll take Janet home, Claire. No worries," said Kanga and he smirked.

There were only about half a dozen boys and girls left on the dance floor now and the band had been replaced by the pianist. The couples shuffled slowly around the floor in a somnambulist manner oblivious to anything and everyone. The bar would close in about half an hour. Above the couples the flashes of coloured light from the round ball had already dimmed. Soon it, too, would be extinguished. Claire stood up. No one seemed to notice.

At the hall, she turned to look back into the room. She still searched in vain for her youngest brother who had not been visible all night. It was then that she became aware of blue eyes looking in her direction. It was the Irishman. He didn't speak but she imagined she saw sadness behind those eyes and wondered why. She thought he smiled at her but she wasn't sure. When she looked again, he had turned his back and appeared to be getting ready to leave as well.

Oisin had noticed the girl at *The Drovers*. Indeed, Claire would have been surprised to know that the Irishman had seen her at all and in such detail for Oisin had decided that here was someone who was different somehow from all the other girls in the room. Older, he thought, from most of them and distant too. While the other girls were busy flirting and getting drunk, she sat composed and straight backed. From the bar he had a good chance to study her in detail. He thought she was the most curious girl he had ever seen what with her round face and short cropped brown hair and her fringe cut to perfection above her eyes. He couldn't make out the colour of those eyes from the distance of the bar. All he could observe was her manner. She hardly smiled and rarely spoke although she seemed to know most of the boys and girls who had gathered around the table. Indeed, when she got up to dance unenthusiastically with the tall awkward youth who sported the untidy red hair, she nodded her head slightly and managed a thin smile to a number of the other couples on the floor. Oisin decided that whoever she was, she was no stranger in the district. And she intrigued him.

He had spent almost the entire night in a kind of existentialist mood and the only outcome of all his thoughts was to wonder what on earth he was becoming? And so, to look at the girl was a slight distraction for him. He wasn't in the mood to be at *The Drovers* and had only agreed to come along at the last minute this time. He thought of Hefty and Matt as mates now. It was good to have them around. Both Hefty and Matt were insistent that what Oisin needed was to find a woman and get away from that old rat-bag Hans, so that's why they dragged him along to the Disco and had done so, every month for nearly a year. Tonight he listened

113

as much as he could to them but trying to hear over the ear-splitting music was difficult. Hefty and Matt eyed up the girls and made suggestive comments describing some of the girls in vivid sexual terms. *To listen to the pair of them*, thought Oisin, *they must have had every girl in Kilgoolga and District!* And the thought of all that sex made Oisin think of Cecy. He wondered what it was like for her with Chuck? Was she as wild with her High School lover, the lover who must be her husband by now, as she had been with him or had she changed and become demure, even pretended to be chaste and inexperienced or something like that? She had very occasionally shown a prudish side. Strange that, but part of her personality and he had even loved her more because of it. She was a passionate and fiery temptress one moment and a Madonna the next. He hated the thought of Chuck being with her and in his mind he visualised the man as some annoying Yank who threw his weight around and spoke louder than anyone else. And he pictured Cecy, smiling and listening to every word that came out of the Yank's mouth and forgetting what she had been like when she was a student in Edinburgh, free and loving and passionate with her quiet Irishman from Ballybeg, West of Ireland. *Maybe being away from home had just been a fling for her and nothing else,* he thought crossly. And, thinking of it all again, he hated that man even more, remembering how she had said, 'I'm going to marry Chuck', even now, after a year, it still hurt him, the thought of the two of them at it. He sometimes got as mad as hell thinking about it.

So as his eyes followed the girl when she left the table, all he could think about was sex. He noticed the way she walked. Prim. And the manner in which she held her head. *Defiant somehow and just a bit superior,* he thought. Looked as if she wasn't part of the Disco scene and it was somewhere she didn't frequent all that much. The way she clutched her handbag, over her shoulder, it was her possession and no one was allowed to go anywhere near it. When she got to the door leading into the hall, she paused and looked around. Her eyes swept over the room as if she was trying to find someone and she frowned slightly. She was annoyed, he could see that. Then she turned towards the bar and saw him. He smiled but she hardly noticed him, he thought, for the next moment she lifted her head once more and disappeared from sight along the hall.

Driving back from the Disco, Oisin had trouble concentrating on the road and once he had to brake to avoid hitting a giant red kangaroo. Almost blinded by the car lights the huge creature appeared like some ghostly apparition in front of him, and then with one magnificent leap across the road, it disappeared once again into the night. Oisin stopped the car and got out. The kangaroo was nowhere to be seen. After that, he drove more slowly and carefully than he usually did on the straight and sometimes narrow tracks. All the while thoughts kept spinning around in his mind and although the night was clear, he was sober, unlike Hefty and Matt who had been left at *The Drovers* to sleep it off. Oisin had managed to make enough money working for Hans to buy a second hand bright yellow Ford Capri from Matt who worked at the garage in Kilgoolga. The car gave him a certain amount of freedom. Freedom was something he felt he was getting less of as the time spent with Hilda and Hans took up most of his life. Lately, he had begun to question his whole existence from the moment of his leaving Cecy and Edinburgh to arriving out here, a stranger in the vast and lonely space that was the Outback. He parked the car at the barbed wire fence and climbed over the metal gate which was the only way into the Weisental station. Hans steadfastly refused to give him the keys to the two padlocks that secured the gate and the only time he managed to get hold of them was when he was allowed to go into Kilgoolga, usually to collect something for Hans or take Hilda with him on shopping days. Most times, after a night out he would walk the two miles to the homestead and, once when he had been too drunk to care, he ended up sleeping in the car. It was this idea in Oisin's mind that Hans was controlling him by refusing to give him the keys to the padlocks and thus keep him tied to the land that had been troubling him lately.

It was a beautiful night. Clear and crisp. Overhead, the sky glowed with trillions of bright stars while the Milky Way created an almost heaven-like glow. He located the Southern Cross, the constellation so loved by Australians and he kept walking. The clear night sky made seeing his way easy. As he walked along the track with the sky above and the full moon giving light, his thoughts walked with him. He sometimes felt uneasy in this empty space and tonight, sober and lonely, he couldn't help but wonder whether this was the case for all those white settlers who had tried to control and tame this remote and ancient land for this land held so many secrets. Could they ever, in fact, ever truly understand it? His thoughts turned uneasily to Hans for here was a white man whose sole purpose was to conquer the space that he owned and try to tame it, and in so trying, subdue the land and do so with all the fanaticism of a zealot. The manner in which Hans went about his daily tasks certainly made Oisin feel uneasy and it was his employer's almost obsessional need to fence the land in that disturbed him the most for no sooner was a new fence erected than another one was proposed and all the time, the two of them were at work mending and straightening other fences. It occurred to Oisin that it was not possible, no matter how hard the farmers tried, to truly understand the land that they reigned over. And even the black folk who had no

116

concept of fences and property and the ownership of land and who had walked and survived here long before the white men and women came, were merely wanderers over the land too. In fact, both the first inhabitants who wandered and the settlers who merely scratched the surface of this land were one of the same because even if they all were to remain here for many more centuries, living and working, in time the land would revert to its primeval past if it should happen that some catastrophic event took them all away, and there would be hardly a trace left of all that human endeavour and sacrifice. Was it not possible that both black and white were merely custodians to an empty space?

He could see the dark outline of the homestead with the black shapes of the trees behind it and the windmill and tank next to it which helped guide his way. He stopped and sat down on a log beside the track. He wanted to escape from his thoughts. If there had been a way to take all his thinking away even for just for a moment, he would have agreed to do it and quickly too, such was his state of mind. It was as if all varieties of his thoughts were competing for space in his head. Firstly, there had been Cecy and sex and the girl at the Disco and then Hans and the fear of what was happening there and finally esoteric musings about the country in which he now lived. And all these thoughts had come about because he was lonely and sometimes angry too. Angry at himself for what had happened to him. When Cecy had betrayed him the only thing he had wanted to do was to get as far away as he could from her and from any memories of her. Australia had seemed the answer because there wasn't a place so far away. But tonight he felt trapped in its unending desolate world; alone and so remote from anything he had known before. He cursed Cecy for what she had done to him but then he grew angry, too, remembering his life before her, his early life in Ballybeg, out of step with everyone around him.

117

He heard the rooster crow in the chook hut beside the homestead and, in the eastern sky he could see the early glow of dawn. It was Sunday and Hans would insist that they all three go to the Lutheran church on the hill. Hans had never asked Oisin anything about his religion and Oisin hadn't felt the need to discuss the subject any further. In fact, he was glad not to have to explain anything like this. He preferred to remain silent about this aspect of his life and to keep his past to himself. Better that way, to be an enigma and then no one need know anything. Everyone in Kilgoolga and District knew one another or were related somewhere along the line, just like it had been back in Ballybeg. Oisin knew he was the outsider here and he was likely to remain so no matter how long he was to stay in this place. Let Hans and Hilda think of him just as a young Irish friend of Wolfgang, nothing more. Hans had never enquired about his past life and although Hilda liked to hear his stories about Ireland and Scotland, it was just to get the conversation onto how much she would like to travel. He had lived with them for a year now and they knew nothing about him really. It was a strange situation indeed. As far as religion and church going were concerned, he had noticed the Catholic church in Kilgoolga, a grey wooden building set back from the road and surrounded by shrub-like trees, but that's as far as it went. He no longer felt any desire to go to Mass or to meet the priest either. He knew his mother, Annie back in Ireland would be horrified and his elder brother, Father Frankie would have been even more mortified but in actual fact, he concluded rather sombrely, the only one of his family who could possibly have understood his present lack of any interest in religion would have been his Uncle Mick, God rest his soul; the same Uncle Mick who had renounced his faith in such a dramatic manner so long ago and who was just a childhood memory now. It was quite a liberating thought, in fact, to be so far from any of his family when he pondered all this religion. So in actual fact, and after Cecy, to

118

go along with Hans and Hilda to a Protestant church wasn't too alien an idea for him. The congregation bored him to tears but being there filled in the morning and in his present frame of mind, this was indeed a good thing. After the service, Hans insisted that all three of them spend the rest of the day in contemplation as it was the Lord's Day and no work must be done and if, because of the nature of farming and the weather, something had to be attended to, it was to be done quickly so they all could return to contemplation and rest. And this arrangement suited Oisin just fine as well. Having a rest from thinking about his current predicament and what he was to do next, was a good idea. He slowly got to his feet and wandered towards the homestead. He had learned how to avoid waking the blue and grey cattle dog and get to his bedroom without disturbing either Hans or Hilda, asleep in their separate rooms. He sunk gratefully onto the bed for he would only be able to get a few hours' sleep before Hilda knocked on his door. As he shut his eyes, a round face with short cropped brown hair appeared in his mind. He smiled despite his despondency. Perhaps there could be hope somewhere, sometime?

CHAPTER SEVEN

Hilda was proving to be an ally for Oisin. She began to disagree with her brother if she thought he spoke too harshly or expected too much. At those times, she raised her head as she always did when she was annoyed. She was a small woman but at those times, she could be quite stern and this was most evident when she felt her brother had delivered an injustice or demanded too much of Oisin. It was her way of defending Oisin. Times like these her words would hang in the air and Hans would sulk but nine times out of ten, he took the line of least resistance and agreed with his sister. Oisin felt caught between the two of them. He was bound into a kind of emotional trap that had been laid for him, carefully at first by Hans and then he would be rescued by Hilda. Hans did demand much of everyone, physically and mentally. He was distant most of the time and when he and Oisin worked together, he rarely spoke. Sometimes his only words were instructions as to how to do the work and then the two men would spend the rest of the day without speaking and because of this lack of communication; it wasn't an easy time between them. The whole day might pass without any feeling of companionship or connection in any way. Sometimes it was only at mealtimes and after he had said his prayer that Hans uttered more than a few words. The days' work or the weather were the most discussed but Hans, who always instigated the conversation at this point, would mention something political or grumble about Pastor Ernst. The pastor often came in for some harsh words. Oisin thought the latter to be rather strange behaviour on the part of Hans. After all, Hans was definitely a committed Christian with a giant capital 'C'. However, most of the words were left for the ritual of the Bible reading. Oisin observed that Hans spoke quite normally every other time but when he prayed out loud and read from the Bible, his intonation changed to a sonorous and sometimes an almost fervent pitch. It was all a bit disturbing.

And there was the matter of the biscuits. Hilda baked delicious German biscuits. She explained to Oisin that they were called *kekse* and the recipe had been modified and handed down for generations, in fact way back as far as Great Great Great Aunt Lotte who had arrived in the country with her brother, Heinrich and Pastor Uncle Albert. Hilda had taken to adding a few extra of these mouth-watering chocolate covered biscuits whenever she packed a lunchbox for Oisin. Her brother, on the other hand, was allocated less. It was a tiny gesture from Hilda of favouritism and it seemed to suggest to Oisin that she didn't care much for her brother or indeed, for his somewhat strange behaviour patterns although she never spoke about any of them. And there was another thing that was amusing. Oisin now received bigger portions of food for meals and always two helpings of pudding. Whether Hans was aware of this or not, and whatever Hilda's reasons were, the relationship that she now enjoyed with Oisin was of a mother to a son. And, although liking Hilda as much as he did, this new development was of further concern to the young man from Ballybeg who now began to view his situation at Wiesental station with just a little more trepidation.

The problem was further highlighted one morning a few days after Oisin had been to the Disco night at *The Drovers* with Hefty and Matt. It all happened after breakfast, when Hans, instead of issuing the usual orders for the day, beckoned both Oisin and Hilda to sit down at the kitchen table. Hilda was vexed because the table still had the breakfast plates and cutlery on it and she had the two goats to milk and the washing to do. So she perched, rather reluctantly on the edge of her seat. Oisin, on the other hand, was quite willing to sit down. It had been another hot night and sleep hadn't come to him till well after midnight. The peculiar nightly sounds outside had kept him awake and once, he had got up from his bed and investigated. All he could see was a sky full of stars and hear the howl of a distant dingo.

"I've something to show youse two... something that's important and all of us must be aware of and it's a very serious matter."

Hilda and Oisin glanced at each other as Hans laid out a large piece of white drawing paper onto the table. It was a map of the property of Wiesental station. In black ink, Hans had carefully drawn out the lines of boundary fences and all the other fences that stretched throughout the property. Clearly drawn was the main gate with the two padlocks marked as 'Entrance' and a thick black line marked the road up to the homestead. Gullies and the creek were illustrated as well as all the outbuildings including the chook house. Even the various windmills on the property were carefully marked. The Kinleven Road to Milberra was coloured in red and drawn as a straight line along one of the boundary fences. Both 'PATERSONS' and KILGOOLGA had a directional arrow to the left and, at the bottom of the page, also coloured in red, two lines to the 'BRADSHAWS'. All these names were written in large capital letters and thick black lines marked out the fence boundaries on the map.

"See here," Hans said and as he spoke, he tapped his index finger onto the map at the top where the boundary fence ended. A few days before he had belted this finger with a hammer and he had wrapped a plaster around the wound so now the finger looked larger and more threatening. He repeated his words and he kept tapping his finger onto the paper as if to add further emphasis.

"See here. We'll have to strengthen the fence here and here," and he pointed to the fence line which divided his property from the Patersons. "Then we'll need to do some repairs to the old woolshed so it can be used again. We'll be able to see them comin' from there... no sense stayin' in the homestead... we'll have to be ready for them, ya know... and the sooner the better. Think we've got time but they're cunnin' bastards!"

Hans paused and nodded his head. He appeared to be thinking what to do.

"Oisin, go into Osborne's today and buy barbed wire, nails, more fencin' wire, think we're nearly out of that, aren't we?... I'll check... oh yeah... and we'll need to get wood for the shed and more nails for the roof... bit of repair needed there... we must make the property secure."

All the time, Hans rested his right foot onto the chair and lent over the map. Then he stood up and looked first at Hilda and then at Oisin. He was somewhat agitated for his words came out in a rush and, what with the finger tapping and the shaking of the head from side to side, he didn't seem to have much control of either his speech or his movement. When he stood up, all six foot of him, the space around the table diminished. Neither Hilda nor Oisin answered for neither of them were sure of what was expected of them. They gave each other a furtive glance. Finally, Hilda, perching awkwardly on the side of the chair, spoke first.

"What do you mean, Hans?" She frowned. Although she was used to her brother many times she wondered what was going on in his head and this was one of those times. Hans turned towards her. He looked somewhat surprised as he stared disbelieving at his sister.

"Why, Hilda," he answered and shook his head in disbelief, "haven't you heard the news? There's a war on... in Vietnam? Don't ya know anything, woman?"

"A war, Hans?"

"Yeah, yeah. Vietnam. Vietnam. Them Commies are comin' down to take over, don't ya know? Tell you what, though, they'll have trouble when they meet me. Yeah, I'm not havin' them yellow bastards comin' down to take my land away. Bloody heathens the lot of them!!"

"Oh, Hans, really! Who on earth are the Commies and where's this place... Viet... what's it called...? You're making it up! Now, I've got work to do. And youse two have as well... and I'm not going to listen to any more of this nonsense."

Hilda's words seemed to antagonise Hans. He thumped his fist down hard onto the table with such force that the milk spilled out of the jug and a trickle of the liquid landed on the edge of the map just where the fence line to the BRADSHAWS had been so carefully drawn. So now there was a milky blob and less of the fence.

"I TELL YOU... THE COMMIES ARE COMIN'!"

Hilda was not in the least bit bothered. Whatever Hans was on about, it could wait. He could shout and bang the table for all it's worth. She could hear the goats bleating. They needed to be milked. She turned to Oisin and said confidentially but so that Hans could hear,

"If Hans wants you to go into town, can I come? That's what you said, wasn't it, Hans... that Oisin had to get something from Osborne's?" She got up from her chair and added,

"And there's another thing too, Hans, while I think of it. When are you going to give Oisin the keys to the front gate? It's about time. It's absolutely ridiculous him having to leave his car at the gate and walk."

If she had expected an answer to any of these remarks from Hans, she didn't get any. He seemed to

124

dismiss her words out of hand and not worthy of a reply for his whole attention was now focused once more on the map he had drawn with such care. It was as if he hadn't heard anything except what he wanted to hear. He mumbled under his breath, 'The Commies are comin'... the Commies are comin...'

As Hilda left the room, she glanced at Oisin. Even if she had been dismissive of her brother's strange behaviour, there was just a slight hesitation in her glance as if she wanted to say more but thought better of it.

"Youse two better get to work. It'll be time for tea before you even get started," was all she said. But Oisin observed that she frowned after she spoke.

However, Hans didn't seem to hear his sister's words or to even notice that she had left the room. Oisin sat very still while all this was going on. He thought of the young soldiers he had met on the train to Kilgoolga. They were laughing and getting drunk then. He wondered if any of those boys had already left for... what was the name of the place? Vietnam, that's right. Vietnam. He debated with himself whether he should question Hans further about the reasons for this sudden turn of events and if they were true, that the country was about to be overrun with thousands of these 'Commie' invaders, where did all this information come from in the first place? As far as Oisin was aware, the only news Hans received came from the radio and the weekly newspaper, *The Kilgoolga Echo*. The pages of the latter were filled with local farming news, sports results and last week's issue had on its front page, a larger than life photograph of a prize bull which had just changed hands for a considerable sum; hardly anything of international importance and definitely nothing about a war or a possible invasion was ever reported. Oisin had read the paper from cover to cover as there wasn't much else to read in the Wiesental homestead. Books were a rare commodity here much to his annoyance. He liked to read. And as for the radio, well Hans rarely listened to it anyhow. So thinking of all this, Oisin doubted very much the veracity of the Vietnamese Army suddenly arriving in Kilgoolga with their one object to take Wiesental by force, murder Hans and rape Hilda. But he decided to remain silent because Hans sat down again and started to tap once more with his index finger onto the map where he had drawn a square to represent the old woolshed.

"Here, here... can't you see, Oisin? Think about it, we'll need to get barricades up round it... here and here," Hans paused. For a moment he seemed confused and his blue eyes lost the expression they had just a few moments before. It was as if he was thinking out this important strategy before he could verbalize any more words. Oisin was at a loss as to what to say and he wished that Hilda hadn't disappeared quite so quickly. *Least with Hilda around, there was some sanity*, he thought. Now it looked as if they would have to secure the old woolshed and fortify it enough to withstand the might of a modern army and all because Hans Seefeldt had decided that his land was about to be taken from him. Oisin, looking at the old farmer in front of him, began to have misgivings about the whole situation and now with a little more urgency than he had had before. Maybe Hefty and Matt were right after all. Was Hans 'off his rocker'?

The old woolshed was situated about half a mile from the homestead and in a slight gully. In a circle around the woolshed, the gidgee trees grew taller and the tightly packed line of black trunks and dense green foliage provided some camouflage for the old building. Was this was why Hans had been so adamant that here was the place where the three of them would be able to take a stand against the imagined enemy or was it because his memories of the place, gave him a sense of security? After all, the old woolshed was falling to bits. To renovate it at all seemed a wild fantasy. Daylight could be easily seen between some of the timber on the grey

126

outside walls. At various times, in a valiant attempt to keep the building watertight, galvanised iron tins had been nailed down to cover some of the holes and to try to keep out the weather. The woolshed had not been in use for many years, ever since the Seefeldts had sold their sheep, so now the whole building had the appearance of an empty and forlorn shell. But neglect and time had done the damage for it was only the human memories of Hans that kept the old place alive. The woolshed stood on metre high wooden stumps, many of which had become victim to termite attack, so that walking on the floor inside could be hazardous. When Oisin pushed open the wooden door and climbed over the debris which had collected in front of it, Hans was already there and wandering around the building. And he looked pleased. It was as if he had reclaimed something of importance to himself and just being inside the building, as derelict as it now was, gave him cheerful memories of a happier time.

"Ya know, I sure as hell miss ma sheep and all of this," he said when he saw Oisin. "Times I just come in here and think on them days. All change... them cattle ain't the same somehow... make a sort of livin' out of them, ya know but I reckon it's not the same... do miss ma sheep, Oisin. Them ewes make wonderful mothers, ya know. There's somethin' about sheep, I can't explain it but I always had me favourites. Some of them old ewes would follow me round like a dog. Bloody things wud drop down dead soon as look at ya, though. I wish I still had ma sheep. We had a mob of two thousand Merinos when ma Dad was alive. Great times. 'Once a sheep farmer, always a sheep farmer,' ma Dad used to say but not many round here understand that now... least of all you, young fella, being from Ireland... but sheep get inta ya blood, don't ya know?"

Hans was a different man from the one who, just half an hour ago, was hell bent on a sort of Custer's last stand against the yellow hordes and the old and decaying woolshed was to be the place where the final battle would be

127

fought. He shook his head and pointed a grimy finger to the line where the shearers had toiled for hours and hours so many years ago. At each man's post the openings in the walls that led to the pens outside remained intact. It was a sunny day and shafts of light and dark cast shadows onto the inside walls and onto the greasy floor where tufts of wool were still visible on the wooden boards. A heap of unused wool bags lay abandoned in a dark corner. Rats and mice had nibbled countless holes in them and left their mark. In another corner the dark wooden table on which the fleeces used to be sorted remained as a symbol of a time when the woolshed was filled with the whirr of the shears and the shouts of the men and boys. Hans had stopped pacing the floor and now leant on the wall nearest the door. Beside him, and piled into an untidy heap, were empty drums that used to be filled with tar and next to them, a brush for sweeping up the bits of wool. The bristles of the brush were almost worn away. In an attempt to try to relate somehow to the latest turn of events, Oisin started to speak but he was hesitant as he did so for he never knew what effect his words would have on Hans. It all seemed different today as if memories had been awakened in Hans and there was a possibility, if just a slim one that Hans might listen to what Oisin had to say and the two of them could have a connection of some sort. He cleared his throat and said quietly,

"Must have been an exciting time when all the sheep were here and the shearing started. Hilda told me a bit about what used to take place. Ye must have had plenty of work then?"

Oisin formulated his words carefully in his mind before speaking in order to avoid a possible backlash from Hans. It had happened on a few occasions when he had tried to speak. It was safer to stick to agreeing with most things.

Hilda had indeed talked of the happier times when she and Hans were younger and their mother and father were alive. Then Wiesental station filled with so many

128

people at shearing time for all of the men, including one or two of the Aboriginal boys, had come to the big house for meals. There used to be a tin shed beside the woolshed and that's where all the men slept, Hilda told him but it had blown down in a big storm, years ago now. The Aboriginal boys slept outside, she remembered but that's just their way, they preferred to be under the stars. But it was in the homestead where it all happened. Some of the other shearing gangs brought their own cook with them but the men who came to Wiesental preferred the meals that Hilda and her mother and old Aggie prepared. Better than any shearer's cook, they said and she remembered hearing one of them say this to her mother. It had made all the women happy, just to hear this. Everyone had laughed and sang together then, not like now, with just her and Hans. She could play the piano and after the evening meal, the shearers would insist she play to them. They loved to hear the music after their day's work. They smoked and drank beer and laughed and teased Hilda when Hans wasn't around. There used to be lots of laughter then because the shearers and their gang of roustabouts worked hard and liked to enjoy themselves after all the sheep had been shorn and before everyone moved on to the next station. Hans still prayed, she had whispered to Oisin, when everyone was here and after they left, the prayers got longer. But that's just Hans and he wouldn't change. Not then, not now. 'The Lord was always with Hans,' she said because that's what Hans told her and he knew about these things. He disapproved of the drinking, even then but he admired the way the work was done and for that reason, he turned a blind eye to the revelry that took place at the end of the three weeks of shearing. We all loved our sheep. They're such interesting creatures, you know and when the lambs come, why that's a magic time. Used to bring the orphans into the kitchen and keep them warm in front of the fuel stove. Some of them survived but if one of the mothers abandoned a lamb, it wouldn't live no

129

matter what you tried to do. The ewes know if something is going to live or die. Hard work, though and Hilda smiled, a sad smile it was too, remembering. But Oisin couldn't join in to talk about all these memories although he would have perhaps liked to for he rather enjoyed listening to this little woman. All he could do was smile too and agree that life might have been a whole lot more fun then. *After all, it must be a lonely life now*, he thought, *for the two of them, brother and sister.* This is a lonely country, he decided, out here, miles from anywhere with only the sounds of the bush for company and he wondered if Hans was perhaps remembering these happier times now when life wasn't quite so lonely. But then again, Hans hardly spoke to anyone, anyway so he mightn't feel the isolation. No one knew what Hans thought; even Hilda was wary sometimes of speaking when her brother was around. They're both a bit strange, he decided, but maybe the bush does that to you after a while even if you've been reared to it. He knew he wasn't anywhere near understanding the country and being here amongst all this isolation, he sometimes felt like an intruder somehow and he would never ever become a part of it, no matter how long he remained. It was hard to put these feelings into words. Perhaps he never could, being an outsider.

He stood beside Hans, waiting for a reply but none came. Instead, Hans took hold of one of the rusty shears in his right hand while his left curved around an imaginary sheep. Everything in the woolshed was as it had been the day the shearers left all those years ago. The line of blades still hung from the wheels above. The imaginary sheep shorn and, as if to complete the picture, Hans stood up and bent his back to straighten it and then he whistled a tune that Oisin hadn't heard before. Hans pushed the phantom sheep away from him. It disappeared through the opening in the wall and re-joined its naked companions. Outside in the pens the imaginary woollen ones awaited their fate and

130

stared uncomprehendingly at the changed appearance of the other sheep that now huddled together in a separate pen, wondering what had just happened to them in so short a time.

"This here's the exact spot that Davy Morgan sheared two hundred and ten sheep in one day. What a day that was! And what a shearer that bloke was. Hardly ever nicked any of 'em. Davy took pride in what he did not like some of the others. We timed Davy once, Dad and me, he could take the wool off a sheep in less than two minutes. Got him in the end though. His back gave way and he spent the rest of his days in a wheelchair, poor bugger."

Although Hans looked directly at Oisin, he gave the appearance that he didn't realise there was anyone else in the woolshed but himself. All that was here were ghosts of the people and the sheep and the constant whirr of the blades. Outside in the sunlight, the pens were full of the spirits of hundreds of sheep, all crowded together. Inside, in the cool of the woolshed, there was just the memory of it all. As if to bring the whole story back into the present moment, Hans picked up the imaginary fleece in both hands and carried it over to the sorting table at the end of woolshed. He shook it onto the table and then he looked once more at Oisin and it was as if he had come back to seeing him again for he spoke in a light hearted manner and rubbed his hands together.

"Well, that's done! Sorted and into the bags and away. Now, what are we goin' to do to this old shed, young fella?"

"Could be patched up a bit, I guess."

"Right ho, that's what we'll do! We've plenty of hard yakka, ain't we? Ya told me ya could use a hammer... "

"Aye. Back in Edinburgh. I worked as a joiner there."

"So ya said. Couldn't be better then, mate. We'll get started tomorra. Off ya go. See if Hilda's got some work for ya. Just want to stay here by meself for a bit," he paused. He

131

looked tired. "Took a lot of gettin' used to, ya know, not havin' ma sheep."

Outside, the sun was climbing higher in the cloudless sky and it would soon be time for tea. Oisin wandered along the track towards the homestead. It was a sort of aimless wander. He was still thinking about the events of the morning. It might be an easy enough job to renovate the old woolshed, he decided but he still couldn't understand why he would be doing it for the whole idea of making it into a fortress against a possible invasion, seemed to him to be bordering on paranoia on the part of Hans. And an image flashed once more into his mind and it was of Hans when he held the gun so close to Oisin's head at their first meeting and the fear and uncertainty of all that. 'This place leads to too much thinking.' He said the words out loud. And he grinned. *Maybe I'm going a bit off my rocker too*, he thought, *in all this space and stuck here with just these two old ones for company*. It was a sobering thought and one that should be addressed later on but not today, he decided. The track from the woolshed to the homestead led up a slight incline and there were two sets of gates to open. As he approached the homestead from this direction, he viewed it in an altogether different light. This was the back of the property and it certainly was more run down than the front entrance. Some semblance of order was evident in the front of the property but here was nothing but accumulated clutter from generations of Seefeldt farmers. As he closed the second gate, he heard a commotion and such pandemonium in the chook run that he stopped and stared. And then, feeling a little uncertain as to what was happening, he ran towards the noise.

He was surprised to see Hilda amongst the hens and she had a spade in her hand. Circling her, and flapping their wings and running in every direction were the frightened, panicked and confused chooks. It seemed everyone one of them was intent on escape. In their panic a few of the more agile managed to propel themselves over the wire and into the outside yard. They huddled together in a small group and nervously viewed the scene that was unfolding in their run. The less fortunate ones flew like suicidal bombers onto the wire. Feathers of brown, white and red fluttered everywhere. Oisin hadn't heard such frantic confusion and alarm amongst poultry since he was a boy back in Ballybeg when it was the turn of a hen to be captured for the pot! Hilda was oblivious to all the confusion. She wielded the spade above her head and, with mighty movements kept hitting the ground over and over again. Finally she stopped and lent back onto her spade, still looking at the ground. Gradually the chooks calmed down and resumed their clucking. Some of the more curious ones approached Hilda who shooed them away with the spade. When she noticed Oisin, she called out to him to come into the yard. He pushed the gate open. A brown hen, on seeing the open gate, let out a loud cackle then stretched out her wings and sped past him to the safety of the outside. Hilda was triumphant.

"This is the culprit," she cried. "I knew something was eating the eggs!"

"What?"

"This!!"

Hilda scooped a mangled object onto her spade and held it close to a very cautious Oisin. It was a brown snake. She had savaged the head of the creature to such an extent that there was nothing much left of it but a flattened and bloody shape where once, just a few seconds before, there had been life. Now the glistening body of the snake lay still and dead on the spade. She had wielded the spade with such force that she cut through the top of its body to the cream underbelly and the wound, now visible was covered in blood. The brown body of the snake seemed to shine like diamonds in the sunlight. It was a young snake not fully grown.

Oisin hated snakes. He had an irrational and inordinate fear of them. Snakes lived in this country and

133

there were many of them. Once he had disturbed one under a tin and he had leapt back and away from it. Alarmed at being disturbed, the frightened snake quickly disappeared into a hole in the ground but Oisin trembled for minutes after. And another time he had come across the translucent and crushed remains of a skin. He had picked it up and examined it. It felt paper-thin and delicate and a strange object to hold in his hand. This skin had once held a body of a creature that Saint Patrick had removed from the Ireland of Oisin's birth. No snakes in Ireland. It was a kind of triumph to repeat this. Oisin had even boasted about it and now, he held a snake's skin in his hand and to all intents and purposes, he was surrounded by them. He never knew when or where he would come across the next one. It could be found sliding along dry tracks or hiding in the grasses or even curled up in a heap like the one he had disturbed under the tin. That one had been a long dark brown shape that uncoiled itself with such rapidity and disappeared just as quickly so that Oisin, his heart thumping in his chest, felt that it could have been a figment of his imagination. But the snake that Hilda had just killed was no allusion. This was real and just the sight of the creature filled Oisin with nervousness, and the fact that it lay dead on the spade did nothing to allay his fear.

Hilda, holding the spade horizontally away from her body, strode purposefully out of the hen run and through the open wire gate. Oisin followed meekly behind her, just a few paces behind. He looked to the left and to the right but there was no other snake lurking there, ready to strike and wanting revenge. His rational mind was about to take over his thoughts and reassure him that all was well but, at that precise moment Hilda pushed the gate further open and the spade on which the snake balanced so precariously, hit the corner post and the snake, now almost cut in half slipped onto the dust of the dry ground. As soon as this happened, a fierce grey and white hen of enormous size lurched towards

134

it and started to peck furiously at the wound in the snake's belly. Three other hens approached the unfortunate snake now minus its head. At first the three were more timid than their rival grey hen but very soon all the hens managed to peck away at the snake. The body was soon covered with various pin holes. Hilda was having none of it. Her spade became a weapon and she belted the enormous grey hen on her wing. Feathers flew and all four hens retreated rapidly to the other side of the track.

"Here," commanded Hilda and handed Oisin the spade. "Take the head!"

She picked up the tail of the snake and held it upright. A few drops of blood dribbled into the dust on the ground. There was a kind of surreal beauty in the object, for that was what the dead snake had become, its body now a dazzling and luminous mix of yellow and brown and cream.

"Hurry!" ordered Hilda. There was no time to lose.

Oisin obeyed. He scooped the head onto the spade. Both the eyes and forked tongue now flattened and bloody, were covered with dust and tiny stones. Hilda, with the body of the snake held tight between her fingers marched towards the fence. Oisin, holding the spade horizontally in front of him trailed after her and behind him the four hens with the giant grey one leading the way made up the rear. The little procession reached the fence. Hilda catapulted the snake over the wire and then Oisin tipped the head into the long grass. The four hens, thwarted now, ran back and forth along the fence in a vain attempt to get through the fencing wire. Their enemy, now despatched on the other side of the fence would remain there until time brought decay or a carrion crow received sustenance from it.

Hilda's brown and wrinkled face was alive. She smiled at Oisin. Puzzled that the incident had caused him such anxiety, she patted him on his arm to reassure that all was well.

"You're not to worry about the snakes," she spoke softly and in a matter-of-fact way. "They're more frightened of us than we are of them. Least that's what they learned us in the school. You'll learn to live with them if you stay round here. That poor thing was just in the wrong place at the wrong time. It's life, Oisin, you know. Nothing to fear. It's just life and death, Oisin."

Oisin wasn't reassured. The image of the headless and strangely beautiful creature would remain with him for the rest of his life. Hilda might have done her best to explain it all to him but he remained nervous around anything reptilian and if he kept it this way, he hoped he would be able to avoid having any contact with any of them, ever. It was just another danger to face in this vast and unforgiving land.

He woke in the night about two o'clock. His sheets had become a sweaty tangled mess. He had dreamed of snakes. Dozens of the things – black, brown and gold – all of them a writhing mass around him, their tongues exploring the air, their bodies entwined. And there was Hilda shovelling more and more of them into a hessian bag which Oisin had to hold. He got out of bed and looked through the wire mesh at the window. It was another star filled night. The air was cooler at the window and he took deep breaths. He could feel his heart pumping wildly from the effects of the dream. It was peaceful outside and despite the drama that had just unfolded in his dream, he felt a curious peace. This strange and distant country could sometimes evoke a wonderful feeling of awe within him when he least expected it. He sighed and crept back to the bed. When he woke in the morning to the sound of the roosters in the chook run, he wasn't thinking of snakes anymore. Cecy had come into his mind, fleetingly and then just as quickly, she disappeared.

If Oisin had thought that Hans would start the repair of the woolshed, he was wrong. Instead he set about moving twenty black cows to a fresh pasture. The beasts were compliant and glad to have a change of scene. They ran amongst the new grass and some kicked up their heels. As soon as the cows were moved, Hans announced they would set about straightening the fence where they had been grazing and so the two men set to work once more. No mention was made about Vietnam or an invasion or anything else. It was as though that had never happened and they were back to fence building again. Oisin had become quite a good hand around the place but Hans never paid him the slightest of compliments but he didn't criticise him either, so there had to be a blessing in that somehow. The days slipped by.

Oisin spent most of his time at Wiesental. He became ensnared in the routine of Hans and Hilda with the only variation the Sunday visit to the church and the fortnightly drive into Kilgoolga. The nightly Bible reading was a ritual to be endured rather than enjoyed and he usually found his mind wandering as Hans droned on and on. Once the book was shut firmly and returned to the shelf, Oisin knew he was free to go. Life with Hans and Hilda lacked any variety or indeed, any joy. It was a difficult situation. Twice he had ventured to the *Drovers* and looked around for the round-faced girl with the short cropped brown hair but she wasn't anywhere to be seen. He felt a pang of disappointment but didn't know why and he kept this to himself. Hefty and Matt would have enjoyed teasing him and no doubt, they would have filled him in about the girl. He still didn't know who she was.

A few days later, Oisin drove the Land Rover to Kilgoolga. Hilda sat beside him and clutched her straw shopping basket close to her chest. That morning she had got up early and plaited her grey hair into a stylish bun. She looked rather smart, sitting straight backed beside Oisin. She had dressed carefully and put on her new lime green cotton dress and white sandals. Hilda liked her fortnightly visit to the town. It was like a breath of fresh air for her, just leaving the homestead for the day. Because it always took a day to get everything done and it had all become more enjoyable over the last few months with Oisin beside her. Made her feel proud and almost like a mother with a son but she didn't want to think too much about that. Just having someone else to talk to rather than her brother was good enough and it made a great change too. And this young Irish boy was a help around the place. Always willing to tackle anything that was asked of him and he seemed to accept Hans's peculiarities, even take them in his stride although he never mentioned anything of them to Hilda. He was a good boy and she would miss him when he left them. But she wasn't going to think about that today. For today she was going to enjoy herself. Oisin could have the day to himself too. She would do her messages and Oisin could collect the feed from Osborne's and they would meet back at the Land Rover after all this was done. Her friend from the church had invited her for lunch and the two of them would have a great old gossip as they always did. Her friend was a great cook too and she always baked a cake just for Hilda. They had known each other all their lives and her friend had married Jack's brother. They could have been sisters-in-law if Jack had lived. It would have been so different. Hilda's life would have been different. She might have even have had a son like Oisin, if only Jack had lived. Hilda sighed and looked out the window of the Land Rover for she felt the tears behind her eyes, just thinking of Jack and what might have been. She didn't want Oisin to see her cry but one tiny teardrop escaped from her left eye and trickled down her cheek. He didn't notice. She wiped the tear away with her

138

white linen handkerchief just as he turned into the main street of Kilgoolga.

Oisin, too, enjoyed the fortnightly escape from the homestead and away from Hans. He had become quite fond of Hilda and felt a bit sorry for her. Hans was difficult beyond belief sometimes. The relationship between the brother and sister was complex. He wasn't sure who depended upon whom and what would happen to the two of them when they got too old to stay out at Wiesental. He parked the Land Rover at an angle just outside Louis's Drapery Shop and he and Hilda climbed out. It was an overcast day and it looked as if rain was on the way. There hadn't been much of it lately but the creeks still had enough water in them after the floods and the breaking of the two year drought six months ago. In fact, there were patches of green grass in Kilgoolga and the place looked less parched than when he had first arrived here. Seemed as if he had been here for eternity, he sometimes thought, as if he was just treading water somehow, not really getting anywhere, just surviving. But at least here people recognised him and he didn't stand out quite as much anymore. His white Irish skin had turned a light brown and he wore shorts and heavy boots, most of the time, and fitted in. With his felt hat and tee shirt, he could have passed for an Aussie except when he spoke and that usually brought some response. Some of the locals called him 'Paddy' but if Charlie happened to overhear them, he put them right: 'His name *is* Oisin' followed by: 'He's a good bloke'. This young Irish bloke who'd appeared out of nowhere was indeed a good bloke, quiet but OK, everyone agreed. No worries. If Charlie said so, it must be right. Charlie had many friends and more relatives around the place and no one disagreed with Charlie George, least not often. He could see through a bloke, could Charlie and his judgement was invariably spot on.

So now, and it had a lot to do with Charlie, Oisin could walk under the awnings in the main street and be greeted warmly by a few locals, something which had taken him many months to achieve. He discovered that there was more to Kilgoolga than he had first thought. On his days off, he had explored the town and crossed the railway track, past the garage where Matt worked and then to wander along the streets to wonder at the lives behind those brightly painted weatherboard houses that balanced on round wooden stumps. High television aerials glistened in the hot sunlight on red, green or silver roofs. They resembled lines of towering alien spears, lined up precariously on the tins roofs. Past neat gardens where gardeners struggled to get flowers to bloom and other gardens where there was nothing but dry grass and bushes that needed no care. Past palling white fences and wire fences with gates that were shut and others that were not. Four streets on the other side of the railway track and then the flat and empty space beyond the fences for the fences were there to mark out property and could never totally tame this untameable land. On the other side of the railway track he also found, to his delight, the School of Arts Hall where, at the back of the building he discovered the library, open on weekday mornings and a friendly librarian to go with the books. Next door was the part time office of *The Kilgoolga Echo,* also only open in the morning and not at all on Wednesday. Further along from these buildings and sitting neatly in an acre of ground stood the small District Hospital and the doctor and dental surgeries next to it. He figured, when the town was being built, there was enough space in this vast emptiness to build where you wanted to without having restrictions of any kind. But his favourite place of all was the park next to the War Memorial at the end of the main street. Here he would sit on the wooden bench and absorb the unmistakable sights and sounds of the Australian bush for even here in the town, the sweet smell of the eucalyptus was everywhere. He usually bought his lunch from the takeaway menu at the ABC Café and he would sit quite happily on the wooden park bench sometimes for an hour or so. Just thinking at times and at other times, he'd pass the time reading a library book. He sat so often at the War Memorial that he had memorised the names on the monument and could recite them off by heart if he ever had been asked to do so. Life for Oisin had become a dull routine and if at times, when he wondered if he was living in a sort of time warp, out in this alien land, he would shrug his shoulders as if by this gesture he could dismiss it all and he would find it was just a dream. The Dreamtime, the Aborigines called the forgotten past. Maybe, he too, was now living in a dreamtime and one day he would awake with no memory of any of it. He had no plan for his future. He merely existed and when the lonely thoughts invaded his mind, Cecy was never far from him then and he cursed her, just remembering. He had no anchor to hold him. No one to guide him. No one to comfort him.

He had arranged to meet Hilda later in the day so when he finally arrived at the War Memorial it was already the middle of the afternoon. He had spent most of the morning collecting supplies from Osborne's and after that, a visit to the barber in the main street. With his hair cut and his beard trimmed, his appearance changed. He was no longer the long haired bearded young man. Instead he was now a rather handsome Irish lad even if the sadness was always there behind his eyes. For the few astute beings who knew about these things that was easily to discern. He settled himself on his favourite bench and took a bite out of his sandwich. It was a good place to sit because there was always something happening. The War Memorial had been positioned on the grassy piece of land in the middle of a very wide street. The street was named Bradshaw Avenue. Two signs indicated this grander name. By deliberately positioning the War Memorial where it was, it had made it a focus for the town and from here, on Anzac Day, men and women would march, turn left into the main street and finish the day at The Kilgoolga Arms Hotel. The pale yellow

141

weatherboard Post Office and the Police Station, painted in the same colour were directly in front of him on the other side of the street. Both buildings had red galvanised iron roofs. Matt's garage was also visible near where the main street crossed the railway line. There was always something happening at the garage. It sold the only petrol for miles. The Police Station was on the corner of the street which led to the Kilgoolga High School. From his bench he could hear the noises coming from the school and sometimes, if he happened to be sitting there at lunchtime, the trail of boys and girls, all in their own adolescent world and heading for the Main street. Some of the girls giggled when they passed by him but the boys hardly gave him a second glance. All in all, it was a good place to sit.

His plan had been to eat his sandwich and then head back to the Land Rover and Hilda for he just had half an hour or so before their agreed meet up time. He ate his sandwich, drank the can of lemonade and got up to leave. It was then that he noticed a girl coming towards him from the direction of the High School. She was in a bit of a state. She had a large briefcase in her right hand and a white handbag clasped protectively to her left side. The strap of the handbag balanced awkwardly over her shoulder. The strap kept falling down and she had to stop every few steps to reposition it. She wore white shoes with high heels. The shoes also seemed to be giving her difficulty because she wobbled rather unsteadily along the uneven footpath. As she tottered towards Oisin, he noticed with some surprise that she was the girl with the round face and the short cropped brown hair whom he had first seen at the Drover's Disco at Milberra a few weeks ago. He could barely believe it. She looked a bit of a sight and not half as prim as she had appeared to be at the Disco. He took a deep breath and shouted to her,

"Hiya, looks like you're having a spot of bother?"

142

The girl was now just a few paces from him. She stopped and looked at him directly. It was not a comfortable sort of look but rather a superior sort of one.

"I'm not!"

"Bit heavy, that briefcase, isn't it?"

"No."

"Looks like it to me. Do ye need a hand?" Oisin grinned.

"No... thank you."

"Didn't I see ye at the Drovers a few weeks past?"

"I don't frequent it much. It's not a place I like!"

"So... it was ye!"

"Could have been."

"Ah... thought so. Well, we've been introduced then, haven't we?"

"I don't think so. Now... I really must go... "

"Have ye far to carry that thing?"

"It's OK, honest."

"Well, now... what do ye say, I'll walk with ye to the main street... I'm headin' there anyway."

"Suit yourself."

"I didn't catch ye name... ?"

"I didn't give it." He noticed that a red flush had appeared on her neck and was heading towards her face. He tried again.

"Let me at least carry yer bag to the main street?"

"It's OK. I can manage."

"My word, looks like the Aussie lassies are a tough lot!"

The girl glared at him.

"We have to be!" she said.

Oisin grinned. He was having fun. He hadn't enjoyed himself quite as much for a long time.

"Well, then... will I see ye again?"

"You're rather presuming, aren't you?"

"It's Kilgoolga."

143

"Well, you're not from Kilgoolga, that's for sure!"

"That I'm not. Now where do ye think I come from?"

"I wouldn't know. Now, I really must... "

"At least, let's introduce ourselves." He held out his hand to her. With her briefcase in one hand and her handbag in the other, it was impossible for her to reciprocate.

"I've work to do."

"Well, I'll introduce meself then. I'm all the way from Ireland and the good priest baptised me and I got the name, Oisin Kelly!"

"You're a Catholic then."

"Lapsed," he said.

The red flush had travelled all the way up her face to under her left eye and Oisin thought the slightest hint of a smile had appeared at the corners of her mouth. He tried again.

"Well, now that's religion out of the way," he said. "How about your name?"

"Persistent, aren't you?"

"Well?"

"I suppose so! Claire Paterson. Happy now?" It seemed to Oisin that she was becoming just a little bit flirtatious as she spoke these words and he held out his right hand again.

"Well, we're introduced properly then. Shake on it?" Oisin grinned.

Claire Paterson put her briefcase onto the footpath and they shook hands. He had expected her handshake to be delicate but it was firm. They held hands for a few seconds longer than usual and then they broke away.

"Now we've been introduced, can I carry your bag?"

"You don't give up, do you?"

She smiled.

"Wow! What's in this? Weighs a ton!"

"Books, test papers to mark... "

"Ah, yer a teacher then?"

"Clever, aren't you?" she said.

"That's why ye were coming from the school!"

"Told you, you were clever, didn't I?!"

They both laughed. At the corner of Bradshaw Avenue and the main street they stood outside the blackened remains of the Commercial Hotel. It looked forlorn and was waiting for a buyer to come along and bring it back to life but no one had appeared.

"I'll have the bag now, please... and thank you," Claire said.

Oisin grinned. He had a cheeky grin when he felt happy.

"Which way are ye going?" he asked.

"Across the railway... I can carry it OK... used to it!"

"Will I see ye again?"

The red flush appeared once more on the side of her neck. She didn't want to look at him and she stared at the ground instead. She was flustered.

"Kilgoolga's a small place... "

At that, she tottered across the road to the garage at the end of the main street and towards the railway line. She was dressed in a tight grey skirt to the knees, a thick black vinyl belt around her waist and a white blouse. Oisin decided it was quite an agreeable view from behind and he thought to himself, *If she turns round, I'm in with a chance!* He watched her struggle with the briefcase and the handbag as she wobbled along on her high heels. At the railway crossing sign, she stopped and put her briefcase down. Then she turned and looked in his direction. His heart missed a beat! He grinned again and blew her a kiss with his hand. When she saw him, she put her nose in the air, turned her back and crossed the railway line without looking towards him again.

Hilda was sitting quite happily in the Land Rover when Oisin climbed into the driver's seat. She smiled when she saw him,

"You look pleased with yourself," she said.

Oisin grinned and started up the engine. He crunched the gears as he put the vehicle into reverse. As they drove out of town, past the Catholic church on the left and the convent on the right, he started to whistle. It was a tune his Uncle Mick used to whistle. He remembered the tune and Ballybeg. He smiled.

"Aye, Hilda," he answered, "that I am."

CHAPTER EIGHT

Oisin had learned to be cautious around Hans. It was a survival strategy that he suspected Hilda used as well because brother and sister hardly seemed to communicate with each other except for the usual day to day banalities. And then it was usually Hilda who did most of the talking. So it was with some trepidation that Oisin agreed to accompany Hans on a walk on Sunday afternoon. Usually Sundays were reserved for the church in the morning and lunch at noon. The afternoons were the best time of all for Oisin because he had free time and could do what he liked. He often walked for miles around the property or sometimes if he felt tired, he would just take a book, stretch out in the comfortable squatter's chair on the veranda and nine times out of ten, fall asleep. He would awake to the shrill and noisy calls from the varieties of parrots that seemed to constantly fly over the property. Or it would be Hilda shaking him gently to inform him that she had made a cup of tea and some fresh scones and would he like some?

Hans certainly appeared to be aging a bit lately and Oisin was sure that the old farmer was becoming more and more unpredictable in his behaviour. Ever since the map and the woolshed, Hans had retreated into himself even further, had never mentioned the events that had led to the imagined Communist invasion and, even more worrying, he rarely spoke to either Hilda or Oisin. When he did, it was only to issue an order or direct them in some other way. He prayed at mealtimes, stumbled over his words sometimes and read from the Bible every day but even these rituals appeared to be decreasing. The Bible readings had become brief - they were over in ten minutes usually – then Hans would shut the book and, without making the slightest comment, return it to the shelf. After that, he invariably disappeared towards his bedroom leaving Hilda and Oisin to talk amongst themselves. So when Hans asked Oisin to come with him, it was no wonder that the young man felt very unsure and decidedly nervous. They set off towards the woolshed and still Hans didn't speak. Instead, he walked at a leisurely pace with his head down and Oisin slowed so as not to appear to be rushing ahead. This would not please Hans if he thought the younger man was trying to show off and by walking faster, highlight the age differences between them. When they got to the abandoned sheep pens, Hans stopped. He was breathing heavily as he leaned on the top rail of the fence.

"I've been doin' some thinkin' lately. Been doin' a lot of thinkin' actually about what's goin' to happen to this place after I'm gone," he paused and took another breath. "This place is all I've known. Me and Hilda, well, we've lived here all our lives, ya know. Wouldn't like to think the Commies would get it... or anyone else for that matter! So, I've been givin' the whole situation a lot of thinkin' and been prayin' about it too and ma prayers have been answered, in a manner of speakin'. I think the Lord has sent me a message from on high." Sometimes when Hans focussed his pale blue eyes on people, it made people nervous. This was one of those times and Oisin, looking into those eyes could feel his heart beating. It pumped so hard that he was sure Hans must have been able to hear it.

It was so silent, standing there, that Oisin was certain his hearing had become finely tuned to such a level that he could have made out the slightest noise from a mile away. He wondered what was coming next. Wispy white clouds appeared in the sky and he watched them rather than look at Hans. The clouds looked as if they had been drawn there and the sky was an enormous bright blue canvas behind them. The only sound to break the silence came from Hans. He leaned on the fence and after a few moments, he finally started to breathe more evenly.

"It's about time, I reckon, that I did something for ya... " He paused. The expression on his brown wrinkled and furrowed face grew more thoughtful. It seemed that whatever he was about to say to Oisin was of such great importance to him and for that reason he had to think out his words very carefully. Oisin waited.

"Hilda's been at me again about it! So, I prayed an' I've come to the conclusion that you should have the keys to the padlocks at the gate... ya know the front paddock... that's if ya want them?"

This was the last thing that Oisin had expected to hear and the thought of having the freedom to come and go as he pleased certainly did please him. Keys and fences and boundaries seemed to be a deep seated problem for Hans and Oisin guessed that the old farmer would have spent many, many hours pondering about the repercussions if he allowed someone else to have the keys to the main gate. In fact, it had got to such a point lately that no one from outside came to the property. If anyone ventured to Wiesental, the usual course of action for them was to ring the homestead first and if Hans decided that they could set foot on the place, either Hilda or Oisin were despatched with the two keys to the gate. Consequently, getting in and out of the place was becoming more and more problematic and less and less people took the trouble to come. The last visitor arrived about six weeks ago. That had been a haulier who loaded about ten of the black cattle into the lorry for the market. Even he, a huge beast of a man, had appeared nervous and didn't spend much time talking. Just loaded the cattle and was away within the hour so for Hans to offer the keys to his young employee must have meant a lot and certainly there would have been some amount of soul searching before the decision was made. Whatever the reasons for this unexpected windfall, Oisin was in no mood to argue and eagerly accepted the offer. He would now be able to drive his car to Kilgoolga or Milberra and not have to walk the two miles back and forth from the gate. He could park his car at the homestead and not at the fence.

"That's very good of you, Hans. I'd like that," he said. He didn't want to appear too excited at this unexpected prospect of freedom.

"Well, then... I'll get a set of keys cut for ya... or mebbes ya could do that next time ya in Kilgoolga? Think they cut keys at the grocery store in the main street along from the ABC Café? I don't much like goin' into that place anymore. Old Smith's a right old crook, if you ask me, make sure ya get a receipt, won't ya? Don't like goin' into Kilgoolga much these days... they're all a bunch of crooks in that place. What do ya say then?"

"That'd be OK. Sure. No worries."

"If ya lose them keys, mind, I'll tan ya hide to an inch of ya life!! Now, be off with ya, I've some thinkin' to do!"

Oisin Kelly now found himself in another dilemma. And a most unexpected dilemma it was too! Certainly one he had never anticipated. The problem was all to do with the appearance of Claire Paterson and his thoughts afterwards. He had managed to divorce himself from his past life to such an extent that family, friends and place were now a kind of weird distant memory for him and, if by chance he caught

150

himself thinking about Cecy, or even his mother back in Ballybeg, he was able to almost instantly delete these thoughts from his mind and turn them into something more appropriate to his present circumstances. Living in the west had hardened him and its remoteness had strengthened him. The very nature of his present life living with Hans and Hilda Seefeldt had changed him. He was not the person he had been before. That person had been an innocent one whose naivety had made him vulnerable. In fact, that person did not exist for him anymore and it had a lot to do with Cecy for in that one painful moment she had taken all his old certainties away from him and with them gone all his hopes and plans were removed from his mind as well. She had left him feeling naked and bare. This is how he had felt. Many times he tried to forgive her but he could not. She had destroyed his innocence. And destroyed his innocence in a way that was more than just sexual, she had ripped all hope away from him in that one cruel stroke. Although he now thought less often about her, he still could not let her go, at least not entirely and that was why meeting Claire Paterson, the very prim and totally different person from Cecy, had caused the dilemma that he was now facing.

He was unsure about his next move. If he wanted to meet Claire again, and he had to admit to himself that he was intrigued by her, how on earth could he go about it? After all, he had sat on that bench at the War Memorial for over a year now and he hadn't seen her before. He could sit there, every week or so and not see her again. She insisted that she didn't frequent *The Drovers* so that option was out. And anyway, he was tiring of *The Drovers* and the almost religious intensity of the drinking that took place there and he hadn't met any girl whom he would have liked to get to know further. Not until Claire. If he hung around the High School, hoping to bump into her, chances are this behaviour would be viewed as suspicious, even in Kilgoolga and he might find himself being cautioned by the friendly police sergeant. And that would never do. He was unsure as to what the authorities would make of his even being in the country. He hadn't bothered with visas, after all. He might be asked to leave and then, where would he go? Back to Edinburgh? No chance. And the thought of returning to Ballybeg and the West of Ireland filled him with horror. No, he had quietly disappeared from everybody's radar out here in the west and he was certain that it was best that it remain so. At least, until he could plot his next move. And thinking all this, it suddenly occurred to him that he was beginning finally to start to plan once more.

He wasn't sure why the brief meeting with Claire Paterson had made him feel happier again. She certainly didn't encourage him. Rather the reverse. But there was something about her that interested him. He had never expected to meet anyone out in the west, least of all in the remote little town of Kilgoolga. But Claire seemed to enter his head more frequently than he imagined any other woman would be able to do, after Cecy. And so he began to plan how he could meet her again? He decided that it would be foolhardy to ask Hefty and Matt. They would tease him and embarrass him. He thought of Hilda. The two of them got on well enough and they were growing closer the longer he stayed at Wiesental but Hilda was old enough to be his mother and it was really too personal a thing to discuss with her. He wasn't sure how she would react to such a revelation. Then there was Charlie George. But Charlie was old too. He liked Charlie but there was the age difference between them and this would make discussing a girl rather awkward. He couldn't think of anyone else he could ask.

People had been quick to let him know that there were three families in Kilgoolga – the Bradshaws whom he hadn't met; the Patersons and the Seefeldts. These were the three important land owning families in the district and by far, the most powerful of the three were the Bradshaws, in particular Eleanor Bradshaw. But whenever Eleanor's name came up in conversation or any of the Bradshaws for that matter, a brief silence usually followed. And Oisin was alert enough to observe that very quickly the subject changed. No one really wanted to talk about the Bradshaws. But the Patersons were a different kettle of fish altogether. Hefty had spoken at length about the story of *The Drovers* and how it used to be the family home of the old Patersons. He went on to say that the Patersons owned Milberra and their financial interests extended into Kilgoolga as well. They owned land, houses and shops in both places. So Oisin reasoned that Claire Paterson had to have something to do with this land owning clan. The problem was how to find out about her but not appear too eager. For if she was indeed a member of this family, the thought of her becoming involved with a nomadic Irishman from the other side of the earth might lead to difficulties. He had lived his childhood in a close knit community in the West of Ireland. He knew the pitfalls and dangers that a stranger in their midst could pose. His own English mother had been evidence of that. And then again, after all this, Claire Paterson might not have the slightest bit of interest in him. She had certainly been aloof when they spoke. She might already have a boyfriend and if he were to approach her, he could quite easily be rebuffed. Given his fragility as far as the female sex was concerned, he wasn't sure he could cope with this. After all, he had tried for months now not to think of women! It was all rather difficult.

His dilemma remained much the same until one late Saturday afternoon when, perched on a stool in the Public Bar of the Kilgoolga Arms, the conversation turned to events that had apparently happened the night before. He had already downed two beers and was drinking his way through the third when Bella, who up to that point had been kept busy washing and drying glasses, suddenly started to laugh. In fact, it was more of a chortle than a laugh. Hefty, Lefty and Oisin were the only men in the bar at the time and all three had fallen silent and were busy with their own thoughts. So Bella's chortle startled them and awoke them from their contemplation.

"Hell, Bella," exclaimed Lefty, "what's ya laughin' about? We was all three thinkin' some pretty deep thoughts, wasn't we, boys? Like when's our next drinks comin'?" And he winked at Oisin.

"I was just thinkin' about last night," said Bella and she poured Lefty another beer. She plonked the glass down in front of him and some of the white froth spilled onto the bar.

Lefty drank half a glass of the beer in one gulp and then he lit a cigarette before saying anything. Finally he said,

"Well c'mon then, Bella ma love, better enlighten us. We're not goin' ta get any peace until we hear what happened last night 'cause ya gonna tell us anyways."

"Well... ," said Bella slowly. She had the men's attention and she was enjoying it. "It was young Harry Paterson... the youngest one, ya know?"

Lefty and Hefty nodded. They knew Harry Paterson. Oisin, on hearing the name 'Paterson', focused his eyes on his glass and so avoided looking in Bella's direction. He didn't want to appear too interested in case it aroused any suspicions. He figured his best course of action was just to sit quiet and find out about this Harry Paterson.

"They're all wild blokes them Paterson boys but Harry's the baby and he has to be the wildest one of the three of them, whaddaya reckon?"

"Too right!" agreed Lefty.

"Well, Harry's gets in here about closin' time an' he's soundin' his mouth awf as usual. Big timin' himself. He's blotto already an' I says to 'im, 'Harry Paterson, youse had enough!' but he wouldn't hear of it, 'Just give'z another one, Bella,' he says, 'one for the road'. 'NO!' And I meant it. Well, crikey did he hit the roof after that! A few blokes were in 'ere at the time an' Billy Anderson, he says to Harry, 'That's no way ta talk ta Bella, mate.' An' at that, Harry takes a swing at Billy an' all hell broke loose!"

"Jesus, Bella!" This from Lefty. Everyone liked Bella.

"Next thing, some of the blokes gets hold off Harry an' boots him out the door. Harry's swingin' punches left, right and centre an' he can hardly stand. We all traipse out but there he is, tryin' to get inta his car. Just then along comes the cop car with all the blue lights flashin'. The sergeant's got the inspector from Brizzie here that's why. Happens every year, Oisin. Watch that you stop at the railway crossin'. The sergeant has to get some convictions... to keep his job, whaddaya reckon, Lefty?"

"Too right. Bella. Watch that crossin', mate an' keep yer speed down. It'll all be back ta normal next week!"

"Anyways, the sergeant says to Harry, 'Where do ya think your goin', Paterson?' 'Kinleven,' says Harry. 'You're in no fit state. Give me the keys now.' Well, think the sergeant's wantin' ta impress the inspector who was just standin' there seein' all this. Funny bloke, the inspector. Them city cops, all alike! Anyways, I was sayin', the sergeant says to Harry, 'Well, Paterson ya not drivin' this vehicle. Ya got a choice 'ere, mate. The cell or I'll take ya round to Claire and ya can sleep it awf there'."

Oisin at that point had lost interest a little in the conversation because invariably Bella's stories rambled on and on and brought in so many people he didn't know, that he usually quite happily went back to his own thoughts. However, when he heard the name 'Claire', he felt his face reddening and he looked up. This had to be the same Claire! There couldn't be two Claire Patersons in Kilgoolga. And Claire must live in Kilgoolga too. Suddenly his world changed. He listened. He wanted to hear what happened next. Lefty and Hefty did too. All eyes were on Bella.

"Well, Harry started to mumble 'bout goin' to Claire's. 'Ma sister doesn't like me,' he says. 'Your choice, Harry,' says the sergeant. 'Think Claire's place might be

155

more comfortable for ya though even if she gives ya some amount o' ear bashin'!' Well, ya can imagine, we all burst out laughin', even the inspector. Then Harry's like a kitten, 'OK, Serge,' he says, 'take me round to ma sister. Least she'll feed me!'"

Bella poured another glass of beer from the tap and handed it to Hefty. He, too, like his father, emptied half the glass in one gulp.

"What happened then?" asked Oisin. He wondered how he could find out where Claire lived. This would be a move in the right direction, he figured.

"Well, Oisin, Harry gets into the cop car, meek as a lamb an' awf they go 'cross the railway line to Claire's. But I can tell ya this, that young bugger's not welcome in here an' I mean it. Least not till he can get a civil tongue in his head. Don't care if he's a Paterson or not!"

"Yeah, ya right there, Bella," said Lefty. "That young fella's got away with blue bloody murder over the last couple o' years. But they get over it. Big brother, Tony used to play up like hell remember, an' he's a changed man now that he's got himself engaged to that young Janie."

"That's what all you men need, Lefty, a good woman to keep the lot of youse in line!" Bella laughed.

"You've got a point there, Bella love," said Lefty nodding his head. "Best be gettin' back to the missus or she'll have the fryin' pan after me!!"

"Oh, Dad... you're safe an' ya know it!" murmured Hefty and then he grinned at Oisin. "Mum's never laid inta him yet... mebbe it's 'bout time she did!"

"That's enough out of ya, son. Drink up and let's be headin' home ta ya ma," replied Lefty good-naturedly. He had a happy home life.

Oisin thought this had to be the moment when he could carefully ask about Claire. Everyone was in good spirits. No one should notice a casual remark. He cleared his throat and trying to keep his voice steady and then he said,

"Harry sounds as if he's a bit of a stirrer, sure. Not met any of the Patersons yet but I've sure heard a bit about them! Sounds like this Claire keeps them in line though. What happened next? Did he get to her place after all?"

"Right enough there, mate. The Patersons think they own Kilgoolga along with Milberra. Strewth, they've always been a wild bunch an' most of them are OK, I guess. They're a helluva a lot better than that lot over there," said Lefty and he pointed to the sepia photographs on the wall behind him.

Ever since he had first set foot in the Kilgoolga Arms, Oisin had wondered who they were. He wanted the conversation to get back to Claire but he was curious about the photographs, so he asked about them. He pointed to the photograph of the severe-looking gentleman with the whiskers along the side of his face to his chin and the receding hair. Bella was happy to tell him the story. She had become quite fond of the young Irish bloke who had appeared out of nowhere a year ago. It was good fun to see his face when the jokes were being bandied about in the bar. Sometimes the men made up stories just to get his reaction but everyone liked Oisin. He was easy to tease and he took it all in his stride, almost as if he belonged here sometimes.

"That's Lord Cyril Bradshaw and the woman's his wife, Oisin," she said seriously.

The woman looked just as severe as her husband. Her long black hair was arranged in plaits on the top of her head and she wore a white blouse with frills to her neck. She looked as if she had never known any happiness in her life. Oisin felt rather sorry for her, just studying the photograph.

"Lord Bradshaw's wife's name was Lotte an' she was a Seefeldt, same as Hans and Hilda but the Seefeldts were never a match on the Bradshaws. The Bradshaws own The Kilgoolga Arms and most of the town... they own a helluva lot more than anyone else round here, don't they, Lefty?

"Yeah."

157

"That photo in the middle... that's the bullock drays in the early days of Kilgoolga. They must 'ave been some people comin' all this way an' tryin' to make a livin' out here. They say the crows fly backwards in Kilgoolga!" she chuckled.

"Too right, Bella," added Lefty with a cheery grin, "an' by the time them crows gets to Milberra where the Patersons are, the bloody things have dropped down dead!"

Everyone laughed, even Oisin.

"Right enough, Lefty. Not much from then on except the snakes an' the flies! If the snakes don't get ya, the flies will, hey! But guess ya'll meet a few of them one day, Oisin, the Bradshaws that is an' the snakes too! That's if you're intendin' to stay out here. But gettin' back to young Harry. Heard he sobered up and was as good as gold the next day. Even heard he mowed Claire's lawn for her after all the carry on of the night before."

Hefty and Lefty got up to leave. The combined height and width of the two of them in the bar dwarfed everything around them. As he passed Oisin, Hefty gave him a playful punch on the arm. Oisin was getting used to these playful punches. It was a bit like getting greeted constantly by a giant and enthusiastic St Bernard dog. Hefty grinned,

"See ya round, mate," he said. "Glad ta see that old bugger's let ya out at last!"

"Aye, I must have caught him on a good day. Catch up with you soon, Hefty!"

Oisin thought how good it was to have a mate like Hefty. Even the bruises on his arm from the playful punches were worth it!

He still didn't know much about Claire Paterson but at least another piece of the jigsaw had been revealed. He now knew the names of the photographs on the wall. Perhaps more importantly though he had learned that Claire had three brothers and she lived over the railway line in

Kilgoolga. He thought that was about all he could hope for at the moment.

"Hey, Oisin, before ya go!" It was Bella. "Ya was askin' about Claire Paterson. She's got her hands full with them three brothers, ya know... well, she's the oldest... an' her mum's not well. The Patersons are OK if ya ask me. Take no notice of what Lefty says about them... he had his eyes set on Claire's mum but she ended up with Rusty Paterson. That's another story. Anyhow, if ya want to know where Claire lives, she's the third street from the railway, opposite the tennis court. There's a camphor laurel tree in the front and a low hedge. Ya can't miss it!"

And then Bella winked.

Claire Paterson woke up suddenly when she heard the hammering on the door. She was in a deep sleep and it took her a few moments to realise where she was. Claire lived alone and she kept the front door firmly locked with a key and a chain. 'You have to be careful, even in Kilgoolga', her mother insisted so both the front and back doors were locked securely all the time. Just to be on the safe side. You never know. She was sleepy and it took her a minute or so to get the key into the lock. Then she had to unlock the wire mesh door. The catch on it had jammed and she gave it a hard twist to open it. In her haste to get to the door she had hurriedly put on her cream fleecy dressing gown. The gown kept slipping off her left shoulder and in her half-awake state, she hadn't been able to locate her slippers so when she opened the door, she was bare footed and heavy-eyed. She switched on the light at the porch and the first thing she noticed was the blue light of the police car. It was a dark

159

night and the street light opposite had flicked off a while back and no one had arrived to fix it so the blue light, flashing on and off, dazzled her sleepy eyes. It took a moment for her to realise just who was at her door. When she recognised the three men, she pulled her dressing gown tighter around her waist. It was the police sergeant and the inspector from Brisbane and between them, and held firmly by both men, was her young brother, Harry. Harry, it appeared could hardly stand up straight and his head fell onto the sergeant's right shoulder. This wasn't acceptable to the sergeant who kept pushing Harry's head back but to no avail for as quickly as he did, Harry's head dropped down again. Claire opened the wire door. She glared at her brother.

"Got a prezzie for ya, Claire," announced the sergeant.

"Harry!"

"G'day, sis!"

"Harry Paterson was in the process of attempting to drive a vehicle under the influence of alcohol," said the inspector in his pompous way. "Rather than confine him to a cell for the night... which is the usual procedure in these circumstances... we have allowed him to come here instead. The keys to his vehicle will remain at the police station and can be collected and signed for by him tomorrow. Do you agree to this man being here, Miss?"

The inspector was a stickler for the letter of the law. He knew things happened differently out in the west but this was one case that he decided needed a firm hand and his was that hand. He had been an observer up to this point but now his patience was wearing thin. Although he rather liked the young sergeant and he was aware that the law was not always upheld in the correct manner out here, he would have to write a report about it. His report would highlight a few of these issues but on the whole, he knew it was best to leave most things as they were. It was a remote community, after all and a close knit one at that. The sergeant was a Kilgoolga boy and the locals seemed to like him. But to be liked was not what a policeman necessarily signed up to be. You have to have discipline otherwise there's anarchy. The inspector was very big on anarchy. He also was very big on drinking and driving. He thought the sergeant had handled this situation in a reasonably professional way given the circumstances. By exhibiting firmness, with the appropriate authority and by allowing a certain leniency which was necessary in the small community, he had won the respect of the other locals who had gathered outside the pub to witness the event. This young drunk would sober up overnight and be let off with a caution when he collected his car keys. He would put all this in his report when he got back to Brisbane.

"Well, Miss?" The inspector was waiting for a reply. He had thought it best to let the sergeant take charge of the situation but he would still have preferred to have seen the young hoodlum spend a night in the cell."

When Claire saw Harry with the police officers, she was flustered. Everyone in the district was always on edge when the inspector arrived for his annual visit and to think her young brother was now the object of his scrutiny, angered her. She would have liked to have pounced on Harry and given him a talking to but instead, she tightened the cord of her dressing gown around her waist and said meekly,

"Yes, Inspector. This's my brother, Harry and I suppose he can stay here tonight!"

She glared at her brother. In fact, she gave him one of her famous withering glances. Harry grinned.

"Ma sister's worth her weight in gold... don't ya reckon, Serge?"

Harry lurched towards Claire and the wire door. He swayed somewhat unsteadily and he only managed to save himself by clutching hold of Claire's arm. The movement caused her dressing gown to slip even further from her shoulder and expose the top half of her breast. Now she was both embarrassed and furious at the same time. She grabbed Harry by his collar and dragged him into the hall where he stood, drunken and dishevelled with a foolish grin on his face. He bowed slightly to the two policemen now that he was safely through the door.

"G'night, gentlemen," he said. "Thanks for the lift!"

"HARRY!"

Harry smelt of stale beer and dry vomit. He meekly followed his sister to the bedroom whereupon he sat on the edge of the bed. The black metal frame of the bed creaked as he fell down. There was no sympathy from Claire. She pulled his shirt, with its traces of vomit, off his shoulders and threw the offending garment into a corner of the room. Harry sunk gratefully onto the bed and in a few seconds he started to snore. Claire studied the face of her brother. He lay there, dead to the world and she couldn't help thinking that he was just as endearing as he had always been, even in his present drunken state. Harry, with his blond curly hair and cheeky grin was by far the most handsome and spoilt of her three brothers. She remembered when she had seen him first. She'd been ten at the time and her mother had given birth to Harry at home with just the help of the midwife. Claire had wanted a baby sister so very, very much and when she saw Harry for the first time, she was furious. So furious in fact that she had rushed outside the house and grabbed her bike and rode along the dirt track from Kinleven towards Milberra. She had finally stopped at the old gum tree and there she threw her bike down onto the dry ground. Bursting into tears, she had yelled at God for giving her a baby brother and not a sister. She had prayed every day and look what had happened. Claire was ten years of age at the time but she never forgot that moment for in that moment, she gave up on God. But after that, she discovered that Harry wasn't quite so bad after all. In fact, it was good sometimes having a baby brother that she could boss around.

Claire eased one of Harry's boots from his foot and then the other one. She placed the boots neatly under the bed. He didn't stir. She fetched a cover and threw it over him for it was a chilly night. Then she left him to sleep it off. In the morning she knew he would be contrite and would offer to do anything she asked of him. It had always been the way. Claire, no matter how hard she tried, could never stay angry with her baby brother for any length of time. As she drifted off to sleep, she planned what she would get him to do the next morning and she smiled.

Sunday afternoons in Kilgoolga were always sleepy. In fact, not much happened on Sunday. The folk who went to church went to church and those who did nothing, did nothing. Others took themselves off to the bowling green or the tennis court and others just wandered around or if you were male and young, you drove up and down the streets revving the engine of your car and generally making a nuisance of yourself. In fact, life in Kilgoolga on Sunday was practically the same as it was during the week, just with less to do. Least during the week the shops opened. But on Sunday all doors were shut along the main street and you could wander under the awnings and not see another soul. Sunday was a sort of non-event type day.

Claire Paterson either spent Sunday at her parent's place at Kinleven or sometimes she played a game of tennis with the boys and her friend Janet. She liked to keep fit and the tennis court was across the street from her place in Kilgoolga. The girls played doubles with the boys. Kanga was always up for a game and he was often joined by Matt and Hefty. Hefty had a mean and powerful serve and usually won the match. The girls preferred to partner Hefty. It was safer not to have to be at the other end of that powerful serve. The boys and girls had known one another all their lives. It was a comfortable arrangement for all of them and it gave everyone something to do on sleepy Sundays in Kilgoolga.

After the incident with Harry and the police Claire was even more careful about keeping her door locked, day and night. So when she heard a gentle tap on the wire mesh door one drowsy Sunday afternoon, she was cautious. She had just emerged from a cool shower and she wasn't in the mood to be disturbed. She was at her most primness at times like this. The gentle tapping continued. Annoyed, she hastily slipped on a pair of jeans and a tee shirt and then ran a comb through her short cropped hair. From the hall she could make out a figure behind the wire mesh and when she got closer to it, the red flush spread quickly around her neck. The figure belonged to the Irishman she had met at the War Memorial a few weeks before. Her first instinct was to run back along the hall but he had already seen her through the mesh door. She twisted the catch to open the door and there he was. He looked different. He had shaved off his black beard and tidied his hair. He grinned.

"I was just passin' by," he said, "and I says to meself, 'Wonder if this is where that lassie lives who didn't want to be introduced an' I was after thinkin', perhaps we could get better acquainted'? "

The young Irishman was trying very hard to sound familiar but she could see he was nervous. She felt the warmth of the red flush and she bit her lip. He had dressed carefully, she noted that. His blue jeans and blue cotton shirt had been ironed. Her heart beat louder.

"How did you know where I lived?" She was becoming primmer every minute. She wondered whether she should invite him in?

"It's Kilgoolga, ye told me!"

164

"Yes… but I didn't expect you to arrive on my doorstep!"

"Is that a problem for ye?"

There was a pause; a long pause.

"No," she said quietly.

"Well…?"

Claire lowered her head but he kept looking at her. He kept looking at her for what seemed to be an age. She had to answer him but she tried to be as distant as she could possibly be. After all, that's what being prim does; it puts an invisible barrier around a person. *But he was different from all the other boys* she thought. *Maybe just maybe that might change things somehow.* She opened the door further and this time she didn't give him a withering look but a slight and shy smile.

"Guess you can come in then."

And with that invitation, Oisin Kelly stepped over the mat and into a new life.

CHAPTER NINE

The Commercial Hotel was once a landmark in Kilgoolga. Its position on the corner of the main street and Bradshaw Avenue and the fact that it had been built almost as soon as Cyril Bradshaw had taken up the land around, had contributed to its iconic statue in the hearts and minds of the locals. This grand two storey building with bars and restaurant and rooms upstairs to accommodate at least twenty guests stood for tradition and solidity. People liked the Commercial. Sometimes the rooms were full. When the Agricultural Show and the races took place people descended on the small township from far and wide and the Commercial was the place to stay. In fact, the only place to stay! The Kilgoolga Arms at the other end of the main street had just two rooms to let and there were very few people in the town who offered bed and breakfast. The Commercial Hotel was built in the style of a rather magnificent homestead with its red galvanised iron roof, a wide veranda upstairs and the twenty foot long red and white sign which hung from the white wrought iron railings upstairs.

From upstairs the guests could look out over the railway station to the lines of houses and beyond them to the flat landscape that stretched into the distance. There was something enduring about the Commercial in the minds of so many and everyone expected that the oldest building in Kilgoolga would be a much loved landmark forever.

166

So the night that the fire took hold of this much loved old hotel and reduced part of it to a blackened ruin was a sad event for all in Kilgoolga and a reminder of the impermanence of human existence. A red glow in the night sky was seen as far away as Milberra. The flames had leapt so high and the intensity of the heat was so intense that at one point the other buildings close by, including the bank next door, were in possible danger as well. Fortunately, it had rained a few days before and there was enough water to contain the blaze to just the hotel. The hoses of the Kilgoolga Fire Brigade combined with buckets of water brought in convoys by the locals from the river managed to put out the fire before it spread to the rest of the building. So in the morning when the smoke cleared, the questions began and these were followed first by speculation and then finally accusation. In that one night, flames had destroyed something that was as much part of Kilgoolga as the railway line and the line of colourfully painted shops nearby. The fire had allegedly started downstairs in the kitchen and a faulty electrical wire was blamed. The flames quickly spread upstairs. It was fortunate that the only occupants had been the owner and a couple who had been on their way back to Brisbane. All were unhurt.

However, it was Eddie, the owner who was under a cloud of suspicion. Everyone suspected arson. A faulty electrical wire seemed unlikely no matter what the insurance report said. In the minds of the locals Eddie was the culprit for everyone knew that Eddie had no interest whatsoever in the Commercial Hotel. It had always been his wife who had been the driving force behind the enterprise and it was she who kept the accounts and provided the business acumen needed for such a hospitality industry.

The fire had all to do with the scandal. Scandals happened rarely in Kilgoolga. Life for most was as arid as the land around them. When the population of Kilgoolga first heard the news that Eddie and his wife, Betty had parted, eyebrows were raised, not because Betty had left him but that she must have been so desperate as to leave him for that grain merchant. 'It was like jumping out of the frying pan into the fire,' Bella from the Kilgoolga Arms was quick to announce. For the behaviour and character of the grain merchant, who after all, was just a mere travelling salesman and who had his shoes under many a woman's bed, was even more untrustworthy than the poor owner of the Commercial. 'And no one could argue with that', Bella concluded sagely.

After the love life of the unlikely trio became common knowledge, word spread as rapidly around the district as a dust storm in the desert. In fact, it was Eddie who received some sympathy but it very quickly become apparent that he had no desire to talk about the event nor would he answer any enquiry about his wife and the circumstances of her hasty departure. The weeks passed and Eddie withdrew even further into his own secret world and was rarely seen. So the adult population of Kilgoolga were left guessing. For all his shortcomings Eddie was a good employer and he paid his three members of staff well so it appeared that the Commercial might survive after all. The three workers were loyal and local. They would keep the place going. Eddie retreated further from public view. Time passed and the scandal became less talked about until finally people stopped speaking about it altogether. But then the fire changed all predictions and nothing was certain after that.

It was unthinkable that there had been a fire at the Commercial that had blazed into the night and caused such damage but it was unimaginable what happened next! A few days after the fire and, with some of the black tarred boards still smouldering where the kitchen used to be, workers erected an eight foot high wire fence which surrounded the entire building on all sides. 'DANGER' and 'KEEP OUT' signs appeared. A week later the three loyal workers were paid off. Tongues started to wag seriously after that. Then

168

Eddie disappeared. Efforts to trace him proved futile. Speculation grew. Wild rumours spread as wild as the fire that had destroyed the Commercial a few weeks before. To all intents and purposes, the hotel and the owner would suffer the same fate. Eddie no longer existed. His hotel would gradually fall into disrepair until finally the building would be deemed unsafe by the authorities. It would be demolished. Then a space and a special part of Kilgoolga would be gone forever. There would be nothing left of it but the old folk's memories. The young folk would never know. Life would go on.

When Oisin Kelly arrived in Kilgoolga, the Commercial had stood like this for over a year. The iconic Commercial Hotel sign had blown down in a summer storm and left the once proud building, decaying and nameless on the corner. People passed by and tried not to think about what had been there before. Nature was vigorous in taking hold and was busily reclaiming the land. A variety of fledgling trees had taken root where the kitchen used to be. Competing for space were the invasive grasses, kangaroo and the like, which had spread throughout, even growing under the floorboards. All these factors contributed to the once majestic Commercial Hotel looking a very sorry sight indeed.

Oisin knew very little of what life had been like in Kilgoolga before the scandal and the fire. The wire fences were always there as far as he was concerned and the blackened and decaying building that used to be the Commercial Hotel was just a forlorn part of the main street for him. Most times he passed by the burnt out ruin on his way to the park bench at the War Memorial. Lately, he had taken to having his lunch with Claire on the days he spent in town. So he was surprised one hot summer's morning to find some activity on the corner of the main street and Bradshaw Avenue. Four people had gathered there behind the wire fence. All of them seemed to be involved in a serious conversation but the one person on whom Oisin focussed the most was a short woman of about fifty years of age. She stood in the centre of the group of three men and she was quite definitely in charge. Her short statue did nothing to hinder her presence within the group and Oisin observed that the three men appeared to listen when she spoke. In fact, it was she who did most of the talking. In one hand she held a clipboard and with her other hand she pointed to the old building behind her. Oisin recognised one of the men as Louis Bercault, the amorous Frenchman who owned the drapery shop in the main street and whom he had heard about from Bella on his very first night in Kilgoolga. The Frenchman was tall and thin. He was at least a foot higher than the woman in the centre of the group but he, like the other men, didn't interrupt her. Oisin who was a polite lad most of the time and he didn't like to stare or to bring any attention to himself but he really was mesmerised by the unexpected scene in front of him. Instead of walking towards the corner of the street, he stopped and pretended to tie his shoe laces. In this way, he could study the group in front of him without being observed. Crouched down he could hear something of the conversation as the short woman spoke loudly with what he decided was an educated Australian accent. She was like no one he had ever encountered before.

The woman stopped talking for a moment and the men stepped back to allow her to pass for it looked like she was about to leave and the men would follow her but instead, she walked over the dry grass that had grown in front of the entrance to the Commercial and entered the building. The men followed. Oisin stood up. He was puzzled by what he had witnessed and intrigued as well. He had lived long enough now in Kilgoolga to know that things happened slowly and strangers were a rare sight in the town. He had been a stranger himself a year ago and he recalled the wariness of the locals towards him then. But he decided

170

that the woman and the three men were not strangers to the town. Rather the opposite. He walked on towards the park bench and Claire but his mind was on the short woman with the black hair and the loud voice. Something within him knew that he would meet her again. The idea intrigued him and slightly unnerved him at the same time. He decided it was best to ignore these feelings for after all, what would a woman of about fifty years of age have that would interest him in the slightest?

Claire was sitting on the park bench waiting for him. She and Oisin were no longer strangers but there was a peculiar kind of wariness on the part of them both. Neither of them at the moment wanted to cross that invisible divide that exists sometimes and often, between a man and a woman. She studied him as he came towards her and she softened just looking at him. *He was certainly becoming more comfortable in his new environment every day*, she thought. Although she couldn't help but worry about him being out there with Hans and Hilda in that lonely surreal world that the brother and sister inhabited. She had never let him know her feelings about the Seefeldts nor did she speak about them. That she could not do. How could Oisin Kelly, an Irishman, ever imagine what people in Kilgoolga thought of Hans Seefeldt? The Irishman was a stranger in their midst and would always be one however long he stayed. It was good though that he could get away sometimes and he was able to do so more frequently now that the two of them had become friends. But it was not her place to offer any advice. She smiled. Somehow when she smiled the primness disappeared for a moment to return just as quickly when she frowned. But she was pleased to see him. They usually took their lunch to the river at the end of Bradshaw Avenue. It was easier that way and she didn't have to put up with the sniggers of her students as they passed by the bench. Miss Paterson, the Maths teacher with that Irish bloke, what a joke? She flinched just thinking of what was

171

being said behind her back. So it was easier to walk with Oisin to the picnic table at the river and sit under the shade of the acacia trees away from the prying eyes of Kilgoolga folk and her students too.

The sun was high in the midday sky and the heat rose from the ground. From the riverbank it was possible to hear the laughter and chatter from the High School grounds as the straggling lines of adolescents made their way to the shops in the main street. A few of them usually ventured to the riverbank and if they happened to see Miss Paterson with her man, they would giggle for this was something to report to their friends afterwards and something to savour. For everyone had decided that Miss Paterson was dedicated to her Mathematics and how could she possibly have any interest in sex? And more giggling would follow as they speculated about that subject; a subject which was much more in their minds than any mathematical equation could ever be?

"Penny for your thoughts, Oisin," Claire said when they had eaten their sandwiches.

Oisin thought Claire could sometimes be perceptive. So he told her about the short woman with the black hair and the three men he had noticed at the Commercial. She shrugged and changed the subject.

"Kanga's having a barbie on Sunday arv. Do you want to come?"

"Am I invited?"

"Yes."

"Well... OK then. I've been thinkin' I should try to get out of Sunday church sometime."

Claire gave him one of her famous penetrating stares which seemed to go right through him but she didn't answer.

"This church business," Oisin continued, "it's just like being back with my Uncle Mick. He stopped going to Mass and all hell broke loose, if ye pardon the expression!"

"Uncle Mick?"

"Aye, my much misunderstood Uncle Mick. I'll tell ye about him one day."

"I'd like that," Claire replied quietly.

The bell rang out from the High School. Claire got up and packed the thermos flask into a bag she had brought with her. She placed the two enamel mugs beside the flask. Lunch was usually tea and sandwiches when she was with Oisin. She was very organised. It all came from being a Maths teacher, her brothers told her. She put her hand on Oisin's arm, gently as a mother would to a child.

"I'll have to go," she said and then she looked around. There was no one else on the riverbank except the two of them. She leant over and kissed Oisin on the cheek. He smelt the delicious whiff of her perfume and he wanted her to stay and keep kissing him. The second bell rang.

"Be careful, Oisin," Claire whispered.

"What do you mean?"

"Of Hans... I must go... I've a class of the great uninterested to cope with!!"

"I'll see you on Sunday then? At your place?"

"Yes... I really must go."

Claire swung her handbag onto her left shoulder. It was a hot day and she was quite smart. Her bright summer dress and white sandals looked good on her. Her dress had wild patterns of colourful blue and red hibiscus flowers all over it. Oisin thought how amazingly attractive she was sometimes and he smiled. As she started to walk away, she suddenly stopped and, frowning slightly, she called to him,

"The woman you saw at the Commercial would have to be Eleanor Bradshaw."

"Eleanor Bradshaw?"

"Has to be! There's no other!!"

He watched her as she turned towards the High School grounds. At the corner of the street, she looked back and waved. He grinned and blew her a kiss. The gesture had become their little secret message. It was exactly what he needed. He wondered if she was beginning to like him after all but still he was wary. Thoughts rattled through his mind and they all arrived there without any warning. Cecy and his mother and Uncle Mick, all jumbled up together and then an image of Claire in her summer dress with the hibiscus flowers, the dry landscape in front of him and then, almost like a flash of lightning, sharp and vivid, came the image of the woman at the Commercial – Eleanor Bradshaw. And with the flash of light there came an unexpected premonition and he knew at that precise moment that he would sometime and somewhere meet this mysterious woman called Eleanor Bradshaw and that she would change his life in some unimaginable way just as living in the remote place called Kilgoolga had already done.

By any standard, Bellington Hill Homestead and the surrounding property was impressive and the Bradshaw occupants who had lived there continuously since the arrival of their distant ancestor, Lord Cyril Bradshaw, also viewed themselves in much the same light and with as much self-importance. It had been the view of successive Bradshaw generations from that time on that they were born to rule. After all, it was their family who had been the first significant white settlers in this black land and it was entirely due to their enterprising and courageous ancestor, namely Cyril. That same Cyril who had been so much part of that venerated English upper class and who had brought civilisation to this small corner of the Empire. It was he who had brought a little bit of England into this heathen land for all the generations of Bradshaws that followed knew that Bellington Hill was the name of that far distant mansion

174

from which Lord Cyril had sprung. The Bradshaws had arrived first and, as the ownership of land being their reason for being, it was only right, according to them, that they should be the chosen ones to rule. The wandering black souls who had lived and struggled in the same country for centuries had no concept of property or ownership or the erecting of fences to keep everything in or out. Therefore, with a logical argument etched firmly into the collective consciences of past and future generations of Bradshaws, these first inhabitants had no apparent reason for being there. They had not shaped the land or done anything towards changing it. The logic then followed that it was the white settlers that had achieved everything in this unforgiving land and all credit should be given to them. That was the view of Lord Cyril for this assumption was a popular one then and now. The fences built in haste around his vast acreage and recorded in some dusty volume of a Land Register implied by law that this land was his, to do with how he wished, and the legal fact of ownership brought with it responsibility which converted into paternalistic behaviour that was still evident even today. The Bradshaws, by their own definition, were born to rule.

When Cyril Bradshaw married his German wife, Lotte and brought with him this so-called civilisation and built a fine homestead in which to live which thus provided a tangible example of this civilising philosophy, he did so with the belief that the land on which they lived was secure for generations to come. Bellington Hill had two fine homesteads and both were built with status in mind. The original one was built by Lord Bradshaw and the second homestead had been erected in the boom years of the 1890's by the enterprising grandson of Cyril and was by far largest dwelling for miles around. In fact, in its heyday, Bellington Hill station was a complete township in itself with homes for the workers, a church and a school. The original homestead was still a fine building, if a little the worst for wear and although the church and school no longer provided their original services, the buildings remained. Years ago, the school had been converted into a house for the head stockman and his wife and family. The church unfortunately did not receive the same fate. Services were no longer conducted within its four walls. The once sacred wooden building now stood, empty and falling into ruin a mile from the homestead. Those Bradshaws who did attend church drove the fifty kilometres into Kilgoolga to the Church of England where they were significant contributors. English traditions ran deep.

Bellington Hill in England was an impressive stone building with pillars at the front entrance and a view to match. Situated on a hill and overlooking a verdant valley, the mansion was solid, permanent and powerful. Here was a visible exhibit of wealth and privilege and, to the successive generations of Bradshaws, a statement of authority. The second Bellington Hill homestead in western Queensland was a mirror image of their ancestral home even though it lacked the pillars. Somehow this grand homestead did not have the sense of permanency that the English version exhibited for everyone to admire. The colonial version, built with weatherboard timber and a green galvanised roof and situated not on a hill but rather a slight incline, conveyed material wealth without the continuation of class so entrenched into English society. But the colonial Bradshaws did their best. They were the undoubted successors of the old pastoralists and even during those times when economic troubles threatened to topple them from their lofty position in Kilgoolga, they always managed somehow to benefit while other less prosperous farmers faced ruin and loss of land. This was most apparent in the dealings between Hans Seefeldt and Eleanor Bradshaw because even though Eleanor accepted the fact that her distant ancestor had indeed been one of the German Seefeldts, she dismissed that side of her family as being of no consequence. The power and privilege she believed in so very strongly as a civilising force belonged firmly to the Bradshaw side of her family. For this reason, she was dismissive of Hans and Hilda Seefeldt and saw them as an eccentric pair and just a little above peasant farmers. She had no wish to be reminded in any way to that part of her genes which were Germanic. Wiesental station, after all, consisted of a mere two thousand acres on which to make a living which was nothing compared to the vast acreage that Bellington Hill covered. When Hans had to sell all his sheep after Britain's demand for Australian wool decreased dramatically, it was the Bradshaws who stepped in and it was Eleanor who had encouraged her father and her brother to buy all the Seefeldt stock. Hans, for all his Biblical certainty, was not able to easily forgive his neighbours, the Bradshaws for this act which he saw as humiliation. It was a wound that would fester within him for a long time and, from the moment that the sale of the sheep was completed and the stock removed from Wiesental, Hans refused to talk to any of the Bradshaws. His animosity was directed the most to Eleanor. He refused to speak her name and if, by chance, he happened to see her in Kilgoolga or Milberra, he would cross the street to avoid having any contact with her. He instructed Hilda to do the same. Hilda, more forgiving, would smile nervously if she happened to meet Eleanor in the street, bow her head and scurry away hoping that Hans would not become aware of her intransigence. Eleanor, for her part was blissfully unaware of the behaviour of her neighbours.

So it came as no surprise to the people of Kilgoolga that Eleanor Bradshaw with all the Bradshaw money behind her had bought the Commercial Hotel and that she intended to bring it back to its former glory and with much more besides. Eleanor now owned the Kilgoolga Arms at one end of the main street and the Commercial at the other. The bigger mystery for everyone was how Eleanor had managed to persuade the disinterested former owner, Eddie to sell and how she had managed to track him down in the first place. However, all agreed that Eleanor always got what she wanted and she usually stepped in as a financial saviour when people were down on their luck. Even those who disliked Hans Seefeldt, remembered the story of his sheep. Eleanor Bradshaw could be ruthless at times. She was a mysterious woman but she was quite definitely a formidable one. But Eleanor's acquisition of the much loved hotel on the corner had to be commended. She would most certainly make more money through the purchase of it but that was to be expected for her business prowess was legend in the district. The positive outcome would be that the locals would once again have the Commercial to drink in and be able to socialise there. At least Eleanor would turn it into a going concern and she was a local. It would have been dreadful if it had been allowed to fall into ruin or even worse, to be bought up by an absentee landlord with no real interest in the place except to make money. It had been bad enough putting up with Eddie for all those years! Everyone knew that Eleanor wouldn't have bought the place had she not intended to make a lot of money out of it. How she managed the sale was left to conjecture but it was tempered with just a little admiration too. Eleanor Bradshaw always got her way.

If the locals had known how Eleanor had been able to achieve this sale, their grudging admiration may have turned to amazement. The whole thing was the stuff of a detective story. Eleanor had recently become a secret lover of the Frenchman, Louis Bercault, that amorous individual whom women found irresistible and who bestowed his favours quite liberally around the district. Even though Eleanor was in her fifties and Louis just thirty-five, their fascination for each other made them ideal partners, had anyone guessed. In fact, despite the age difference, Louis quite liked the dominant Eleanor. She owned his drapery shop and he paid her an over inflated rent for it. Once they had become more than friends, she reduced the monthly rent by a few dollars!

Even if it was only by a few dollars, Louis judged that it had been worth his while. He had used all his Gallic charm to pursue Eleanor and when this had been achieved, he wasn't disappointed. Both agreed that the exact nature of their relationship would be best left secret. They were friends. That would be enough for the prying eyes and the gossips. Even though Louis had a reputation, no one could possibly believe that he had been able to seduce the powerful Eleanor Bradshaw. A friendship was just feasible, an affair highly unlikely. And if Louis was seen more often at Bellington Hill and he was sometimes still there in the morning, no one in Kilgoolga suspected that anything would have happened between them other than good food and agreeable conversation.

In order to track down Eddie, when all the other individuals and some authority figures had failed to do so, Eleanor enlisted the aid of her new friend, Louis. The people of Kilgoolga had long suspected that the Bradshaws owned more than just their vast property in the west but no one had ever been able to prove just how much. After all, the Bradshaws had put themselves so far above the local population in property ownership and influence that, had more assets and money become apparent in other places, it was doubtful if many of them would have bothered to speculate about how all this fortune had been accumulated. Many would have assumed it had come from somewhat dodgy pursuits because you don't amass a fortune without treading on toes or being entirely truthful to the taxman but had anyone known just how vast a fortune it was, they would have been staggered. The truth, however, would remain hidden for that is often the way in financial matters and in this, Eleanor Bradshaw, in particular was true to her class.

Eleanor's life was unfathomable to the people of Kilgoolga and the reason for some of this mystery was entirely due to the fact that she had left the district at an early age, firstly to go off to boarding school and then, at nineteen she disappeared entirely. Conjecture and rumour kept the locals interested for a time. It was indeed probable that somewhere along the line she had acquired a husband. She had spent a lot of her time in England. Everyone speculated it was there that she had found this possible husband. As no one knew for sure if this had happened and, as is usual in the matter of gossip, whatever the truth was the story had become greatly exaggerated so that Eleanor's husband varied from being an English aristocrat one minute to a successful horse breeder the next. Those who disliked Eleanor decided that her husband was neither one of these but had to be just an idle waster who she had more than likely picked up at one of those events that the toffs go to, probably in the South of France. That sounded just about right and they pictured Eleanor lying in the sun on some outrageously expensive yacht, cruising around the Mediterranean, drinking cocktails and demanding attention from all and sundry.

Eleanor had indeed married a rich man but it had not been a very happy arrangement. They had little in common and the age difference between them of twenty years or so had soured the relationship almost as soon as the marriage vows were spoken. Eleanor became bored. A divorce was inevitable; the pay out to Eleanor, considerable. In England Eleanor visited Bellington Hill, the home of the Bradshaws. Here she had hoped to learn more about her ancestral relations. She was deeply disappointed. No one had heard of Lord Cyril Bradshaw. Even though Eleanor trawled through all the birth and marriage certificates of the time in an attempt to have written proof of his existence, it proved hopeless. Instead, she discovered that Bellington Hill was now the property of the National Trust and there was no sign of any living Bradshaw anywhere. So she spent time wandering around the crumbling mansion, admiring the silver and staring at the lines of vacuous faces of her ancestors who adorned the walls of the great hall. It was a sobering experience. Ever after, she was defensive in regard to the existence of Lord Cyril but instead of consigning him to obscurity; she elevated him in her mind and would speak of him in a haughty sort of way and often compared herself to him. Favourably, of course. This fanciful version of the life of Lord Cyril became more noticeable to others after she eventually returned to Bellington Hill and as the years went by it was as if her distant ancestor was alive, at least in Eleanor's mind. This sort of talk generally went unheeded in the small community but it did contribute to the opinion that it was possible that Eleanor herself was able to tap into an unseen world. The sceptics viewed all this with amusement. There was no one in Kilgoolga who knew the reasons why Eleanor Bradshaw had come back to resume her earlier life in the remote place of her birth. After all her years away Kilgoolga had to be a boring sort of life for her, everyone thought. They were not to know what the impact of having Eleanor Bradshaw once more in their midst would mean for them for her return was to be a dramatic one. The first thing she did was to set about modernising and expanding Bellington Hill and she would listen to no one least of all her younger brother by ten years, Joseph.

Joseph Bradshaw was a different nature entirely from his sister. Whereas Eleanor had relished boarding school and the years she had spent in England, Joseph had hated every moment away from Bellington Hill. He was a farmer through and through, practical and hardworking, everything his sister was not. After the deaths of his elderly mother and father Joseph was free to pursue his dream to modernise the property and it was his passion to keep the traditions of the old pastoralists alive. There was no one else left in the Bradshaw clan to do so. The various other family members had dispersed far and wide and no one knew where his sister Eleanor was and if she would even care one jot what Joseph did on the property. None of his other relatives had any great interest in Bellington Hill except to deposit cheques into the bank when the going was good. Consequently, by the time Eleanor had established her place once again at Bellington Hill and indeed within the wider community, Joseph had matured enough to take over the total reins of authority. His sister's return annoyed him and at times he resented her for what he called 'her bloody interference'. He was married to a country girl and the two of them lived quite happily with their three young children in the big house. Eleanor's return was not to Joseph's liking. Eleanor believed that she had the right to be in charge. Her argument being that she was the eldest and that she had the experience of travel behind her. She liked to remind Joseph that it was she who had seen Bellington Hill in England and traced Lord Cyril. It, therefore, followed in Eleanor's mind that she was the rightful heir. It had been an unbroken long line of Bradshaws after all, she said and it was always the eldest who took charge. The result of all this was that the two of them argued incessantly and about anything. Neither would give in.

Eleanor was still an attractive young woman when she returned to Kilgoolga and, as she was just thirty-six years of age, it was assumed that she would one day marry again. She did not. She preferred to take the occasional lover. In this she was discreet. Fifteen years later, Louis Bercault was the latest and the most unexpected. Louis was a mystery man himself but he had somehow managed to fit into the tight rural community of Kilgoolga and almost, on occasion, become a part of it. He was conceited but full of charm and wit and this was just what Eleanor Bradshaw liked. She would tire of him but at the present moment, they were soul mates and had been together in another life. At least, that's what Eleanor told Louis and he agreed even if it seemed a bit far-fetched to him. He wasn't very interested in the afterlife and what might happen to him there. His present life was enough for him, he thought. He liked women and enjoyed their company and in the male

182

dominated outback town, he was happier to be with the female sex. In his time, he had made many conquests and if Eleanor thought they had been lovers in some other life, well, you never know, it might just be true! He found her unfathomable and a challenge for any man. Louis was quite pleased with himself for conquering the enigmatic Eleanor. Their sex life, however, was rather irregular and not at all what he had hoped for. He knew, and he accepted this reality with a philosophical shrug of his shoulders. He hadn't conquered her at all.

When Eleanor decided to buy the Commercial Hotel her first problem was to find and persuade the owner to sell. Because Louis was now a willing partner and would agree to whatever his new mistress decided to do, it was an easy matter to enlist his aid. The plan was simple. 'No one disappears without a trace,' Eleanor told Louis and Louis, hanging onto her every word, nodded approvingly. His wife in France and his mother didn't have a clue what had happened to him but he assumed if either woman had wanted to find him, they would have been able to so it followed in Louis's mind that people could be found.

'All that is needed to locate the owner,' Eleanor told Louis, 'was to get the right contact and then it would be easy after that'. Eleanor made much of her contacts in the right places; she repeatedly reminded Louis that she was on familiar terms with an Anglican Bishop in Brisbane and a barrister in Sydney. Always handy to have both of these on hand she insisted. Louis just had to agree. He always did. So the two of them set off from Kilgoolga one hot summer's day to drive the six hundred miles or so to Brisbane because that was where they should begin their search, Eleanor said. Louis drove his green and white Holden station wagon while Eleanor sat beside him and talked. In fact she seemed to talk the whole way. The miles slipped by as Eleanor revealed more and more of her plans to an intrigued and captive Louis. Her ideas included the complete refurbishment of the

Commercial and at that point, she told Louis that he would have to take charge of the soft furnishings, the upholstery and the curtains. Louis was flattered. He often boasted to the women who came into his shop that he had been the principal buyer of fabrics in a famous Parisian fashion house. Whether this was true or not could never be proved by anyone but in any case, the women who came into his drapery shop in outback Kilgoolga couldn't help but be impressed. To have such a famous person amongst them was exciting at times. Louis could tell such stories of chic and beautifully clad women and their equally fashionable men who frequented the boulevard cafés. Here the talk went on and on along with the parties that never seemed to end for life didn't stop at ten o'clock like it did in Kilgoolga. Life was never dull, just listening to Louis. If only they could be sitting in those cafés, drinking red wine and wearing fine clothes and not stuck here in Kilgoolga, amongst the dust and the flies. All the women decided that Louis the Froggie knew how to talk to their sex, something their husbands and boyfriends could do with learning.

Brisbane was hot and sultry. Overhead, the black clouds threatened a downpour and the forked flashes of lightning followed by the rumble of the thunder signalled that the daily afternoon storm was on its way. The storms were as regular as clockwork during the summer months. Both Eleanor and Louis were relieved to have arrived at the Bradshaw family unit at Kangaroo Point just before the heavens emptied their bounty and the air cooled. They were tired and dusty from their journey and both glad to have reached their destination without having any major problem. You could never be sure with Eleanor that there wouldn't be a problem, major or not. She had a way of making things seem significant when perhaps they were not.

The next day they set to work. A visit to Eleanor's solicitor provided the necessary legalities with regards to the acquisition of the Commercial Hotel. A study of the Electoral Register revealed the name of the owner's wife. A drive to an outlying suburb located the address. It was amazing how effortless the whole enterprise had been so far. Eleanor and Louis sat in Louis's car outside the old Queenslander house and studied it. It was Eleanor's plan to take stock of the situation before venturing any further. The house was built on high rounded black timber stumps with cream painted wooden lattices between them. It was a typical Brisbane house of the time, dull yellow weatherboard with a red galvanised iron roof. Twenty wooden steps with a railing on both sides led up to a small porch and the front door. A few of the louvre windows were open so it appeared that someone was in the house. Somewhat incongruently the front door, also a lattice design, was covered with bright red gloss paint. The paint was peeling off in places. The bright red rather clashed with the rest of the dull yellow exterior walls and Eleanor commented that taste wasn't much in evidence here. Louis nodded. His expertise was in fabrics but he had an eye for colour and design and this wasn't a building that had much to recommend it. *In fact there was an air of neglect surrounding the property,* he thought.

Eleanor, with Louis following dutifully behind, opened the small iron gate and the two of them proceeded to walk along the red concrete path towards the front steps. Half way up the steps, Eleanor paused and leaned over to pick a branch of the yellow and white frangipani flowers. Two of these bushes grew on either side of the steps and the small yellow and white flowers intoxicated the senses with their sweet perfume. She picked one of the flowers and held it under Louis's nose.

"Smell!" she commanded and Louis obeyed. He felt a sensuous pleasure just holding the flower.

"Be careful of the sap. It can irritate the skin. The scent's stronger at night than during the day. What do you think?" And she threw the small branch with the remaining flowers into the bush without waiting for a reply. Louis took another brief sniff of his flower and then did the same. Eleanor rang the doorbell.

A few minutes later a rather large woman of about forty-five opened the door. She looked as if she had just emerged from her bed and hadn't had the time to comb her straggly dyed blonde hair or to improve her appearance in any way. She held a cigarette between her fingers and when she saw who was at the door, she took a puff and blew the smoke up into the air and in the direction of Eleanor. She did not smile.

"Well... Eleanor Bradshaw... this is a surprise and you've brought Louis the draper with you... I am honoured."

"Can we come in?" Eleanor was annoyed. She glared at the woman in front of her.

"Well... it's a free country. Didn't expect to see anyone from Kilgoolga ever again. Thought I'd seen the back of that bloody place!"

The woman shrugged her shoulders and stepped aside to allow Eleanor and Louis past. Louis was unsure of what to do next but Eleanor had recovered her composure and was now in complete control of the situation.

"I want to know where Eddie is, Betty," she said when she and Louis were seated around the kitchen table. Betty stood in front of them, folded her arms and leaned against the kitchen sink. She shrugged again.

"That no good piece of shit!" was all she said.

"Maybe so. I need to speak to him though... as a matter of urgency."

"Well... he's not here. Is that all?"

"No! Have you his address?"

Betty sniffed and said,

"Heard he's gone troppo. Up north. Past Port Douglas. Good riddance to bad rubbish, I say."

Eleanor looked at Louis and winked.

"What do you want to see him for?" Betty was curious. Eleanor Bradshaw was the last person she had expected to see on her doorstep and with the Frenchman in tow, well that was a surprise too.

"I'm buying the Commercial."

"Are you now? I've some say in that, ya know."

"How much?"

"Fifty-fifty."

"Well, will you sell your half?"

"Depends."

"On what?"

"What's the offer?"

"If Eddie agrees to a sale, you'll get half. It's between you and him," Eleanor said. She sensed victory.

Betty lit another cigarette. She was thinking of her next move. This could be a windfall.

"Didn't think you'd have much interest in the Commercial but I suppose you're extendin' your business interests," she said sarcastically.

"I am."

"If Eddie agrees then... say thirty-five thousand dollars."

"Thirty," argued Eleanor.

Betty tried not to smile. Fifteen thousand would suit her just fine. She was renting this place and the money would go towards buying it. She was on her own now. The useless grain merchant had disappeared and left her a few weeks back but she wasn't about to be defeated. No man had ever been able to do that!

"If Eddie agrees then, you've got a sale. How's that?" she said.

"You're sure you don't know his address?"

"OK. Why not? He's dropped out, the bastard. In a hippie colony outside Port Douglas. Livin' on coconuts and smokin' pot! Shacked up with some bird half his age. I told you he was useless, didn't I? Only good thing he ever did at the Commercial was pay them their wages on time... I did all the work. He can rot as far as I'm concerned. Men!" And she glared at Louis who gave her a suggestive wink in reply.

"He'll sell. But I'll get my half, mark my words. You get the paperwork done and I'll sign. Now, is that all?"

Three days later Eleanor and Louis seated on a wooden park bench and looking towards the calm blue waters of the Pacific Ocean, ate ice cream and contemplated what to do next. At least Eleanor did. Their search for Eddie, the missing owner of the Commercial had led them north to Cairns but it was here that they had drawn a blank. It was hot and humid in Cairns and Louis would have liked to have remained in the hotel room, lying on the double bed and cooling off under the overhead fan but Eleanor would not hear of it. When they booked into the hotel along the Esplanade, the receptionist eyed them a little suspiciously for they did seem to be the most unlikely of couples. But the receptionist said nothing. When strangers met Eleanor they rarely made any comment about her. It was the way she went about it. In fact, whatever opinion people might have had about Eleanor, they usually kept this to themselves. There was just something about Eleanor that kept people at a distance. It was not only that she appeared always to be in charge of any situation, it had to have a little to do with the fact that Eleanor Bradshaw was used to having her own way.

But this time, she had encountered a problem. No one they spoke to had heard of a hippie colony anywhere near Cairns. If Betty had been right and her estranged husband was indeed living in one, it now appeared they had hit a dead end as to where he was. Louis was no use at all. Eleanor had allowed herself a certain amount of days to locate the owner and negotiate the deal and she wasn't about to be distracted by a petulant Louis. So the two of them sat in silence under a palm tree and took in the surroundings. It was midday and there weren't many people around.

"We'll have to go further north," Eleanor said at last. They hadn't spoken to each other for about a quarter of an hour. The silence had finally broken just a few minutes before when a lone seagull arrived and, hoping for a handout, took up position a few feet away from them. The bird was busy walking backwards and forwards just far enough away to be safe and yet close enough to snatch some crumbs. Eleanor threw the remaining end of her ice cream cone onto the ground and the seagull gulped it down and then flew away, squawking.

"Yes," she continued, "I think we'll find Eddie further north. Port Douglas, Betty said... but I think she's wrong."

"Wrong?"

"Wrong."

She stood up and stared at the sea as if she were seeking inspiration there. She became very still and folded her arms across her chest. To Louis, she appeared like a diminutive goddess and the embodiment of all that was female.

"What is it?" he whispered.

"Yes. I know where he is. Come on!"

"How do you know?"

Eleanor didn't answer him. Instead, she picked up her handbag from the bench and started to walk in the direction of their hotel. He had to walk quickly to catch up with her and when he did, she had a look on her face that

189

meant that she had no desire to discuss the matter any further. He was in awe of her.

Two days later they found Eddie. Eleanor was right and Betty was wrong. Eddie wasn't living amongst the hippies after all but by himself in a beach hut which he had built himself underneath some coconut palms. Louis never knew just how Eleanor had managed to find Eddie and how she had been able to find their way to this remote spot so far from Port Douglas. But a few days before Eleanor had disappeared into the general store in the small township and when she emerged from it, she knew where Eddie was. And she told him there was no time to lose.

Eddie recognised them both when he saw the two of them coming towards him. If he was surprised to see two people from far away Kilgoolga, striding over the soft white sand in their unsuitable shoes, he did not show it. But he did not smile either. Eddie's skin was as brown and as weather beaten as the outside walls of the hut where he had made his home. He hadn't bothered to trim his grey beard for months so that this was now about a foot long and heading towards his waist! Naked, except for a pair of khaki denim shorts, he stared towards the clear blue sea and, whatever his thoughts were at that particular moment, he did not turn his head when the two people from his past arrived to stand in front of him and thus obstruct his view. His old life and the new life he had made for himself could not have been more disparate. In Kilgoola, he had grudgingly inherited a hotel in which he had not the slightest bit of interest and married a woman with whom he had nothing in common with whatsoever. In actual fact, the fire had given him freedom.

He had had many days beneath the hot tropical sun to ponder the good fortune that the fire had bestowed upon him. Contrary to popular gossip in Kilgoolga, he was relieved when his wife upped and left him for the grain merchant and after her speedy departure, he hadn't given her a second thought. He was an honourable man and he settled the legal separation with her amicably enough but when the fire destroyed the property a few months afterwards, it was as if a door had opened in his life which said, GO!! And he did. He now lived off the land as much as he could and only ventured into Port Douglas when he had to. Twice a year he made the trip to Cairns and stocked up on supplies but he was happiest when he was away from civilisation. Contrary to what his wife had thought, he lived alone without any woman to restrict him in any way. He had become a hermit and loved it. He didn't speak to Eleanor or Louis but continued to stare through their legs towards the sea. Eleanor wasted no time.

"Eddie," she said curtly dispensing with the usual civilities, "I want to buy the Commercial. What's your price?"

Eddie didn't answer.

"Well, Eddie? I've talked to Betty and she's willing to sell her half… "

Eddie didn't reply but tugged his beard as if the movement of his hand would give him an answer. Eleanor tried again whilst Louis, with his white panama hat, white shirt and his cream linen trousers ironed to perfection, stood looking rather like a lost puppy who would have much rather been away from the heat and preferably sitting at a bar, sipping Pina Coladas.

Still Eddie made no movement. Just a shrug of his shoulders.

"I'd like an answer, you know!"

Eleanor was getting annoyed. She wanted to get this over and done with it as quickly as she could.

Now Eddie looked up. He shaded his eyes with his right hand and shrugged again.

"Guess you've got an amount in mind? The Bradshaws are known for their dealings with all things financial?"

"Twenty-five thousand dollars!"

Eleanor knew how to get a bargain. Betty would never know the difference in the amounts. What's five thousand dollars? Better in Eleanor's hands anyway.

Eddie shrugged. He couldn't have cared less.

"It's a deal," he said and held out his hand to her. "Guess you've got the paperwork all ready to sign? Eleanor Bradshaw doesn't come empty handed!"

Eleanor ignored the comment. From her handbag, she pulled out the paperwork that her solicitor had drawn up in Brisbane a few weeks before and handed them to Eddie. He didn't give them a second glance.

"Sign here and here," she said, " Louis'll witness the signature."

Eddie stood up. He walked over to a wooden seat he had built in front of the hut and here he placed the papers. Eleanor handed him a black pen and he signed. They shook hands again. Eddie spat on the ground.

"Give me your bank details and I'll deposit the money there, Eddie. It should take about a week or so to go through."

Eddie shrugged.

"No problem," he said. "Betty can have the lot. Don't need a bank account up here!"

CHAPTER TEN

Three months later Eleanor Bradshaw reopened the Commercial Hotel. No longer a blackened out ruin, standing sad and forlorn on the corner of the main street and Bradshaw Avenue, it was now a fine old building restored to its former splendour and looking even the better for it. And what a day it turned out to be for the people of Kilgoolga! Everyone agreed that all the credit had to be given to Eleanor for it was she and she alone, who had somehow persuaded Eddie to sell and anyone could see that she had spared no expense in the restoration of the building. It was refreshing to know that some of the Bradshaw money was being put to good use as well. All believed that the Commercial restored and in use again had to be a good thing for the town and even if Eleanor had never been liked or understood much by many folk, in the matter of the restoration of the Commercial, she received her moment of popularity. It was, however, to prove to be a fleeting moment.

The Commercial now boasted an impressive lounge, public bar, and a huge dining area. A breeze block wall had been constructed behind the newly planted line of fast growing acacias along Bradshaw Avenue and it was here that Eleanor decided that there should be a beer garden, complete with a see-through roof and a barbeque area. The acacias would in time provide much needed shade and the six foot fence erected on the boundary line of the property would give all the security and privacy needed for such a public place. Eleanor thought of everything. The beer garden was capable of seating fifty or so customers and it was to prove to be one of the most popular places to eat and drink in the whole hotel. There was a feeling of opulence especially in the dining area, in particular, with its brightly coloured curtains and paintings of old and present Kilgoolga on the walls. Most of the upstairs had been damaged by the fire so all the twenty rooms for the guests had been rebuilt from scratch and here Louis Bercault was in his element, choosing different fabrics for every room and all colours co-ordinated to perfection. Now some of these rooms even had en suite facilities. Eleanor, knowing that she was about to make her mark once again in Kilgoolga, hired a chef from Sydney who knew how to cook and a very competent manager who understood the joys and the pitfalls of hotel management. As well as employing these two newcomers she had, by reinstating the previous staff and adding a few more, received approval from most of the population of Kilgoolga – except perhaps for Hans Seefeldt who muttered that the new hotel would fail and fail totally because of Eleanor Bradshaw. 'Just like that woman to splash her money around when everyone else was tightening their belts because of the drought,' he declared. But then anything that the Bradshaw family did and more so, if Eleanor had anything to do with it, was always under suspicion according to Hans. He disagreed with everything that his neighbours did. But even Hans had to concede that having the new hotel there was far better than the blackened ruin that had stood for a year or so. But no way was he about to put a foot inside the building, refurbished or not and he forbade Hilda to do so as well. Hilda nodded her head as she always did when Hans issued her an order but in this matter, she had no plans to obey her him. The next time she and Oisin went into town she had already arranged to meet Jack's sister in the

Commercial for a bar meal and a glass of white wine. Hilda felt quite pleased with herself, just anticipating her outing. No doubt Oisin would keep quiet about it too. He didn't say much to Hans either. It was all very exciting.

The Commercial now employed twenty people. They all seemed to be happy to work there and, if there was to be any rumblings of dissent as there would have to be given human nature, this would surely happen in the future and definitely not during the optimistic days surrounding the reopening. It was a sight to see with the newly painted bright red iron shimmering under the hot summer sun and the weatherboard walls, covered with two layers of bright yellow gloss paint added just the right touch. The old hotel began to take on a whole new character and this was further enhanced by the Commercial Hotel sign with its black background and carefully painted Roman letters in white. Eleanor had much to say about the positioning of the large sign and she ordered it to be displayed along the white wrought iron railings of the first floor and in just a way that it would be noticeable from many angles. The sign was much talked about and it was an impressive sight. Visible from the railway station platform and even from some of the houses in the street behind the railway line, the Commercial sign was designed to be noticed by as many people as possible. Because of the layout of the hotel with its entrance being at a diagonal, the sign was hung so that it could also be viewed even further along the main street. The people of Kilgoolga were happy. The Commercial was back in business and Eleanor knew just how to make it pay.

On opening night, Oisin didn't arrive at the Commercial until about nine o'clock. For some reason, Hans had spent longer on the nightly Bible reading than usual and this had meant that Oisin was running late. He drove into Kilgoolga with his foot to the floor and when he walked into the Commercial, he discovered that the meals had all been served in the dining area. Shrewd Eleanor Bradshaw offered a ten percent discount off any meals and drinks on the opening night. This proved so successful that the kitchen staff ran out of food about half past eight and then there was nothing left to eat but burgers and sausages from the barbeque area. Serious drinking was well underway. When Oisin arrived, the lounge, the beer garden and the public bar were packed with merry people in various stages of intoxication and everyone appeared to be as excited as schoolchildren about to go on a summer outing. The noise in the lounge almost drowned out the music as Tommy George, the pianist from *The Drovers*, sweat pouring down his face, thumped out the popular tunes on the recently purchased piano. A few couples slid around the small polished pine floor in front of him. Most people, however, sat at the tables in the lounge and most had jugs of cold beer on these tables. The room was alive with the energy that comes when good food and drink leads to good cheer.

Oisin pushed his way through the crowd of drinkers to the bar and asked for a beer. He saw Charlie George and his wife sitting at a nearby table with Lefty and his wife. All four smiled at him. Oisin took a sip of beer and nodded his head but he wasn't in the mood for socialising. Janet and Kanga sat at another table. The two of them spent all their time fondling and kissing each other. Oisin wondered what the sex was like for them with all that public display of affection. Wondered, and then he thought of Cecy and thinking of her put him in a bad mood. He finished his beer and bought another full pint. He had rushed from Wiesental to get to the hotel for the much discussed opening and now he was annoyed with himself because there didn't seem much that he wanted to do. Everyone sat or stood in their own small groups and he felt a bit of an outsider, once again. Claire's two brothers, Tony and Geoff were seated at a table near the entrance to the beer garden. The two of them looked settled with their girlfriends beside them. One of the girls caught Oisin's eye and she smiled at him but the boys took no notice. He wondered where Claire was. He had arranged to meet her outside the hotel but she was nowhere to be seen. This annoyed him even more. *It was probably because I was an hour late*, he thought, *but she could have waited*. He had drunk the two beers quickly and he was beginning to feel the effects. And his bad mood wasn't getting any better. He bought another beer and headed towards the beer garden hoping to locate Claire.

It was cooler outside than in the dining area and not quite as busy. A group of six or seven men stood around talking near the barbeque area while most of the women and a few of the men sat at the tables. Nearly all the chairs were occupied. A gang of children of various ages ran past and through the gaps between the tables. They were noisy and every now and then one of the mothers yelled for them to 'Come here and sit down!' and the children would stop for a moment, panting and giggling, collapse beside their mothers and then after a minute or two continue their games just as noisily as before. The beer garden area covered about half an acre. There was nothing to obstruct the view to the open plains, only the rugby field with its white goal posts and the trees beside the river beyond that. Oisin was relieved to be outside and away from the smoke filled and jam-packed lounge. He took another sip of his beer and walked over to the barbeque area. A young man whom he recognised as Johnno was slowly turning over burgers and a few sausages on the grill. He looked bored but brightened up a bit when he saw Oisin and said, 'G'day mate, what'll ya 'ave?' Oisin suddenly felt hungry. His three beers had gone to his head and the burgers smelt so tempting that he ordered one and then covered the meat with a liberal squirt of thick tomato sauce. He didn't recognise anyone. Claire was nowhere to be seen. He was about to return to the lounge when he felt a tap on his right shoulder. It was Louis Bercault.

Louis was tall and thin and Oisin had to look up to him. It was the closest he had ever been to the Frenchman.

Louis appeared as elegant as ever. 'LB' in navy blue was embroidered on the pocket of his light blue cotton short sleeved shirt. The four top buttons on his shirt were unfastened and revealed a black hairy chest. Wearing cream trousers with the creases ironed to military precision and highly polished tan leather shoes, he stood out amongst all the other men. He was so unsuited to Kilgoolga. A stereotypical Frenchman, he even held a glass half full with red wine in his right hand. His hands, too, didn't fit in for his nails were neatly manicured and his long fingers smooth. The difference between the two men's hands was noticeable as Oisin's hands looked part of the country these days. His work on the farm had roughened them and there was often dirt under his nails.

Oisin knew of Louis's reputation. Even Hilda giggled after a visit to the drapery shop. He had often wondered about Louis and his business and how the Frenchman had managed to make a living out here in outback Kilgoolga and so far from Paris. *But then there wasn't another draper for three hundred miles, so in the scheme of things, Louis was most probably doing very well all things considered*, he thought. The Frenchman had dark brown eyes and olive skin and an interesting face with a slightly crooked nose. No wonder women were intrigued. With his pronounced accent and his penchant for adding words from his own language into the conversation, Louis Bercault had become an interesting personality in the small town and now that he was often seen in the company of Eleanor Bradshaw, he was even more of a mystery.

"You approve of the appearance of the Commercial 'Otel?" Louis couldn't pronounce the 'H' and he waved his left hand in the air as if to insist that Oisin look around, too, and particularly at the furnishings and the curtains in the lounge area.

"Suppose so."

"Ah... a man of few words... I thought that all the Irish had the gift of the Blarney...!"

"Some of us do, I guess."

"You like it here? We two are strangers in this country. It is for that reason that Eleanor has asked me to invite you to tea on Sunday afternoon at Bellington Hill."

His invitation was totally unexpected. Oisin hadn't even met Eleanor Bradshaw. What interest could she possibly she have in him? Louis gave that particular Gallic shrug of the shoulders and then continued,

"You are puzzled, Monsieur. But we are both of us a long way from Europe... and for that reason... ? "

The Frenchman shrugged his shoulders again and Oisin nodded. *No one could argue with that statement,* he thought.

"So... you will come, Monsieur?"

Oisin looked around once more hoping to see Claire but she definitely wasn't anywhere to be seen. *She's not here*, he thought crossly. He felt himself getting angry again. Louis was waiting for an answer.

"OK. What time?" Oisin replied after a few seconds. He really couldn't have cared less at that moment and it seemed the easiest option given the circumstances.

Oisin had hardly spoken a word to Hans and Hilda on the Sunday morning before his visit to Bellington Hill. Unable to think of either a suitable or a believable excuse in order not to attend the Lutheran church with the brother and sister that morning, he had squeezed uncomfortably onto the front seat of the Land Rover next to Hilda and tried to avoid making conversation. This was a fairly easy thing to do as Hans and Hilda didn't speak much to each other anyway and they spoke even less when they were going to and coming back from the church. In fact, Hans had once mentioned that Sundays were best spent in contemplation and preparation for the week ahead. The young Oisin thought this was a great arrangement. Sometimes the whole situation he found himself in with Hans and Hilda was stifling to say the least and to have some time to do what he liked without interference gave him some much needed space. Being able to have his own thoughts without interruption had always been an essential requirement for Oisin and his own wellbeing. Even in Ballybeg, his most precious moments had been when he had been able to get away from everyone and ride his faithful old pony, Bess along the strand. So Sundays had become the best day of the week for him despite the ritual church attendance. For some reason, he felt it best not to mention to either Hans or Hilda that he had been invited to afternoon tea at the home of Eleanor Bradshaw. It just seemed safer that way.

He set off for Bellington Hill just after Sunday lunch. The gravel road, with just two slight bends to break the monotony and, even though the road ahead was as straight as a die, driving along it required some concentration. The countryside looked so dry again. No rain had fallen for six months and the endless holes in the road made driving difficult. To avoid them Oisin drove more slowly than usual. Trails of dust rose behind him. For miles there was nothing to see but coolibah trees and brown grass. Then the trees thinned and the view ahead changed to the flat open spaces that had become so familiar to Oisin. Fences, some with the barbed wire strung between them and others just posts and rough split wood connecting them, appeared on both sides of the road and the road narrowed. Oisin stopped the car and stretched. There was nothing to disturb his view. He hadn't passed another vehicle or seen anything remotely interesting for miles. Bellington Hill was about forty miles from Wiesental as the crow flies. He figured he still had another five miles or so before he finally arrived there. The intense heat of the early November afternoon made him feel thirsty. He always carried a flask of water with him these days. The water was cool and refreshing. He drank and as he held the flask to his lips, he noticed something move through the grass a few metres from where he stood.

It was a dingo. The creature stood still and both man and wild dog stared at each other. At that precise moment and, as if to add another dimension to the scene, a lone kookaburra appeared from nowhere and came to rest on a wooden fence post beside Oisin. The bird could have been a living sculpture. Now there were three living things, all watching one another. The dingo had black eyes and brown body. It showed no fear but stood rigid and alert, waiting. If the man or bird moved, the dingo would run and disappear as mysteriously as it had appeared. It was a beautiful creature, wild and free, alone in its natural habitat. The Irishman from the other side of the earth was the interloper here and the dog and the bird, the ones that belonged. They were the survivors without a doubt. The man would move but the dingo and the kookaburra would stay. Oisin walked towards the car, his flask in his hand. By the time he turned around to look once more, both the wild dog and the bird had disappeared. He got into the car and started the engine. As he drove slowly along the gravel track towards Bellington Hill, his thoughts were on the scene that he had witnessed. He did not know what was before him or how he would react to this stranger who was Eleanor Bradshaw. Seeing the dingo and the kookaburra felt like an omen and he wasn't quite sure what it meant. By the time he arrived at the gates to the Bellington Hill station, it was as if his anxious thoughts had completely taken over his body and he began to wonder, quite irrationally, whether he should just turn back. No one would be any the wiser. He could make an excuse to Louis when he next saw him. He hadn't even been introduced to the mysterious Eleanor and he still couldn't think what possible interest she could have with him. *This whole country* is *driving me insane*, he thought.

The contrast between the entrance gates to Bellington Hill and those two padlocked ones at Wiesental could not have been more pronounced. Here was an entrance that was designed to make a statement. Two heavy black posts and slab wooden fences, all of them covered in brown creosote had been erected on either side of a cattle grid. Two slightly thinner vertical posts on the left, also creosoted, were nailed onto one of the horizontal wooden slabs and, perched on top and secured to the high uprights, was a carved stone sculpture of a ram. The ram was a proud figure with two large horns. Below the ram an oblong sign and eight inch letters painted in white announced that this was BELLINGTON HILL. Ahead lay another gravel track with a line of acacias on one side. The trees and the road stretched to a distant horizon. Oisin drove carefully over the cattle grid and slowly along the gravel track.

The land on either side of the road was more prosperous looking in every way than the Seefeldt property where Oisin had laboured for over a year now. Instead of fences being in constant need of repair and derelict machinery lying rusting in the sun, Bellington Hill looked reasonably well maintained, despite the present drought. It also had water. When he crossed over a bridge and looked down at the creek, a reasonable amount of water still flowed there. He noticed three windmills with their circular metal blades gently moving in the slight breeze and beside them, the corrugated iron tanks and troughs full of water for the animals. There was evidently enough money available at Bellington Hill to ensure that the vast property would be able to continue even if market prices should fall or severe weather disrupt. No wonder the Bradshaws were so much talked about. The gravel track started to climb gently from the creek and at the top of the slight hill, Oisin saw Bellington Hill homestead for the first time.

The homestead looked impressive. He parked his Ford Capri beside a jungle green Holden utility truck which looked the worse for wear. This was the side entrance to the spacious colonial mansion. With beautifully designed wrought ironwork around all of the three wide verandas, this was a typically built country house of the time. The white wrought ironwork triangles which decorated the tops of the twenty or so pillars supporting the veranda roof further contributed to this overall feeling of genteel elegance from a bygone age. The wrought iron alone must have cost a small fortune. It had been wealth that had built this place. It was no surprise then that the noble ram was so visible at the entrance gates for it seemed likely that sheep had brought prosperity to Bellington Hill. Six steps led up to the front entrance and here under the green iron canopy roof there was an even more elaborate design in wrought iron with the date 1868 incorporated into the pattern. The front door was open and Oisin rang the bell. There was no answer. In fact the whole place appeared to be deserted. The wide windows on either side of the front door were open. All the windows had fine wire mesh in front of them as did the door. Oisin rang the bell again. Puzzled, he decided to explore further. He saw another set of steps at the end of the veranda and headed in that direction. A garden with various shrubs and a climbing rose had been planted at the side of the house but all the plants and grass looked parched and dried up from the lack of rain. It was very hot. He began to wonder what he should do next and whether he should just get in his car and go when he heard voices coming from behind a line of oleander bushes - then a zing and thud followed by clapping.

He had arrived at the tennis court. A mixed doubles match was in progress and as Oisin hesitantly approached the court, a short stocky chap wearing a white cap, slammed the ball across the net, just missing his partner, a rather agile young woman with a pony tail. His opponent seeing the ball coming at great speed towards him somehow managed to connect racquet to ball and he deftly lobbed the ball back over the net. White cap, however, was quicker. He waited and as the ball began to descend towards him, smashed it with such fury that the ball landed on the line just near to where Oisin stood at the side of the court.

"It's in... game over!!!"White cap cried and threw his racquet in the air.

"No, it's still on... missed the line... " and his opponent seeing Oisin, standing there, looking helpless, yelled, "you saw it, mate, didn't ya? Missed the line by a bloody mile!!"

He was a thick set character, built like a bullock and with a mass of ginger hair and he shook his racquet at Oisin. It had been a hard game and he wasn't about to give in. Sweat ran down his face and his tee shirt, equally wet, clung to his body. Oisin, who didn't have a clue about tennis, just looked helpless. Thick set tried again.

"Look... blind Freddie could see it... ball was out ... game's still on!!!"

"Give it up, Reg," and his partner, a freckled face girl of about twenty grinned at Oisin. "Come on... have a beer... there's a bottle in the esky... want one?" she said to Oisin who shook his head.

But Reg sulked. He stalked over to the line and tapped his racquet on the clay court. Dust rose.

"It's only a game, Reg," another woman spoke from the lean-to at the side of the court. She had seen the whole game and thought the ball had indeed landed on the line. Reg was a bad loser. Everyone knew that. She grinned at Oisin and winked at him. She had a stubby of cold beer in her hand and she thrust the bottle towards Oisin.

"Like a beer , mate... ?" and then she said to Reg. "Have a beer, Reg... for Chrissake... give it a miss!"

Everyone acted as if they had known Oisin all their lives. He felt a bit at a loss as to what to do next but the stubby of cold beer thrust into his hand looked inviting to say the least. *If beer were currency*, he thought to himself, *this country would have to be the richest on the planet!* But he took the bottle and drank. It was hot and the cold beer tasted delicious. Reg threw his racquet into the corner of the lean-to and sat down on the plank of wood that served as a bench. He glared at Oisin as if it were he who had been the cause of the lost game. The woman who had handed Oisin the beer, smiled at him and said,

"Haven't seen you round here before? Fancy a game? Don't mind Reg... he'll get over it, won't you, darl?"

She put her arms around Reg's neck. He scowled.

"He's really a big softie, ya know!!!" She enjoyed teasing him.

They all laughed except Oisin. He was wondering how to get out of the proposed game of tennis. Tennis, however, seemed to be finished for the day and the serious drinking was beginning.

"'Fraid I'm not much good at tennis," he muttered and hoped that the statement might somehow diffuse the situation with Reg who now appeared resolved to the fact that he had lost the game.

"I'm bushed," Reg said. "It's too bloody hot for running round like a chook with its head off!"

He lifted the lid off another bottle, spat on the ground and glanced at Oisin who reddened as six sets of eyes stared in his direction.

"I'm looking for Eleanor Bradshaw..." Oisin said. He felt rather awkward.

The six sets of eyes, as if as one, all turned away.

"You won't find her here then." The man with the white cap answered. "Well, mate "she's my sister, you know."

"Oh... "

"No problem. You weren't to know. You'll find her at old Bellington Hill... about a mile up the road, keep going to the horse paddock... on the right... past the hay shed on the left... then you'll see the sawmill and the house's on the right. You can't miss it. Eleanor moved out of the big house six months ago. We had a right old barney before she went but that's history now!"

Joseph's words seemed to amuse everyone because they all laughed and he yawned as if the whole episode had been a bit of a bore.

Reg, who had now drunk two stubbies of beer very quickly, got slowly and slightly unsteadily to his feet. He held out his hand to Joseph and he grinned. It was a bit of a foolish grin.

"Joseph, mate," he announced, "I'll settle the game with you next time... and we'll get a bloody umpire up there then." He pointed to the umpire's perch at the end of the net. "Mebbe we should ask Eleanor to do the honours! She sure as hell will keep us all in line! I might even win if she's scorin'!"

They all laughed, even Joseph. Everyone, that is, except Oisin.

As Oisin drove along the wide bitumen road towards the old Bellington Hill homestead, he was aware that the land on either side of him was more fertile and the sheep grazing in the distance looked as if they were surviving in somewhat better conditions than others were in the district. The drought had started to bite and the grass burnt brown but here was better land. He could make out the line of trees in the distance where the creek had to be. If the creek dried up as it must have done during the dry times, it looked as if there would be enough bore water to keep things going on the property. He could see irrigation pipes bringing the life giving water. Where other farmers would struggle and some might even give up, at Bellington Hill there would be the means to continue until conditions improved. All the fences, too, were well maintained and Oisin, having spent over a year erecting and patching up fences for Hans, could now appreciate the difference between the two properties. On the far right side of the road and behind a slab wooden fence was the horse paddock. Here a splendid white Arabian horse drank from an iron water trough which was connected to the windmill. Two other fine looking horses, a grey and a bay, their coats sweating in the heat, stood as statues under a shady white gum. Further on, Oisin drove past a hay shed and four timber framed buildings on either side of the road. The heat rose from their iron roofs. There was a slight dip in the road and on the left, beside a large heap of cut logs stood a sawmill housing a cross cut saw and a tractor in a shed. He drove on. About a half a mile along he came to a smaller bitumen road to the right, and he got his first sight of the old Bellington Hill homestead. Lord Cyril had chosen the site well for the old homestead had stood on this spot for a hundred years. This is where the Bradshaws had begun their empire and it was here that many generations of them had lived and died. The old homestead was smaller than the grander new one but it was still an impressive building with its wide verandas and a silver iron roof with a brick chimney. Tall pines, their seeds brought long ago from England, surrounded the homestead and gave the much needed shade. The blades of the iron windmill at the back stood motionless. Oisin got out of the car, stretched and looked around. No fence surrounded the property, just a red concrete path to the steps and the front door. On either side of the path, oleander bushes covered with pale pink flowers and the long green pointed leaves between the flowers provided the only bit of colour for everywhere else there was just dry brown grass. Oisin walked slowly along the path and under a metal trellis stretching in an arc over the path. A

207

climbing rose, devoid of bloom, had been planted to grow over the trellis but under the hot sun the leaves had curled through the lack of water. It looked a sorry sight. Six steps led up to the open veranda and the open front door. Louis and Eleanor were waiting for him. Both were on the veranda and seated on bright red and green striped canvas outdoor chairs. When Louis saw Oisin, he stood up and called out:

"Ah... Monsieur, you find us!"

Oisin climbed the six steps to the veranda and got his first close up view of the much talked about Eleanor Bradshaw.

She was shorter in height than he remembered and stouter. An attractive woman as well and even though her curly black hair had strands of grey throughout and the lines on her face were deepening from age and the summer sun, she would never allow her advancing years to weaken her. There was a defiant determination within her to keep going no matter what and when age finally caught up with her, she would face this prospect with an admirable strength of character which would make her the envy of others. At least, this was the impression she liked to demonstrate to those about her.

"Good afternoon," she said politely to Oisin. "We need another chair, Louis." She placed her hand on the Frenchman's arm.

Louis disappeared immediately into a room off the veranda to return a few moments later carrying another red and green striped canvas chair. He placed it beside his own chair and motioned Oisin to be seated. Eleanor studied the young man in front of her. Her brown eyes didn't seem to blink. Instead, they dug into his head and a rather uncomfortable silence descended upon the small group. At least this is what Oisin thought was happening to him but both Eleanor and Louis appeared oblivious to his discomfort or indeed to the stillness about them. Oisin coughed slightly to try to break the silence and then he began to wonder rather anxiously what he should do next. He had become used to the silence of the plains but not to the silence that comes sometimes between people when there doesn't seem to be much they have to say to one another. He looked down at his brown leather shoes and ran a nervous hand through his black hair. Eleanor continued to stare at Oisin and Louis studied his nails. Louis had chosen his clothes carefully as he always did and, especially more so, when he was with Eleanor. With Louis everything always looked perfect and today was no exception. He had dressed for the heat and wore a loose cream cotton shirt, the pocket embossed with his initials, fawn shorts and tan leather sandals. He was tanned and handsome. Occasionally he would look up and give a sort of conspiratorial half smile to Eleanor. This gesture between them suggested intimacy. Oisin was nervous and comparing his own appearance and dress sense to the immaculate Louis, made him feel even worse. His blue jeans had a small hole at the knee and his tee shirt, bought in Sydney and with a dyed picture of the Harbour Bridge on it, had seen too many washes. The tee shirt clung to his body and he was conscious of his sweat underneath it. Even his brown leather shoes were covered in dust. No one spoke and Oisin, feeling more awkward by the minute, decided to try to make some sort of conversation. He remarked about the heat and the lack of rain. This seemed to waken Eleanor because she threw her head back and laughed.

"Louis tells me you're Irish," she said, ignoring Oisin's feeble remark about the weather, "and that you work for my neighbour, Hans Seefeldt?"

"That's right," he mumbled. He still felt very uncomfortable and was beginning to wonder how he could make an exit. He was hot and thirsty and, after having driven so far, he had hoped to have been offered a drink at least but none seemed forthcoming.

"Another time we'll talk about Hans but not today. Now, we must have some tea. Louis?"

The Frenchman rose obediently and headed along the veranda in the direction of what was probably the kitchen. Oisin turned his head to avoid Eleanor's gaze and he focussed his attention instead on a small brown bird that hopped from branch to branch of one of the oleander bushes. A slight breeze ruffled its feathers and the bird flew off. The heat had not relented and Oisin's mouth was dry. He wondered if he should ask for a glass of water and then changed his mind. Droplets of sweat settled on his brow and his tee shirt felt damp. It was so hot that he had difficulty breathing for the air was warm. The early afternoon heat brought with it an overwhelming lethargy. To move required physical effort. He wondered how they had managed to run around the tennis court in such heat. And he wanted his eyes to close. He wanted so much to close his eyes for the heat and the penetrating eyes of the woman in front of him were both of such intensity that he would have given the world to be away from both. He cleared his throat.

Eleanor leaned towards him. She was dressed in a lemon and white striped silk blouse with a pleated white linen skirt and a wide white belt around her waist. A few buttons of the blouse were undone and Oisin could see her cleavage. He didn't want to look but he couldn't help himself for she leaned towards him in such a way that he was unable to look away. He could feel his face redden under the sweat. His hands felt clammy and he placed them together on his knees and studied them in an effort to avoid both the cleavage and the dark brown eyes. Eleanor noticed the boy's discomfort and she smiled. She was well aware of the effect that she had on men and she used it to her advantage.

"I can help you... "

"Help me?"

"I knew you needed me from the first moment I saw you... at the Commercial... "

"You saw me at the Commercial... I... I didn't see ye."

"I see people. Strangers are easy to notice. You were easy."

He felt trapped. *Why doesn't Louis arrive with the tea? Where was he?* This conversation was unsettling to say the least. He didn't know what to do. There was nothing else for it but to try to change the subject but Oisin, in his vain effort to diffuse the intensity of the moment ended up chattering in a confused and disjointed manner about the Commercial and the renovations and how good it all was and what a great thing it must be for Kilgoolga to have the old hotel back and running again. Eleanor continued to stare at him.

"Don't be nervous. There's nothing to fear," she purred. "Tell me about this girl you loved... the one who hurt you."

Oisin felt his heart miss a beat. No one knew about Cecy. He had kept the precious secret to himself when they had been together and when they parted, it had been a hidden shame. How could anyone know? He hadn't even told his mother about Cecy or even unburdened the story to a stranger. Now this woman with the black hair and the intense brown eyes, years older than him, had brought it all back again. He had hoped he was getting over it and especially lately with Claire but then he hadn't heard from Claire in a week, not since the opening of the Commercial and he wondered what was happening between them. But Cecy. How could he escape from the memory of Cecy? She had invaded his soul and sometimes it was too much to bear and now he had to think of it all again and he hated it. He clenched his hands and made an effort to get out of the chair but the brown eyes held him captive. He sat back and didn't speak.

"How do ye know about that? I've told no one. It's been over for a year now since it all ended."

"I know things," she murmured the words softly and all the time she stared at him with her unblinking eyes.

The two of them sat, not speaking until they heard Louis's steps along the veranda.

Louis had finally arrived holding a tray with fine china cups and saucers, a sugar bowl, milk and a silver tea pot. He laid the tray on the small occasional table in front of Eleanor and disappeared once more to return a few seconds later with a plate on which sat a thick sponge cake with a generous covering of white icing. Eleanor clapped her hands and taking a knife, she cut three pieces of cake. She plonked each piece of cake somewhat unceremoniously onto three small plates and then whispered to Louis,

"You be mother and pour the tea."

Louis obliged. Glad of the distraction, Oisin sipped his tea and was grateful to have a drink at last. He took a bite of the cake. It was delicious. Eleanor wiped the corner of her mouth with a white linen handkerchief.

"Louis," she whispered, "your culinary skills are divine. The cake is baked to perfection."

Her next words were unexpected to say the least.

"You were late," she said and looked directly at Oisin, "I don't like unpunctuality. It indicates an untidy mind. Have you an untidy mind?"

Louis giggled. He could see that Oisin was nervous and he rather enjoyed the sight. Eleanor could do this to people. She sometimes did it to him.

"Eleanor likes people to be on time, Monsieur," Louis sounded rather superior.

Oisin was getting tired of this sycophantic Frenchman and his theatrical manner. He hesitated before replying, weighing out his words.

"I got lost," he said, "I went to the big house first at the creek and then got directions from some people who were playing tennis... at the side of the house."

"Tennis? Oh... competitive sports... the problem here is there has to be a winner and a loser. The winner feels superior, the loser devastated. For this reason, I don't play

212

tennis. You must have met my brother, Joseph then?" asked Eleanor somewhat disdainfully.

"I… I think so."

"He rather indulges himself in competition. Always has done. But, as I said, I don't like competitive sports. And I can see that you don't as well. Do you ride?"

"Aye. I used to… in Ireland… was very fond of my old Connemara pony, Bess, I called her. All us kids had ponies. Da insisted."

"Then you and I will ride. Louis refuses to get on a horse, don't you, dear?"

The Frenchman shrugged. He raised his hands in the typical Gallic gesture and not looking at Oisin but at Eleanor, he murmured under his breath,

"Ah, ma chérie… you are *so* right… I prefer that both my feet stay on the ground… to allow myself to be on top of such creatures… NON!"

He poured himself another cup of tea without asking if anyone else would like one. Oisin, despite the circumstances of this strange encounter, found himself relaxing slightly. The tea and the cake had revived him and he suddenly wanted to talk. It was a strange feeling. He just wanted to talk.

"In Ireland… we lived in the west, at a place called Ballybeg and we all used to ride… I've two brothers and a sister, ye know. My best moments I remember were when I rode Bess along the strand. Sure, that's heaven… she was a wonderful wee pony, I sometimes miss her. Haven't ridden since then… that's when I left the west. Bess died. They're all gettin' old in the west now… my mammy too. But Declan's married and runs the farm. He's got two wee children, a boy and a girl and then there's my sister, Mary… she's in Dublin, an artist."

"And you have another other brother?"

Oisin reddened. This woman knew everything. *How could she have any inkling about Frankie, my elder brother*

213

Frankie who had become a priest and no one had heard from in years? And Frankie had always been in charge. Frankie was competitive too, just like those tennis players at the big house. Frankie hated to lose, Oisin thought, *and he never let me win anything. Frankie always made sure of that. Why is this woman getting me to talk about all these things?*

"How do ye know all these things? Frankie's my eldest brother... became a priest." He avoided the dark brown eyes and looked instead into the middle distance and saw Frankie's face, just for a moment. Frankie, a young man, handsome, confident and off on the train at Ballybeg, to the seminary with the whole of Ballybeg there to see him off.

"I know these things because I have a gift. The gift of second sight. You're Irish, you'll understand."

Eleanor's voice was calm, controlled. Then she turned to Louis and asked him to refill the teapot. It seemed to Oisin that she wanted to get the Frenchman out of the way, just for a moment. Oisin could feel his stomach churn. *This woman knew more about me in a few moments than others had in years, including Frankie,* he thought suddenly, *even if Frankie was a priest and my brother. Frankie never understood. Always just thought of Frankie.*

"I told you I will help you," Eleanor leaned towards Oisin again. He caught another glimpse of the cleavage and blushed. Now all he wanted to do was get away. Get away before Louis returned with the teapot and before anything else was said by this strange woman. But Louis had returned and without asking, poured both Eleanor and Oisin another cup of tea. The drink was refreshing even on such a hot day. The silence descended once more. The little brown bird returned to the oleander bush and started to twitter away. Oisin was glad of the sound. He was about to say something about the twittering as a way of breaking the silence when Eleanor, for the first time since he had arrived, stood up abruptly and walked to the edge of the veranda. She turned

214

her back to the two men and seemed to be studying the distant horizon. She was deep in thought. No one spoke.

Now Oisin had another chance to study her. Both he and Louis watched her for neither knew what she was about to do next. This was Eleanor's way. She liked to be in command and she also liked to ensure that no one was ever sure of her next move. The little brown bird flew away once again and the only sound to be heard, thought Oisin, was the beating of his own heart. Eleanor turned round and he felt her eyes bore into his head once more.

"Now you must go."

She walked slowly away from the two men. At the far end of the veranda she opened a door and disappeared from sight. Louis shrugged.

Oisin got quickly to his feet. He was taken aback by the unexpected exit of this strange woman who appeared to have no manners at all. Given her obvious status in the community, he was surprised by her sudden withdrawal. He had expected her to continue the conversation given that she had been able somehow to tap into his subconscious. Her remarks and observation about him had been uncannily spot on. This in itself was a tantalising prospect for Oisin for we are all slightly in awe of anyone who appears to be able to look at us and give us some hint of where we are heading. He didn't know whether to be relieved or disappointed but he did know that he had no wish to stay any longer and have to make awkward conversation with the Frenchman.

At the big house, Joseph and the man called Reg waved to Oiasin who drove slowly past them in his yellow Ford Capri. The game of tennis was over and they had been discussing the next match. They were competitors on the court but best of friends off it. In fact, they were first cousins. Joseph indicated Oisin should stop the car. Oisin put on the brakes. Joseph took off his white cap. He had black curly hair, just like his sister but his brown eyes were kinder.

"G'day, mate," he lent on the side of Oisin's car, "guess you found my sister OK by the look of you."

Joseph and Reg both grinned. Oisin suddenly felt cheerful too. The two of them seemed normal.

"Sure, I met your sister and the Frenchman was there as well."

"Ah!"

"See you round, mate," said Reg. And he winked at Oisin.

Oisin arrived at Wiesental in time for tea and Bible reading. When Hans opened the leather bound Bible and read the passage that spoke of Joseph's dreams, Oisin began to wonder if indeed Hans was right and that there was some divine intervention at work. Hans believed that when he opened the 'holy book', he would be guided to the page and the passage that was relevant for the day. Oisin had always been sceptical of this ritual for that was what he had decided it was, just an unbending ritual. At times, he had even laughed to himself at his employer's fervour and conviction but tonight he was just a little bit subdued. In fact, he actually listened carefully to the reading for the first time in weeks. When Hans closed the book, Oisin remained seated.

The kitchen at Wiesental was without doubt the centre of all activity and the largest room by far in the whole homestead. Here the meals were cooked and eaten and the plates washed. At the far end of the room in a corner and always covered in piles of paper sat the carved wooden oak desk that had been bought years ago at an auction in Brisbane. A gun rack hung on the wall with two shotguns and a rifle. In front of the desk, and looking a little the worse

216

for wear, four rather uncomfortable lounge chairs were arranged in a circle and faced a large window. From here it was possible to see a few of the farm buildings and the windmill and ridged iron tank which provided the water for the homestead. Hans, Hilda and Oisin always sat on the chairs at the window for this is where the Bible readings always took place with Hans sitting on the largest and least uncomfortable of the four chairs. A routine had been established and Oisin always sat in front of him facing the desk and the gun rack. His thoughts were often elsewhere. He observed that Hilda's mind, too, must wander a little because she fidgeted a lot on occasion and looked out the window a lot. But nothing was ever said and at the end of the reading and on most nights, all three would retreat to their various rooms.

Sometimes, however, Hilda would take her knitting and she and Oisin, who liked to read, would stay seated on the chairs for they had become comfortable with each other's company. But if Hans indicated that he wasn't about to move, both Oisin and Hilda normally found some other place to be.

The heat had died down and the large window at the end of the kitchen where the chairs were arranged was open and the curtains moved slightly with the light breeze. Oisin felt quite comfortable just sitting there but he kept thinking of the events of the afternoon and these thoughts didn't seem to want to get out of his head. He half wondered if he should mention Eleanor to Hilda but then he thought better of it. There always seemed to be a hint of animosity in the air at Wiesental whenever any of the neighbours were discussed. He had purposely kept his relationship to Claire Paterson to himself and this had been more so since Claire's cautious warning about Hans. He was uncertain what either Hans or Hilda would say about the Bradshaws, especially Eleanor, who appeared to the subject of much discussion wherever she went. After meeting her this afternoon, he was

217

even more determined to keep the whole episode to himself and he decided that he wouldn't mention the visit to Claire either. He made up his mind that when he next saw Claire, they would keep things on a friendly footing and not get into anything too deep. Having resolved all this in his mind, he was about to get up and retreat to his room when the phone rang. The phone, too, sat on a table at the other end of the room next to the door to the outside. It was Hilda who answered the phone. Oisin watched her face. She appeared flustered and when she put the receiver down, her face was flushed.

"It's for you, Oisin."

The phone didn't ring much at Wiesental and there had only ever been a few calls for him in the whole time he had been there. Hefty had rung and Claire, once or twice. Claire had been at her most prim and Hilda, who usually answered the phone, had not known who it was and Oisin had not enlightened her. He picked up the receiver.

"Monsieur Oisin... " It was Louis.

Oisin could hear the Frenchman's breath. There was a moment's silence and then he heard his voice.

"Monsieur, Eleanor asks me to telephone you. The next Sunday to invite you to dine with her at the Commercial 'Otel for lunch at twelve noon exact."

"Oh... will you be there?"

"Non, Monsieur. It is the Sunday I go to see my friend, Maudie. She is a great cook. She cooks for me a traditional Australian meal... roast lamb, roast potatoes. She makes for me the perfect gravy. Monsieur, Eleanor wishes to do the same for you. She says to go to the bar and ask to see her. Eleanor has her own apartment at the 'Otel and you will dine with her there. And now, I go for there are matters I need to do at the shop for tomorrow."

Oisin put the phone back on the hook. He didn't know whether to feel pleased or alarmed but whatever

218

emotion he felt at that particular moment in time, he knew that he would accept this unexpected invitation.

CHAPTER ELEVEN

Claire Paterson was angry. And when Claire was angry, all the primness disappeared and was replaced instead with a frown, tight lips and an acerbic tongue. Everyone about her had become expert in judging the tell-tale signs. At times like this, one look from Claire was enough to silence the strongest of critics. At the Kilgoolga High School her students became as angelic as it was ever possible for teenagers to be for they all knew that when Miss Paterson issued an order, it would be a very foolhardy and unwise person who would not jump to attention. A visit to the Head's office would most certainly be the outcome. Even Claire's wild and incorrigible three brothers took heed when their sister was in this mood. One of them once remarked, in jest, that their sister's temper could fell a man at ten paces! All in all, it was best for all concerned just to put the head down and hope the storm would pass by. This time the reason for Claire's anger had all to do with men.

It had started when Claire, alone with her parents at Kinleven station one late Saturday afternoon was handed a letter addressed to Harry. Her mother was in tears. Her father, on the other hand, was quite upbeat, even jovial. When Claire read the letter, her first instinct had been to screw the offending letter up and throw it in the paper bin. She thought better of it and instead, she banged the piece of official looking paper onto the kitchen table and let out a most uncharacteristic expletive for someone who was normally so prim. The temper had risen within her and exploded like artesian water from a bore hole. Neither her mother nor her father made any attempt to pacify her. Her father chuckled and her mother sobbed a bit louder.

The letter required Mr Harold Evans Paterson, 'in accordance with the provisions of the National Service Act', to submit to a medical examination and to present himself on 22nd January 1970 at the National Service Registration Office to ascertain if he was suitable for compulsory military service for the duration of two years.

"What does Harry think of all this?" asked Claire. It was very difficult. She hated to see her mother crying like a baby. Another enormous and uncontrollable tear ran down Mrs Paterson's cheek.

"He thinks it's an adventure... he's just a baby! My baby! He's never been out of Kilgoolga... why him?" sobbed her mother.

Mrs Paterson wiped the tear away with a wet tissue and then looked at her husband. It was a look that a person gives to another in the vain hope that the other person will be able to provide them with a suitable answer and solve the problem for them by speaking a few well thought out words. It didn't happen. Mr Paterson was quite pleased to think young Harry was about to stand on his own two feet at last. He didn't know what to say when women cried. He made an attempt to bring some sort of practical male sort of wisdom into the conversation.

"C'mon, Mum... it'll make a man out of him. I did my bit the last time... "

"But that was different." Mrs Paterson glared at her husband. He always made a joke out of everything and yet she knew he wasn't able to cope with anything serious. Just went to pieces and she had to manage. Her daughter might give some reassurance. After all, despite the primness, Claire

221

usually knew what to say. She was good in a crisis, always had been.

"Make your father understand, Claire... it's different. Two years is a long time for a twenty year old... he's got his whole life ahead of him... and what," Mrs Paterson paused and bit her lip, "what if they want to send him to that Vietnam place?"

"It mightn't come to that, Mum. There might be an end to it soon... there's Moratoriums going on all the time in Sydney and Melbourne... " but Claire wasn't too sure of this. She was so against the war that she had wondered about marching too but thought better of it. It wouldn't do for the school to find out and she needed the job. But the whole idea of war and suffering made her angry. Such a waste and this enforced conscription just made her even madder. And she hated seeing her mother so upset. The whole family knew that Harry was her mother's favourite.

"You know they just brought all this in without telling anyone... this national service malarkey... and you know how they do it? Just select names at random... they've got a whole lot of numbered marbles with birthdates on them... and Harry's birthdate must have come up. I read how they do it in the paper so it must be right, but why our Harry? There's dozens of twenty year olds in the district... why him?" Mrs Paterson blew her nose furiously. "Maybe he'll not pass the medical?" And she looked hopefully at her husband.

"Pass the medical, Mum? C'mon... Harry's as fit as a Mallee bull... now stop your blubbering, woman, he'll be OK... do him the world of good... be an adventure for him and he'll meet new mates... be good for him to get out of the place while he's young enough to enjoy it... the Army didn't do me any harm, now did it? And think how popular Harry'll be with the women... you all like to see a bloke in uniform!" And he winked at Claire who returned the wink with one of her looks.

222

"But he's never been away from home... " Mrs Paterson wasn't convinced.

Mr Paterson got up from the table. He whistled to his West Highland terrier, Hamish. The dog opened a sleepy eye.

"Up ya get, Hamish, me old mate... time you and me did the milkin'."

The old dog got slowly to his feet. He was twelve years of age and his joints were stiff but he loved Mr Paterson with a devotion that was evident to all the humans. This was the routine. The Patersons had a small dairy herd and every day about this time he and his master herded in those large brown creatures to be milked. He wagged his tail and hobbled behind his master.

When her father left the room, Claire got up and put her arm around her mother's shoulders. Mrs Paterson's smile was sad. When she looked at Claire, it was as if within her pale blue eyes the whole human story of life and death, of fear and faith was told, but above all else, behind those eyes there was the sacrifice of a mother's love.

"Why do men like war so much, Claire?" she asked her daughter sadly.

Claire might just know the answer. Claire was the cleverest by far in the family and she always had something to say about most things. People listened to Claire, Mrs Paterson thought. But Claire didn't have an answer. Instead, she squeezed her mother's shoulder just a little bit harder and kissed her softly on the top of her head.

Claire's anger did not improve when she saw Harry. In fact, Harry wasn't in the least bit troubled about leaving and he didn't have a clue why his mother and sister were getting into such a state about him. He'd talked to his father about what the Army was like and his father had told him about all the good things that happen. *You have to do what you're told,* his father said, *but you'll make some good mates too. Just be careful, mind, keep your head down and*

223

don't rock the boat. The officers don't like to see you rocking the boat. Do your bit, son. Proud of you. And Harry beamed from ear to ear when he heard these words. He hadn't ever thought of the Army, had never really thought of anything much but now he had the letter and he was going to be a Nasho, well, might be a bit of fun and Dad said the girls really fancy you when you're in uniform. *That would be almost worth the two years*, thought Harry. He couldn't get enough of the girls and he was running out of talent in Milberra and Kilgoolga. Be good to meet some of those city birds that he'd heard about. They might be just a bit easier than the locals. He didn't want to go off to this war in a place he'd never heard of but 'guess a man's gotta do what a man's gotta do.'

"Be OK, Claire, honest," he said. "Dad said it'd be OK."

"Harry, you don't know anything!" Claire wanted to throttle her baby brother and her father too. *Men are so stupid sometimes*, she thought.

Claire hoped that Oisin might at least understand just a little bit more, but she was deeply disappointed because it seemed that Oisin, too, thought that it was a good thing if young Harry went off to the Army. Oisin didn't exactly say that the experience would 'make a man out of him', in the words that her father had used, but he hinted as such and that hint angered Claire even more. She had thought that the gentle Irishman would at least agree with her but instead he just made a joke about Hans keeping them all safe from the invading Vietnamese hordes so Harry mightn't be needed anyway. And he told her about how Hans was busy building fortifications and renovating the old woolshed at Wiesental. That did not go down at all well with Claire and she retorted, pursing her lips in that characteristic manner of hers, that everyone knew in the district that Hans Seefeldt had 'kangaroos loose in the top paddock' and Oisin should have realised that by now. And she didn't speak to him for ten minutes or so. Oisin, although preoccupied with other matters, puzzled about the expression for it was one he had never heard before and it seemed so uncharacteristic of Claire, the prim schoolteacher, to launch into the colourful idiom which came so naturally to most Australians.

The outcome of all this was that Claire despaired entirely of the male sex and their constant competing against one another. She couldn't help but worry about Harry though. He was her baby brother after all. But it was when she stopped worrying about Harry and thought of Oisin, however, that she grew increasingly concerned. Oisin was different somehow. She had wondered about inviting him to the Paterson holiday home at Noosa for a week or so of the summer holidays if Hans would allow him time off. The sun and the surf would do them both the world of good, she decided and she knew that Oisin hadn't seen anything of the country, just Sydney and the train trip through New South Wales to Queensland and outback Kilgoolga. Australia was such a vast and diverse place. *It must be so different from Ireland for him*, she thought. At one point she had hoped that there was the possibility of something more than friendship developing between them but lately, she had begun to wonder where their relationship was heading. It just made her feel even angrier and more annoyed at men. She decided that instead of asking Oisin, she would take her mother for a fortnight's holiday to the beach and then, well, she might just go down to Sydney and march against the war and if there were any repercussions from that, she would face the consequences. At least, if that happened she wouldn't have to worry about men if she got put in the gaol!

Oisin ran his hand through his curly black hair. This was a nervous gesture of his and, as he stood outside the Commercial Hotel, he began to worry about whether to go in or not. No one would know. He could just make some excuse when he saw Louis again and the likelihood of running into Eleanor Bradshaw again would be pretty remote considering that he had lived in Kilgoolga for over a year now and their paths had not crossed in all that time. He wondered whether it would be better just to forget all about the invitation and go round and try to make it up with Claire. He had a feeling that Claire was annoyed with him but he wasn't quite sure why. It had to have something to do with Harry and his call up. He knew that she was protective of her brothers but he couldn't think it would do young Harry much harm spending a year or so in the Army. *Might do the young lad some good*, he thought. He tried not to think of the names on the War Memorial. Wouldn't want to see Harry's name there! But then they just carved names from the two World Wars on the memorial as if all the other conflicts didn't count. Claire's three brothers were all great lads, he liked them all and of course, they'd be able to fit into any situation they found themselves in. The three of them liked to party, that's for sure but they meant well and none of them shirked from any work. Claire should realise that. No, Harry would be OK. He would try to explain all this to Claire when he saw her next but that wasn't today's problem.

His moment of indecision passed and taking a deep breath, he entered the Commercial. It was one of those moments that if he had not gone in but ran away, his life would have taken a different course entirely. This other path he would never know because the decision to go was made in that split second and there was no going back after that. Later in his life, he would sometimes wonder what would have happened to him if he had not gone to the Commercial that hot November day but gone instead to Claire. His eyes took a moment to adjust from the glare of outside. The November heat was unforgiving. It was cooler in the lounge and the four overhead fans, all set on full power hummed in unison to circulate some of the hot air. There didn't seem to be any one about. His instructions from Louis were to go to the bar and ask for Eleanor. His heart beat faster. The boy from the barbeque was behind the bar. He was busy setting out the glasses ready for the day's drinking. When he saw Oisin he grinned.

"She's expecting you," he announced with a smirk. "Follow me, mate."

Oisin followed.

The boy walked quickly towards the stairs which lead to the second floor and then along the front veranda. Oisin just had time for a quick view of the railway station and the houses behind. He could make out the high fence around the tennis court and he wondered what Claire was doing. Suddenly the boy stopped. They had come to the end of the veranda. Here was a chain with a wooden sign hanging from it which said PRIVATE. The boy unhooked the chain and knocked on a dark mahogany door a few paces along.

"Leave you here, mate," he said.

The boy started to whistle and then with a spurt of youthful vigour, he leapt over the chain. A few seconds later he was gone. Oisin ran his fingers through his hair once again and tapped on the door.

When the door opened and Oisin saw Eleanor standing there, he felt his nervousness disappear and to his surprise, a strange feeling of well-being seemed to start at his head and move all the way through his body to his feet. Eleanor smiled. In fact, her whole appearance and manner looked so different from how she had looked at their first meeting. Eleanor had chosen her red and black flowing kaftan deliberately for it was always her intention to make a statement and this was especially true when she first met strangers. The kaftan with its colourful patterns of circles,

227

squares and triangles gave her an air of elegance that made her look years younger than she actually was. On her feet she wore white leather sandals and she had painted her toenails in bright red varnish. A necklace of large crimson balls with complementary earrings completed her outfit. Her manner and her appearance seemed so out of place in outback Kilgoolga but then Eleanor was used to being different. Powder covered her entire face and the lids of her brown eyes were thick with bottle green eyeshadow. Dark black mascara and thick eye liner meant that her eyes were even more compelling and when she studied Oisin as he stood at the door entrance, he felt himself reddening slightly under her gaze. Her lips, too, were heavily made up with a very red lipstick. She held out her hand to Oisin and he took hold of it. The handshake was firm. Here was a woman who knew who she was and would, by the force of her personality, always see that she got what she wanted.

Eleanor smiled and gestured with her hand that he was welcome and then she stepped aside to allow Oisin to enter the room. He entered Eleanor's private world. As this part of the hotel had been totally destroyed by the fire, she had been able to design an entirely new area and rebuild from scratch. Her decision to make this part of the hotel her private quarters was an astute one. It gave her freedom from Bellington Hill station when she so desired and it was here that she could entertain and, when it became necessary in her view to keep an eye on the hotel, she would stay there for a few nights. For Eleanor intended to make sure that the investment she had made in the buying and the renovation of the Commercial paid off. In this, the hotel was just another of her many business pursuits but the hotel was special to her. Eleanor was a Bradshaw through and through. The acquisition of money ran through her veins and she would see to it that the takings from the Commercial flowed like liquid gold. So far, everything was working out just fine.

228

The room that Oisin stood in was light and airy and he felt immediately at home. This surprised him. He had been decidedly apprehensive just a few minutes earlier. He worried all morning thinking about Eleanor Bradshaw. Her invitation had been conveyed to him by Louis in an abrupt manner and had been issued by him in such a way that a refusal would have been somehow impolite. Oisin had been caught unawares by the invitation and hadn't had time to think up an excuse. The result of all this was that he had made up his mind that the whole thing had to have some sinister motive which he couldn't fathom out in his present frame of mind and the result of all this worry, was that he regretted his decision to come and he wished he could be somewhere else. After all, he had only met Eleanor Bradshaw briefly and couldn't think for the life of him what he would have that such a woman might find of interest. He imagined all sorts of consequences happening and wondered what foolishness had made him accept the invitation and with such alacrity. Now he began to think he had perhaps been wrong. He started to relax. Eleanor was much friendlier than she had been when he had met her a week ago at the old Bellington Hill homestead. She insisted on giving him a tour of her unit starting with the dining room. Here, an oak table had been set with fine china plates, silver cutlery and two elegant wine glasses and a bottle of Chardonnay. *Eleanor certainly knows how to live and has the money to do it*, thought Oisin and he nodded approvingly as they went from to room and more elegant living was revealed. His appreciation of her possessions seemed to delight Eleanor. She explained how pleased she was with what she had accomplished so far at the Commercial and Oisin agreed that she had good taste. She looked even more pleased when she heard these words and he thought for a moment that she was about to kiss him. But she didn't. Instead, she hooked her arm into his and opened the large glass sliding door. The view from the balcony looked over the barbeque and to the paddocks beyond. Inside in the lounge two overhead fans cooled the air but outside on the balcony a belt of warm air hit them. It encircled them like a cloud. There was no sign of the drought ending soon and the earth lay dry and parched beneath the unforgiving heat of the summer sun. They could hear voices and a whiff of grey smoke rose from the barbeque. Everything else was still. Neither Oisin and Eleanor spoke but it wasn't an awkward silence between them, rather it seemed to Oisin that it was one of those moments that are best enjoyed without talking. He no longer felt uneasy. Although he had only met Eleanor a few moments before, a peculiar kind of peace came over him, standing there on the balcony and looking out over the dry plain. He had discovered that sometimes this country did this to you. The vast empty spaces and the flat plains which stretched for miles and miles cast a spell on you and you didn't know why it should happen nor could you even attempt to explain any of it. And it always happened that something would occur which would disturb your daydream and it came this time in the form of a red-tailed black cockatoo.

The huge bird shrieked like a banshee and landed somewhat awkwardly in the eucalyptus tree at the side of the balcony and just a metre or so away from where Oisin and Eleanor were standing. The cockatoo was joined immediately by another bird of about the same size and the two of them flapped their wings and screeched in a fury at each other. As both birds tried to balance on the smaller branch, it caused the slightly larger branch to move and for one split second, it looked as if both branches would snap under their combined weight. Eleanor clapped her hands and both cockatoos stopped their screeching for a second. When they saw that the noise had come from a human who was close by, one of the birds squawked even louder and then both of them rose as one, flapped their wings and flew in the direction of the rugby field. They landed on one of the horizontal posts and there they continued their argument. Eleanor chuckled. Oisin relaxed even more.

Then Eleanor started to speak and she did not stop. She told him that the back of her unit had to be totally private unlike the front entrance off the veranda which just had its chain barrier. She insisted that the spiral set of steps were necessary here and her balcony had to be physically removed from the back veranda where the guest rooms were. However, from her balcony she could keep her eye on the barbeque area and also the guests who sometimes stood on the veranda to admire the view. This suited her purposes just fine, she said. Oisin wondered what those purposes could possibly be as she seemed to be in control of much of Kilgoolga and beyond. What did she want? Eleanor Bradshaw was becoming more of a mystery every moment for him. But he began to feel that she was possibly the most interesting person he had ever met in his entire life. There was something about her that he was unable to explain to himself in a rational way. He listened to her every word.

The lounge and the dining room were contained into one large room with four comfortable looking leather chairs, television set and oak sideboard. It was when they were seated at the table and had finished the meal which Eleanor assured him she had prepared all by herself that she asked him what he thought about the two photographs on the wall above the sideboard. She emptied the bottle of Chardonnay into his glass and sat back in her chair. She was satisfied with the way everything had turned out. The meal she had prepared was just the sort of food for a hot Australian summer's day – cold melon to start with, followed by a ham salad with a generous helping of new potatoes and to finish it off, a delicious pavlova with lashings of cream and fresh pineapple. Oisin appreciated the food so much that he politely, if somewhat nervously, asked for a second helping. Eleanor seemed delighted with the request and she loaded his plate with a generous helping of ham and potatoes. She

231

fancied herself as a cook and loved to experiment with new dishes. To be the recipient of such hospitality was a joy for Oisin as he had a great appetite. He felt that he was being treated to something quite special and he was rather pleased with himself so he sat back in his chair and wiped his mouth on the white linen table napkin and smiled at his hostess for the first time. In fact, despite his earlier nervousness, he now felt totally at ease. He studied the photographs on the wall. He had noticed them when he first entered the room and said so.

"Well done, Oisin!" and she patted his arm. "This is a photograph of Bellington Hill, the ancestral home of the Bradshaw family. I lived in England, you see... well, for a time... and when I was there I was invited to visit the Bradshaws, I got to know some of the family, you know... "

As she spoke, Eleanor pointed out various architectural features of note in the photograph which was set behind a rectangular gold frame.

"When I returned to Kilgoolga after my travels, I lived in the new Bellington Hill homestead but because of circumstances beyond my control, I had to move to the original homestead... old Bellington Hill, we call it. You saw the two houses, didn't you? Old Bellington suits me just fine. Unfortunately, this country hasn't the traditions of England. Lacks history! No way could a building like this be built in this country and especially not in outback Kilgoolga!" And she sniffed dismissively at the thought.

Oisin got up and studied the photograph of Bellington Hill. The building was similar in design to all the other Georgian stately homes he had visited years ago; every one of them had concrete pillars at the entrance and the large porch area and solid oak door. The photograph had been taken from the driveway and it did look to be an impressive piece of architecture and he said so. This observation was greeted by Eleanor with even more rapture and she talked non-stop about the various hidden features of the building and why it had been of such importance for her, just spending time there, she said, was inspirational. In fact, she became quite animated especially when she started to talk about the great hall with all her ancestor's portraits hanging there. Then Oisin's attention turned to the sepia photograph set in an antique oval frame and hanging next to the gold frame of the stately home.

"I've seen this man before," he said. "Isn't there a photo of him with his wife at the Kilgoolga Arms?"

Eleanor's reaction to these words was totally unexpected. She nodded her head, smiled and then she kissed him on his cheek. She had to stand on tip toe to do it. She tapped the oval frame with her finger. Her finger nails were perfectly manicured and covered in bright red varnish. She tapped the glass in the manner of a strict school teacher explaining something that needed to be understood to an inattentive child.

"I knew when I first saw you, Oisin, that you were special." She seemed to be excited for some unknown reason that he had noticed the photograph and realised that there was a similar one at the Kilgoolga Arms. It was important to her. She had rescued the photograph with its frame from the attic when she left new Bellington Hill after the argument with her brother, Joseph. Her brother had no sentiment about his ancestors or any of their history for that matter. Joseph was a philistine, according to Eleanor and could only think of sheep and for that reason; he had no right to anything of value and especially, valuable family history. It's a wonder the photograph had survived his purges. His wife would have made sure it went on the fire, had she known. Eleanor had discovered it just in time. She would explain all this to Oisin at another time.

"Do you know who he is?" she asked. But Oisin couldn't remember what Bella had told him at the Kilgoolga Arms and he just murmured that the photograph of the severe man with the whiskers which grew down the side of his face to his chin, had to be a Bradshaw, one of the pioneers to the district, he thought. He had noticed two photographs at the hotel, he said, one of a man and a woman and the other one with a team of bullocks. The bullock dray was laden down with possessions, he remembered.

"Ah... yes, you're right and now you see him, he's an older man here... this is the Lord Cyril Bradshaw and he was more than a pioneer. He brought civilisation and culture to the outback. Cyril was the man who built Kilgoolga! In fact, he owned Kilgoolga."

She pronounced the words 'Lord Cyril' slowly and deliberately.

"I heard the story of Lord Cyril when I met the Bradshaw family in England," she continued speaking and, as she did, she tapped the glass once more with her red fingernail. "They said I bore a striking resemblance to him. What do you think?"

Eleanor faced Oisin and looked severe, just like her ancestor in the photograph. Oisin paused before answering. He thought he'd better be careful not to offend but he had to admit, there was a slight, a very slight similarity between the two, especially around the eyes and he said as much. His remark delighted Eleanor and he thought she was going to bestow another kiss on his cheek but she smiled and nodded her head, murmuring,

"Yes, that's what I thought, that's what my relations in England thought as well. You are astute for one so young."

She sat down on one of the leather armchairs and asked to Oisin to sit next to her. This way they were both able to continue looking at the two photographs. Eleanor wanted to talk about Lord Cyril. In fact, she could have spent hours and hours talking about him. Sometimes she looked at the photograph and spoke to him. She was totally convinced that there was an invisible connection cord that bound the two of them together.

"Lord Cyril was definitely the most famous of all the Bradshaws," she said. "He's so handsome. And definitely the most adventuresome of any of them and just look at those eyes, he's so very intelligent, don't you think? I wish he were alive today. You know sometimes I think when I look into his eyes that he is. What do you think when you look at the photograph, Oisin? I'm sure he's telling me what I must do... and you, too... this isn't fantasy, there's more in heaven and earth, you know. There's an unseen world we are a part of and a few of us can tap into this."

Oisin had never given the possibility of an invisible world much thought. He looked even more closely at Lord Cyril. He wondered if Lord Cyril would think he was astute as well. As he stared at the photograph on the wall and focused all his attention onto the eyes of Lord Cyril, he felt a very peculiar sensation. He had heard people say that in some of the great houses when you studied a portrait for too long, the eyes of the person moved. He stared at the sepia photograph behind the glass. Lord Cyril stared back. He had never had this sensation in all his life and he found the experience rather unsettling and uncomfortable. He wondered whether he should mention what had just happened to Eleanor but then thought better of it. At the present moment, although he was now more relaxed and at ease in her company than he had expected to be, he still had a few reservations about her. He wouldn't have been able to explain these reservations either so instead of answering her question about Lord Cyril, he decided that the best course of action was to look away from the eyes and as soon as possible change the subject. Eleanor obviously felt some sort of bond with her distant ancestor and, if she thought that Oisin too, was able to experience a similar sort of supernatural feeling, she no doubt would find reasons to explain what it all meant. It was all rather bewildering. He decided to change the subject.

"He's got an interesting face, to be sure," he answered and turned his head so that he didn't have those eyes looking at him. Instead he looked through the sliding glass door and away from Lord Cyril. The sun was low in the western sky. It surprised him that he had been with Eleanor for so long. Time had slipped by. If anyone were to ask him how he felt about the afternoon he would have found it difficult to explain. It had certainly been a relatively relaxed affair; he had enjoyed the meal and he had found Eleanor Bradshaw to be one of the most fascinating people he had ever met. There hadn't been much in the way of intellectual companionship in Kilgoolga after all and Eleanor certainly was intelligent and she had seen a world away from the grassy, flat plains. Sometimes Oisin had a hankering for the sights and sounds of home so it had been good to talk about these things to Eleanor who had even spent a few months in Dublin, or so she said. He had no reason to doubt her as she knew lots of the places that only someone who had lived there would know. It was always the little details that mattered. He told her he sometimes missed the soft rain of Ireland and she laughed and said there was no such thing here. When the rain came, there was nothing soft about it, just a downpour and then the inevitable flooding. She hoped the drought would end soon. The sheep and cattle were suffering and the river levels were low. Oisin must know how dry it is. It was a pity he couldn't bring them some of the rain from Ireland. She laughed then.

He thought it was about time he got ready to leave. But something seemed to keep him rooted into his chair and he sat back again. He felt a strange sensation behind his eyes and he turned his head once again and this time towards Eleanor. When he looked at her he could have sworn that it was Lord Cyril's eyes who stared back at him. He glanced at the photograph and then back at Eleanor. The moment passed and he told himself he was being an idiot, that there was no way that could have happened. On the wall was a dead person and beside him there was someone who was very much alive. No way could a dead person's eyes turn into the eyes of a living being. He got up to leave. But Eleanor would not let him go. She insisted he stay for coffee and cake and so, a little reluctantly this time, he sat down again but he deliberately avoided looking at the photograph of Lord Cyril.

Eleanor disappeared towards the kitchen and he heard the kettle boil. When he looked outside he realised that the sun had set and everything was dark. He had been with Eleanor for hours. A few minutes later she reappeared with a tray holding a percolator of coffee, milk and sugar, mugs, plates and thick chocolate cake. She placed the tray on the side table near where he sat and asked him to pour the coffee. The coffee was strong and he had to add another spoon of sugar to it. Eleanor cut two generous slices of the chocolate cake and the two of them ate the cake. Neither spoke. For most of the afternoon, Eleanor had talked constantly and at times, with great animation but now she seemed to drift into a sort of dream. She finished eating and sat back in her chair and shut her eyes. Oisin wondered what to do next but he, too, found that his eyelids were growing heavier and he wanted to shut his eyes too. He tried to resist but somehow he could not. He closed his eyes and slept.

It was the screech of the black cockatoo outside the door that woke him. The bird had returned to the same branch and was busy reclaiming his territory. Oisin opened his eyes. He could hear no other sound. The two curtains in front of the sliding door were shut and he went over and peeped through the gap between them. There was a pink glow in the sky and he realised that it was dawn. He must

237

have slept all night. He ran his fingers through his hair and felt the stubble on his face. He needed a shave. The clock on the wall said half past five. Eleanor was nowhere to be seen. He went into the bathroom and then to the bedroom door. The door was ajar and he quietly looked inside. The bed had not been slept in. He frowned and returned to the lounge and the dining area. He had to get back to Wiesental and start work at seven. It would not do if Hans and Hilda realised that he had not been back all night. If he left now, he would get there in time and they would be none the wiser, he hoped.

Everything had been cleared away. The table where they had eaten their meal was bare. Lord Cyril stared out from his photograph on the wall and Oisin avoided gazing into those eyes. Instead, he looked at the sideboard and there he received a surprise. A pink envelope was propped up against a tiny ornament of a collie dog and written on the envelope, in purple ink and with a flourish, his name, **'Oisin Kelly'**. He picked it up. The envelope was sealed and he ran his finger along the fold to open it. He frowned. Inside he felt a key and there was a note. The note, also written in the same flowing hand, said:

Take the key. It unlocks the sliding door. Always come in from the balcony entrance. Feel free to come and go as you wish.

He put the envelope with the key back onto the sideboard and ran his fingers through his hair once more. He stared at the key and the note. His could feel his heart pumping in his chest. He didn't know what to do. Outside, the black cockatoo let out another shriek and he heard the rustle of the leaves in the tree. He bit his lip. Then he made a decision. He took the key and the note and put them back inside the envelope. Then he took the envelope and shoved it into the front pocket of his jeans.

CHAPTER TWELVE

When the schools broke up for the summer holidays Claire Paterson and her mother went off to Noosa for two weeks. Their holiday home overlooked the beach and every morning for the two weeks Claire plunged into the clear blue sea. She dived through the waves and with pure hedonistic delight let the rush of water sweep her towards the shore. Then she emerged from the cool, clear Pacific Ocean to sit on her beach towel and let the salty water dry on her tanned brown skin. Patches of sand clung to her wet bikini. She shielded her eyes from the glare of the sun with a large straw hat and always wore sunglasses. Here on the beach, Claire Paterson was sublimely at peace with her world and so very far removed from the dry, dusty plains of Kilgoolga.

It was on the beach that Claire made up her mind that she would not think anymore of Oisin Kelly. He was like all the rest of the boys after all. She had hoped for something more but she refused to let her disappointment ruin her present moment. She also made up her mind that she would not allow her fear of what might happen to influence what she saw as the right thing to do any longer. She was only one but she *was* one and with that thought in mind, she decided that when the two weeks of joyful physical indulgence were over, she would go to Sydney to march against the war in Vietnam; a war that she believed was morally wrong and completely unjustified. There was a cousin of hers, Jim and his wife in Sydney. Jim was active in the trade union movement and known to the security services. Jim could be relied upon for he had the same moral courage as Claire and he was against the war and the conscription of the twenty year olds as well. Claire decided that she would ask Jim if she could stay with them for a few weeks and do what she could to protest. Then she would return to Kilgoolga to say goodbye to Harry. And by doing all these things, she would definitely not have time to think about Oisin Kelly!

To say that Oisin was baffled by the circumstances which now surrounded his relationship with Eleanor Bradshaw would have been an understatement. He had taken the key to her rooms at the Commercial without thinking what it all meant and it was only afterwards that he began to wonder what had been her motive for offering him the key which would mean, if he were to take her up on her offer, that he could come and go as he pleased. He did not have long to wait for an answer because the next day Louis rang him again at Wiesental to say that Eleanor had invited them both for tea once more at old Bellington Hill homestead. It would be on Sunday afternoon again at one o'clock. Oisin accepted the invitation without a moment's hesitation because the thought of meeting Eleanor again intrigued him and added to this was the exciting feeling of suspense. His usual Sunday afternoons lately had been spent with Claire but the last time they spoke to each other, she had made it quite clear to him that she would be busy with the end of term activities and needed to work most weekends. After that, she and her mother were going to Noosa and she didn't know when she would be back in Kilgoolga but it definitely wouldn't be till the end of January when the schools started again. Oisin took this as a rebuff. He hadn't mentioned his meeting with Eleanor at the Commercial to Claire or to anyone else for that matter and he thought that it might be best to keep it that way, at least for the present. Eleanor was a mystery to him but there was something about her that he was drawn to and this feeling would not go away. He found himself thinking of her at odd moments and sometimes just before falling off to sleep, the events at the Commercial would go round and round in his mind. The whole story Eleanor had told him of the Bradshaw family intrigued him and he decided that the next time he had a drink at the Kilgoolga Arms he would study the photograph of Lord Cyril and his wife, Lotte, more closely. If Lord Cyril's eyes followed him around at the hotel, he would be on the alert, that's for sure.

Oisin could not deny that he found Eleanor an attractive older woman but that was as far as their relationship would go. Eleanor was certainly a powerful personality and to Oisin's mind neither her age nor her gender mattered one jot to him. In his wildest imaginings, however, he could never think of having a physical relationship with her and if, as popular gossip had hinted, she and Louis were indeed having a sexual relationship, this was entirely their own affair and he had no wish to find out the veracity of these claims. In fact, given his sometimes prudish nature, he found the whole idea quite distasteful. He was much more intrigued with Eleanor's obvious intellect and her command of any situation she seemed to find herself in. It flattered him that she had noticed him at all and that she had welcomed him into her inner circle with herself and the flamboyant and slightly sycophantic Louis. He decided if the three of them were locked together in this tight little group, he might even find himself liking Louis a bit more. After all, Oisin reasoned, Eleanor certainly had shown a profound knowledge and astute judgement of her fellow human beings. Therefore it was logical to conclude

241

that there must be something about Louis which had to appeal.

Their first obvious connection was the fact that both he and Louis were strangers to Kilgoolga. It might be good to have someone to talk to who knew something more of the world away from the dry plains. Although Oisin now felt relatively at home in Kilgoolga by virtue of becoming friends with a few of the locals, particularly Hefty and Matt, and lately Claire and her brothers, there were many times that he knew he was an outsider. He felt this most when discussions took place between them all about times past and unknown people. So having Louis to talk to might even prove a blessing in the long run. Oisin considered himself at this point in his life to be a drifter. At least Eleanor and Louis would be a safe harbour for him while he was here.

And as far as the matter of the key was concerned, it mightn't be ·such a bad thing to have it anyway. In the sometimes stultifying environment of Kilgoolga, it would be good to have a bolt hole which no one knew about. For all these reasons, he looked forward to his next visit to Bellington Hill with a tinge of excitement.

On Sunday afternoon, Bellington Hill station was deserted and the only signs of human habitation were a few cars parked at the new Bellington Hill homestead. It appeared that tennis was off for the afternoon. Oisin had thought that tennis was something that happened every week and he had half wondered if he should wander around to the court to introduce himself once again. Eleanor's brother, Joseph and the group had seemed friendly enough and he felt sure they would welcome him. He had planned to do this in a casual sort of way and hoped that a little bit more information about Eleanor might have been forthcoming. So he was slightly disappointed when there appeared to be no one about. He drove on through the property to old Bellington Hill. Louis's car was parked in the driveway and when Oisin got out of the car, a large German shepherd dog appeared from behind one of the oleander bushes, barked and then ran to the back tyre of Oisin's car and cocked his leg. The dog then trotted purposefully ahead of Oisin towards the homestead. Oisin followed. The dog led him along the path. Every now and then the dog stopped and sniffed the dry grass and then kept going in the direction of a large gazebo. Around the wooden lattice frame a sorry looking purple wisteria was attempting to survive the drought. Oisin heard voices and when he came to the front of the gazebo, Eleanor and Louis were there. The dog ran up to Eleanor and received a pat on the head for its trouble. Both Eleanor and Louis were seated on a large tartan rug spread out on the brown grass. Behind them were four wooden garden chairs and a small table. A large jug of what looked like lemonade sat in the middle of the table and arranged around the jug were four blue plastic glasses. Louis lay on his back with his head in Eleanor's lap. Every few seconds she picked one of the grapes from the ceramic bowl next to her and Louis opened his mouth. Then she popped the grape into his mouth. Neither Eleanor nor Louis acknowledged Oisin and he just stood there, feeling rather foolish. The whole scene looked like something out of an Edwardian theatre set. Oisin didn't know whether to giggle or say something significant. He thought better of it so he just stood in front of them with the sun beating down on his head and all the time gradually beginning to feel more out of place as well as becoming hotter.

Finally Eleanor stopped feeding Louis and she looked up. Louis remained in the same position. He closed his eyes.

"Have a grape?" she asked in a rather languorous way and at that, she pushed the bowl of grapes towards Oisin.

He shook his head but decided instead to sit on the tartan rug next to her. Seeing the boy on the rug, the dog got up from its position at the back of the gazebo and plonked

243

its large frame down beside Oisin. The dog put its head onto Oisin's knee and shut its eyes. Almost instantly it started to snore gently. Now both Eleanor and Oisin were trapped beside each other by a dog. Eleanor was more casually dressed than she had been at the Commercial and with Louis's black hair and tanned face positioned so intimately on her white slacks; they were oblivious to everything and everyone about them. To further add to the picture, Eleanor's tight red and white striped blouse had a few buttons undone so that her large breasts dangled provocatively over Louis's head. She didn't speak but stared into the distance and as she did, her left hand stroked Louis's hair. Louis did not say a word. The heat rose from the ground and sitting on the rug, Oisin observed a line of ants heading towards the table on which sat the jug of lemonade. He wondered whether the ants would attempt to climb the leg of the table to the jug. It was that sort of hot summer Sunday afternoon when nothing much happens and when the observation of a line of ants is the only thing of particular interest. Eleanor and Oisin must have sat there without speaking for about twenty minutes or so before she started to question him and when she did, he felt his face redden.

"Tell me about this girl of yours... " she asked and as she spoke, she brushed away a fly that was attempting to land on her face. The fly flew to the top of the dog's head and walked towards its ear. The dog opened a sleepy eye. Oisin was trapped. He didn't answer.

"It would help you to talk about it, you know. It's called catharsis. Then you'll move on. You've courage, I can see that but this hatred you feel towards this girl is keeping you on the lower plane. You need to free yourself from its power. She hurt you a lot, didn't she?"

"Well, I met her in Edinburgh and I asked her to marry me," he said.

"Go on."

"That's it. She was engaged to someone else."

"Ah... this has you trapped, this hate you have towards your rival?"

"I don't know what you mean. I just felt... I don't know how I felt. Just didn't care, I guess. All I wanted to do was get away and Australia is the furthest away from anywhere. It all happened a year or so ago. It's just that I'd never felt like that about anyone before and it sort of broke me up. You'll think I'm weak?"

"No."

"Well, I try not to think about her. Try all the time but somehow, I can't stop. She comes into my head and she won't get out of it. It's like a deep wound that doesn't seem to want to heal. I thought I was getting over it a bit, sure I really thought I was but... well, I don't know now." He thought of Claire.

"Close your eyes."

"What?"

"Do as I say!"

Her dark brown eyes seemed to penetrate into his brain. He felt his eyelids getting heavier just as they had at the Commercial when he looked at the photograph of Lord Cyril. He tried to keep his eyes open but something seemed to say to him that he must close them. He tried to resist those brown eyes but he couldn't. He held the body of the dog a little tighter and then he felt his eyes closed.

He didn't know how long he sat with his eyes shut or what was said. When he opened his eyes the dog was no longer on his knee and Louis was nowhere to be seen. Eleanor sat on one of the chairs and she had the glass of lemonade in her hand. She smiled at him.

"Now you can have a drink. It will help. You'll be thirsty now."

She poured a drink into the blue plastic glass. He drank. The lemonade was cool and it tasted delicious. He emptied the glass in one gulp and she refilled it. He

245

experienced a strange sensation of lightness in his head. Even with Cecy, he had never felt this release of everything. It was a minor explosion that started at his head and worked its way down his entire body to his feet. The world around him seemed clearer and more vivid than it had ever been before. The blue glass in his hand was a vibrant colour. Before, it had been a rather dull blue. He looked at the sky. He thought he had never seen anything as bright even though the sun was making its speedy exit to the horizon and it would soon be dark. Eleanor stood up. She had a faraway look in her eyes and she didn't look at Oisin. Instead, she took the empty jug of lemonade and stacked the four glasses into one. It was time for Oisin to go, she said.

He didn't want to leave. He wanted to stay with her and talk and talk. He wanted to know what had happened to him. What powers did she have that she could do this to him? One moment he had been speaking to her and then he couldn't remember anything except when he opened his eyes, he was free. If he thought of Cecy now, it would be just the happy times. How could this have happened in such a short space of time? For months he had hated Cecy and now could it be possible that all that anger and bitterness had been washed away from him? He wanted Eleanor to talk to him and explain.

"When can I see you again?" he asked.

She looked at him now and he couldn't bear it. Instead he looked down to the dry ground to avoid her deep brown eyes. He remembered Lord Cyril's eyes and the photograph. Yes, these were the same eyes. He should have been frightened thinking of all this but instead he felt calm. He couldn't bear to think that she mightn't want to see him again for the thought of not being in her company seemed to be unimaginable at that moment. He wanted to learn so much from her. Here was someone who was wise and even if her behaviour would be considered strange by others and misunderstood by many more, she said she would help him and he believed her. For the very first time in his life, he thought he had met someone who really did understand him. Even Cecy hadn't been able to find that part of him. This woman had entered his soul.

"Louis will give you a ring. If you need me at any other time, I want you to ring Louis. I'll see you at the Commercial next time... you have the key?"

"Aye."

"Use it any time you want. Just make sure you go to the balcony though, not through the hotel, like last time."

"Aye. It's good of you."

"Don't try to contact me at old Bellington Hill. Louis'll make arrangements and I'll tell him when. You'll feel tired tonight. Try to sleep. I have some herbal tea I'll give you, that will help. You've a lot of hurt inside you but this is the beginning. It gets easier but the hurt has to come out first. When you think of this girl next you will begin to think of all the good times you had with her. You can tell me her name now?"

"Cecy Stanworth. An American from upstate New York. She was in Edinburgh for a year... at the university... studying English literature... a very clever girl. She'll be married now... to a guy named Chuck."

It no longer hurt when he talked about Cecy and when he said the name, 'Chuck' he didn't feel his old anger.

"I couldn't stop thinking about her. It's odd. Perhaps she did love me in a strange sort of way and I've never thought that she did before?"

"You're beginning to understand."

"What happened?"

"She didn't mean to hurt you, you must believe that. I think you're right, yes, she did love you. How does that make you feel, that she may have loved you after all?"

"Happy... and free."

"Ah... anything else?"

247

"Aye. I'd like to write to her and wish her well for her life. I think I really did love her and I want to put the record straight."

"Tonight before you go to sleep, write her a letter and try to put all this down. If you can't write tonight, make sure you do so before I see you again next week. Then bring me the letter and we'll read it together. It's a release. There's no need to send it to her. It wouldn't do any good. There are relationships that are worn out and no longer serve any purpose in our lives; this is one of them for you."

"I don't think I can do that... let her go, that is."

"You have already. As you go through life, you will understand that people come into your life for a reason and some of them go. You learn from everyone. Sometimes we learn the most from those who hurt us. It's all part of a divine plan and we only begin to understand any of this when we become free. Freedom is letting go. Cecy taught you a lot. If you hadn't met her, you wouldn't be here. Think about that. There will be more women for you. And I'm not talking about sex here. The next one could be a man... "

"I don't understand."

"Sometimes the ones who cause us the most pain are the very ones who in the end give us the most blessing. It's necessary to meet these people. We learn from every experience. As I said, it is not conditional on age or gender. We need to understand our parents too."

"It's not easy."

"No one ever says it's easy. We all tend to desire a comfortable life after all."

"All I wanted was to marry Cecy and have a family with her. I didn't think that was too much to ask."

"Who are you asking?"

"I don't know... maybe God. I don't think I believe in all that anymore."

"Do you blame God?"

"I don't know. Was it too much to ask then? I mean, most people achieve these things... marriage, family, a purpose in life because of this."

"Of course."

Eleanor handed him the empty jug of lemonade and the glasses. She picked up the bowl which now had no grapes in it, just a few stalks and then she lifted the tartan rug from the ground, shook it and placed it over her arm. She walked slowly away from the gazebo to one of the back doors of the homestead. Oisin followed. He wanted to know more. They entered the kitchen and Eleanor placed the empty bowl on the sink and threw the tartan rug over one of the chairs. The kitchen was large and about the same size as the one at Wiesental except this one was tidier and everything had a place. Eleanor liked order.

"Can I see you next Sunday?" he asked. It was a plea.

"Ring Louis. Bring your letter... the one you'll write to Cecy."

"How do I start it?"

"You'll know. This is the beginning for you. It's important to write it down so you'll be free. Now you must go."

When Oisin returned to Wiesental, he went straight to his room. Hilda had kept a meal hot for him on the stove but he said he wasn't hungry. The Bible reading was over but Hans made no comment about Oisin being late. Hilda wondered what had happened but she kept quiet. If there was a problem that Oisin had, he might talk about it to her later. *They had become friends*, she thought. She had noticed a change in him. Lately he had talked less to her and went to his room more. He was away from the house most Sundays and sometimes she knew he didn't come in till late at night. He had become such a part of her life and even though Hans wouldn't admit it, Oisin did most of the work on the farm these days. She couldn't bear to think he might leave her. *Life would be so empty without him*, she thought. *Maybe he's had news from home and that could be the reason. Perhaps it's his mother or something like that although he doesn't talk much about his family in Ireland.* Hilda fretted just thinking about it but she didn't say anything. She took his meal and fed it to the dog.

Oisin sat on the bed and looked through the wire mesh window to the dark night. There was hardly a star visible. Thick clouds covered the night sky and he wondered if it meant that the rains might start again soon. It had been so hot and dry lately, it would be good to think the drought had broken at last. Times like this he missed the soft rain of Ireland. His mind went through the events of the day. He had a letter to write that he would not send and he didn't know how to begin it and thinking of writing this letter brought Cecy into his mind again. He lay on his back and stared at the ceiling. And then he closed his eyes.

When he woke in the morning his first thought was about Cecy. He remembered how she had been during their two weeks in the Scottish Highlands and when he thought about that time, the memory was good. It surprised him because the last time he had remembered this, he had been so angry with her. It had been during their holiday together in the Highlands that he had made up his mind to ask her to marry him. Now instead of the anger he usually felt because of the events that came after this, there was a different sort of feeling. He couldn't explain it but it felt good.

He whistled as he came into the kitchen and Hilda, busy preparing the breakfast, smiled at him.

"G'day young man, you're lookin' very pleased with yourself this mornin', aren't you?" she teased. "Looks like

250

you're ready for a good breakfast... and an extra rasher of bacon is called for, what d'ya reckon?"

Oisin could hardly wait to see Eleanor again. On Sunday he climbed the steps to the balcony at the Commercial and tapped gently on the sliding door. The curtains were drawn back and he could see inside the room. He noticed that the table had been set for two and there was a crystal decanter and glasses on the sideboard under the photo of Lord Cyril. He tapped again and then slid the door open and stepped inside. It was slightly cooler in the room and although the rains had not come during the week, the black clouds promised to bring the afternoon summer storms soon. Oisin was glad of the slight respite away from the heat. It was slightly unnerving to be alone in the room. He deliberately kept his eyes away from the photo of Lord Cyril and cleared his throat to announce his presence. There was no answer. He called out softly. In a strange way, he was pleased with himself to be back in Eleanor Bradshaw's rooms and to have written the letter that she insisted that he must write. It had been difficult to get the words down at first. It had taken him quite a few attempts to get it right. A few times he had stared at the blank page and fiddled with his pen only to screw up the paper without writing anything at all. It had all changed one night when he woke suddenly about three o'clock in the morning. It was a clear night and he heard the roosters crowing. Something or someone seemed to propel him from his bed to the small desk that sat in the corner of his bedroom. He sat down on the chair, picked up the pen and wrote:

Dear Cecy,

251

This is difficult to write. I have spent all this time trying not to think of you and I've failed every time because I love you, still do despite everything that happened. I don't know whether it's over for me at last but...

He covered the page and the next one and kept on writing and writing until, exhausted with the effort, he threw the pen onto the paper and stood up. He looked at his watch. It was four o'clock. He read the last lines twice and then he picked up his pen and finished the letter:

I hope you are happy with Chuck and I want you to know, that I wish you both (he thought for a moment) *every blessing. We'll never meet again.*

Your friend,
Oisin Kelly

He folded the pages and placed them neatly inside a plain white envelope. Then he wrote on the envelope*: Cecilia Mary Angela Stanworth , upstate New York,* and smiled.

After he had written the letter, things had seemed better somehow and life had been a little more bearable that week with Hans and Hilda. He thought of Eleanor now and not Cecy. In fact, if Cecy popped into his mind, it felt good. He wondered what Eleanor would say about the letter. It was somehow important for him to tell her how it had been for him after he had written it. He touched the envelope inside his trouser pocket and called out again.

He heard her singing and then she was there beside him. She greeted him with a kiss and told him to sit at the table. They both sat down. Oisin looked around the room and wondered where Louis was. He was glad the Frenchman wasn't anywhere to be seen. He had Eleanor all to himself.

"I've written the letter," he said proudly.

Eleanor placed a pair of tortoiseshell framed reading glasses onto her nose and read. When she had finished reading, she folded the pages carefully and handed the letter to Oisin.

"Burn it!"

252

He hesitated.

"Did I do the right thing?" he asked. He was a child again, wanting approval.

"We'll put a match to it!" She paused.

He didn't know what to say. He had wanted her to talk about the letter, to give him some reassurance. He frowned.

"Did I do the right thing?" he asked again. "Writing the letter, I mean... "

Eleanor didn't answer. Instead she went to the kitchenette and opened a cupboard door. She handed him a box of matches.

"Burn it. Over the sink. We don't start fires outside in this country. Burn it."

He lit the match and took the first page of the letter and held the flame to the corner of the paper. The flame curled upwards, destroying the words and the page. Then he took the next page and the next until all that was left in the sink were blackened pieces of paper and a spiral of smoke in the air. Finally, he took the envelope on which he had written the words with such a flourish just a few days before, *Cecilia Mary Angela Stanworth, upstate New York*. He lit another match and held the flame to the corner of the envelope. The burnt and blackened envelope dropped gently into the sink and landed on top of all the other pieces of burnt paper. Words and memories lay there, destroyed.

Eleanor scooped all the black and burnt pieces of paper into a dustpan and carefully placed them in the grey pedal bin underneath the window of the kitchenette. She didn't blink as she looked at Oisin nor did she smile.

"Now you are free of her," was all she said.

253

A few weeks later, Oisin was in the saddle and at perfect peace with his world. The yellow plains over which he rode were still bone dry from the months of drought but thankfully the heat had eased just a little and a soft breeze cooled the air. It was heaven to be in the saddle again and feel the strong movement of the fine Arab horse beneath him. Oisin felt like a boy again and as he rode memories of his childhood came into his mind. His thoughts were of the lost halcyon days when life was less fraught with day to day problems and the sweet nostalgic remembrance of those past times and in those few precious moments; he wished he was back there astride his pony, Bess and cantering along the strand near his home at An Teach Ban with the wind with the soft rain on his face and the ever changing clouds above. The mare on which he rode was a much finer beast than his beloved Bess of childhood days and more temperamental by far. This horse had character and courage and needed a firm hand on the reins. Oisin had spoken softly to the mare and stroked her neck gently before swinging the saddle over her back. This seemed to do the trick and the horse relaxed slightly. She finally allowed Oisin onto her back and the two of them had developed respect for each other in a very short space of time so that now both man and beast were enjoying that wonderful feeling of rhythm that comes with such mutual understanding. Oisin was a natural when he was astride a horse and the mare sensed this and responded in a positive way. She maintained a steady canter most of the time but occasionally Oisin would give her a gentle nudge in the ribs and a few words of encouragement and allow the mare to break into a gallop if he saw there was a straight stretch of land with just a few tussocks of grass to hinder their progress. Then they would almost fly through the air just like Bess used to do on the sandy beach at Ballybeg and with the wind in his hair, Oisin felt his world had come full circle.

254

Eleanor Bradshaw rode beside him. An expert horsewoman, she sat straight in the saddle and held the reins loosely in her hands. She only needed to give a gentle nudge and a slight tug on the reins to guide and control her white stallion. The horse stood at fifteen hands high and with his intelligent eyes and finely chiselled head, he was a noble animal indeed. Eleanor was exceedingly fond of her horse. He was named Amir from the Arabic for trustworthy and he was devoted to Eleanor. The woman and the horse understood each other and as so often happens, a special bond had developed between them. She had cared for the horse since he was a foal and the horse repaid all those hours with the same sort of devotion. Amir would not allow anyone but Eleanor to ride him. He was a proud animal. Oisin and Eleanor had not spoken to each other for about half an hour. They rode on Bellington Hill land. It was a silent world except for the clip clop of the horses' hooves on the parched soil and the screech of the occasional flock of white cockatoos that appeared out of nowhere then vanished just as quickly, a flash of a hundred white feathers against the clear blue and cloudless sky. Every now and then they heard the lonesome call of a crow. The sound seemed louder on the silent plain. Once they glimpsed a dozen or so wallabies grazing on the tough grasses and when they got closer to them, the animals bounded away towards the safety of a line of gidgee trees. Oisin was still enthralled by the sight of these creatures. Whenever he saw them, he had to remind himself that he was definitely in another country and a long way from the Ireland of his childhood. Life there was tamed and the landscape controlled. Here, in this vast space, these strange creatures, free and untethered, bounded across the plains. He decided that their freedom was indeed a thrilling thing to behold and just another allure that this incredible and arid land had.

It was Saturday and a near perfect day for Oisin. For weeks he had hoped that Eleanor would invite him for a

255

day's riding and she finally had. Her invitation was given in a matter of fact way so that there was no chance of him not accepting it. Not that he would have anyway. To be with Eleanor was becoming an addiction for him. He looked forward to their meetings with all the excitement of a child about to go on a Sunday picnic and since the episode of the letter to Cecy, Oisin and Eleanor were in each other's company a lot more. In fact, Oisin's life now consisted of the weekly work with Hans and Hilda and any spare time he had was spent in the company of Eleanor and sometimes Louis. It annoyed him when Louis was there and the way the dynamics of the little group changed when the Frenchman was about. Eleanor was always in charge and sometimes Louis sulked. The best time was when he had Eleanor all to himself.

They rode all morning until the sun was high in the midday sky. It still seemed incredible for Oisin to think that they could ride for so long and still be on one family's land for there was no boundary fence that announced the end of the property anywhere to be seen. He thought how his father and uncle had slaved to eke out a living on the few acres they had at Ballybeg and he wondered what they would have made of all this empty space. The land around Bellington Hill homestead was more fertile than the open plains over which they now rode. In the vicinity of the homestead Merino sheep grazed on the more nutritious grasses which grew over the acres and acres of fenced in land but here there were no signs of either fences or sheep for the kangaroo grass that grew in tussocks over the plains would provide little nourishment.

They rode towards a group of six or seven acacia trees which grew along the river bank. Here Oisin slipped from the saddle and held the reins of his horse. The horses were hot and thirsty. Just a trickle of brown water flowed along the gully where the river was and here and there the tops of the rocks were visible in places because of the

256

drought. He tried to lead his horse to the river but she refused to move.

"Take them back along the creek. They won't drink here!"

Eleanor turned Amir and the horse walked cautiously along the bank over stones and rocks and both horse and rider had to be careful. Oisin followed. He was puzzled. Horses sometimes had a sixth sense and nothing you could do, would persuade them to move. This looked like one of those times. About a hundred metres from the original stop, Eleanor dismounted and, talking gently to Amir, led the horse to the water. More water flowed here and the horse picked his way over the stones and rocks to the river. Oisin and his horse followed. When both of the horses finished drinking, Oisin tethered them to a large acacia tree and they stood there, grateful to be under the shade and able to rest for a while. But Eleanor would not stay with them. Instead, she walked back to the original spot and here she arranged the tartan travelling rug on the ground underneath a large acacia and then handed Oisin a sandwich made from two thick slices of white bread with an equally thick piece of yellow cheese and a rather limp lettuce leaf.

From her hessian saddle bag she produced two bottles of orange cordial. She arranged the bottles neatly in the centre of the rug and then she sat down. Under the acacia it was cooler but Oisin felt a peculiar wariness about the place and wondered why. He still puzzled about the horses. He could see them in the distance. They looked content and were obviously enjoying the rest in the shade. He could see nothing around him that would have produced this odd feeling as it was a near perfect day. The sky was a cloudless blue and the plains were still. In the faraway distant horizon his eyes focussed on a mirage for the heat rose from the dry ground and he thought to himself how tantalising the sight of this would have been for the white explorers of old. How seductive and yet so cruel to have imagined that water was so close and yet not there. It was another example of how this country could torment you one moment and seduce you at the same time. He took a sip from the bottle of cordial and a bite of his sandwich. The uneasy feeling did not leave him and he wondered what was causing this as he couldn't think of a rational reason for it at all. Eleanor didn't speak. He had noticed that sometimes she wouldn't talk to him for what seemed ages and during those times; he had learned to be quiet also. He wanted to know what was making him feel so incredibly uneasy and he wondered if there was something about the place that she might be able to explain the reason why. For such a hot day, it felt cold under the tree.

"It's cool here," he said for want of something to say.

Eleanor didn't answer. Instead she reached into her saddle bag and threw him a red apple which he caught with a quick movement of his right hand. She shut her eyes and lay back on the rug and covered her face with her straw hat. He thought she had fallen asleep. He took a bite out of the apple and looked around him once more. All was still. There wasn't even a bird to be seen in the sky. The whole place was remote. It felt like another planet.

He had no idea how long Eleanor remained silent under her hat but just as he was beginning to wonder whether to wake her or not, she suddenly sat up and pointed her finger over the river towards a distant line of hills.

"That's Paterson land that way and over there's where the Seefeldts join up with the boundary fence. We're still on Bradshaw land now! Tell me, what do you make of Hans Seefeldt?"

The question came out of the blue and Oisin, caught unawares, frowned slightly. How could he explain Hans to anyone?

"I'm not sure... he's fine one minute and the next... well, he can change just like that. I don't think I'd be able to

258

stay out there except for Hilda... she's OK." It sounded rather lame.

"Do you think he'd sell?"

"What do you mean?"

"He's getting old."

"Aye, I've often wondered what will happen to the two of them when they can't manage anymore. Been thinkin' a lot about it lately. I seem to be doin' most of the work these days. Although Hans's still the boss!"

"Do you think he'll sell?" She asked again.

"I doubt it. He's got a bee in his bonnet about a Communist invasion from the Vietnamese Army. For the last few months, he's spending most of his time in the old woolshed. He can be irrational at times."

Oisin remembered the shotgun.

"It's common knowledge in the district that Hans Seefeldt throws a few wobblies from time to time. Some say he's even mad," Eleanor remarked casually.

"Don't know what he used to be like."

"The Seefeldts have caused the Bradshaws a fair amount of grief... over the years. It would be best for all concerned if Hans sold Wisental."

"Where would he go? And Hilda? I get the impression that his land is everything to him. I don't think he would leave."

"We'll see."

Oisin felt uneasy again. It had been a great day but now this talk of Hans and this peculiar feeling wouldn't go away. He decided to ask Eleanor about this place and to change the subject at the same time. He didn't want to talk about Hans Seefeldt. Despite his failings, Hans had been good to him most times after all.

"Ever since we've been here," he said, "I've felt a bit weird. I'm not too sure about being here... can't explain it. Why wouldn't the horses drink over there?" He ran his fingers through his hair.

"You've got a sixth sense."

"What do you mean?"

"It's a place where something happened a long time ago. I brought you here to find out whether you could feel it. I thought you would. As I explained to you the other day, we are soul mates, the two of us. It is possible that we were lovers in another life. You know that Louis is my soul mate, too, but I doubt if he'd have had the same sort of awareness that you have. He thinks a bit too much of the flesh and it is weak, as the Bible tells us. But you're right, no one knows what happened here but something did... and it wasn't plcasant."

"Would that explain the cold feeling under the tree? It's weird... after all, it's so hot."

"There are places in the world where evil has occurred. The evil hangs in the air there. Then there are other places which hold pleasant memories. Something good has taken place there and people feel at peace just being in the vicinity. When I was in Italy I visited the place where Saint Francis of Assisi prayed. I was at peace there. I noticed that everyone about me was happy too. There was joy. It almost felt that Saint Francis was still there, praying. People said that to me. You know it's always been good and evil since time immemorial. It's the same old story. But evil throws a deathly shadow and its power is harder to bear. We can become intoxicated with its power, drugged by the evil some might say. Difficult to explain to you but that's why this place feels eerie and why you think something happened here."

"Do you know what it was?"

"Yes. A death."

"How do you know?"

"You have to open your mind and then you will know as well."

"Not sure I want to know."

"It's not for you to say. There is a higher power."

260

"God?"

Eleanor laughed.

"We are part of everything there is. When you feel the wind in your hair or the soft rain on your Irish face, you come alive with the life force that's within you. If you want to call it God, that's fine. Why do you think the horses refused to drink here?"

"They were spooked. I know horses. I don't think I like it here either."

As he spoke, a slight breeze ruffled the leaves of the acacia. It unnerved him even more.

"You say something wicked happened here. What was it?"

But Eleanor didn't answer. Instead she turned her head away as if she wanted to conjure up an image of what had happened at the river bank all those years ago and if she looked out there in the middle distance she would find the answer. She smiled.

"I told you... a death... a long time ago."

"You know what happened then?"

"Perhaps."

Oisin stood up. He wanted to move. This place was getting to him. He suddenly felt the loneliness of it all. They had been sitting on the tartan rug under the tree for two hours. It surely was time to head back to Bellington Hill. The horses were rested now and would be ready to go home too.

"I don't like it here anyway," he said. "I'd like to go now."

"Ah... you're sensitive. No wonder Cecy caused you such pain!"

"I don't think about her anymore," he replied sulkily. "I just want to go."

He walked back to the horses. They were pleased to be released from the tree. He led both of them over the stones once again to the water and they drank. A small flock of grey cockatiels flew overhead and then, as if as one, the whole flock swooped down to drink. They were noisy and when they saw the man with the horses they all rose once again into the air and were gone. Oisin watched them fly off. He wondered what it would be to like to be able to fly. *It would feel like freedom*, he thought, *not being restrained by gravity*. He took hold of the horses' reins and led them back to Eleanor. She had packed the saddle bag and folded the rug.

"We'll leave this place then," she said. "Are you glad you came?"

Oisin hesitated. Her questions often appeared to have another deeper meaning and he was sometimes confused.

"Aye. I just don't like it here, that's all. Been amazing to be able to ride again though."

"You're a good horseman. You ride well. It's been necessary that you see this place, that's all."

"Why?"

"You ask too many questions! Now, the horses are ready to get a move on. My Amir wants to get home, don't you, my darling?"

She stroked the horse's neck and ran her fingers through the white mane. Amir nudged her shoulder. Then she put her foot into the stirrup and in a quick movement, she was astride Amir's back. She looked down on Oisin who had not mounted his horse yet. She looked magnificent.

They hardly spoke to each other on the way back to the homestead. The horses were eager to get home to be fed. Oisin and Eleanor allowed them to gallop most of the way and only slowed them down when they came to fences and gates. By the time they arrived at the stables the sun was almost on the western horizon. For Oisin it had been a memorable day in so many ways. He was weary and stiff from hours in the saddle but he was undaunted by the experience. It had been great to feel that sense of freedom once again. He had been too long at Wiesental station, he

262

decided and had forgotten what it was like to have nothing to think about all day. Just to enjoy life and Eleanor's words came back to him in a pleasant little rush of memory – *to feel the wind in your hair*. It was funny how he had thought of Ireland as he rode. He hadn't thought much of Ballybeg lately but with the horses and Christmas coming, well, it's natural, he concluded. Eleanor had asked him to spend Christmas with her at old Bellington Hill and he had said 'yes'. Louis would be there, of course but it would be a change from being with Hans and Hilda and feeling lonely. He had been lonely last Christmas but then he had still been thinking of Cecy then and hadn't really cared. This year would be different. He wondered what Claire Paterson was doing. He hadn't heard from her for weeks. Still, maybe it wasn't meant to be. He hadn't mentioned Claire to Eleanor. She would probably know anyway, she seemed to know everything, he concluded. It was amazing how she could speak about the future as though it was already there and he was intrigued that she seemed to know details about his own life long before they had ever met. This was fascinating but a bit bewildering to him all at the same time.

Their horses were tired. The dark had come down in that sudden way that still intrigued Oisin. The evening star was a bright sparkle in the night sky by the time they had finished with the horses. They walked slowly back to Oisin's car. Eleanor paused and looked up to the sky. More stars had appeared, white shinning dots in a black sky.

"Now, what do you think of all this? Is that heaven up there?" she asked and pointed towards the evening star. Oisin hesitated before answering.

"Feels as if it could be," he replied. "It's so incredibly quiet. Peaceful. There's been no evil here, has there?"

His mind was on the river bank and the gully and that weird feeling.

"No, of course not. I told you Lord Cyril was the first white man here and everyone who came after him looked up

263

to him. He was a shining light in the district. Others envied him you know, particularly the Seefeldts and the Patersons. But yes, you're right as far as evil is concerned. No great evil has ever happened at Bellington Hill station but there's been times, evil has waited... perhaps still waiting in the wings, ready to strike."

"Now you're worrying me."

"I told you we must be vigilant. You'll play your part... when the time comes."

Oisin was troubled, hearing this. It sounded like an omen and he didn't like it.

"I don't know what you mean... "

"Ah, you've a lot to learn about life. Dark times are coming and we must be careful. There are people out there who don't understand and they would rip the heart out of you if they feel threatened. You'll find out who they are, soon enough but there's much to do before that happens."

It all sounded shadowy and slightly worrying. Eleanor often spoke in riddles and this added to her mystery. Oisin ran his fingers through his hair as he always did when he was nervous. This was another of those times.

"Well, I haven't met anyone in Kilgoolga who would fit that description," he said.

Eleanor shook her head.

"They're here though. You just haven't been aware enough to see it but this is where I will guide you. I told you I would help you. For starters, you don't think about Cecy anymore, do you?"

"No."

"Well, then. We've had a good day, haven't we? We'll ride out there again. I often do. Next time we meet I want you to tell me about Hans Seefeldt."

"Hans?"

"Yes. What do you make of him? And Hilda?"

"They seem OK... most of the time. Hilda's been good to me, mothers me, you know. Feel a bit sorry for her though."

"Why?"

"Well, must be lonely out there. I think she would have liked to have been a mother and had people to look after. She's a sweet wee woman. I know I can move on but she's sort of stuck out there, you know what I mean."

"That's why I want you to tell me all about Hans. What does he do these days? Does he go out? Except to the church, he's always been obsessive about religion. He's known in the district for his intransigence. People know he's stubborn and narrow minded to boot."

Oisin grinned. This is what Eleanor did to him. One minute she spoke in a way that confused him and the very the next minute, she joked and those feelings passed as if by magic.

"Aye, ye are right," he said. "I know what ye mean about the religion. I've found it the best course of action is to be quiet when anything's said on that subject. But I'm used to that, after all I grew up in the West of Ireland and the priests had a way of telling ye what was right and wouldn't hear any argument against them. I must tell you about my Uncle Mick sometime. He caused bedlam when he decided not to go to Mass anymore. Ye would have thought World War Three had been declared! But Mick never went to church after that, he was true to his word. In fact, Hans sometimes reminds me of old Father O'Malley in Ballybeg, I can just remember him, he wouldn't hear of another opinion either. Stubborn man, too, just like Hans."

"Well, then, you know what to do. Keep an eye on Hans and let me know what he's thinking."

"That's a tall order," he laughed. "Doubt if anyone knows that."

"You do. You're an observer. Don't worry."

265

"Lately all he does is sit in the old woolshed. I told you about the Vietnamese. He's still on about it when anyone will listen. But I'll keep my ears open. You never know."

"Good."

Eleanor kissed him on the cheek. Sometimes she did that; other times he was dismissed with a wave of her hand. He opened the car door and slipped into the driver's seat and turned the key in the ignition.

The next week Oisin watched Hans a little more closely. Eleanor was right, Hans was slowing down. Even in the short space of time that Oisin had lived with him, Hans had grown older. He still worked from dawn to dusk but he rested more during the day. Sometimes he just went to the woolshed and told Oisin what to do. Those days no one saw him. If a stranger had come to Wiesental on one of those days, they would have assumed that it was the young Irishman, Oisin Kelly who ran the place and did all the work for the old farmer was nowhere to be seen. Oisin wondered what Hans did all day in the woolshed and what his thoughts were while he was there. It was all very well for Eleanor to instruct him to work out what Hans was thinking. Hans hardly spoke to either Oisin or Hilda at any time and on those days when he disappeared to the woolshed, he didn't speak to them at all. After a day in the woolshed, even the prayer Hans said at the dinner table and the Bible reading afterwards were brief. Then he would get up and head for his bedroom without so much as a 'goodnight' leaving Oisin and Hilda to clear the table and wash the dishes. So it was difficult for Oisin to work out what he would say to Eleanor

266

about Hans the next time they met up. He wondered why she had suddenly become interested in Hans and what her motive was in asking.

Oisin decided that his best course of action was to see if Hilda might offer something that might shed some light on what was going on as far as her brother was concerned. He could talk to Hilda about most things and she had a bit of the dry Australian wit about her sometimes that he enjoyed. She often had him in stitches of laughter and usually it was about some mundane incident that others would not even have noticed. In this, brother and sister were at odds with each other. Hilda had a sense of humour that often bubbled to the surface. Hans, on the other hand, rarely joked about anything. It was all duty with Hans and laughter appeared alien to him. If he joked it was usually about something quite obscure. In all the time Oisin had known him, he couldn't remember Hans laughing much about anything or anyone, for that matter.

He cornered Hilda one late afternoon when Hans was nowhere to be seen and all the work was done. He found Hilda with her goats. She loved her little herd of goats and called them names. There was Gertrude, Heidi and Gruff. They all had personalities and Hilda fussed over them like a mother hen. Oisin had got used to drinking goat's milk. Hilda did all the milking. Neither Gertrude nor Heidi would allow Hans or Oisin anywhere near them at milking time.

"Need any help, Hilda?" Oisin asked, knowing full well that the answer would be 'No'. "Have you seen Hans?"

Hilda paused. She was in the middle of coaxing Heidi to stay still. Heidi could be flighty and sometimes objected to being milked, even by Hilda. Gertrude, on the other hand, was always extremely grateful.

"He'll be in the woolshed, I suppose," she replied. "We don't see much of him these days, do we? I've noticed, you're doin' most of the work. What would we do without you?"

"You'd manage. I've discovered the women are a tough breed out here!"

"You know what we've got to put up with then? Sure the Irishwomen are the same. Bet your mother kept you all in line. Women do." Hilda laughed.

"Aye. My mother was English but guess it must've been hard on her sometimes out there in the west. It's a long way from London where she was born." He had hardly mentioned his mother to Hilda. It had never felt appropriate and this wasn't one of those times. He carefully steered the conversation back to Hans.

"I've been wondering lately if Hans is feelin' OK. He seems awful silent most of the time."

"Ah, Hans's always been like that. Ever since we was kids. Don't worry about it." Hilda frowned. "But what made you think that?"

"Well, I don't think he looks well. I know I haven't known him all that long but he seems to get tired a lot these days."

"We're all gettin' old, young man. Hans won't admit it though."

"Would ye stay on here, do ye think, Hilda? I shouldn't be asking, I just worry about ye, that's all."

This delighted Hilda. It felt good to have someone asking about her. Hans never did.

"Hans has said that he will never leave Wiesental and I believe him. He loves this place."

"And ye?"

Hilda frowned. "I try not to think about it. Guess I'm like Hans in that way, I can't imagine livin' anywhere else. Not like you, been everywhere!"

Now it was Oisin's turn to frown.

"I wouldn't say that," he replied. "I seem to have got stuck here too!"

"I hope you stay a bit longer." She looked sad.

"Aye. It's been good... knowing ye."

Hilda blushed. She thought of Hans.

"That's kind of you," she said. "I know Hans can be difficult at times. I'm used to it but you must wonder sometimes… ?"

"Just wonder what he's thinkin', that's all. Do ye really think there's goin' to be an invasion… like Hans said… the Commie Army comin' down and all his plans for fences and barricades?"

"Oh, take no notice. That's all nonsense. Who would want to invade Wiesental? It's not exactly on the beaten track! Next stop Bullamanka!"

She laughed.

"Bullamanka?"

"Haven't you heard of Bullamanka? It's past the black stump, you know."

"No, I didn't know. So ye don't think the Viet Cong will have the run of the place then? What should we say to Hans? I think there's another trench to be dug near the top paddock!"

"It's best to go along with him, Oisin. He doesn't like people to disagree with him. If he thinks there's goin' to be an invasion, he won't hear anything said against it… it's gospel as far as he's concerned. Makes up his mind and he won't change it. Well, he gets a bee in his bonnet and won't let it go. He's always been like that, ever since he was a kid. Just go along with it. I don't know what's going on in his head. Although this Vietnam thingy doesn't sound right to me. Don't understand war, do you?"

"No."

"Still, guess the pollies know something we don't. Hans hates them though… the pollies."

"Pollies?"

"Politicians. Them blokes down in Canberra what makes all the rules. Hans says they should all be lined up and shot. As I said before, don't argue with him. He's always

269

right. Though he could have a point as far as the pollies go, don't ya reckon?"

"I don't know much about politics... especially here," Oisin replied somewhat thoughtfully.

"Well, that's fair enough. My sentiments exactly!"

Hilda nodded her head and then almost as an afterthought, she said in a sort of reassuring way and as she spoke, she patted his arm,

"Don't you be worryin' yourself about the fences and the barbed wire that he's gettin' you to put up. Think about it for a minute, them foreign soldiers have Buckley's of making it to Kilgoolga... that's why we've got an Army and a Navy, haven't we? And they're callin' up the boys too, just like the war before... but you're too young to know anything of that one, aren't you now?"

Hilda often rattled along and this was one of those times.

"Buckley's?"

"Buckley's chance. No way will them Vietnam fellas get to Wiesental but if Hans wants to put up more fences and he thinks they will, well, let him, I say. I know he's my brother, but sometimes!! Goodness, is that the time? He'll be in for his tea. He's always on time for his tucker, haven't you've noticed?"

Hilda often got into a fluster when she thought of her brother and remembered mealtimes. Oisin had observed this. Hans demanded that his evening meal was on the table for him at six thirty on the dot. His nights were a holy routine even if his days had been rather unplanned lately. Hilda handed the bucket of goat's milk to Oisin to carry and then she scurried off towards the homestead as if there wasn't a moment to lose. Oisin followed slowly behind her. His thoughts were on Hans and what he would say to Eleanor next time they met. He felt pleased with himself that he had at least done what she had asked him and found out a bit more about Hans Seefeldt. He couldn't imagine why she

270

would be interested in the old farmer but it always made him feel better when he was able to do what Eleanor asked him to do. It was a strange feeling he had to admit that to himself. But then when he was with Eleanor Bradshaw, he often didn't know what was going on anyway.

A few weeks after Christmas had been and gone and the summer storms arrived in a downpour of rain that once again brought green grass and swollen rivers, Oisin received a surprise that changed the pattern of his life; a life that was beginning to follow as much a routine as the one that Hans and Hilda Seefeldt lived by. And the shock came one evening after Hans had gone to his bedroom leaving Hilda and Oisin to tidy up once again. It was all the result of a phone call. Hilda answered the call and then she handed the receiver to Oisin. She was puzzled and a little curious for it was an unknown voice on the phone. She didn't know whether to leave Oisin by himself or just stay and try not to listen in. She stayed.

Oisin picked up the receiver and then he heard a voice in his ear from a long time ago and the voice just said:

"Hiya, Frog. It's me!!!"

CHAPTER THIRTEEN

Oisin put the phone down and then he walked over to one of the kitchen chairs and sat down. His mind was all of a muddle. He didn't know whether to feel pleased or annoyed. He ran his fingers through his hair once and then again.

"Well, what a thing that is!" he said and looked at Hilda.

Hilda had tried very hard not to listen in but she could be a nosy sort of woman sometimes. She was also polite and didn't want to appear too eager so instead, she wiped her hands on the towel which hung on a hook beside the sink and then she sat down beside Oisin at the kitchen table.

"That was my brother... Frankie," announced Oisin in his quiet sort of way.

"I didn't know you had a brother called Frankie?"

"Aye. My big brother. Sure it's a surprise to hear from him. Haven't heard a peep out of him for years."

"That's wonderful then... isn't it? You must get lonely for your family sometimes, don't you?"

"Aye. Frankie and I never got on though. Ye would never believe it, Hilda," he said confidentially, "big brother Frankie is here in Kilgoolga!"

"In Kilgoolga?"

"Aye. Staying at the Kilgoolga Arms. Bella's taken him under her wing just like she did with me. She's put in the room at the back. Sure now, isn't that the most crazy thing? Frankie in Kilgoolga. Wants to see me."

"Well, of course he would. You'll have to ask Hans for some time off though. You brother has come such a long way and you'll both want to spend some time together, won't you?"

She smiled in a reassuring sort of way. Oisin nodded.

"Aye. Guess it's not every day ye get a blast from the past, is it now?"

It was not that Oisin didn't want to meet his brother; it was just that Frankie had a way of taking over and making everyone feel useless somehow but that was Frankie and it was doubtful that he would have changed much. *It was a shock though*, Oisin thought. *Frankie here in this outback place when no one had heard from him in years.* The two of them were always at loggerheads and it was no surprise that they hadn't kept in touch. His first thought had been to tell Eleanor. What would she make of this unexpected visitor from the other side of the earth? No doubt she would be charmed by Frankie. His big brother charmed everyone even if he was a priest.

He had arranged to meet Frankie at the ABC Café the next day if Hans would allow it. Oisin had wondered whether it would have been a better arrangement if Frankie and he had met on neutral ground, perhaps at the War Memorial but then he thought better of it. At least in the café there would be people about. The Commercial would have been a possibility too but there were a lot of prying eyes there as well. The Commercial was always busy these days

273

thanks to Eleanor's business prowess. In the end, the ABC was the safest bet and Frankie seemed happy with the idea.

Hans had been surprisingly agreeable to the idea of Oisin taking a day off. So agreeable, in fact that it worried Oisin just a bit. He thought the old farmer was becoming more and more amenable these days and the reasons for this weren't apparent to anyone. In fact, Hans had told Oisin to take Hilda with him into town, saying that the day off would do his sister a lot of good as well.

"The old bugger's mellowin' in his old age", was Charlie George's summation of this new turn of events when Oisin and he had spoken bricfly to each other a few weeks back. It was all a bit mysterious.

In the end, Oisin drove Hilda to town in the Land Rover with Hilda chattering all the way and Oisin as silent as the proverbial church mouse. He had become comfortable at last in his new surroundings so far from anywhere out here in Kilgoolga. Frankie's unexpected arrival was sure to bring on problems. It had always been this way between the two of them. He walked slowly along the footpath underneath the awnings, past Louis's shop and to the ABC Café. Here he waited.

A few people spoke to him briefly and Charlie George stopped in front of him, scratched his head and lit a cigarette.

"G'day, mate," he said. "Hear your brother's in town? Been talkin' to him the other day about you. He's a bonzer bloke, ya brother. We had a great ol' yarn, the two of us, the other day."

This was a surprise. Oisin hadn't thought that Frankie would have met anyone yet but it appeared that most of Kilgoolga seemed to know that Oisin's brother from Ireland was in town and wanted to tell him that they had met him.

"Seems everyone has met me brother," Oisin mumbled. He could feel the resentment rising inside him.

274

Frankie always caused this tension. It didn't help that at that moment Bella appeared and started to gush about how handsome and helpful Oisin's brother was and how it must be great to see him again.

"Your brother's no trouble, Oisin," she continued. She was rather animated. "I says to him that he could stay at the Arms for as long as he likes. He's so obliging and what a man for the story tellin'… why, he had me in stitches the other day with his yarns. Well, must away. Ya comin' in later, Charlie?"

Charlie spat a strand of tobacco onto the footpath and rubbed it in with his foot.

"You bet, Bella ma luvely. Got to have a cool one to quench me thirst in this bloody heat! Be in about five. If Oisin's brother's about, him and me can compare yarns. I've a few meself I can tell, ya know." He winked at Oisin.

That appeared to end the conversation and the two of them wandered off leaving a slightly bemused Oisin standing outside the ABC Café. He didn't know what to make of it all. He took a deep breath and entered the café. It was dark inside after the outside glare but cool. The overhead fans whirred continually and Oisin sat down at one of the tables and waited for Frankie. The waitress saw him and came over to the table. She put a hand on her hip and leaned towards him so that he had a tantalising glimpse of her cleavage. She always did this. It drove the men wild. Oisin reddened.

"Well, Oisin," she whispered, "hear ya big brother's in town. Exciting days for the Kilgoolga girls, don't ya reckon? Two Irish blokes in town!" She laughed.

"I haven't met him yet. Seems everyone else has though!" Oisin replied grumpily. Hadn't Frankie told anyone he was a priest? He glared at the waitress.

"Seems none of ye know that me brother's a priest… probably a bishop by now!"

He thought that would do the trick. Surely that announcement would put an end to all this nonsense about how handsome Frankie was and how he was driving the girls wild. It didn't. The waitress just laughed.

"Well, stone the crows," she said, "he sure don't act like a priest! Why, here he is now... g'day, Frankie, how's it goin'?"

And she beckoned to a tall man who was dressed in a blue and white striped shirt and pale blue jeans to come over to the table. Frankie put out his hand to shake Oisin's. Oisin got rather clumsily to his feet. His brother looked different somehow. Older.

"Hi ya, Frog," said Frankie good naturedly. "Been a long time."

"Don't call me that!" hissed Oisin.

Frankie winked at the waitress who appeared unable to take her eyes off the man in front of her. She giggled.

"He's awful sensitive, my brother. He's lookin' good though, don't ye think? The outback must agree with him, sure."

The waitress looked even more besotted with this stranger from Ireland. She wished there wasn't anyone else in the café and that the two of them could just sit there and talk. He was so good looking. His soft Irish accent just drove her wild. She could have listened to that voice all day. She wondered what it would be like to kiss him.

"What do youse two want anyway? Soup's good today... chicken and mushroom?"

"Sure, that'll do just fine. Two soups. Well, me lad, how are ye?"

"I don't want soup!"

"Oh...!"

"I'll have a bacon and egg roll... and a pot of tea... please."

"Make that another tea for me then and I'll have the soup!" and Frankie grinned at the waitress who giggled again. "Well, brother mine, what have ye been doin' with yerself?"

Frankie leaned back in his chair and studied his younger brother's face. He thought Oisin had changed. The years had matured him. He looked fit and healthy. The life out here must be doing him good somehow.

"This and that," Oisin replied.

He had no intention of telling Frankie what he had been doing. Why, they hadn't seen each other since the day that Frankie went away with the curate to the seminary and all of Ballybeg had come out to see him off. He remembered that day well. He had been so resentful that he had kicked a stone which had hit the train as Frankie and the curate got aboard. What could they possibly have to say to each other after all that time? Although he had to admit to himself that Frankie looked different and Oisin was astute enough to think that perhaps that look wasn't entirely due to the fact that his elder brother had grown older. There was a sprinkling of grey now amongst the black of Frankie's thick curly hair which made him look more good looking and this appeared to make him even more desirable if the behaviour of the waitress was anything to go by. Frankie had always been able to flirt with the women, Oisin concluded sulkily. And he could talk to anyone; that's why everyone had decided he would make such a good priest. He thought he had better find out what his brother was doing in Kilgoolga and then maybe, just maybe, they might have something to say to each other. *They were brothers after all*, he thought.

"Yer the last person I expected to see," he said as a way of starting some semblance of a conversation. "Kilgoolga's not exactly on the beaten track. How did ye find me?"

"Well, mammy is worried about ye. She's frail now and she worries that she doesn't hear much from ye. How about a letter to her occasionally?"

"I write!"

277

"Aye... but I think she wants to see ye again. Ye were always her favourite."

This was a surprise. Oisin had always thought his brother Declan was the apple of his mother's eye and Frankie, too, because he was a priest. He always thought he never sort of fitted in with any of them. He shrugged.

"Thought it was ye... being a priest an' all... an' Declan, of course. I was always left out."

"Well, that's what ye thought. We'll leave it at that. By the way, I'm not a priest anymore."

This was Oisin's second shock in a matter of seconds.

"What do ye mean? Everyone had ye down as a bishop or higher. Da said ye would make Rome!"

Frankie laughed.

"Not an easy decision I can tell ye but the right one. These things happen. A lot of the lads who I met at the seminary have left. I don't want to talk about it. Anyhow, Da was wrong; I'd have never made a bishop let alone Rome. They wouldn't have had me!"

"What have ye been doin' since then?" Oisin couldn't imagine his elder brother not being a priest. It had been pre-ordained by everyone in Ballybeg. His mother must have been devastated. Why hadn't anyone bothered to let him know?

"Teaching. In Dublin. It's a good life. I'm able to get back to Ballybeg a bit more these days, to be sure. It's good to go home to An Teach Ban. Declan's changed the farm, ye know. Da and Uncle Mick wouldn't recognise the old place. There's been a lot of changes since yer been away but there's something about the west, it sort of takes hold of ye. I enjoy walkin' along the strand and seein' the clouds. Ye must miss the soft rain of Ireland?"

"Aye... sometimes. It sure gets hot here. The heat's taken me a bit to get used to and the lack of water. It's a tough place to live, so. Droughts and floods, a never ending battle to survive... that's the outback for ye!"

278

Frankie smiled at his brother.

"Well now," he murmured softly.

The waitress arrived with the soup and the bacon and egg roll. She plonked them down on the table and returned a few seconds later with the teapot and cups. She spent a few seconds longer than was necessary arranging the cutlery in front of Frankie. He didn't seem the least bit embarrassed when she leaned towards him in her provocative way. *The old Frankie would have blushed,* Oisin thought, *this new one looks pleased with himself and irritatingly comfortable.* He felt himself getting resentful again. He took a bite out of his bacon and egg roll.

"Have ye heard from Mary?" he said between chewing. He thought he may as well find out about all his siblings while Frankie was here. Oisin and Mary had been friends.

"Aye. She's in Dublin. I see her sometimes. She's making quite a name for herself as an artist. Don't understand her work though. Bit experimental for me but she's selling well. She never goes home. Quite the city lass is our Mary. She's living with a gallery owner, ye know?"

"No, I didn't know."

It didn't surprise Oisin that Mary had made her own life. She always got what she wanted. It didn't surprise him that she was living with a gallery owner either. If Mary thought it would advance her career, she would do this.

"Well, that's the family all sorted, Frankie," he said. "What are yer plans... now yer here in Kilgoolga?"

"Thought I'd stay for a bit. Keep an eye on ye. People are friendly."

"Ye'll get bored. Not much happens."

And Oisin thought of Eleanor and Louis. Everything happened when he and the two of them got together but he had no intention of introducing his brother to Eleanor. Their relationship was a private affair between the two of them. Not even Hans or Hilda had any inkling of it. But Frankie

279

wasn't convinced. He rather liked Kilgoolga and it was fun to see his young brother squirm at the thought of his staying on. He grinned.

"Sure, by the look of ye there's something in the air round here that's doin' ye good. Think I'll stay on for a bit," and he took a spoonful of his soup.

In Sydney over the summer holidays, Claire Paterson marched with the anti-war protestors, attending meetings, stuffed leaflets into letterboxes and had been propositioned by an American soldier as she sat on a park bench in Hyde Park looking at the fountain. The soldier was on R and R from Vietnam, high on something and high on testosterone. He had been drafted in to fight and he hated it. A country boy from Iowa he couldn't understand any of it. Claire agreed with him on the matter of the war but on the other matter of sex with a stranger, she was as prim as she could be. So in the end, the soldier wandered off and left Claire sitting on the bench thinking about her future and the whole sorry mess of living through a war, a war that was being fought so far away and therefore invisible. She felt sorry for the soldier. He was just a boy, like her brother, Harry, in the Army now too and far from home. She hated the thought of Harry being called up to fight in this stupid war. Harry was such an idiot sometimes. He would probably volunteer to go to Vietnam just to be a hero. She wondered what he would make of it if he knew she had marched the other day against the war. He probably wouldn't understand any of it, just like the young American soldier from Iowa. Claire felt the weight of the world's problems on her shoulders. She was a Maths teacher, after all, not a politician. No one was asking her to

280

save the world all by herself. She had come to Sydney to do something about it but being here, in the city, had done something to her as well. There are moments when an idea comes out of nowhere and the sudden decisions which are made then in a split second can change a person's life forever. Claire had one of those moments that hot summer day. She glimpsed her future life in a sudden tantalising moment of self-awareness and when she rose from the park bench, she knew what she had to do.

A few weeks later she was back at the Kilgoolga High School and the safe predictability of her daily routine was established once again. But Claire was a changed person. She had hardened. When she walked in to the ABC Café that early afternoon the last person she expected to see was the person she had spent the last few weeks trying not to think about. There he was sitting at a table with a stranger. Claire had decided on a few things and Oisin Kelly was one of those things. She didn't hesitate but walked over to the table where Oisin was sitting and stood in front of him and stood in such a way that he had to speak to her. She came straight to the point.

"Oisin," she said, "are you going to introduce me?"

She looked Frankie in the eye as she spoke. Oisin was caught unawares. The last person he had expected to meet in the ABC Café, too, was Claire Paterson and a Claire Paterson who had the look of someone who knew what she wanted and was determined to get it. He spluttered. He felt as trapped as a schoolboy caught smoking a cigarette at the back of the bike shed.

"Oh, hiya Claire, didn't expect to see ye in here… this's my brother, Frankie, he's staying a few days… all the way from Ireland!"

Claire sat down and she smiled at Frankie. Oisin noticed that the red flush had appeared on her neck but that was the only slight sign of unease. Frankie, for his part was delighted with this attractive intruder. He grinned.

281

"Well, seems my young brother's been keepin' a few things hidden! Pleased to meet ye," he said.

Claire blushed slightly but she wasn't put off. She thought Frankie was one of the most handsome men she had ever set her eyes on.

"Ye've been hiding yerself away too, Claire," Oisin broke in.

They glowered at each other.

"School holidays. I'm back now." She turned to Frankie. "Have you been in Kilgoolga long?" she asked politely.

"A few days. Came out here to see what this young rascal's been doin' with himself. Think he needs to come home."

"To Ireland?"

"Aye."

Claire looked at Oisin. He was furious, she could see that.

"Are you going back... to Ireland, that is?" she asked Oisin.

He didn't answer but glared at Frankie who seemed completely oblivious to the tension his remark had caused.

"What are the sights I must see in Kilgoolga, then?" Frankie looked at Claire as he spoke.

"There's not much! You're in the outback here. There's more in Kilgoolga than Milberra, by the way... that's the next place, hardly a town, is it Oisin? And then after Milberra, there's nothing for miles!"

"Maybe you could give me a tour?"

The red flush appeared on Claire's neck.

"Well," she replied, not looking at Oisin, "perhaps. As I said there's not much to see but there's a few places, I guess."

"Grand. Let's make a time. Are you coming, Frog?"

"Frog?" asked Claire.

"Don't call me that! No, I'm working. I have a job."

282

"Well, then it's just ye and me, by the sound of it, Claire. Ye make a time an' I'll be there!" said Frankie with a grin.

"Where are you staying?"

"The Kilgoolga Arms Hotel."

"You'll have met Bella, then?" asked Claire to make conversation.

"Aye. I think I may know everyone in Kilgoolga by now!"

"Or if you don't, everyone will know you! Bella will see to that."

Frankie and Claire laughed. Oisin glared at them.

"I've noticed," said Frankie. "What time suits ye then, Claire... for the grand tour, that is?"

"Afternoons are best. After four. I teach at the High School."

"Well, then, tomorrow afternoon? I'll wander along to the school if ye like."

"No need for that. There's a bench at the War Memorial. I'll meet you there."

This was too much for Oisin. He stood up and as he did, he knocked his half empty cup of tea. The contents spilled into the saucer and on the tablecloth.

"I'll have to go," he said. "I've Hilda to meet!!"

It didn't help Oisin's mood when he scrambled into the driver's seat of the Land Rover beside Hilda. She was looking extremely pleased with herself and she couldn't wait to tell Oisin the news. As they drove out of town towards Wiesental, she remarked,

"Jack's sister told me she's met your brother, Oisin... the other day at the Post Office. 'A lovely boy', she said. 'So polite'. We'll have to get him out for a meal, won't we? You'd like that, wouldn't you? I'll make sure Hans behaves himself. We'll be alright as long as religion or them Commies don't come up in the conversation! I'm sure your brother wouldn't say anything about either subject. 'Such a nice young man and full of the Irish wit,' Jack's sister said that too. You must be very proud of him!"

Oisin crunched the gears into top and put his foot down hard on the accelerator. The Land Rover spluttered slightly and picked up speed. And Oisin didn't say a word.

Oisin didn't see or hear from either Frankie or Claire for a week. In that time, he brooded. He couldn't wait to see Eleanor Bradshaw again. Maybe she would be able to explain to him why he always got on the wrong side of Frankie and why they were always seemed to argue. *It has to be something more than sibling rivalry*, he thought. He was annoyed at Claire too. For all her primness, she had drooled over Frankie and Frankie had responded in his usual irritatingly way. It all seemed most unfair. He decided that if he spoke to Eleanor she might be able to help. So far, everything she had done with him had proved a success. He hardly ever thought of Cecy these days, for instance. Cecy had become a distant memory and if she ever came into his mind, he remembered all the good times they had enjoyed together. The hurt seemed to have disappeared. This new way of thinking had all to do with Eleanor. She could explain things to him which made sense. When he was in her company he felt safe. It was a peculiar sort of feeling. Eleanor Bradshaw just did that to people and Oisin was glad he was one of her selected people. She had told him that and he believed her. Maybe they had been lovers in another life, who knows? But in this life, she was proving to be an ally and a dear friend, despite their age difference.

It didn't even matter anymore to Oisin if Louis was there. In fact, it was fun sometimes when the Frenchman joined them. He made everyone laugh and laughter was something that Oisin didn't hear much of these days living as he was with Hans and Hilda in their crazy isolated world. And then he thought of Claire again and got as mad as hell. She was a teacher after all and Frankie was one now apparently. They would have a lot in common. What could she possibly see in Oisin anyway? He was hiding himself away out here in the remote place that was Kilgoolga and living with Hans and Hilda was making him even more inaccessible. His only change of scene was when he was with Eleanor at Bellington Hill station or when he drove into Kilgoolga with Hilda for the weekly or fortnightly shop. He hardly saw Hefty and Matt these days and never went to *The Drovers* anymore. He had even stopped going to church as much with Hans and Hilda. This had proved a bit problematic at first and he had been nervous bringing up the subject to Hans but in the end, Hans didn't seem to be over bothered which rather surprised Oisin who had thought that this was an essential part of his employment. Hans was certainly becoming more amenable. That had to be a good thing at least.

Seeing Claire again had surprised him and he realised how much he had missed her. But then Frankie had taken over as usual. Claire was clever. Frankie was clever. It seemed more than probable that they would get together. *That was the logic of it all*, thought Oisin. However, it didn't make it any easier for him, thinking of them together. Frankie always got his way and if his brother set his eye on Claire, he would win her, ex-priest or not and with this thought in his head, Oisin got even angrier. Surely if he spoke about all this to Eleanor, she would help him. She had said she would and this is what he made up his mind to do next time they met. She had wanted to know about Hans. Well, Hans could wait. This business with Frankie was more important, he decided.

He met Eleanor at the Commercial in their usual place. For once, Louis wasn't there and Oisin was pleased to have Eleanor all to himself. They were sitting on the balcony overlooking the barbeque area when he brought up the subject of Frankie.

"My brother's here in Kilgoolga. Bit of a surprise to be sure. I haven't seen him in years."

"That's your brother, Frankie," replied Eleanor.

"Aye. How did ye know?" Everyone seemed to know about Frankie. He could feel the anger rising once again.

"It's a small place and a stranger in town stands out."

Eleanor laughed. She could see his discomfort and his jealousy too.

"Do you like him being here?" she asked.

"No. I haven't seen him for years and he turns up, out of the blue and unsettles things like he always does."

"You're annoyed at him?"

"Aye. It was good to see him, I suppose... at first that is. He had a few surprises for me though."

"Such as?"

"Well, he's my eldest brother and I was just ten or so when he went away. He went off to be a priest, ye know. All of Ballybeg came out to see him off. Everyone expected great things of Frankie. Well, guess what? He's left the priesthood and now he's a teacher. Didn't tell me why he left but no one else did, for that matter. My family, that is, none of them bothered to let me know."

"Looks like I'd like to have a long talk to your brother, Frankie."

"Don't know how long he's stayin'," Oisin replied grumpily.

"Well, we'll have a meal together, the three of us, downstairs. I'll ask Louis to come along. He sees things sometimes I can miss!"

This was a surprise. Oisin assumed that Eleanor was almost omnipotent, at least that's the way she liked to appear. He frowned.

"I'm not sure... "

"About Louis?"

"No. Don't know about Frankie though... "

He didn't want Frankie to take over. Frankie was sure to impress Eleanor. He wasn't sure he wanted that. *I'd much rather keep Eleanor a secret and keep the two of them apart,* he thought but she was insistent.

"That's decided then," she said. "Next Sunday. Twelve o'clock. Downstairs."

He wanted to argue but he never could with Eleanor. If he tried to change her mind it always proved futile. Most times he went along with it but occasionally he sulked if she requested something of him that he felt unable to do. This was one such occasion. He tried again to change her mind.

"I don't know what Frankie's doing on Sunday," he said, "or even if he'll be in Kilgoolga. He said he wanted to see the sights." He thought of Claire.

"Oh, he'll be here," Eleanor replied in her all knowing way. "I spoke to him the other day!"

"What?"

"I told you Kilgoolga's a small town. He came into the Commercial and I happened to be there. I introduced myself to him. I said I knew you. Then he told me he was your brother. It was easy after that. There's not many Irishmen turn up here after all."

Oisin suddenly felt very angry. For the first time since they had met, he was annoyed at Eleanor.

"You must remember that Kilgoolga's a small place and I'm always kept informed about what's going on. I own the Kilgoolga Arms too and most of the shops along the Main street to the Commercial. Surely you know that?" Eleanor asked. For all her astuteness she didn't seem in the least bothered about Oisin's discomfort.

287

"Aye, I knew that but I don't like to pry. Well, then if ye have already met Frankie, what do ye think of my brother?"

"He's an interesting man. I'm looking forward to discussing a few things on Sunday. Twelve o'clock. You be there!"

So it was decided and poor Oisin felt a bit like an unfortunate pawn in a game of chess, the result of which had been already decided.

On Sunday he arrived on time at the Commercial. Earlier in the day, he had attended the church service with Hans and Hilda and given his apologies once again because he couldn't stay for the midday meal. Hans didn't say a word to him but Hilda was pleased that the three of them had at least been to the church together. She liked it when Oisin came along. It was even better when he was able to dine with them for Sunday lunch. It felt like a family having Oisin there. When it was just she and her brother together at mealtimes, the silence between them could be deadly.

Oisin entered the Commercial and it was already busy. Ever since the opening night, people packed into the hotel and often the rooms upstairs were full of guests. He nodded to a few people he recognised and looked around for Eleanor. He hadn't seen Frankie all week and he didn't know if the drive with Claire to see the sights had taken place. He tried not to think about it. He had hoped that Claire was perhaps different but it looked like she was just the same as all the rest of the women he had known and, as far as she and Frankie were concerned, she would prefer to be with Frankie rather than Oisin. He felt a bit sorry for himself. He

288

had tried so hard to distance himself from his past life but now it appeared some of that hurt had come back to haunt him and in a way he could never have imagined.

Sitting at a table in the corner of the large dining room, he saw Eleanor, Louis and Frankie. It seemed as if they had been there for a while as the bottle of Burgundy on the table was half empty. Eleanor appeared to be in high spirits and all three looked as if they were getting along just fine. Oisin felt a bit of an intruder. All his old insecurities had suddenly reappeared in him and they were like so many dark phantoms haunting him still. The table had been set for four but the food had not yet arrived. He sat down beside Louis. Eleanor was in the middle of talking to Frankie and she didn't acknowledge him. This made him feel even more miserable. Eleanor and Frankie were having an interesting discussion about the afterlife. *Quite deep for a Sunday afternoon*, thought Oisin. But Eleanor was like that. You never knew what she would be on about next. He tried to follow the thread of the argument.

"I think the reason why you have such doubts about the transmigration of souls, Frankie, is because of your earlier indoctrinations from the Catholic church.You'll need to examine the whole problem with a dispassionate eye and not allow yourself to be clouded by dogma of any kind. Then you'll be able to think about the subject more on a subjective level. You'll have to agree with me that it is indeed possible, even probable. Why could it not be so? You've a great intellectual understanding I knew that from the moment we met. But you also have a mind that reasons first and this is where your difficulties lie. Everything you see is in black and white; it's the sign of an analytical mind. I'm right, aren't I? I am puzzled though. Why did you decide to be a priest?"

Eleanor refilled Frankie's glass with wine and pushed the bottle towards Oisin who emptied the bottle into his own glass and then he looked at Frankie. His brother frowned slightly. Everyone waited for Frankie's answer.

"It was certainly a decision that I didn't take lightly, both entering the priesthood and leaving it, ye are right there."

"Ah, I know I'm right. But you haven't told me why you entered the priesthood in the first place. I can see why you left. As I said before, you have an analytical mind. I can see that you agree with me on this. It would have been impossible for you to settle to the confines of a doctrinal approach to all things and follow that dogma slavishly. It must have been difficult for you at times," Eleanor said in her omnipotent way. Oisin suddenly felt inadequate. But he wanted to hear what Frankie had to say. It was a mystery to him that Frankie had become a priest and an even greater mystery that his brother had left. Louis, for his part, sat back in the chair and looked at Eleanor in much the way that an adoring dog views its master. It was evident that Louis thought Eleanor could do no wrong. Frankie was very quiet. He, too, appeared to be under Eleanor's spell. The conversation had taken an interesting turn.

It was Louis who spoke first. He had spent most of the time sitting back in his chair and drinking the wine.

"Surely it is the duty of a priest to give succour to his flock, Monsieur. There must have been some souls you helped," said Louis and as he spoke he tapped the index finger of his left hand on the edge of the table as if to add emphasis to his words.

"Aye," replied Frankie thoughtfully, "There were a few I helped, I guess and there was an old man once. He said I'd given him hope but I doubt that I did. I was at that place in my life when the doubts were gaining ground in me. I still think of the old man though. He was rather special."

"Do you think you will face judgement, Monsieur? For your decision?"

"That's in God's hands. I still believe in a higher power, ye know."

Frankie turned to Eleanor.

290

"Ye want to know why I became a priest," he said thoughtfully. "I got caught up with the whole idea of it. Somehow, it seemed the right thing to do at the time and it made my mother proud, didn't it, Oisin?"

Oisin, watching his brother closely, noticed a sadness come over his face that he would never have believed could happen to Frankie. He wanted to ask his brother what being a priest had been like and why it all went wrong. He suddenly felt a stab of guilt for all his thoughts about Frankie who mightn't be as sure of himself as he liked to portray.

"How long did it take ye... to decide ye weren't cut out for the job?" Oisin asked. He felt his brother owed him some explanation and it was as good a time as it could be to ask the question surrounded by these people. Frankie smiled.

"Ah, brother mine," he said, "ye were always the one to ask the questions, weren't ye, now? A long time is your answer. These aren't decisions made in the spur of the moment like ye would buy a new hat!"

Everyone laughed even Oisin. So his brother had suffered too in his own way. This was quite a surprise. He had always assumed that Frankie was somehow immune to problems that beset other folk.

At that point the waiter appeared to take the order. He was on his best behaviour because of Eleanor and deferred to her at every opportunity. She was in her element and gaily ordered T-bone steaks from the barbeque accompanied by baked potatoes and a green salad for everyone. Neither Louis nor Frankie seemed in the least put out that she had made this decision without consulting either of them. Oisin, for his part had got used to Eleanor making decisions for him. He knew that the food would be delicious if she had anything to do with it. If Eleanor decided to order steaks, then the steaks would be the best thing on the menu. She would have informed the chef that she and her guests were in the dining room. Everything would be done right so Oisin settled back. He was the observer once again.

"So your decision to leave the priesthood did take a long time for you, Monsieur? In many ways, I think to hear this I am pleased. It would not be right to hasten such a decision," said Louis.

The Frenchman took a sip of wine from his glass. In everything he did, he was precise. Frankie nodded his head.

"Aye. I can't remember the exact moment when the doubts overcome the faith. All I know is that when there were more doubts it was time for me to go."

Frankie said quietly. He looked at Eleanor as he spoke.

"Maybe the transmigration of souls ye talk about came from my Uncle Mick. I might have gained part of his soul? Maybe it was Mick who somehow brought me to reconsider my faith."

"This Uncle Mick of yours must have had a significant impact on your life, Frankie. I would have liked to meet him," replied Eleanor.

Frankie nodded. Eleanor was right once again. His Uncle Mick had been an important person in his childhood. He turned to Oisin.

"What do ye think, Oisin? About our Uncle Mick, that is? Have ye any memory of Father O'Malley and the night he tried to save our uncle's soul? Quite a night, wasn't it?"

Oisin didn't answer. He did remember that night. He had a flash of recall and saw himself clinging to his uncle's leg for he had witnessed the fury of the priest and it was frightening. All the family had been frightened, everyone but Mick. This was the only memory he had of that night, the fear of the priest and the look in his uncle's eyes. It was something that the family never forgot and none of them spoke about it much after that night. His mother had been distraught but then she had loved Mick.

"Aye, I remember," he answered quietly.

Eleanor turned to look at Oisin. When she looked at him, he often thought her eyes could see right into his very being and here they would discover all the hidden parts of it there. Those parts that were best kept hidden. She could be the most unsettling of women sometimes and the most fascinating at other times. He was surprised that Frankie seemed to appear so comfortable in her presence. He hadn't known how his brother would react to this intriguing stranger but it looked like they were getting along quite well, at least on an intellectual level. *Eleanor could always be relied upon to strip you bare, at least psychologically,* he thought. It looked as if Frankie was receiving the treatment and even to be enjoying the experience for his brother beckoned the waiter to bring another bottle of Burgundy to their table. It occurred to Oisin that maybe Frankie had been starved of any intellectual stimulus over the years. The years as a priest may have been lonely ones.

"Ye have some interesting ideas," Frankie remarked to Eleanor when the bottle of wine arrived. "Do ye think it's at all possible that we are connected somehow in some gigantic loop and we are joined together in life and in death? Our souls are eternal? That we just keep on recycling ourselves somehow. Do ye think that is how it happens and God is the glue that keeps it all together... the recycling, that is?"

"I'm sure of it. Souls split in the infinite. I know part of my soul is joined to my ancestor, Lord Cyril Bradshaw. I've spoken about Cyril to you, haven't I, Oisin?" replied Eleanor and she stared at Oisin without blinking an eyelid. He didn't reply. Instead, he had a picture of the much discussed Lord Bradshaw in the photograph above the sideboard in Eleanor's apartment and wondered if this man had really been all that his descendent assumed him to be.

How could she be so certain of this man's character from so long a space in time but then, maybe Eleanor was right? She may be part of her distant ancestor and therefore would know him better than anyone else.

"Lord Bradshaw?" asked Frankie, puzzled.

"Yes, Frankie, Lord Bradshaw," replied Eleanor with some animation. Whenever the opportunity to talk about Cyril came up, her enthusiasm was evident to anyone who cared to listen.

"His story is an inspiration to us all. I do believe that he must have been as an advanced and enlightened soul as I am. Do you know that he brought a team of men and bullock drays from Sydney right through the bush to Kilgoolga? In those days, there weren't many roads and the aborigines were hostile in some places. Legend has it they threw spears at them. When he finally got to Kilgoolga, it was a matter of felling the trees and trying to survive but then that's where all that breeding came in. He was a natural leader of men. Kilgoolga owes its existence to him. I'll show you photographs one day, if you are here for awhile, that is? Oisin found them interesting, didn't you, Oisin?"

Oisin nodded. He wasn't sure if he found the photograph of Lord Bradshaw interesting. In fact, quite the contrary. The eyes worried him still.

"Did you know that Lord Bradshaw was the first white man to set up camp in Kilgoolga, Frankie? He claimed the land as his and named Bellington Hill station after his ancestral home back in England. I managed to visit it and you wouldn't believe it but some of his descendants are still living in the original mansion! Can you imagine it? They could trace the Bradshaw family tree back to the twelfth century. This is what we lack here in Australia, all that history. They were the most charming people and I must say they made me very welcome. They couldn't do enough for me. I really wondered whether it would be better that I stayed in England as I felt so much at home there but I had

294

to come back to Kilgoolga. Joseph was getting himself into a real mess and I was needed. But I would have liked to spend longer in England. The English countryside is very beautiful, so very different from here. All that green everywhere but of course you boys know all about that, don't you?" she tittered and then continued her story. "Cyril's highly regarded over there. Books have been written about him."

"He does sound interesting," murmured Frankie. *Eleanor's fascination for her ancestor was puzzling,* he thought and he glanced at Oisin. It was a slightly amused look but then, that was Frankie. He could be relied upon to see many sides of the same coin. *Maybe he hadn't been such a bad priest after all*, thought Oisin, *even with his analytical mind.*

"There's some people who are remembered long after they're dead and gone and I fully believe that Cyril is one of these. Of course, I'm the only one in my family who thinks about him like this. My brother says I'm delusional and he thinks that I give our dead ancestor too much attention and this worries him. It's extremely foolish, he's always telling me, but then my brother has a lot to answer for... in my opinion. It's best he sticks to his sheep and doesn't venture into any deep thinking especially if it's philosophical or intellectual, I've told him that many times. My brother is an intellectual dimwit! I'm sure Lord Bradshaw would have agreed with me about Joseph. My soul and Cyril's are bound together, you see. In fact, I sometimes think I hear Cyril's voice speaking to me when I talk about these things, guiding me somehow. I doubt whether he would have liked Joseph much either. At times I often wonder if Joseph is actually my brother, we are so different!!"

She was wearing a pearl necklace and as she spoke, she fingered the pearls. The pearls, too, probably had some significance in Eleanor's eyes. This was her way. Everything she said and everything she did had a message or a symbol.

"But what of evil?" Oisin suddenly blurted in and everyone looked at him. "What about the people who commit the deadliest of sins, do their wicked souls get recycled? Or do they face punishment? Isn't that's what Hell is for?"

"There is no escape for them," replied Eleanor. "Evil can return but sometimes in other lives there is a cleansing but it can often take many recycling lives before that happens."

Oisin wasn't convinced. Given his present state of mind, he would have liked to see some punishment after evil deeds.

"And what about those people who appear to be 'holier than thou' and yet hide deadly and horrible secrets within themselves?" he asked.

"I said there's no escape for them either. That's what God is. He can see into every heart," whispered Eleanor.

"Then what about this war then?" Oisin wanted an answer. He was getting tired of Eleanor's riddles. He wanted to hear something concrete, not words, the meaning of which could not be understood. "What about the politicians who start the wars and get people killed, and for what? It's all very well for them, isn't it? They sit in their comfortable offices and never have to go near any of it. They have a lot to answer for. And another thing, this war they're fighting now in Vietnam for an ideology. How do ye justify that?"

"Oui, Monsieur we all of us like to 'ope that there comes a day of reckoning," murmured Louis. "I do understand what you mean, Oisin, mon ami. War is hell and this war is one of the worst. My countrymen leave many problems in that poor land.I am, how you say, not proud of my colonial French ancestors and what they have done to that part of the world. It is easy to feel superior when an army marches in and says, 'I want this land! It is mine; it does not belong to you!' " He gestured with his hands and then he pointed his index finger towards Eleanor.

296

"You talk about wicked souls. What about the wicked souls of the politicians or the kings or the queens, Eleanor? And then there are the dictators. We suffered in France because of a mad dictator just a few years ago. Did we not? Tell me, what about them? These men rule a country and tell everyone that their way is the right way and then the people begin to hate those people who were once their friends because of what the dictator says. It is these evil people who cause all the wars not the ordinary man in the street. I do not think anyone really wants to kill another human being but when they are ordered to do so, they do it. This is the result when the evil souls make the wars. I speak the truth, do I not? What a sad history of mankind!" he shrugged his shoulders in the manner of a Frenchman. For all his peculiarities, Louis Bercault was a kind man and he hated the thought of anything cruel.

"Of course you are right, Louis. There's a lot we don't understand. War is another matter entirely... " murmured Eleanor.

"And it is written in the Bible that 'Thou shalt not kill'. Is that not one of the Ten Commandments we are meant to live by?" Louis added.

Frankie had been listening closely to what the Frenchman had to say.

"You're right about war, Louis. I don't know whether it's ever justified. We always pray for peace. But these evil people ye talk about, Louis, do they reap what they sow after all? I believe that God can see into every heart just as ye said, Eleanor, and it's not for any of us to judge. And if, what ye say is true about the transmigration of souls, souls that split in infinity, it's likely that there is a judgement day after all and that the good will always prevail over the evil even if it is not seen by any of us in our lifetime, more's the pity!"

"I see that we agree about many things, Monsieur Frankie. You speak as a priest does. This gives to me the hope. Perhaps there is a justice in the world after all and

297

who knows there is a God. What do you think, Oisin? This talk, it has made you have the hunger?"

"I'm thinking, Louis. I'm thinking," Oisin said softly. "Perhaps..."

"Let's leave all this talk till later, Oisin," Eleanor interrupted him somewhat rudely for at that moment, she saw steaks the size of dinner plates coming towards her. She clapped her hands. The waiter carefully positioned the plate in front of her and stood back while a waitress brought the rest of the food to the table. Without waiting for anyone else to start eating, Eleanor attacked the steak in the manner of someone who hadn't eaten for days. Oisin had observed that sometimes she was like an excited child and would delight in the unexpected especially if the unexpected had to do with food. There were some people who considered her a glutton. On many occasions, she had taken food from another's plate and shovelled it onto her own. She never thought this behaviour was at all unusual. In fact, she couldn't bear to see food wasted and would eat and eat until there wasn't a scrap of food left on her plate.

With the three men she was the centre of attention and for Eleanor this was what she was born for. So skilfully had she steered the debate to questions beyond the everyday that the men listened without interrupting her. She liked to portray herself as a mystic. When she spoke of that unknown world she assumed the mantle of a woman with mysterious powers and when she spoke, her words contained wisdom beyond the understanding of her acolytes for it was these people who listened the most to what she had to say. Over the years, there had been many men and women who had fallen under the spell of her powerful personality and the three men who listened so attentively to her at the Commercial were just three of many. This was an art that Eleanor had carefully cultivated from an early age believing as she still did, that the name of Bradshaw gave her certain rights and responsibilities and she was the proud bearer of that name. It was no accident that she used her name to add credibility to some of her more outlandish views. The fact that she was a Bradshaw and her belief that this was an ancient and venerated name, all thanks to the one and only Lord Cyril, meant that she refused to believe that anyone could possibly disagree with her. In that unseen world that she liked to talk about so much there was no room for either argument or scepticism. It was easy for her then to dismiss as misinformed all those so called unenlightened souls who found her ideas strange and challenged her version of 'The Truth'. In that way, she was able to continue to exert an almost hypnotic control over the ones who held onto her every word, her followers. It was no accident that those who were led to believe that she had a greater knowledge than anyone else were called 'enlightened' by Eleanor Bradshaw. It was an easy matter for her then to malign and find fault with all those others who did not agree with her including her own brother, Joseph. She had occasionally mused on the possibility that Joseph was not even a Bradshaw but an adopted orphan whom her parents had felt sorry for. No credence was put on this supposition by anyone else for Joseph's appearance and manner indicated that he was a true Bradshaw, the spitting image of his father. It was more probable that Eleanor would have liked to be the most important member of her clan, past and present, a worthy descendent of Lord Cyril and having Joseph around rather spoilt that.

When the meal was finished and the empty plates cleared away by the attentive waiter, Eleanor got up from the table. Four bottles of Burgundy had been drunk and she was feeling a little light headed but she was still very much in charge of the group and it was her hotel. In the manner of a matriarch she led the three men towards the entrance to the hotel and, just as she got to the door, she ran her fingers along the wooden rail which acted as a decorative feature in the dining room, and here she discovered dust. This discovery annoyed her. She expected perfection in her hotel. This was a fact. She, Eleanor Bradshaw had refurbished the Commercial and saved it from its ruined fate and everyone in Kilgoolga should be grateful. However, this gratitude had to be visible and the sight of dust could not be tolerated. She beckoned the waiter and told him by gestures and words that much more attention had to be given to cleanliness and she expected the matter to be rectified immediately. By the time Eleanor's little group got to the door; Oisin noticed that one of the girls was busy wiping a rag along the offending rail and trying not to smile.

Outside it was slightly cooler for they had spent a long time over their meal and it was already four o'clock in the afternoon. Louis got ready to leave. He kissed Eleanor's hand and murmured something in French that Oisin didn't understand. Eleanor was flirtatious and it looked as if their goodbyes might take longer than was usual. Oisin and Frankie stood a little apart. The sight of the younger man and the older woman in such an intimate display of affection in a public place was awkward but then most of Kilgoolga must know by now of their relationship. Eleanor cultivated lovers and Louis was happy to oblige. Frankie coughed slightly to draw attention away from the unlikely couple.

"I think I'll go for a walk along the river," he announced. He wanted to be alone. Oisin could see that. *Probably the result of the discussion over the meal*, Oisin thought. Frankie had said things there that the younger Frankie would never have even questioned before. He would have liked to know what his brother was thinking about. Eleanor had made quite an impression on his brother, he was sure of that. He watched Frankie walk slowly along the main street to the corner of Bradshaw Avenue and then turn right towards the War Memorial. His brother didn't look back.

Louis, seeing Frankie leave, set off towards his shop in the main street. Unlike Frankie, he walked briskly with

300

his head held high as though he was prancing along a busy street in Paris leaving Oisin and Eleanor to stand on the footpath in front of the Commercial. He wondered what Claire would make of it if she happened to see him and Eleanor together outside the hotel and if it would even matter to her in the slightest. A man and a woman came out of the hotel and said 'G'day' to Eleanor. Oisin didn't recognise either of them but standing there under the afternoon sun, he began to feel as if many eyes were studying him and making a judgement. This was the first time he had been seen so publicly with Eleanor Bradshaw.

"Come with me," ordered Eleanor as if she read his thoughts.

She led Oisin towards the back entrance to her apartment and he followed her. He looked to the left and right but there was no one about. They climbed the stairs to her balcony and she slid the glass door open.

Oisin relaxed. He sunk into the canvas chair on the balcony and shut his eyes. Below he could hear the murmur of voices and the clatter of plates. The staff were cleaning up after the Sunday lunch and getting things ready for the evening meal. He could feel his head spin slightly from the effects of the Burgundy. The thoughts which ran like wildfire through his brain seemed to jostle one on top of one another and refuse to leave him. He had so many questions he should ask Eleanor for he had abandoned any thought that there could ever be any other person likely to come into his life who would have the knowledge or the wisdom that this enigmatic woman possessed. He felt that he could sit and listen to her forever.

When Eleanor brought the silver tray with the coffee and two mugs and laid the percolator onto the mosaic top of the small table, he opened his eyes. She smiled at him and it was that sort of smile meant for just the two of them. This pleased him.

301

"What do ye think of my brother?" he asked when the coffee had been poured for he was sure she would have the right answer to any question he might ask and Frankie had been his nemesis for as long as he could remember.

"Ah, he's very handsome!"

"Well, sure ye have to be right there. But what do ye make of him? Really?"

"You're a lot like him."

"Me? Yer joking! He's handsome an' clever and all the things I'm not!"

"Sounds like you're just a bit jealous of him?"

She took a sip of her coffee. It was still hot and she laid the mug back on the table and looked at Oisin. He frowned slightly.

"Well, he's always got exactly what he wants. That's what annoys me about Frankie. I sure was surprised him findin' me out here. I'd never have thought he'd even bother about me let alone track me down to Kilgoolga!"

He suddenly remembered what Eleanor had said to him, just a few moments before.

"What did ye mean? Him bein' like me? No one's ever said that to me before."

"An observation. He likes you."

"What?"

"You heard."

It was quiet downstairs and the staff had evidently finished what they were doing in the barbeque area. Soon everything would be noisy again as people arrived for their evening meal. The Commercial was proving to be popular in the district and its success story was just beginning, all thanks to Eleanor Bradshaw.

"Frankie's changed a bit, I guess. Ye know all the family and that includes me thought he'd end up the greatest priest ever. Even become a bishop or a cardinal. Certainly get to Rome like Da said. We all know Frankie's clever enough! Surprised he left. That might have changed him. What do ye think?"

"Yes. He did go through a dark night of the soul. Try to be more compassionate. It wasn't an easy decision for him."

Oisin felt his cheeks redden. It was a slight reprimand and he didn't like it. Seems that Eleanor, too, preferred Frankie.

"He wants me to go back to Ireland, to Ballybeg." he said sulkily.

"You have to go."

"I'm not sure that I do. There's nothing for me there except the view!"

She laughed.

"And what's here for you? The dust, the flies... me?"

"All three," he answered seriously.

"Well, we'll see! You can only stay hidden for so long, Oisin. People can find you even out here. Frankie proved that to you, didn't he?"

"Aye, I suppose yer right as usual. Maybe I'm jealous of him like ye said. Just that he always gets his way!"

"Is there anything else you want to tell me?"

He wondered whether he should mention Claire Paterson and the fear he had that Frankie might take her away from him. He felt angry just thinking about it. After all, it was a stupid thought. Claire probably didn't want him anyway.

"No, there's nothing else," he replied quickly.

In the western sky, the sun was sinking behind strands of thin red and yellow clouds and soon it would be the night again. The sunsets in the Kilgoolga sky were dramatic and memorable. Sometimes he watched the sun go down and thought perhaps there might be a God after all for no artist's palette in the world would ever be able to compete with the colours Nature could display. The natural world was truly a miracle. He loved to see the sun set in Kilgoolga although he rarely saw it rise. He often recalled the sunsets over the strand at An Teach Ban. The sky was softer there. Here the light was so intense that sometimes when the sun set, its glow turned half the western sky a vibrant red. The end of the day was defined just as everything was in this vast country by the light and the dark. He had known the soft light of northern skies. Often the glare that rose from the ground in this southern land almost blinded him. He watched the sun drop like a round red stone behind the faraway horizon and then he got up to leave. In just a few moments, all would be dark.

"There is something, Eleanor," he said. "Aye, there is something, right enough."

She stood up and faced him across the coffee table.

"What is it?" she asked gently.

"There's no need to fear death, is there now?"

He thought of the afternoon and what had been said then. It seemed as if all that had happened a very long time ago. Eleanor Bradshaw smiled.

"No," she said. "Only not living."

CHAPTER FOURTEEN

The next time Eleanor saw Oisin, she wanted to discuss Frankie. It was becoming obvious to Oisin that she thought Frankie was somebody who she could have deep and meaningful discussions with and given time, she might even be able to bring him around to her way of thinking. Oisin, for his part, was rather sceptical that this could happen. Frankie had always held rather dogmatic opinions and even if he had changed somewhat over the years, Oisin was certain that the old Frankie was still there and just as unbending as always. If the truth be known, he was just a little bit jealous of the attention that was now being bestowed onto his older brother by Eleanor. Oisin was blissfully unaware of the influence that Eleanor had already made upon him. To him, Eleanor was a trusted friend and an intelligent one at that and he hadn't found too many people in the world so far who could fit into either category. Others who were not so closely involved with Eleanor may have questioned her motives in befriending a stranger from the other side of the earth.

Frankie, for his part, stayed in Kilgoolga and even if he had plans to move on, he did not discuss these with his younger brother. So Oisin was left rather hanging. When Frankie and Eleanor were together their conversation invariably turned to esoteric matters and it was religion and spirituality that were the most discussed. Oisin listened attentively and tried to follow the lines of argument but often he was at a loss of words and he began to think that his opinion didn't matter much anyhow. But every now and then, Eleanor would turn to him and say something that brought him back into the conversation. When this happened he sometimes thought that even Frankie listened to what he had to say. This was certainly a new development between the two brothers. Frankie didn't interrupt quite so much and this in itself was unusual for that had never been Frankie's way with him when they were children. His elder brother had, in the past, normally been dismissive of Oisin's opinion about anything. In fact, Oisin had decided long ago that he didn't really have much to say to Frankie and it was better that there was distance between them. It suited him fine, not having much to do with his elder brother for whenever they met, there would invariably be rows. So if nothing else, this was the best thing that had happened between them in years. It was the first step in a sort of new sibling bonding and for that reason, it was encouraging. If Frankie could try to understand Oisin just a little and, if the two of them could find some common ground and resolve some of their differences, they could at least try to be friends if possible. They could go their separate ways then. But Oisin was still not prepared to allow Frankie to come between him and Eleanor and for that reason; he was a bit reluctant to discuss anything about his brother with her. However, if Eleanor decided that Frankie should be the subject of their conversation, there was little that Oisin could do about it. Through the sheer force of her personality, she usually got her way. Just like Frankie.

"Frankie is still a priest, you know," she said to him one afternoon when the two of them were alone at old Bellington Hill. They were sitting on the veranda and Eleanor's dog had his head on Oisin's knee. It was a peaceful sort of afternoon and nothing much was happening around and about.

306

"What do you mean, 'still a priest'? He's left. He's been teaching in Dublin now for a few years," Oisin replied. He was rather surprised. He didn't feel like discussing Frankie on such a sleepy afternoon.

"I've observed him. He still thinks he's in charge of peoples' souls."

"Well, he's not in charge of mine!"

"Oh, Oisin. Don't you understand your brother at all? I know you're often angry with him. The two of you are so alike." She sighed.

"Ye have said that to me before but I can't see it somehow. Look at the two of us. Frankie's handsome, clever, can do just about anything, physically or mentally. I still don't know why he became a priest but whatever he set his mind to do; he'd do it better than anyone else. That's just Frankie. Not me," he concluded with just a trace of his old bitterness about his brother.

"You're right about all those things but Frankie isn't all that you have thought him to be. He's often depressed."

"Frankie? Depressed? I think you're right on most things, Eleanor but I've got my doubts about this one. He's never shown the least sign of being depressed. How can you tell?"

"I've told you. He still worries that he should have stayed a priest after all. I think his decision to leave troubles him no matter how hard he tries to hide it. Maybe you should talk to him? I think you might see another Frankie then. Not the brother who can do everything but someone who has doubts. Why don't you try?"

"He would never listen to me. Remember he calls me 'Frog' and he knows I hate it. Just does that to annoy me. So why would he listen to me? Anyhow, he'll be moving on soon and I probably won't see him again for years."

"You'd like that?"

307

"Well, yes and no, I guess. We've been gettin' on a bit better this time. Have to admit that. Livin' out here in the bush has helped me, ye know. I feel stronger."

"Yes. You're a lot stronger now than when we first met. Physically and mentally. I don't think someone like Cecy could hurt you quite so much now. I'm right, aren't I?"

"You're always right, Eleanor. Thanks to ye, I don't think about Cecy much now. If she comes into my mind, I just remember the good times we had together and try not to be angry about it anymore. It happened. Got me to Kilgoolga and that had to be a good thing. Glad you made me to write that letter, it sure did the trick! I never imagined a letter not posted could help so much!"

"You were ready to move on, Oisin. I just showed you the way. That's what a good teacher does. There's enormous power in the printed word, you know. Cecy was a big part of your life but not anymore. You're a different man now. No longer a boy. If you met Cecy today, you wouldn't know what to say to her. She'd be a stranger. You mightn't even recognise her at first. I'm correct, aren't I?"

"Aye. Sure ye are right. I would find it awkward now, wouldn't know what to say to her. She's moved on just like me but in different directions. She'd hate it out here. Cecy's a real city lassie. At the moment, I couldn't imagine livin' anywhere else."

"You're learning."

Eleanor reached over and patted her dog's head. The dog opened a sleepy eye and wagged his tail. He stretched his large frame and Eleanor broke a biscuit in two and gave half to the dog and ate the second half herself. The dog stared unblinkingly but as there were no more biscuits coming his way, he lay down at her side, sighed and shut his eyes.

"Yes, Oisin. You did well. One thing is in your favour. You obey. You didn't argue with me when I asked you to write that letter to Cecy. It was important for you that we didn't post it but burned it the kitchen sink, and now you see, you're cured of her. She no longer has any power over you, has she? You've let her go. And this is all because you didn't argue with me," she nodded her head and then continued. "Frankie argues and that's his problem. He knows he's clever and when he argues he thinks it gives him control over others, as long as he wins the argument, that is. You can help him to see that if he stepped back a little from this notion he has, of always having to be right, if he thought in a different way, the way I've taught you to do, he would be cured as well, both of his depressions and his doubts. It wouldn't be necessary for him to pretend that he's something he isn't. This is the major cause of his depressions, you know. But he hides all this very well. Maybe it has a lot to do with the fact that he's the eldest in the family and has always been the centre of attention. With two younger brothers, he'd assume he was in charge. I can see by your face that you weren't aware of any of this. Doubt if he would ever let anyone know that he may have a weakness. Definitely he wouldn't let *you* know! It might surprise you to hear that I think you are a more advanced soul than your brother, Frankie."

"Me?"

"Yes, you."

"How can I be compared to Frankie in that way? Everyone in my family knows that Frankie is the genius! Not me."

"Ah, Oisin. You've a long way to go. Stop telling yourself all these negative things. You owe it to Frankie to help him, the way I've helped you."

"I thought ye would be the one to get Frankie to come around to yer way of thinkin'. He'd never listen to me!"

"I agree he's becoming less argumentative with me the more we are together but I think it has to be you who will change him, not me."

309

"Well, I'd be surprised if I could do anything. Frankie always gets his way. Doubt if he'd listen to me about religion or things like that. What do I know?"

"What I've taught you. You're happier now, aren't you? Of course, you can discuss religion with Frankie. You've had plenty of it these days, haven't you? With Hans Seefeldt, that is!" She laughed.

"Going to church, if you mean that," replied Oisin, somewhat grumpily.

"I'm talking about life and you know what I mean. I was only joking about Hans. That's someone I want to talk to you about another time but not now. Hans has problems too and I'm sure you're aware of some of them but today we're thinking about your big brother, Frankie Kelly, the ex-priest and what you can do to help him."

Oisin thought of what Eleanor had said. He had never imagined Frankie in the way that she had described, ever before. He still wasn't sure. He definitely wasn't sure because if Frankie were to think that Oisin thought him less than what he appeared to be and that was, the Frankie who knew everything and got everything he wanted, that would herald a change in their relationship and perhaps not for the better. He couldn't imagine what Frankie would think then. Oisin knowing more than Frankie didn't sound quite right somehow. At least, not at the present moment.

"I don't know, Eleanor," he said thoughtfully. "It would surprise me if Frankie did listen to me but then, you never know in life, do ye now? I don't hate him, ye know. Guess I've just felt small beside him, that's all."

"Small is mighty sometimes, my dear."

Oisin was in for a shock when he went looking for Frankie a few days after his conversation with Eleanor. He decided that she could be right and the best thing was to try to get his brother to talk to him, really talk to him and not in the usual way. He had no clear idea about how to go about this transformational change but he hoped that what he had learned from Eleanor's teaching would do the trick and that Frankie would open up and that they could be brothers, proper brothers and after that they might be able to become friends too. Oisin decided that it would be a good thing if he could feel less of a person than Frankie and it might just be what they both needed if what Eleanor had said was true. Maybe Frankie wasn't the big man all the time. He had planned out the conversation in his head and it had all ended with Frankie listening to him for the very first time and the two of them shaking hands at the end of it but it didn't work out that way because when Oisin went to the Kilgoolga Arms, Frankie was nowhere to be seen.

"He just up an' left, Oisin," Bella told him when he managed to find her. She was at the back of the hotel, stacking bottles ready for collection that afternoon. "Told me he was goin' away for a few days an' not to worry 'bout him. Said he'd be back when he had made up his mind. I think that somethin' was botherin' him. All very mysterious, if ya ask me. Did remember you, though, 'Tell me brother not ta worry, I'll see him later.' So youse not ta worry, Oisin, 'cause I knows how ya worry.I worry too. Everyone's worryin'!" She chuckled.

"It's not like him. Did he say where he was headin'?"

"Not a word! Like I told ya, all he says was, 'not ta worry'!"

It was indeed rather mysterious. Although Oisin had not seen Frankie much for years, his brother had always been very particular about his whereabouts. His mother always knew where Frankie was which couldn't be said for Oisin who often disappeared for hours. Times like that when

311

Oisin returned home not one of his family had even realised he wasn't there. But Frankie was different. Everyone would have missed him. It was just the way it was at An Teach Ban. So why had Frankie suddenly decided to disappear and especially out here in Kilgoolga, miles from anywhere? The Australian bush was different from Ireland. People died here. Frankie wouldn't have a clue what to do if he got lost.

"Did he get on the train, Bella?" he asked her.

"Well, Oisin if it's any comfort ta ya, he left his things in the back room and paid me for another week. Just took a small bag, that's all and no, I dunno where he was goin' an' the train's not due in till next Tuesday so he won't have gone by train."

"We'll just have to wait then, I guess." But Oisin looked worried.

"He's a grown man, Oisin. Ya right, we'll just have ta wait. No sense in gettin' ourselves into a state, is there now? Mebbe ya could ask Claire Paterson? She might know."

"Claire?"

"Yeah. The two of them's been gettin' on like a house on fire. Ya wouldn't know any of this, you bein' stuck out there with that old ratbag at Wiesental most of the week. Yeah, reckon ya should go an' see Claire. She might know!"

Bella's words hit Oisin as if he'd been run over by a truck. How could Claire know what Frankie was doing? At the ABC Café, Frankie had hinted that Claire take him around 'to see the sights' but surely that was just a casual favour to ask from a stranger to a local? Even if that had happened and the two of them had become better acquainted, it was weeks ago now and a few things had happened since then in Oisin's life. He liked Claire. To be sure, they hadn't seen much of each other lately but she had been away all the summer holidays after all. If he thought for one moment that his brother had done anything to come between him and Claire, all that Eleanor said that he must do to try to talk to Frankie, would mean nothing. He just wouldn't do it, no matter what Eleanor directed. He knew he had become mesmerised by Eleanor Bradshaw and he felt happy just being with her. He knew it might be viewed by some as an unlikely relationship but he didn't care. That was just the way it was for him. People wouldn't understand. He was able to tell Eleanor things about himself that he hadn't told another living soul. Eleanor listened to him. She spoke in riddles that he often couldn't understand but he never for one moment doubted her sincerity. He trusted her but in this matter and whatever she said to the contrary, he would not obey her.

He crossed the main street to the barbed wire fence that separated the street from the railway station. Here he climbed over the wire and stepped over the line which served as a shortcut to the streets at the back. This way he was able to avoid meeting anyone in the main street. He was angry and if he happened to meet anyone, he might say something to them that he would later regret so the shortcut across the railway was the safest option. He walked quickly in the direction of Claire's house and as he walked he thought out what he was going to say to her. The red roof and the camphor laurel tree came into view. He stood on the red paving stones that led to her door and wondered whether to knock or not because her Holden station wagon was not parked in its usual place under the awning of the car port. It was Saturday afternoon and he had assumed that she would be at home. This annoyed him even more.

Across the street he heard voices coming from the tennis court and he thought she may be there for she often played a game on the weekend. She was a keen tennis player and he liked to watch her play. She leapt around the court with the agility of a gazelle, pounding the ball over the net and sending many powerful first serves down to her opponent that often resulted in aces. He enjoyed the sight of Claire in her short tennis skirt and frilly white panties and his imagination was often erotic. He couldn't help himself.

The court was sheltered by a laburnum hedge and he had to walk around the side of it to get to the gate so he wasn't sure who would be there.

As Oisin opened the gate that led into the tennis court, he was just in time to see Hefty hit a deadly forehand stroke straight down the middle of the court. The ball travelled at meteoric speed and bounced just near to Janet's feet. She yelped and was about to try to hit the ball but thought better of it and instead, stepped back slightly in order for Kanga to take over. Kanga somehow managed to return it and the ball, now losing some of its power became an easy shot for Hefty's partner, his new girlfriend, who was positioned in exactly the right place at the net and could easily sneak the ball inside the line to win the point. Hefty let out a cheer of triumph and threw his racquet high in the air. With Hefty's height, the racquet shot up to the height of the outside wire. Everyone stopped play and Kanga, realising Oisin was standing at the umpire's stand, yelled to him,

"Jeez, mate, ya look like somethin' the cat brought in! Where ya been hidin'?"

He lent on Janet's shoulders and still holding his racquet in his left hand, he nuzzled her right ear with his lips as he spoke. She giggled.

"He's not getting' any, that's his trouble!" added Hefty and with that, he trundled over to Oisin and gave him the customary belt on the arm. When he saw how distracted Oisin was, he said,

"Bloody hell, ya right, Kanga. Just look at ya, Oisin, me old mate, what ya been doin' with yarself?"

"Where's Claire?" Oisin was in no mood to listen to their teasing.

"Told ya so, he's not gettin' any!!" cried Hefty and with that Oisin's upper arm got another belt.

"Wouldn't get much from Claire," smirked Kanga.

314

"Stop it, youse two," Janet said crossly and then she smiled at Oisin. "I haven't seen her for a week, Oisin. The kids have been off school for a few days, I think. Maybe she's gone on some school trip or other. Really don't know where she is. She's not been in touch. I half thought she might come over today for a game but not a sight or sound of her! Have you seen Claire, Liz?" She asked Hefty's new girlfriend who just shrugged. Liz didn't like Claire much.

Oisin was annoyed at them all. He was even more annoyed at the thought of Claire not being in her house or at the tennis court. She was normally around on Saturday afternoon.

"I'll get goin' then," he muttered almost to himself.

As he opened the wire gate, he turned and called out,

"If ye happen to see her, tell her, I'm lookin' for her!!"

This announcement was met with cheers and more suggestive gestures from Kanga and Hefty. Admonishments to 'shut up' from both the girls led to more teasing from the boys and Oisin, his face burning, stalked away from the tennis court towards the street without saying another word.

He walked slowly back towards the main street and his car. He had parked the car outside Louis's drapery shop and when he got there, Louis was standing on the footpath talking to a woman whom Oisin recognised as Maudie, the Frenchman's 'bit on the side'. He wasn't in any mood to speak to either of them. He nodded at Louis and then reversed the car quickly. His only thought was to collect his thoughts and get back as fast as he could to the security of Wiesental. He never thought he would ever think that way about the place but he had received a few shocks and sometimes when these things happen, the familiar is safe.

At the crossroads where the road branched off towards Bellington Hill and the Bradshaws, he stopped the car. If he continued towards Milberra, he would get to Kinleven and the Patersons. *It might all be innocent*, he

315

thought, *Claire might be visiting her parents*. He got out of the car and walked to the creek. It just seemed like yesterday that he had been sitting in Charlie's old ute with Charlie's dog sitting beside him. They had stopped under the coolibah and ate sandwiches and drank tea. Everything had been dry and he had seen wallabies close up for the first time. Since then, he had grown stronger, he knew that. This wonderful country had made him stronger. He no longer thought much of Cecy or his life back in Ireland. He thought of all the people he had met since then. Eleanor Bradshaw came into his mind first. It was she who had helped him through his past hurt. He believed she had given him a purpose once again for there had been many, many moments since his arrival in Kilgoolga that he had felt adrift, a loser who had had nothing to hold him anywhere. If she had given him nothing else, at least she had given him hope and where there is hope; there is the possibility of something better happening. He thought the something better might have been with Claire but now all that seemed to have changed and he wondered if he would be adrift once again. He thought of Claire and then Frankie. It didn't seem possible that his brother could have arrived out of nowhere and taken Claire from him. He decided that he must talk to Eleanor about this new situation. He had kept his relationship with Claire from Eleanor for reasons he didn't fully understand. It had all to do with the fact that he wasn't sure what Claire thought of him and that Eleanor might somehow disapprove. After all, there seemed to be an intense rivalry in the district between the three families, the Bradshaws, the Patersons and even the Seefeldts. If Eleanor realised he was friends with Claire Paterson, it mightn't go down too well. *It was all very complicated*, he thought. However, in this matter if Eleanor gave him some practical advice, he would listen to what she had to say and if she decided that he should let Claire go, then so be it. He would accept whatever she had to say but it wouldn't be easy. Despite everything, he still liked Claire even if she probably thought differently about him now. A sad thought came into his head, for why wouldn't she? How could he ever compare himself to Frankie? Frankie always got his way, whatever Eleanor thought to the contrary. Eleanor had told him that Frankie had suffered leaving the priesthood. Well, Frankie didn't look too bothered about all that now! Frankie hadn't changed one bit! He had just got older and more good looking and Oisin had just got older!

Oisin opened the car door and started the engine. He thought for a few more minutes and then he turned right towards Wiesental and the Bellington Hill road.

When he drove into the yard at Wiesental, all was quiet. The blue and grey cattle dog was running free and when he saw the car and the occupant, he barked, then ran to Oisin and received a pat on the head for his trouble. It was unusual that the dog wasn't tied up on his rope at this hour but Oisin didn't think much about it until he entered the kitchen and saw Hilda. He was surprised by her appearance. Usually she was a neat little woman who took care with her hair and kept it plaited. She sometimes arranged the plait neatly around her head and other times she kept it tidy in a bun. The first thing that Oisin noticed about Hilda was her hair. It looked as if her grey hair hadn't been brushed and it hung in straggly strands to her shoulders. She looked worried and when she saw Oisin, she cried out,

"Oh, Oisin, I'm so glad you're here. Look what Hans has done? He's taken Julius!"

"Julius?"

317

"Yes, Julius. You know. The photograph of Julius, it used to hang above the desk!"

There was a bright yellow rectangular patch on the wall where the photograph used to hang. Oisin frowned. The desk had gone as well.

"Whatever's happened?" he asked for Hilda was in quite a state. She kept wiping her hands on her apron even though her hands didn't appear to be wet.

"Oisin, he's taken Julius away. I must have told you about Julius, Dad's prize Merino ram. Dad won First Prize with Julius at the Ekka in 1930. Julius won so many ribbons at all the local shows but the Ekka was the best one of all! Dad had a photograph taken of him at the Ekka. Dad was so proud. I can remember him hanging the photo above the desk and it hasn't been moved since then and now Hans has taken it into his head that he wants it and he's taken the desk, too."

Hilda looked as if she might burst into tears any minute. It was obviously very important to her. Oisin put his arm around her shoulders.

"Don't worry, Hilda. I'm sure he'll bring it back. Hans loves his sheep too. Julius will be back on the wall in no time, so. How did he manage to move the desk though?"

It was a heavy oak desk and would have taken some strength to move. Hilda shook her head. There was certainly a gap in the room where the photograph and the desk used to be.

"He must have moved it while I was out milking the goats. When I came in, it was gone and the photo as well. I couldn't believe it! There's more though, Oisin. He's taken the guns away." She bit her lip.

Suddenly Oisin felt uneasy. This was a new development and it wasn't a good one. Hans kept two shotguns and a rifle on the rack next to his desk. Who knows what he planned to do with them?

318

"There must be some reason, Hilda. Maybe he wanted to clean them... outside the kitchen?" he said doubtfully. But he wasn't totally convinced. Hans kept a few boxes of bullets on the shelf above the desk. They were gone as well. All that was left on the shelf was the Bible and a few notebooks.

"The Bible's still there," he said hopefully. "Must mean he's intending to come back, Hilda. Where do ye think he's taken everything?"

"Oh, to that bloody shed," snapped Hilda uncharacteristically. She was usually very polite especially with Oisin.

"The woolshed?"

"Yes! He spends all his time in there these days. You must know that! I haven't seen him all day, Oisin. I'm worried about him."

She looked frail and old. Oisin felt sorry for her. He decided he must try to do something to help.

"Do ye want me to go an' look for him?"

"No! I know you mean well but please don't go anywhere near that old woolshed. He might do something. You know how many rolls of barbed wire he's put all around the shed and he has a key to the place that he keeps to himself. 'No one is to go in there', he said. Oh, Oisin, what's happening? What can I do?"

"I don't know, Hilda. Ye said he likes his tucker," he smiled to reassure her. "He'll be in for his tea an' he'll have to give us our Bible readin'. Hans wouldn't miss that, now would he? Wonder what it'll be tonight? I'm sure there's a perfectly sensible reason for all this, ye know."

But he wasn't as sure as he tried to be. Hans had been acting strange lately, even more so than when Oisin had first met him. He remembered Hans shooting a bullet over his head that first day. It still made him feel uneasy thinking about it. The old farmer had got worse since then. Sometimes, he didn't speak to Hilda or Oisin all day. Even the Bible reading had been erratic on many occasions. Often Hans read for half an hour or so, other times he just managed a few lines of scripture.

Hilda didn't seem convinced but she wiped her eyes on the corner of her apron and tried to sound cheerful.

"You're right about the tucker, Oisin. He's always eaten for two! Mum used to say he had hollow legs! But I worry about him, you know," she sighed. "Wish he'd got married but he never showed any interest in girls... "

Oisin looked quizzical. Hilda must have sensed his question because she blushed and said,

"Nor anything else, Oisin, either. All Hans ever thought about was the land and the sheep. He hates them Aberdeen Angus's, you know. He'd put the sheep back if he had the energy but guess all that's gone now. He's too old to start again. It's just been Wiesental and the church, that's his life!" she sighed. "He's always liked goin' to the church but he's had plenty of barneys with the pastor and he gets a set against some of the ones that go there. But he loves his Bible, doesn't he? That's got to be something, Oisin, hasn't it?"

"Aye, Hilda. That's got to mean something," he said gently. "He's got his faith, that's for sure."

Hans had his faith, thought Oisin. *Everything was arranged in black and white in Hans's brain. There was no room there for any doubts as far as God was concerned.* He wondered what Hans and Eleanor would say to each other if they ever got together and talked about religion but then, Hans didn't talk to anyone anymore so that probably wouldn't happen.

Hilda patted Oisin's hand as if to reassure herself that he was someone who understood.

"It was a great day for me when you came to Wiesental, Oisin. You're a good person. Are all Irish people as kind as you? I do worry about Hans though but I'm so very glad you're here."

320

Oisin didn't answer because at that moment he heard a meowing at the door and Hans's large ginger cat sauntered into the kitchen and proceeded to demand to be fed. It meowed and rubbed its body against Hilda's legs. She had prepared the food earlier because Ginger was as regular as clockwork and always arrived at the same time every evening. It was a routine they both lived by and it had been going on for so many years that if, for any reason there was a change to the timing and the cat did not appear, Hilda would call its name loudly and scold it when it finally arrived. When that happened the cat was not at all put out and it usually gained a few extra morsels from Hilda for its tardiness. Hilda was fond of the old ginger cat but it kept its allegiance for Hans and only used Hilda as a supplier of food. Automatically she placed its dish onto the floor and the cat purred a 'thank you', sniffed the offering and then proceeded to chew the meat slowly as it had lost most of its teeth due to its advanced age.

"Hans likes his cats too. He's always spoilt old Ginger rotten as you know. Guess that's something, isn't it?" A look of such sadness came over Hilda's face that Oisin couldn't help but feel sorry for her. He really didn't know how to answer. Hilda seemed to be almost defeated by it all. She had the look of someone who wanted to give up and just shut her eyes and it would all be over. He had become fond of Hilda and he would miss her when he left because at that moment, he knew that he would have to leave her soon before he became more and more entangled into the emotional web that spun like a tight cord around the brother and sister. This web was threatening to engulf Oisin as well and if he were to stay with them too long, he might become like Hans with nothing to strive for and consequently, nothing to live for. Hans and Hilda were old and tired with their lives behind them. Oisin was young and could escape. He knew there was no possible way that he, a stranger from the other side of the earth, could ever give Hans and Hilda back all those lost years nor was it right that he should sacrifice what years he had ahead of him in order to ease their unfulfilled and thwarted desires, whatever they may be. It must not be allowed to happen.

They heard footsteps on the path outside the kitchen window and Hans entered the room. He slowly walked to his chair, sat down and put his head in his hands. He looked weary. Hilda glanced at Oisin. No one spoke. When Hilda put the plate with four pork sausages, mashed potatoes and peas in front of Hans, he didn't acknowledge her or make any comment. Instead, he remained with his head in his hands. It looked as if he wasn't going to eat the meal nor was he about to say a 'thank you'. This was so uncharacteristic that both Oisin and Hilda glanced once more at each other and this time, both were puzzled.

"Is everything alright, Hans?" asked Hilda.

Hans did not reply but he put his hands on his knees and stared at the food on his plate. His face was grey and lined and everything about his manner suggested that he, along with Hilda, was beginning to show evidence of their advancing years. He had the appearance of a man who was about to give up. He pushed the plate away.

"I'm not hungry, Hilda," he said. "Don't feel like eating."

"That's not like you, Hans. You've never missed your dinner for as long as I can remember, except that time you had the measles when we was kids and that was only one meal! You know you've always enjoyed your tucker. Are you sure you're feeling OK? Do you want me to ring the doctor for you? Oisin could drive you in to Kilgoolga if you can't drive?"

Hearing this, Hans stood up and growled at his sister,

"Stop fussing, woman," he said. "The cat can have the sausages. I'm going to bed."

And with that, he strode out of the kitchen. They heard his bedroom door slam shut.

"Oh, dear," murmured Hilda. She frowned. "What do we do now?"

After they finished their meal, Hilda cleared the table and Oisin helped her wash the dishes. Neither spoke. When they sat down on their lounge chairs at the far end of the kitchen, everything seemed different. Every evening since Oisin had lived with Hans and Hilda, Hans had read from the Bible and they had sat on these chairs. Now there was a space where his desk and his chair had been. The gun rack was still on the wall minus the guns. It all looked so bare.

"Hilda," he said, "I'd like to make a phone call."

She looked at him. He hardly ever used the phone. In fact, the phone rarely rang at Wiesental.

"Of course you can, dear," she replied.

Oisin dialled the number.

" 'Allo?"

"It's me. Louis, can you get in touch with Eleanor please? It's urgent!"

"Is that Monsieur Oisin?"

"Aye. Ask Eleanor to meet me at the Commercial. Let me know what time is convenient for her and I'll be there... "

"But of course, Oisin. I telephone to her now. Is there anything I can do?"

"No... thank you."

"Very well."

Oisin replaced the receiver and went back to his chair.

"I might be able to help, Hilda," he said. "Try not to worry."

It was all because Eleanor Bradshaw had become such a dominating force in Oisin's life that he thought of her first. The sight of Hans with his head in his hands and the reaction of Hilda when she saw her brother was just enough for the warning bell to go off in Oisin's head. Something was wrong. Something was dreadfully wrong with Hans and he needed help. So it was natural in Oisin's mind that he should turn to Eleanor. She listened to him. She gave him advice when advice was needed and soothed him when he was distressed. In everything he had discussed with her, she had shown herself to be a loyal friend and for this reason he was certain that she would be able to help Hans. He fully acknowledged that there were other people in Kilgoolga who were not nearly as captivated by Eleanor as he was and that even her own brother, Joseph viewed some of her more outlandish ideas with a certain amount of scepticism. In Oisin's mind, this was totally acceptable. There are often leaders of men who, because of the very strength of their personality, create envy and malice in others. The leader is constantly under threat from these people. This is how Oisin viewed Eleanor. She was this powerful and all-knowing leader of her select group of which he now was one. A charismatic leader like Eleanor takes no notice of any dissent of disagreement. In the minds of both Eleanor Bradshaw and Oisin, she was the most influential person in the whole of Kilgoogla for she had in equal measure, knowledge, influence and wealth. It was no wonder, then, that the gentle Irishman from Ballybeg, lonely and confused, would fall under her spell and in fact, be rather proud that he had been added to her little band of followers. With Eleanor both his loneliness and his confusion disappeared. It was as if she had swept a magic wand across his whole body. She had given him a reason to live and with that idea firmly fixed in his brain, a purpose as well.

However, when Oisin met Eleanor, as arranged, in her unit at the Commercial, he was unsure of what to say to her. This was rather surprising given the fact that just a few hours earlier he had been confident that Eleanor would be able to provide some answers or even offer him a few clues which could help to explain some of the behaviour of Hans. She talked about things that he had never thought about before and when he listened to her, he glimpsed a world so very far removed from anything that he could ever have imagined. Knowing her had widened his understanding of the world about him and he now thought more deeply than he had ever done before about life and in what direction his own life was taking him. Added to all this, Eleanor Bradshaw was such a powerful personality in Kilgoolga and district. She had known Hans Seefeldt all her life. Their two properties were joined by a boundary fence that stretched for miles. So, all things considered, these factors combined should give him some answers and then he would know what to do for the best. He would listen to what Eleanor said. Although he was now seriously contemplating leaving Wiesental at the earliest opportunity, he couldn't help but be concerned for Hilda. He rather liked the little woman and he didn't want to think of her having to face her irrational brother all on her own and so far from anywhere. Hans was becoming an increasingly worrying problem, anyone could see that. Even if there was nothing to bind Oisin in any way to either of the Seefeldts, he was grateful to Hilda and even to Hans. They had taken him into their home on trust and made him feel welcome in their own ways. Right from the start Hans had shown many odd behaviour patterns but there had been a few pleasant occasions when he had been friendly. Oisin had learned a lot from the old farmer on those rare times when they had been able to communicate with each other and then they were almost brief companions of sorts. He now knew how to build fences and look after Aberdeen Angus cattle. Every day, he was becoming more at

325

home in the Australian bush and even to understand it, just a little. The vast empty spaces no longer worried him to the extent that they used to and at times, he couldn't imagine being anywhere else in the whole world. Hans had taught him all that. He had gained so much knowledge from the old farmer that now he was practically running the Wiesental station, all two thousand acres of it. For these reasons, he didn't immediately want to start talking about Hans when he met Eleanor. Instead, they sipped tea and ate biscuits and spoke of mundane things. He had become a frequent visitor to Eleanor's flat and sometimes, if he found himself at a loose end in Kilgoolga, he would spend an hour or two alone there. Eleanor's unit was a welcome relief from the heat of the day and as far as he was aware, no one ever knew that he had the key and could come and go as he pleased. This fact, in itself, flattered him that a woman such as Eleanor had freely given him a key to her private world. So he was both flattered and grateful that she had agreed to see him so quickly after his call to Louis. But he still hesitated before speaking about Hans until Eleanor suddenly said with some exasperation in her voice,

"Well, Oisin. What do you want to talk about? You had to see me, that's what Louis told me and he said it was urgent too."

"It's Hans," he said. He hadn't mentioned anything about Hans to Louis when he spoke to the Frenchman over the phone.

Eleanor smiled as if she knew it all. She had cultivated this certain smile in order to add mystery to any conversation she might have. This enigmatic smile made her appear to be different from others because people then assumed that she had could see into the future and was therefore, a person with special powers.

"There could be nothing else. I told you we needed to talk about Hans. There's a right and wrong time for everything and now is the right time! Speak!"

326

"He frightens me."

"Ah."

"We think he's getting worse, Hilda and me, that is."

"Tell me."

So he told her all about Hans. How Hans had fired a gun over his head on the very first day when he arrived at Wiesental and how Hans had insisted on Oisin attending his church even though Oisin had no interest in it at all because after all Oisin was a Catholic, even if he was a lapsed one, but he hadn't told Hans any of this for on that subject he felt sure Hans would be irrational and threatening. Everything was black and white with Hans; his religion being the most unwavering subject of all. He had to admit that he had learned a lot about the farm work from Hans but Hans would sometimes go all day and never speak a word to Oisin and that had been hard to bear because Oisin liked to talk. He was Irish, after all and loved the banter but Hans had no sense of humour in him. None whatsoever. It was all duty and work and more work but now Hans doesn't do any work at all but spends his whole day and sometimes the night, alone in the woolshed. Neither Hilda nor Oisin are allowed anywhere near the place for Hans has the only key and he keeps the place locked and now this has to be the final straw, Hans has taken his desk away from the kitchen and also a black and white framed photo that had sat above the desk for over thirty years of a prize ram called Julius. Had Eleanor heard of Julius? But the worst thing of all and the most worrying was that Hans had taken the guns away. This frightened Hilda the most, Oisin said, because Hans was a good shot and knew how to use them. How the fear of the Viet Cong invasion and the barbed wire entanglements and the trenches dug were irrational to say the least but Hans was so adamant that Wiesental station would be overrun with these 'yellow, slit-eyed Commie bastards' and they would take his land away from him, murder him and rape Hilda. It all seemed crazy. He had maps drawn up and battle

327

plans worked out. 'Retreat to the woolshed', he said. Oisin had helped Hans to repair the outside of the woolshed and make it water tight. He had enjoyed that work because he liked the carpentry side of things but as soon as that was done, Hans refused to let him go inside so God knows what's happened in there now. A few weeks ago there was a lot of banging going on inside the shed but that's all stopped now. Oisin hesitated for a minute and lowered his voice,

"To tell ye the truth, Eleanor," he said, confidentially, "I've been a bit scared about even going anywhere near the old woolshed these days an' I think Hilda's the same. Least ye never see her near the place an'she told me not to talk to Hans there."

Then he resumed the story. He told Eleanor all about the matter of the padlocks at the front gates and how Hans would not let anyone near the property unless they asked permission. If he decided that they could come in, Oisin or Hilda had to drive to the gate to unlock the padlocks. Hans would never go. It always had to be Hilda or Oisin. People thought it was weird. Oisin thought it was weird. How Oisin had gone for months not being able to come and go but always having to ask permission for the keys and Hans kept hold of these keys always, until one day, Hilda had said to him, 'Enough is enough' and Hans had reluctantly agreed that Oisin could have keys to the padlocks and thus have some freedom at last.

"And last night," Oisin continued, glad he was able to speak of all these things for he had been so lonely at times out at Wiesental with just Hans and Hilda for company, "last night, can ye believe it, he wouldn't eat anything? Just pushed his plate away an' went off to his room in a rage? And Hilda such a good cook too! Poor Hilda was beside herself with worry when he did that because her brother has such an appetite, 'a strong man needs his food', she tells me this all the time and 'Hans has always been a strong man'. That's why I rang Louis to get hold of ye. That's what ye said

328

I must do, if I ever needed help. 'Ring Louis', ye said. Well, I think I need help now not only for me but for both of them. Hans looks terrible, Eleanor. His face is grey. I've seen that look before with my Uncle Mick back in Ballybeg when I was growin' up, grey and tired. But Mick was never like this, not like Hans. Hans is scary when he goes on and on about the Bible and the war in Vietnam and all these things. Uncle Mick was never scary, ye know. Uncle Mick was just clever an' had no one to talk to, I guess. Hans isn't clever, not in that way. Hans never reads books not like my Uncle Mick. Uncle Mick read every book in the Ballybeg Library, now wasn't that something? But the only thing Hans reads is the Bible and sometimes the *Kilgoolga Echo*. I'm worried, Eleanor. I don't know what to do. I know it's not my problem but that doesn't make it any easier, does it? Ye sort of connect up with people an' that's happened to me with the pair of them. I never expected any of this and just planned to stay for a while and move on after I got my head straight about Cecy and all that, but things happen, don't they? Things happen that change ye. Whether ye like it or not, people come into yer life and stay there an' I guess I just felt sorry for the two of them, so I stayed. Must be a lonely life for the both of them, don't ye think?" Oisin finished his story and sat back in his chair and looked for answers from Eleanor.

He had expected her to give him those answers immediately and then a lot of advice that would help him but instead, she clapped her hands and got up from her chair and cried out in a loud voice,

"Oh, my God! Finally! It's happened at last! How many years have I waited for this moment? You have no idea, Oisin. No idea at all."

She was in quite a state. Her whole face changed. A few minutes before she had been so attentive, seemingly absorbed in what Oisin was saying and listening carefully to every word but now her brown eyes changed. They were

329

even more alert than usual and they twinkled. Her lips, heavily covered with her favourite bright red lipstick, parted, revealing a row of slightly uneven teeth. This was not the reaction that Oisin had expected.

"Just what I wanted to hear, Oisin," she said. "You've done the right thing coming to me. I knew it! I knew it! Now, we must act. And we must act fast before it's too late! There's not a minute to lose. Hans will not wait forever!"

And then she started to hum a tune he had never heard before. She took hold of a feather duster and proceeded to flick the duster over the sideboard and switch it over the framed photo of Lord Bradshaw. Oisin had never seen her quite so animated before. It seemed such a strange thing. How could she suddenly change her whole manner in so short a time? He had expected reassurance. To listen to the story about Hans and then to treat his unexplainable behaviour with so little concern was puzzling indeed. He wanted her to explain.

"Eleanor," he said at last for the sight of this woman dancing around the room was unnerving to say the least, "what on earth do ye mean? Hans is sick. Well, I think he's sick in the head but then I'm no doctor. What do ye mean 'we must act'?"

"Just that, my little Irish boy. Hans Seefeldt will speak to me now," she paused, "and you will make it happen!"

"Me?"

Eleanor laughed then. She patted Oisin's head with her feather duster and said,

"Yes, you! You've been put on the Wiesental station for a reason, my dear boy. We're friends for the very same reason. Everything has a time and a place and if we allow it, the right things happen at the right time. Hans will do as I ask, you mark my words. See, Lord Cyril agrees, don't you, Your Lordship? We've waited a long time, haven't we, Cyril?"

330

And as she said that, she curtsied like an actress on the stage in front of an appreciative audience and towards the framed photograph. Oisin caught sight of those eyes again. He frowned.

"I don't understand," he murmured.

"Understand? What is there to understand? Ah, but there's one thing you must do for me to finish this puzzle... "

"Puzzle?"

"Yes. Yes. It's been a long and complicated puzzle but it's all been worthwhile... at least it will be when it's finally over. I can see the end now. And you'll play your part in this little drama, Oisin Kelly. You're important, you see."

"I don't see. I'm a stranger here. I'm thinking of leaving anyway. I've been thinking a lot about my life lately, maybe Frankie is right; I need to go back to Ireland after all. So what on earth can I do?" He shrugged his shoulders.

"You must bring me the keys to the padlocks on the front gates of Wiesental. That is your mission. Do that for me and both of us will be free."

CHAPTER FIFTEEN

To be told in such a way by Eleanor that she wanted the keys to unlock the padlocks of the front gates of Wiesental was something that Oisin could never in his wildest imaginings thought would be asked of him. Nor was it feasible or even possible. For her to ask him to do this and also to expect that he would happily comply with her request was also a major problem for him. He had no idea what was happening at Wiesental. Hans had so jealously and possessively kept these keys as a means of control over everyone. If the old farmer thought that Oisin had given Eleanor Bradshaw these keys might be the final straw, even dangerous. Hans was unstable at present. Who knows what would happen if Eleanor Bradshaw suddenly appeared on his property? The outcome could be quite tricky.

"Eleanor, I really don't think I can do that for ye," Oisin said softly. He had never refused to do anything that Eleanor had asked of him before.

At that moment, she was busy making them another pot of tea and didn't answer. Oisin could see her from where he was sitting in the lounge room. She was in high spirits and completely unaware that he had even spoken for when she brought out the tray with more tea and biscuits, she said to him in an offhand sort of way,

"I'll need the keys as soon as possible, Oisin. Might be best if you get another set cut for me. This way I'll be able to surprise Hans and you needn't be involved at all. Hilda's of no consequence. I only want to see Hans."

"I can't do it, Eleanor."

"What do you mean? 'Can't do it'?"

"Just that. I've just told ye everything about Hans that I know and I just can't do it. Ye have no idea what those keys mean to him. He's obsessed with them. It's all to do with not allowing anyone onto his property. I don't know why that is, but it just is. If he thought I'd given them to ye, I don't know what'll happen."

"You will give them to me," she whispered into his ear.

For the first time since he had met Eleanor, Oisin felt uneasy. He wasn't sure what to do next. He took a sip of tea and bit into one of the biscuits. The biscuit was hard and he dunked half of it into his tea to soften it. The whole situation had suddenly become worrying and he felt something so unusual was happening that he had never experienced before for Eleanor fixed her eyes onto his and try as he could, he couldn't stop looking into her eyes. She didn't blink. Her whole attention was focussed on him. She whispered again,

"You will give me the keys to Wiesental. You will give me the keys, Oisin Kelly. The keys to Wiesental."

Oisin wanted to get out of his chair and run. He had spent an hour or so telling Eleanor all about Hans and now it was as if none of that had happened. He wondered if she hadn't even listened to him. This was a surprise because at other times, she had been attentive and interested in what he was saying. He had trusted her then. It occurred to him that perhaps all that Eleanor wanted was the keys to Wiesental and she had used him because he was the only one able to give them to her. Was that her only interest in him? He wanted to escape from those eyes of hers but her gaze held him a prisoner and he was even a willing prisoner because the part of him that wanted to run was nowhere

333

near as powerful as that other part that held him motionless and captive. He felt himself getting drowsy. He wanted to shut his eyes but he could not and still she stared at him with unblinking eyes and said again and again and again,

"You will bring me the keys. Bring me the keys."

Oisin shut his eyes.

He wasn't sure how long he had been asleep or if he had indeed been asleep because when he opened his eyes, it was dark in the room and Eleanor was nowhere to be seen. He looked at the table and he saw that his tea and biscuit were still there where they had been before he shut his eyes. Small pieces of the biscuit had risen to the surface of the liquid and were floating on the top like chunks of broken ice on a pond. The tea was cold. Oisin felt cold, too. He shivered. He had no idea what had happened to him but his first thought was that he had to get keys cut; the keys to Wiesental station; the keys to the padlocks that would allow Eleanor Bradshaw to intrude into the weird world of Hans Seefeldt and so do whatever it was that she had to do. He tried to get out of the chair but his legs felt weak and he sat back down, grateful somehow that she wasn't about to see him. He felt as if he had drunk too much and was suffering from an enormous hangover but no alcohol had touched his lips, only tea. Slowly, in the manner of an old man who had been asleep for hours and just woke up suddenly and not knowing where he was, he got to his feet and walked to the light switch. He turned on the light in the lounge and then poured a glass of cool water from the tap at the sink in the kitchenette. The water revived him slightly. He could see into the lounge from here and as his eyes focussed on the wall in front of him, he was surprised to discover that the sepia portrait of Lord Bradshaw, the portrait that Eleanor paid her special kind of homage to on so many occasions, was missing. An oval patch of brighter blue was all that remained on the wall. Now he began to wonder what was going on and instinct told him that he had to get out of the place and somehow find Eleanor. He wondered if some harm had come to her for he couldn't imagine why the portrait she loved so much would be missing. It was the weirdest thing not to see the oval frame on the wall. The room was empty without it. Lord Cyril had commanded attention. Every time Oisin had sat in the chair in front of the portrait, he had sensed those piercing eyes studying him and often Eleanor's eyes had given him that same strange sensation. Their eyes were so similar to each other, one and the same, he had often thought. He turned off the light and headed for the glass door and slid it open. A gust of cool air hit him like a splash of cold water and he stumbled towards the railing and held on tight. He could hear music and loud voices and he smelt the smoke from the barbeque. He saw a wisp of smoke rise in the air, grey against the night sky. The lights from the outdoor area lit up the balcony. Everything looked normal. Only he didn't feel normal. He had no idea what time it was but a few stars were already out and the quarter moon hung like a silver thread in the black sky. He glanced at his watch. It was a few minutes to seven. He must have been with Eleanor for about six hours, he figured. Carefully he negotiated the wooden stairs and out onto the main street. Everything was just as it had been a few hours before. He opened the door of his car and fumbled for the keys. The engine started straight away. He drove down the main street, turned right and then onto the familiar road to Wiesental.

An hour's drive later he was at the iron gates of Wiesental station. The chains were still there with the padlocks hooked through them, making it all secure. He opened the gates and drove his car through as he had done so many times before but tonight it felt different. He locked the gates once again and drove very slowly along the gravel road. Normally, he drove fast on the straight country roads but he had no wish to get to the homestead in a hurry and the slower he drove, the longer it took. It was past nine o'clock when he finally arrived at the homestead. He couldn't see any lights on in the house. Everything was dark, as only a night in the outback could be, for clouds had blocked out the stars and the quarter moon was nowhere in sight. He heard the cattle dog bark a welcome and he saw a movement in the bushes near the steps that led to the veranda. A black shape appeared then disappeared towards the back of the house. The black shape was tall. It was Hans Seefeldt.

Oisin lay on his bed and stared at the ceiling. The pale yellow gloss paint on the tongue and groove wooden ceiling above his head was dull and needed re-doing. He would have liked to renovate the room but there didn't seem to be much point anymore. He closed his eyes. It was a relief to be back in his bedroom at Wiesental. He wondered where Hilda was and what Hans had been doing, lurking around the steps. He was so tired at that moment, he couldn't even think of what to do next. There was only one thing that he was certain that he had to get done and that was to get the keys to Eleanor but first he had to find her. But all that would have to wait until the morning and then he would see what happened then. His eyelids grew heavy and he slept, stretched out on his back and fully clothed. He must have slept for hours. When he woke in the early morning and heard the roosters crowing, it was as if he had been dreaming all night. Strange dreams he had had of Ballybeg and Uncle Mick and keys and a fire that took them all away and left him standing beside Claire Paterson. She was dressed entirely in red. Even her hair had changed to red. They stood next to the barbeque at the Commercial Hotel. They were barefooted and their feet and ankles were covered in the grey ash from the fire. He had a glass of water in his hand. He tried to put out the fire with the water from his glass. He got out of the bed and looked through the wire mess at the window. All was still and the morning air was cool. He knew what he had to do.

336

Eleanor drove her bottle green Citroën car to the two iron gates which led into the Wiesental station. Eleanor was the only person for six hundred miles or so who owned a French car. Everyone else made do with Holdens and Fords and the occasional Japanese models but Eleanor had to be different and owning the latest model Citroën was another visible and tangible sign of who she was. No one else was allowed to drive her car so that if anyone spied the green Citroën on the country roads, it was most certainly Eleanor Bradshaw behind the wheel.

She inserted one of the brand new brass keys into the top padlock. It opened easily. She did the same with the other key and the lower padlock opened just as quickly. The thick chains were rusty and traces of rust transferred to some of her fingers. She rubbed her hands together to remove the brown colour and then she swung the gates open. Eleanor was a country woman and always mindful of country ways. She drove through the opening and shut the gates behind her, making sure that chains and padlocks were locked together once again. She took a few deep breaths right to the bottom of her lungs and surveyed the scene in front of her. Wiesental station. She had not been through these gates for years. Not since Hans Seefeldt had sold his entire flock of Merinos to the Bradshaws. That day, she had accompanied her father and Joseph to Wiesental to take Hans's sheep away. The Bradshaws were rich. They knew they could buy sheep and wait until the markets improved but Hans had no alternative. He had to sell his beloved sheep. If he hadn't done so, the bank would have taken possession of Wiesental and he and Hilda would have had

337

no where to go. Eleanor remembered that the very next day, Hans had chained and padlocked the main gates to Wiesental and after that no one could enter his land without permission from him. Everyone in the district thought that was the moment Hans Seefeldt withdrew from the world about him. Eleanor felt triumphant, just being here.

The land was marginal and in no way as prosperous as the richer pastures of Bellington Hill but it had sustained generations of Seefeldts nevertheless. She drove cautiously along the gravel track, opening and closing half a dozen iron gates until she reached the homestead. Here she stopped the car next to the skeletal-like windmill with its galvanised iron tanks and water trough for the animals. She looked about. From the slight hill, she could see the homestead and its surroundings clearly. Wiesental homestead was situated in the valley and Eleanor was surprised how desolate it looked even in the bright sunshine. The years of neglect were evident. Hans and Hilda had lived here for years now and without much help. It must have been a blessing when young Oisin arrived out of nowhere to lend them a hand but it would require more than one pair of youthful hands to bring Wiesental station back to its former glory when a dozen or so people and hundreds of sheep had made their home here. The iron roof of one of the outbuildings at the side of the homestead had collapsed and rust covered sheets were scattered hither and thither. Eleanor could see two goats nibbling the dry grass in a small paddock at the side of the homestead. Oisin had told her Hilda kept three goats but she couldn't locate the other one. Even the wire enclosure of the chook run looked about to fall down and two or three brown hens had escaped and were wandering around aimlessly. The roosters, unable to figure out how to get out, ran back and forth along the wire in a vain attempt to join the hens. It was a bright autumn day and the sun was already high in the sky. There wasn't a breath of air. Everything was still.

338

She parked her car at the side of the homestead. No one was about but this was deliberate as Eleanor had planned it this way. Oisin had told her that during the week he worked away from the homestead and particularly on Monday and Tuesday, neither he nor Hilda would be about. Hilda usually came with him on those days and did what she could to help him. She brought their lunch and drove the tractor. It was evident that Hans no longer took much part in the day to day work on the station. This was a perfect arrangement for Eleanor for it was Hans that she had come to see, not Hilda. In fact, she didn't want Hilda to be aware of what she had in mind. Nor did she want to see Oisin.

From the back seat of the car, Eleanor took a small briefcase, the same one that she had taken with her when she had located Eddie and bought the Commercial Hotel. She was methodical and kept her important papers in this case. Then she placed a brown paper shape under her arm and shut the door of the car. She knew that Hans would be in the woolshed because that's where Oisin said he spent his days and some of his nights. The woolshed was about half a mile from the homestead. She walked slowly past the clutter from the accumulation of years of Seefeldt habitation which was so different from the order and tidiness of the Bellington Hill station. *It's easy to see what happens to places once there is no one left to maintain them*, Eleanor thought. Wiesental station was in the process of reverting to what it had once been and what it would have looked like when the first white settlers arrived and felled the trees and fenced the land. The only thing that Eleanor could see that indicated there was any maintenance being done at all was the straight lines of barbed wire fences. The fences stretched to the flat horizon. She opened one gate and then kept walking along the gravel track to the next one until she caught sight of the woolshed and the pens which used to hold the sheep before and after they had been shorn.

She had not seen the woolshed for a long time. How different the building had looked like then. She remembered it as it had been. Now the old woolshed, its grey wooden frame and rusted iron roof shimmering under the yellow sun, resembled a Wild West fortress. A six foot deep trench surrounded the building. The wooden rails for the pens were no longer there. They had been replaced with rolls and rolls of barbed wire, rolled up in such a way that it made entry to the shed almost impossible. The wire stretched around the four sides of the building. It was a disturbing sight and whatever was in Hans's mind as he set about changing the innocent building into a war zone and making the building a defence against imagined foreign invaders, was even more disturbing. Eleanor hesitated and thought what to do next. For a moment, she wavered and she wondered whether the plans that she had carefully and triumphantly made just a few days ago, should go ahead. At that moment, she had to make a decision. She usually made decisions quickly and just as quickly made decisions for others to follow but as she studied the old woolshed, now a changed sight, a slight and uneasy feeling came into her mind. The only sound she heard came from a lone kookaburra perched in a distant gum tree. She saw a shimmer of colour against the blue sky as the bird flew off.

She walked carefully towards the back of the building and here she saw that Hans had carefully constructed a means to get into the shed. He had placed a wooden plank over the trench and the barbed wire entanglement was cut in order to allow him to get to the steps and the door. Presumably in his mind he had worked out a plan as he would have been able to quickly replace the barbed wire and remove the plank should the dreaded foreign troops come close to the building. Eleanor stepped on the plank and through the hole in the barbed wire. She knocked on the door. It was new and the clean timber of this new door

340

contrasted with the greying wood of the rest of the building. She knocked again, louder this time.

"Hans, open the door!" she called.

No sound came from the inside. She called again, louder this time.

"Open the door!!"

"Who is it?"

"Eleanor Bradshaw. Let me in!"

"GO AWAY!!!"

Eleanor was not the sort of person who gave up and this was important to her. She put her briefcase and the brown paper shape onto the step and this time, she hammered on the door with both hands.

"I'm not going away, Hans until you open this door!"

"What do ya want?" The rough voice came from inside the shed.

"We must talk!"

"I've nothin' to say to ya. Leave me alone."

"Open the door, Hans. NOW!!"

She heard the bolt being pulled at the back of the door and Hans's unshaven face appeared.

"I've nothin' to say to a Bradshaw," he said.

"Let me in Hans, please."

"We've nothin' to say to each other. How did ya get here anyways?"

"That's of no consequence. I've something to say to you. Now, can we talk?"

The door opened slightly. Eleanor picked up her briefcase and the brown paper shape and then pressed her black and tan sandal firmly into the gap so that Hans had no alternative but to open the door further and allow a determined Eleanor into the shed.

"What do ya want?" he growled.

"I've a proposition to put to you, Hans," Eleanor replied. "May I sit down?"

341

She looked around the shed. Two beechwood veneer chairs both with chipped black metal frames sat side by side along the wall where the shearers used to shear the sheep. The chairs looked the worse for wear but they were the only seating available. She hauled both chairs into the middle of the shed and wiped the dust from the seats with an oily rag that she retrieved from the top of an old hessian bag. She sat down. Hans remained standing. He stood with his arms rigid at his side and his legs apart.

"Now, Hans let's get down to business."

"I've nothin' to say to ya."

"Oh yes you do. Our families go back a long way, don't they now? Ever since Lord Cyril... "

"That bastard!"

Eleanor frowned. Normally she would not allow anyone to denigrate her hero but she knew that Hans Seefeldt wasn't rational these days. *Anyone would have been able to see this, just by looking at him*, she thought. Oisin had filled her in with the visible behavioural signs and also a few details about the paranoia. She decided to ignore the insult.

"So you say," she replied carefully. "Don't you remember that it was Lotte Seefeldt who married Lord Cyril and it was Lotte who walked away from Wiesental?"

"That's history. Who cares now?"

"I care."

Hans shrugged. He remained standing. Eleanor untied the string around the brown paper shape and lifted the oval frame onto her knee so that Hans could see the sepia portrait.

"And he cares, Hans... Lord Cyril cares. Look at his eyes, there's unfinished business there."

"Rubbish. Ya talkin' bloody rubbish, woman but that's what the Bradshaws are. Bullshit artists, always have been, the whole bloody lot of 'em and ya the biggest one of all!"

Eleanor smiled slightly. She refused to allow Hans to draw her into an argument. That would be futile.

"Be that as it may. The Bradshaws, the Patersons and the Seefeldts have been in Kilgoolga a long time. We all of us matter to the district. Our properties have boundary fences. Just because Cyril was the by far the most influential and industrious of all the families doesn't make the Bradshaw descendants any lesser than the Seefeldts... or the Patersons for that matter. And remember, Hans," she murmured softly, "there's only you and Hilda left on Wiesental now!"

"What's that to do with you?"

"Everything," Eleanor replied.

She placed the photograph of Lord Cyril upright on the other chair. Now there were four eyes watching Hans. He remained standing. He still held his arms rigid at his side and both his hands were clenched into fists. His large frame dwarfed Eleanor's small shape but she remained seated. She wasn't in any way intimidated. Rather the contrary. She felt she was winning. She pointed to Cyril.

"Remember Lotte, Hans. Lotte and Heinrich at Wiesental with Uncle Albert all those years ago? Struggling to make ends meet and so far from all they knew back in Germany. You can feel their struggle, sometimes, can't you? You can't escape your genes, Hans. It makes you what you are. A hundred years or so is nothing in the long view of human history and you know and I believe that all the generations of Bradshaws and Seefeldts are bound together by that marriage between Cyril and Lotte. I've always felt that Lord Cyril speaks to me. Do you wonder sometimes, how we all are connected in some way? I know I do."

Eleanor lowered her voice and tried to focus her eyes onto his face but Hans refused to look at either she or the photograph. She wanted him to know just how important it was to her. If she had expected Hans to agree with her or at the very least nod his head and thus give some sort of acquiescence to her measured words, she not only

343

miscalculated but misjudged him because he raised his voice and said in a threatening tone,

"Your bloody Cyril was a bastard. Lotte should have left him. Look at him. Really take a good hard look at him, Eleanor. This is what I think of your Lord Cyril!!"

And as he said the words, he grabbed the oval frame and threw the precious portrait onto the floor of the woolshed. The glass cracked into a dozen pieces. This infuriated Hans even more and he stamped his heavy leather boot down so hard onto the face of Lord Cyril that the paper ripped and the glass fractured into even smaller pieces. Eleanor gasped.

"What have you done? What have you done?" she cried.

She knelt and tried to pull his boot away from the destroyed portrait but Hans grabbed her arm and pushed her back onto the wooden chair.

"What have ya come here for, witch?" he yelled. "Satan's child!!"

Even this action did not frighten Eleanor. She was shaken but still defiant. She had come to Wiesental for a reason and she meant to stay until it was accomplished. In her eyes, Hans Seefeldt was no match for her. Her mental agility was far superior to his physical power. She was in tune with an unseen world and knew things that others did not. That's what she believed. She had special powers. So she remained calm.

"You might have destroyed an image, Hans Seefeldt," she hissed, "but you can't destroy an idea. Now, this is what I have to say!"

"GET OUT!!!"

"I'm not leaving until this is done."

Eleanor reached into the small brown leather briefcase that she had placed at the side of her chair.

"I've had my solicitor draw up the documents, Hans. All you need to do is sign. You can still write your name, can't you?"

Hans appeared confused. He didn't answer and instead, sat down heavily on the other wooden chair. Eleanor, sensing victory, continued,

"Look at this place, Hans," she purred. "Barbed wire, trenches, living in an old shed... what are you doing to yourself?"

"The Commies are comin'," he mumbled. "Need to be prepared for them bastards."

"Now, Hans. Why would they want Wiesental? It's hardly prime land," she added sarcastically.

"It's my land."

"You're so right there, Hans. Yes, you own the land and it's all thanks to Lotte and Heinrich, isn't it? And Lord Cyril had a part to play in it, too, didn't he?"

"First thing that'll happen, ya know Eleanor, is that them Viet Cong fellas will bomb all hell out of the cities and then them soft city bastards panic an' head for the bush, just like it happened in Darwin last time. Them city drongos wouldn't have a clue, ya know. Not city blokes. Couldn't boil water. But I'll be ready for them yellow slit-eyed bastards when they come, ya mark my words!!"

It occurred to Eleanor that Hans had not heard anything she had said to him nor had he noticed the thick envelope that she held in her hand. He had changed in those few moments and was now quite conspiratorial.

"I'll see that Hilda is OK. I've a plan, ya see. Hilda's ma sister, I can't have them fellas doin' things to her. But I have a plan. Ya'll see," he said and he took a step towards Eleanor.

"I'm sure you have, Hans. But you know, you and Hilda aren't getting any younger and that young Irishman will go back to Ireland soon and it'll be hard for you then, won't it? Trying to make a living on this land and," she paused to let the words sink in, "with the Viet Cong coming, you'll find it difficult, won't you?"

"I'm ready for them."

"I know you are, Hans. That's why I've come to see you today. To talk things through."

"I haven't anything to say to a Bradshaw."

"I know that, too, Hans. But as I said, the Bradshaws and the Seefeldts go back a long way."

Hans looked at Eleanor then. He appeared to be thinking. He took another step towards her and he whispered,

"There's them bloody useless Patersons, too, ya know, Eleanor... at Kinleven, don't forget them! Can remember me granddad tellin' me that Jamie Paterson wanted Heinrich's land way back. No one knows what happened to Jamie, do they? 'Abos' probably got 'im, I reckon. But Heinrich wouldn't give up one square inch of his land to the Patersons, I'm right 'bout that, ain't I? Ya know about these things more than me?"

"Yes, Hans. You're right. I've been through the history of Kilgoolga. No one knows what happened to Jamie Paterson. They were hard times. Doubt if we'll ever know. People just disappeared. The bush was a tough place to be back in those days. Still is. That's why I've come to see you today, Hans. To talk."

Hans frowned.

"Well, what do ya want? I'm busy, ya know. Can't waste ma time yabberin' away. Got things to do."

"I know you have," she said gently. "I've been thinking of what you said, Hans," Eleanor could be persuasive and she sensed that this was the right moment, "your ancestor... and mine, too, Heinrich Seefeldt, well, he kept the land and you still have it but now I think it's the right time to think seriously about Wiesental... for the sake of Hilda, too."

"What's there to think about?"

346

"I will give you a good offer, Hans."

"An offer?"

"For Wiesental. It'll stay in the family then, don't you see?"

"I don't understand what your sayin'? Why would I sell Wiesental?"

"Because it's for the best, Hans. For Hilda's sake, too. I've had my solicitor draw up the papers. All you need to do is sign and you won't have to worry anymore. The Commies won't get you and Hilda. You'll be safe."

Even in his present state of mind, she had expected him to agree because it was a good plan and a well thought out one. Eleanor Bradshaw had waited a long time for Wiesental. This is what she had assumed would happen but instead, Hans trampled once more on the photograph of Lord Bradshaw and he clenched his fists. He was in a rage. He swore and then he took hold of Eleanor's shoulders and he shook her. Hard.

"JEZEBEL!!!! DO YA THINK I'D LET THE LIKES OF YOUSE LOT GET HOLD OF WIESENTAL. NEVER!!!!"

Oisin had spent a pleasant, if rather challenging morning, rescuing a young calf that had become parted from its mother. The calf had somehow managed to get through one of the barbed wire fences and had found its way to the creek bank. Here, in the soft soil its foot had become trapped under a fallen branch of an acacia tree. The more the poor animal struggled, the worse the situation became until the exhausted and frightened calf appeared to be losing its struggle for life. Its mother on the other side of the fence was distraught and it was her frantic and plaintive mooing that alerted Oisin to the plight of her calf.

Since Hans no longer did any work around the station during the day and spent most of his time in the woolshed and indeed, most of his nights there, Oisin had taken over the running of the property. A year ago, he would have thought it would have been impossible for him to do all this. At that time, he had lacked any the skills necessary to oversee the day to day work of a farmer in the outback. However, he had learned such a lot from Hans in that year that now, rather than being an inexperienced and rather naïve young man; he had become a competent and well-informed farmer and general labourer. He was physically strong and perhaps equally as important; he now enjoyed the work and the solitude of the bush. So he established a routine every day. He would rise early and eat his breakfast with Hilda. Occasionally Hans joined them but it was no longer the Hans of old but rather a shell of a man, grey and weary who had no interest in the day to day workload and seemed oblivious to the fact that the young Irishman now did all the work. Oisin's first concern was always to make sure the small herd of black Aberdeen Angus were safe. He knew that Hans had preferred sheep, but Oisin rather liked the cattle. He found them interesting and given the fact that the herd was small in number compared to the cattle on larger and more prosperous stations, it made getting to know them a lot easier. He studied them and discovered their different personalities and in this way he learned and his confidence grew when he was about them. There were just enough cattle to make a modest living on Wiesental. Any more would have required that more workers would have had to be employed. The small herd was enough to cope with and when they were ready to go to market, Oisin knew that he had contributed to their well-being and it was his growing understanding that made for good animal husbandry. To add to his expanding knowledge, he borrowed books on cattle rearing from the Kilgoolga Library and talked to local farmers. It was all a world removed from his old life in Edinburgh and Ireland. Often he wondered what that old life had been.

He usually drove the Land Rover over the rough ground to check on the cattle. Hans's obsession with fences meant that there were many gates to open and close but Oisin was agile and it was all part of the routine. As a companion he took the new Kelpie pup, an eager and intelligent little animal named Patch. The older blue and grey cattle dog had retired and spent his days sleeping, untethered and in the shade of the acacias at the side of the homestead, so that the work with the cattle was now the job of the enthusiastic young Patch. Oisin always counted the cattle to make sure they were all there and it was then that he discovered the absent calf and its mother. He drove further through the paddock until he came across the distressed mother. In her valiant struggle to find her calf, she had injured herself on the barbed wire and bloodied her side. Oisin stopped the Land Rover and he and Patch got out. The cow, seeing the dog, let out a plaintive cry but it was this cry that caused the calf on the other side of the fence to answer. Oisin climbed over the fence and walked the twenty metres or so to the creek. A frightened and weakened calf on seeing its human rescuer managed a low cry and attempted once again to pull its leg from under the branch. Oisin ascertained the situation quickly. The calf, although trapped was healthy. It was just a matter of removing the branch and then persuading the calf to climb up the creek bank. The mother on the other side of the fence would do the rest. It took brute strength to shift the branch but Oisin was strong and in about fifteen minutes or so the calf was free. It clambered up the creek bank none the worse for its adventure and trotted towards the fence followed by Oisin and an excitable Patch. Being in charge of Patch required a firm voice and to avoid any further misadventures that might happen to the calf and its mother, Oisin used his stick to control both dog and calf. The barbed wire fence was an obstacle and to solve the problem, Oisin, Patch and the calf made their way along the side to another of Hans's iron gates. The calf limped slightly but otherwise was unhurt while its devoted mother, mooing constantly, followed along on the other side of the fence. Their reunion was something to witness and another reason why Oisin had, during his time at Wiesental, become charmed by the antics of the Aberdeen Angus. It had been a rewarding morning's work.

He had his morning tea and biscuits at the Land Rover. It was another clear day and there was already an autumnal cool in the mid-morning air. Winter was approaching. These were the days Oisin liked the best and these were the days when he thought what an amazing experience it was for him, just being out in the open air surrounded by the solitude and beauty of the Australian bush with not another human being for miles and miles. In the distance he could see a line of trees and behind them was Kinleven, the Paterson property. Miles away to the right another boundary fence marked Bellington Hill station, the home of the Bradshaws who owned more land than the Patersons and the Seefeldts many times over. *These three families with their histories, Kilgoolga would be nothing without them,* he thought. The three families whose struggle over their environment gave them all a commonality of purpose but that had led them to have such different ways of viewing their world for each family regarded one another with either amusement or suspicion and in the case of Hans Seefeldt, hatred.

Oisin drove back to the homestead and he was still thinking about the three families when he got there.

Eleanor Bradshaw's bottle green Citroën was parked at the side of Wiesental homestead. No one was about. Hilda, now that Hans appeared less around the place, often ventured out more. In fact, instead of her weekly or fortnightly visits to Kilgoolga as in the past, she drove her station wagon into the town once a week and sometimes, even twice these days. It was Monday and at breakfast, she announced that she would not be back till noon. So to see Eleanor's car and no Hilda was something that Oisin had not anticipated. He parked the Land Rover and gave Patch some water. Then he looked around and wondered what he should do.

The woolshed was about half a mile from the homestead. This is where Hans would be and there was a high probability that Eleanor would be there as well. She had been determined to get the keys to Wiesental and talk to Hans. *It had all to do with these three families*, thought Oisin but he still had no idea what it was all about. He only knew that Eleanor was here and no one else was around. Out on the silent plains he had felt at peace and at times he even enjoyed the solitude but now that same isolation seemed to him to have taken on an oppressive, even a deathly sensation. He shivered slightly. It was as if someone had walked over his grave. He went into the homestead and looked in all the rooms. There was no one about. The old ginger cat was asleep on one of the lounge chairs in the kitchen. He opened a sleepy eye when he heard Oisin and stretched himself but remained on the chair, watching. The table was set for three. It looked as if Hilda must be planning to return to prepare lunch and she had thought Hans might join them. Oisin went into his bedroom. All was as he had left it, hours before.

He walked outside into the bright sunlight. His eyes took a moment to adjust to the light. He thought that the only course of action now would be to find Eleanor and he set off in the direction of the woolshed. It didn't occur to him that Eleanor might not welcome his intrusion if she was in the middle of a conversation with Hans. But Hans was so ill at the moment and so illogical about most things that neither of them might even notice if Oisin suddenly appeared. It could all be different anyhow and Eleanor might surprise him and be glad to see him.

He had kept away from the woolshed these last few weeks because Hans was insistent that neither he nor Hilda should come anywhere near the place. Before then, he had used his carpentry skills to build a wooden door and hang it for there had been major repairs needed in order to secure the shed to Hans's specification. Hans had appeared to be pleased with the workmanship done and he even gave Oisin a compliment of sorts which was most unusual. Together they rolled out the barbed wire to encircle the shed and then Hans instructed Oisin to go into Kilgoolga and hire a small digger from Matt's garage so that they could dig the trenches. Digging the trenches mechanically was a far easier job than by shovel and spade and he was relieved that the irrational Hans had at least regarded this as the best and quickest option. Oisin had liked digging trenches this way and even if he knew the whole idea of trenches and barbed wire was totally unproductive work and would never be needed, the days spent on the digger had been enjoyable. At the end of the week, for it had taken that long to complete the task, he had become a proficient digger driver. This experience had to be worthwhile even if the work was not. All these varied tasks had taken over a month to complete but once they were done, Hans locked the door and that was that. The place suddenly took on a different atmosphere entirely. Both Hilda and Oisin were now less inclined to go anywhere near the old woolshed.

He went around the back of the shed to his newly made door and saw the plank and the gap in the barbed wire. Everything was still. He hesitated for a moment before knocking on the door. Still no sound and then he heard Hans's voice. Oisin knocked on the door once more.

"Who is it?"

"Oisin."

"Who?"

"Oisin… Oisin Kelly, Hans. Can I come in?"

"Go away!"

"Is Eleanor Bradshaw in there with you?"

"I said, go away!!"

He heard a woman's voice. It was Eleanor.

"Oisin!" she called out his name. Her voice sounded different somehow.

"Eleanor, can I come in?"

"You can't come in, whoever ya are!" This from Hans.

"I'm coming in… "

He tried to shove the door open. He had to push it hard because there seemed to be something jamming it on the inside. He kicked the bottom of the door with his foot and the door opened.

There had been nothing in Oisin's mind that could have prepared him for what he saw in the woolshed. Before it had been an old shed with memories of sheep and shearers and evidence left behind from those happier days. It was dark and it took him a few seconds to adjust his eyes after the glare from outside. The first thing he noticed was the black and white photograph of Julius, the prize Merino. The photograph now hung at the end of the shed and alongside this, and pinned on the wall was the map that Hans had drawn of the fortification plan. Adjustments had been made to the map for now there were dozens of red and blue arrows and all were drawn in the direction of the old woolshed. It looked like a military plan of attack and a detailed one at that. Hans must have spent hours drawing the arrows and the various black lines on the map before he finally decided that it was ready to be pinned onto the wall.

On the wall where the remains of the woollen bales used to be, Oisin could see a bed of sorts made from these old bales and flung over this make shift bed was a tartan blanket with a black and white striped pillow minus its case. This must have been where Hans slept. He had brought tins of food from the homestead and these were stacked side by side in neat rows further along the wall. All the tins were arranged in an orderly fashion and it occurred to Oisin that Hans had stacked them in this way because that was the way Hans had always been, methodical in everything he did and everything having its place in life. The sight of the tins rather unnerved him. A primus stove and a kettle completed the picture of Hans Seefeldt's new living arrangements.

Oisin had taken all this in before he became aware of what really was happening. It was one of those surreal times when the sight of other things comes into your mind before the reality of the actual scene dawns. This is what happened to Oisin for the moment that he became aware of the guns was the moment when he knew something was wrong. The desk that Hans had somehow dragged from the kitchen was now positioned in the centre of the shed. An unlit kerosene lamp sat on the desk. This was the only lighting in the shed. The photo of Julius and the military map were pinned on the wall at the front of the desk. It looked like Hans had positioned the desk in such a way that he could sit at his desk and study both the map and Julius. The two shotguns from the kitchen lay on the desk and beside the guns were the boxes of cartridges, arranged neatly in the same way as the tins and beside them, a row of bullets.

"What do ya want? I told ya not to come in!"

Hans stood in front of the desk and in his hand he held the rifle that had hung for years on the gun rack in the kitchen and he pointed this rifle at Oisin.

"GET OVER THERE!!!"

Oisin didn't move. His feet were like anchors. He couldn't move them.

"I TOLD YA, GET OVER THERE!! NEXT TO THE WITCH!!!!!"

It had taken Oisin's eyes a few moments to adjust to the light in the shed and his whole attention had been focussed on the changes that had been made there. In his bewilderment he hadn't noticed Eleanor. She was at the far end of the shed and underneath the line of shearing shears. She called his name again.

"Oisin! Do something!!"

This was not the voice of the Eleanor Bradshaw he had come to admire and even at times, to love. It was a shaky voice and it was a voice full of fear. When Hans heard Eleanor, he pointed the rifle towards her and he yelled out so loudly that if he had been anywhere else, people would have come running to find out what was happening. But in the old woolshed so far from anywhere and anyone, there was no one to hear and no one to rush to the rescue.

"SHUT UP, YA BITCH. I TOLD YA TO BE QUIET. YOU, GET OVER THERE BESIDE THE WOMAN FROM HELL!!!"

Still Oisin remained in the same spot. He felt the barrel of the rifle on his arm.

"MOVE!"

Then Oisin moved. Closer to Eleanor.

Her hands were tied behind her back with orange baler twine. The same twine had been used to tie her legs and her arms. Hans had twisted the twine so tightly around the back of the chair that she was unable to move her body at all. The only movement she was able to make was to stretch her fingers slightly but even that was difficult. Her legs, too, were bound together in a similar fashion and the twine knotted around the rung of the chair so she was completely restrained. Any movement of her legs would have caused pain. She looked helpless and afraid. This had not been the outcome that she had planned. She had spent most of her life certain that one day she would become the owner of Wiesental station because this is what she believed must happen to complete the task that Lord Cyril had started all those years ago. It was Eleanor's belief that when her ancestor married Lotte Seefeldt, he should by rights have owned Wiesental as well. She had uncovered a diary written by Lord Cyril and he had written this down. He died before he was able to acquire the Seefeldt property but the words in his diary indicated that this had been his goal. In his diary he wrote of his dislike of Heinrich Seefeldt. It had taken generations of Bradshaws to acquire more and more property in Kilgoolga and Milberra but the one piece of land that Eleanor longed for the most and she had coveted it from an early age was the land belonging to her neighbour, Hans Seefeldt. If she could become the owner of Wiesental, Lord Cyril would finally rest in peace. This is what she believed. She had business acumen aplenty bred in her for generations and she had always been a country woman at heart. Hans Seefeldt's land was marginal and in no way would it yield what Bellington Hill did but that wasn't important. What was important to Eleanor was the righting of a wrong and the ownership of land. She had come to Hans with a proposition which she had thought he would not be able to refuse. She had expected him to be difficult at first because that was his way. The whole Kilgoolga district knew what Hans was like. Nothing, however, could have prepared her for the state of his mind. Eleanor tried to reason with him.

"Untie me, Hans! We can talk... please."

"What have I got ta say ta the likes of you?"

"Just let me go and we'll put an end to it."

"It's too late."

Oisin edged nearer to Eleanor. Where she sat, bound to the chair and further from the desk, was the area of the woolshed where the sheep had been shorn before being pushed out through the openings in the shed to the outside pens. All the openings had been covered with thick exterior plywood, nailed down with six inch nails but the rusty shears still remained fixed to the pulleys above. Shafts of bright light shone through dozens of cracks in the wood so that the old woolshed was a mix of speckled light and dark shadows. A larger crack in the wall near where Eleanor sat meant that it was possible to see just a little bit clearer there. Oisin moved a little closer towards Eleanor. He could hear her breathe.

"STAY THERE!!!"

Oisin was now about two metres from Eleanor. Once more the rifle was pointed at his chest. He froze.

"What are ya doin' with this woman?" Hans said.

"She's my friend, Hans."

"Friend!!!" Hans spat on the floor.

"Let her go. Let us both go."

"It's too late."

Hans moved towards them both. He gripped the rifle with two hands. Now Oisin could see his face clearer as Hans stood where a shaft of light shone through. He couldn't believe the state of the man. A week ago, Hans had been different. He had come back into the homestead one evening and eaten a meal with Hilda and Oisin and read from the Bible as he used to. True, he had left abruptly after that and neither Hilda nor Oisin had seen him since then. They thought he would return when the food ran out in the woolshed or if it got too cold to sleep there. This is what they thought would happen. Hoped would happen. This was not the man they knew. This man was a stranger.

Oisin tried to reason. It was the only thing he could think to do. If he brought religion into it, Hans might listen. Perhaps that might be the only way.

"Hans, this is not the way to go about it. Ye go to the church, don't ye now, what would the pastor say? This isn't right. Untie Eleanor and we can talk about it... please."

Then Hans looked at Oisin. He lowered the rifle. And he laughed.

357

"The pastor is a fool. Who takes any notice of him? Why should I let this Bradshaw woman go? What have the Bradshaws ever done for me? Stole my sheep, ya know. The high and mighty Bradshaws stole my sheep when I was down on ma luck. I thought ya knew all this, young fella. Thought I told ya 'bout ma sheep. Miss ma sheep."

"Put the gun down, Hans and we can talk. I know ye miss yer sheep but this isn't going to change anything, tying Eleanor up like that, now is it?"

He glanced at Eleanor. He saw a glimmer of hope come into her eyes. He continued,

"We can all calm down and talk about it properly. Just give me the gun... "

Oisin saw Hans hesitate. He lowered the rifle and sat down on the other beechwood veneer chair but he kept the rifle pointed at Eleanor. Oisin took a nervous step towards him.

"I'm tired, Oisin," Hans said.

"I know ye are, Hans. Give me the gun."

"Can't do that!"

Outside Oisin heard the lonely call of a crow. It must have flown over the roof of the woolshed because the sound was loud. Life was still going on in the world outside. The sudden call of the crow must have startled Eleanor because she said in a clear voice,

"Hans, give the boy the gun. Please. Do as he says. We can talk about this later."

For just a brief moment in time she became the forceful Eleanor Bradshaw whom everyone expected her to be. The Eleanor who was in charge of any situation. The Eleanor who knew how to get people to do as she wished, always. The woman who owned Kilgoolga. The woman who never failed. She wanted to be that Eleanor Bradshaw once again. She fixed her eyes onto Hans but he didn't respond. She tried again.

"Hans, you and I have known each other all our lives. What we have to say to each other is between ourselves. We can talk later. Just untie me and I'll go away and leave you in peace... "

Hans stared at Eleanor. Whether he was aware of what she was saying wasn't certain. He seemed confused.

"It's too late."

"It's not too late, Hans. We can talk later. This is just between us three. No one else need know, not even Hilda."

"Leave ma sister out of it!"

"Of course, Hans. Hilda needn't know." Eleanor glanced at Oisin and nodded her head slightly. He frowned. What did she have in mind?

"Give me the gun now, Hans and untie Eleanor," said Oisin and he held out his hand towards Hans.

The silence in the shed was electric. Hans remained seated on the chair with the rifle. He gripped the barrel harder. Oisin thought at that very moment it was all over. Hans didn't speak. Nor did Eleanor. Nor did Oisin. *Any moment now*, thought Oisin, *he'll give me the gun and I'll free Eleanor*.

"Can't do that!" said Hans and he stood up, all six foot of him.

He smiled. Then he took a few paces towards Eleanor and he still held the rifle. As he got closer to her, he stood once again on the broken glass that lay on the floor. He stared at the portrait of Lord Cyril and at the fragments of glass and the torn paper that once was the face of the most famous Bradshaw of them all. His boot crushed a part of the white oval frame and he kicked the piece away. And he frowned.

"Well, stone the crows," he said, "Lord Bradshaw's dead!"

Then he flicked the safety lock of the rifle with his finger and raised the gun so that it pointed straight at Eleanor Bradshaw's head.

"Stone the crows," he said again, "Eleanor Bradshaw's dead!!!"

"NO!!!"

Oisin didn't think of anything else but Eleanor. He lunged towards Hans and grabbed the rifle with both his hands. His first thought was to lock the rifle again so it couldn't fire. This swift action took Hans completely by surprise and he loosened his grip on the trigger just for a split second but it did the trick. The gun wouldn't fire now. For a second both men were inches away from each other's face. They could feel each other's breath and smell each other's manhood. They were competing stags. The old man and the young one and it was a fight to the death. Oisin was strong. He pushed Hans away and Hans toppled slightly on the greasy woolshed floor. Four hands fought for the rifle now but Hans was not beaten. He still grasped the rifle with both his hands and then he shook it hard, so hard that it caused Oisin to loosen his grip for a brief moment but it was enough. He stumbled backwards and as he did, his feet slid slightly on the built up grease of the woolshed floor. This was to Hans's advantage.He sensed victory. He rammed Oisin with the butt of the rifle. Then Oisin stumbled again and this time he was closer to the floor. The two men still held onto the rifle but Oisin was losing the battle. For a split second, they stopped struggling and stared into each other's eyes. The next moment Hans wrestled the rifle from Oisin's fingers and holding onto the barrel with both his hands, he struck the butt onto the side of Oisin's head close to his left ear. Oisin let out a cry. He stumbled. His knees started to buckle. Then Hans hit him again with the butt and this time the blow landed on his left shoulder. As he fell, he noticed a few tufts of grey wool stuck between the floorboards. The wool must have lain there for years. Then his head hit the floor. He collapsed into the foetal position and tried to cover his head with his hands but Hans wasn't about to stop. He lifted the rifle high above his head and brought the butt

360

down once again onto Oisin's upper left arm, near his shoulder.

The last thing that Oisin saw was Hilda's face at the door and he heard her scream. He heard a click and then the sound of a gunshot... and then another...

CHAPTER SIXTEEN

Oisin opened an eye. He could hear the hum of traffic through the open window. Then he heard the shrill sound of a police siren coming even nearer. He wondered where he was. He wanted to open his left eye but he couldn't see. It was black. When he tried to focus on the open window with his right eye everything around him appeared blurred. Nothing seemed right. He turned his head slightly and noticed the drip. Then he saw the tubes and looked at his right hand. His hand was bruised. He attempted to move his fingers. They did not seem to be a part of him anymore. When he moved his head to the left he could see that his shoulder was covered in a white plaster and there were bandages around his rib cage. He tried to ease his body to sit up but the pain in his side was too much for him. His head sank gratefully back onto the pillows again and he shut his right eye.

He must have slept for when he opened his eye all he could see in front of him was a white shape. The white shape had cool fingers and they held his right hand ever so gently. He moved his head towards the white shape and saw that the white shape had a face and brown hair and on top of the brown hair sat a crisp white cap with two red vertical bands. It was a kind face under the cap. She smiled.

"How do you feel?"

"Where am I?"

"In the General. Brisbane General Hospital. Don't try to move." She placed a thermometer under his tongue.

"How did I get here?" he said when the thermometer was out of his mouth.

"Emergency. You arrived by ambulance from Kilgoolga." Her blue eyes had a twinkle behind them.

"I can't remember anything."

"You're lucky to be here," she said. "Looks like you've got the luck of the Irish!"

"What's happened to me? I can't see out of my left eye... "

"Doctor O'Neill will be along soon. She'll tell you," she nodded. "How did an Irish boy get to Kilgoolga anyway? Thought nothing happened out there in the back of beyond."

"Ye'd be surprised."

"Looks like it!" She grinned at him. "Try to get some rest."

Doctor O'Neill was a stout woman of about forty years of age. She had a wicked sense of humour and everyone loved Doctor O'Neill. She was that kind of person and that kind of doctor. Doctor O'Neill was also very good at her job. When the young Irishman arrived on her ward she was the only one of her colleagues who thought he would pull through. And she was right.

"Well, now, young man," she said and patted his arm gently to waken him, "what have you been doing with yourself? I'm Doctor O'Neill."

Oisin opened his eye. Standing at his bedside was a woman with a mission, a mission to save him. He tried to smile but his face still hurt.

"I can't remember much. I think I must have blacked out."

"You did."

"The nurse said I got here by ambulance."

"That's right. We'll sort you out. We don't keep you in here for too long, you know."

363

"I can't see out of my eye... my left eye."

"I know. We might be able to save it though," she said.

"My head hurts."

"Yes. You've had quite an ordeal out there. Hope it hasn't put you off us Aussies though! We're not all mad buggers, you know!"

Oisin smiled as much as he could.

"I can hardly hear anything. Everything seems far away."

Doctor O'Neill poked a finger into his left ear. The nurse whispered into his right.

"Can you hear me?" asked the nurse.

"Yes."

This time it was the the nurse who poked her finger into his right ear. The doctor whispered into the left ear.

"How about that?" she asked.

"Nothing."

He noticed the doctor and the nurse looked at each other over the bed. He wondered what was happening.

"I know. You'll need to rest but we know what we're doing," Doctor O'Neill smiled.

"Will I be alright?"

"Yes. You're tough. There's just a few things though." Doctor O'Neill paused. It didn't get any easier having to tell patients what they had to face. Sometimes, it hurt like hell. She came around to the right side of the bed and sat down.

"Do you want the good news first or the not so good news?" she asked him.

Oisin Kelly was an Irishman. He knew about suffering. His country had suffered for centuries and the priests and nuns had told him it was all good for the soul. Heaven was waiting.

"Tell me the not so good news first," he said.

"Well, Oisin, it looks like you've lost your hearing in your left ear, I'm afraid. There was nothing we could do.

364

You'll be able to hear out of your right ear though. That's the not so good news. We think your left eye might be able to be saved. We'll do our best. We've a great eye surgeon here. And we think you'll be able to walk. It'll take time and a lot of physio but you're young and strong. See, I'm onto the good news already!"

"I can still see out of my right eye but it's a bit of a blur. I can hear ye a bit though, Doctor. Everything seems OK on the right side. What does that mean?"

"It means, young man, that you're a winner. In time, we're sure you'll be able to hear well enough and you've still got the sight in your right eye. Don't worry about it being a bit blurry. That'll change, I'm certain of that. There's been no major internal damage, just bruises. We'll keep you right with the pain killers but, as I said, it will take time to heal."

Another nurse appeared in front of the curtain. Doctor O'Neill got off the bed and spoke to her but Oisin couldn't make out what was being said. Then Doctor O'Neill came to his bedside. Oisin noticed that the nurses and the doctor were always on the right side of the bed.

"You're giving all my nurses something to talk about, young man," she whispered into his right ear. "It's not every day they get a handsome young Irishman to fuss over. You watch out! And... ," she patted his arm, "you just get better for us. You'll be safer then." And Doctor O'Neill gave him the most devilish wink he had ever received. Despite his pain, he just couldn't help grinning. At least, he tried to grin.

The nurses did fuss over him and Doctor O'Neill was right. It was fun having a young Irishman on the ward. But for Oisin Kelly it wasn't fun. When they told him jokes to make him laugh, he tried to smile but it just didn't work. The jokes didn't seem funny anymore. The porter came and moved his bed to the veranda. It was cooler there but the traffic noise was louder. When the nurses shut the curtains at night, they blocked out the noise but not the noise in his ear. He fretted. He was sure he was losing his hearing in his right ear as well despite what Doctor O'Neill had told him. He began to doubt if he'd ever walk again. They kept him on pain killers so the pain in his side was just a dull, dull ache but it didn't go away. One day they came and took the drip from his right hand. It was slightly easier then. He discovered he could move his hand just a little bit. *At least I have movement there in my right hand*, he thought. His left hand was still covered with a bandage. He wondered if he would be able to use it again. He wanted to weep. At times there were tears in his eyes and then the nurses were even more concerned. They hovered around his bed like anxious hens and tried to comfort him. Every one of them was a professional but they were human too. Some patients they liked more than others and they all liked the young Irishman. They hated to see him in pain for they had heard the story of what had happened to him in Kilgoolga and his bravery there. But Oisin didn't feel brave. There were many times he wished he had never come to this country. If he hadn't met Wolfgang in the hostel in Sydney, he would never have gone to Kilgoolga. It would have been good not knowing anything about the place. Because if he hadn't gone to Kilgoolga he would never have met Hans Seefeldt or Eleanor Bradshaw, for that matter and things would have turned out differently. These were the dark moments. Eleanor would have called them the dark night of the soul. Maybe she was right. She was right about some things but not everything. He wondered what had happened to her. Was she alive?

Gradually the memory of what had happened slowly returned to his mind. He relived the moment when he fell to

366

the floor and one night, he dreamed of Hilda. The dream woke him and when he looked around, it was dark in the ward. He could just see the shape of the old man in the bed next to him. The old man snored and he muttered in his sleep. Words Oisin couldn't understand for the old man was a Greek and hadn't been in Australia very long. It all seemed too much to bear. That night he did weep and he prayed. He hadn't said a prayer of any importance for years but the words just came into his head. It must have been a comfort somehow because after he prayed, he closed his eyes and didn't wake till dawn when the clatter of the ward and the morning traffic woke him.

Although winter was approaching, Brisbane was never that cold. He found the humidity during the day hard to bear. He began to long for the soft rain of Ireland and the cold winter days. He longed to be able to turn in his bed. For life to be as it was. The simplest task became a major problem for him. When he was able to lift his head enough to eat and move his body just that little bit more, he felt he had achieved the grandest thing imaginable. The nurses cheered him on that day and Doctor O'Neill was pleased.

"We'll have you out of here in no time now," she told him.

But he didn't believe her. He wished Hans had shot him in the woolshed and then he wouldn't have had to go through all this. He hated it. He hated his life.

"Will I be able to walk? Ever again?" he asked Doctor O'Neill but he doubted anything she would tell him.

"I told you. You'll walk again. We'll fix you up. We'll send you home as good as new!"

"Home?"

"To Ireland, of course. Don't imagine you'll want to return to Kilgoolga, will you? The natives weren't that friendly, so I've heard!"

"No."

367

He thought of Ireland then and the Ballybeg of his childhood. That was a different life. He wondered what would happen now if he did return. Would he be welcomed or had he changed so much that he would be a stranger in his own country? People move on with their lives and he had been away such a long time. Ireland would have changed because he had changed. He might find it difficult, just being back and having to settle to the old ways again when he had seen so much of the new. How could you explain to people what life was like in a place like Kilgoolga, for instance? They would listen to him for a little while but they would soon grow bored with his stories because they had no experience or any understanding of life out there. How could they? How could they imagine a place like Kilgoolga when they had only ever known the soft green of Ireland? If he tried to explain any of it to the people in Ballybeg they would think that Kilgoolga was on the moon. And maybe they would be right.

Frankie wanted to take him home. That's what Frankie had said but he was never sure about his brother. Frankie might have just been all talk. He was often like that. Maybe no one in his family wanted to see him again anyway. If he couldn't walk or hear much, he would just be a burden to them. They would be better off without him. Everyone would be better off without him.

A few days later he felt a little better. He could move his body in the bed and the pain in his side lessened, just slightly but enough. The sight returned to his right eye and could see clearly out of that eye again. He began to feel some of his old optimism returning. Then Doctor O'Neill came and she was determined. He had to get out of the bed. He protested because his mind had decided that he would never walk again.

"Nonsense", she said.

And she was right. Two nurses held him and Doctor O'Neill gave the three of them their orders. One slow step and then another and another. He walked ten paces and back to his bed again. The old Greek man in the bed beside him raised both his fists in the air for victory and Oisin Kelly thought it had to be the greatest thing he had ever done in his life.

The next day he received an even greater surprise. He had dozed off despite the noise in the ward and he woke to hear a voice speaking softly into his right ear. He opened his eye. A round face with brown eyes was just a few inches away from his face.

"Claire?"

She smiled. A soft, gentle smile for one so prim.

"How do you feel?"

He didn't know what he should say to her.

"Might survive," was all he could think to say.

"Of course ye will. Tough as old boots ye are!"

And there was Frankie beside Claire and at his bedside too. Frankie and Claire together and Frankie looked fit and healthy as if he didn't have a care in the world. He was cheery too.

"Ye are a hero, ye know!" he said.

"What are ye talkin' about? I'm no hero."

"Let me be the judge of that, Oisin. I know about heroes. I learnt all about heroes in the priesthood. They come in many shapes and sizes and ye are one of them!" This was a surprise to hear.

"I don't follow ye," replied a puzzled Oisin. Frankie didn't talk that way to him. Not Frankie.

But Frankie was serious.

"Ye tried to save another's life an' nearly lost yer own. That's a hero in my books, isn't it, Claire?" He looked at Claire.

"Yes," she said quietly.

"Didn't think what I was doin'," mumbled Oisin. He hadn't expected to see them. At least, he hadn't expected to see Claire with Frankie.

"What happened? I can't seem to remember much. Just falling to the floor," he said to Claire.

"We're not sure. Hans shot himself, Oisin. He's dead."

No one spoke for a few minutes. It was noisy in the ward and the visitors were arriving. The old Greek man had three women beside him, all talking in Greek and eating grapes. Oisin looked at Claire.

"I'm sorry to hear that... about Hans, I mean. I don't think he knew what he was doing."

"No. Everyone in the district knew about him but no one thought it was that serious. Everyone just thought Hans was a bit barmy, well, you know."

"Aye."

"Can ye remember anything at all?" asked Frankie.

"Only tryin' to get the gun off Hans. He was too strong for me. I can remember him sayin' that 'Lord Bradshaw's dead' and then 'Eleanor Bradshaw's dead!' That's when I tried to grab the rifle."

"Eleanor's dead too, Oisin. He shot her... then he must have turned the gun onto himself."

"Oh God!"

"She wouldn't have suffered, Oisin," said Claire softly. "Hans was a good shot!"

"He'd tied her to a chair... with baler twine."

"I know."

"She didn't deserve that."

"No."

Oisin could feel the tears behind his eyes. He didn't want Claire to see him cry. Suddenly he had the image of Eleanor tied to the chair. He closed his right eye. The left one was still covered in bandages.

"Do you think we should go?" He heard Claire ask Frankie.

"Give him a moment. I'll have a word with him," Frankie replied.

Their voices seemed to come from far away but that might just have been because of his hearing. They were both at his right side, speaking into that ear but it was still hard to hear every word. *The nurses must have told them to come to my right side*, he thought. He opened his eye.

"Frankie?"

"Yer doin' grand, old son. I told ye, yer a hero."

"I still couldn't save her. I tried, though, Frankie. I tried."

"No one's doubting that."

He looked around. Another woman with two young children had arrived to see the old Greek man. The boy and girl were bouncing on the bed fighting over a box of chocolates. The noise got louder.

"Where's Claire?" asked Oisin.

"She'll be back," said Frankie. "Just wanted a word to ye meself, brother to brother."

"We've never really got on, have we?" said Oisin. He felt quite miserable.

"Can't say we have. Guess I never had time. Ye were always just my kid brother. Someone to boss around. Sorry about that."

"Well. Can't be helped."

"No. Ye know, it wasn't all wrong me bein' a priest, Oisin. I learnt a lot about people but I guess the best thing of all was, I got to know a bit about meself. Ye wouldn't have expected that, now, would ye?"

"No. Ye had everything, I thought."

371

"Well, ye never know about another person. Truly know them, that is."

"Eleanor… " He found it hard to speak her name. The name didn't sound real somehow. Like the person. He tried again.

"Eleanor said it was hard for ye. Leavin' the priesthood, that is. I didn't believe her."

"She was right," Frankie said quietly. "Aye, she was right."

Visiting hour was ending. The Greek contingent was packing up and they were all talking at once. Oisin glanced at the old man. The old Greek had shut his eyes. Oisin suddenly felt very tired.

"Frankie," he said. "Frankie, what do ye think I should do?"

His brother grinned. Frankie always had a cheeky grin. It cheered people up. Perhaps when he left the priesthood, people missed that grin.

"Well, Oisin. Think ye have a few things to think about, right enough but the most important thing is to get better. That's the most important thing for ye. Get walkin' again. If ye think of what happened, be gentle with yerself. It was a helluva thing to go through. Don't know what I would have done but I doubt if I'd have been as brave as ye were. But then," he grinned again,

"Uncle Mick always told ye that ye were a warrior and a poet, didn't he, now? Looks like the old man was right after all, God rest his soul. Now, we all know that ye are a warrior! When are ye goin' to be a poet?"

When Frankie left the ward, Oisin lay back in the bed. He moved his right arm to keep the circulation going and then he stretched his legs. He thought of Eleanor Bradshaw. He remembered the first time he had seen her and how he hadn't been able to keep his eyes off her face. She was so different from anyone he had ever known before. When she decided that he was someone she wanted to get to know, he had felt flattered by the attention. Even getting to know Louis had been an experience. It felt good being part of their little group. Sometimes Eleanor had been kind to him. Other times, an uneasy feeling came over him when she was with him. Uneasy with what she told him but then he never for one moment doubted her intelligence even if her words often baffled him. Perhaps she meant well? There were the good times and the bad times, he decided. He doubted if he would ever understand her. Truly understand. It was right what Frankie had said to him, could you ever really know another person? And Eleanor had so many facets to her character and that made her so much more interesting than anyone he had ever met before or ever would meet again. He thought of what had happened to them in the old woolshed. It was becoming a bit clearer now. Maybe what he had thought that day was right. Maybe Eleanor had used him to get to Hans? Maybe that was all he had been for her, a means to an end. When she discovered that he lived and worked with Hans was that the moment she decided to use him and even manipulate him in some way that would be to her advantage? Was the fact that she needed to own everything and everyone the most important thing in life for her? He thought of her obsession with Lord Bradshaw, a dead ancestor. It had to be strange but then, that was Eleanor. Maybe she got some sort of comfort, feeling that she could communicate with this man. Maybe she was able to? He thought of himself and Louis. Perhaps people were to be used by her and then tossed aside. He doubted if Louis would have been around her much longer.

The last time he had talked to her, she had been critical of the Frenchman so maybe she had been planning that it was time for him to go. No one would ever know now. He would never know what she really thought of him and why she decided that she would befriend a young Irishman from Ballybeg, the least likely of any of her acquaintances. *It was all over now,* he thought. He would try not to remember her in those last moments. She had been so fragile, tied to that chair and scared. And no wonder. Hans Seefeldt was insane. He had just wanted to save her. That was all. It was good to shut his eye. All had become quiet again, at least for a while. That was enough thinking for the moment, he decided as he dozed off.

"The police are here to see you, Oisin."

A gentle voice spoke into his right ear. It was one of the young nurses. She looked smart in her crisp white uniform. Oisin was out of bed and sitting on a chair. He was pleased with himself for every day he had managed to do something more. Every day he could feel himself getting just that little bit stronger.

"There's two of them,"the nurse added confidentially. "I'll bring another chair. Close the curtains, too, if you don't want anyone to hear."

It was the cheerful young sergeant from Kilgoolga with a young blonde policewoman beside him. The policewoman had a folder in her hand.

"Well, Oisin, how's it goin', mate? You're lookin' a helluva a lot better than when I last saw you. Thought you were a goner then. We've got to take a statement from you.

Procedure. Are you up for it, mate?" the young sergeant asked him.

"I... I guess so."

"Can you write?" murmured the young policewoman.

"Don't worry about that. You can do the writin', love. Oisin just needs to sign his name. You can do that, can't you, mate? Not left handed, are you, mate?"

Oisin shook his head. *At least that's something*, he thought. It would have been another thing to learn to write with the other hand.

"Sit on the bed," the young sergeant said to the policewoman. "I'll take the chair! Bloody hell, I hate Brisbane. My feet are killin' me."

"Stop complaining, Serge. He does nothing but complain," she said to Oisin. "Too noisy, too crowded, his feet hurt, does nothing but moan."

"You watch yourself, young lady. Or I'll get you posted to Bullamanka!" said the sergeant, good naturedly.

"Where's that?" asked the policewoman.

"Beyond the black stump! Now, let's get on with it. Speak slowly, mate, she's just learned to write."

"Ha... ha... ha! Think you're funny, don't you, Serge?"

"These young ones. No respect for their elders!" the sergeant leaned back in his chair and grinned. The young policewoman poked out her tongue at him.

That's what I like about the Aussies, thought Oisin. *Everyone's a mate*. He couldn't imagine this conversation happening anywhere else in the world.

"Well, in your own time and in your own words, Oisin. Whatever you can remember, mate?" He was serious now. There was a job to do.

"I'll try to remember as best I can. Where do you want me to start?"

"At the beginning, mate. Guess when you saw Hans and Eleanor in the woolshed. Bloody hell, I'll never forget it."

"Best not to dwell on it," said the young policewoman to him kindly. "We've known each other awhile, haven't we, Serge?"

The sergeant nodded.

"Yeah. You're OK, Constable. We'll make a real copper out of you one day! You know, you could get promotion if you put in for Kilgoolga."

"Oh, perish the thought. Dust, flies, mad buggers out there and I'd have to put up with you! And I'd miss the beach."

"See what I mean, Oisin, mate. No respect. Come on, let's get on with it. My feet are killin' me!"

The policewoman took a clipboard and paper out of her folder. She wrote a few words on the paper. She was good looking with long legs. When she perched on Oisin's bed, both he and the sergeant were able to view those legs at a closer range. It was an enjoyable sight.

"Well," said Oisin as the images of the woolshed came into his mind. He spoke slowly. It was very painful to remember. "Do you want me to start when I first saw them... in the woolshed, that is?"

"That'll do, mate," said the sergeant.

"I saw Eleanor's car parked at the homestead... her Citroën, ye know the one... "

The sergeant nodded. There wasn't anyone in Kilgoolga who didn't know Eleanor Bradshaw's bottle green Citroën.

"Then I went to the woolshed because that's where Hans had been spending his days and most of his nights, too. He'd got me to dig a trench all around the place and we rolled out tons of barbed wire. He thought the Viet Cong were comin' to take his land," he said to the young policewoman. She frowned.

"He was off his rocker," explained the sergeant.

"Well, when I managed to get the door open, Hans had a rifle and Eleanor was tied in a chair. Her arms and

376

legs were tied with baler twine, orange baler twine." Oisin shuddered.

"Take your time, mate," said the sergeant.

"Then I don't know quite know what happened next. I tried to reason with him an' I thought if I could just do that, he might put the gun down an' I could free Eleanor but he got mad. Real mad. I thought he was goin' to kill me. Then he trampled on the portrait Eleanor always had in her room at the Commercial, the one of Lord Bradshaw and... "

"The Bradshaws own Kilgoolga," interrupted the sergeant. He thought it best to fill the young policewoman in with all the details. She was good at her job and very thorough. *She would be interested in the details*, the sergeant thought. He continued,

"Eleanor had a bit of a thing goin' with her old ancestor. That's Lord Bradshaw. Yeah, *I know*. Lord Bradshaw. Bit weird, if you ask me. Go on, mate. Just keepin' the constable informed for when she's transferred to Kilgoolga!" He grinned.

"That'll be the day!" she said.

"Sorry, mate. Can't help myself. She always rises to the bait, don't you, love?"

Oisin thought for a moment. It was difficult to try to remember everything. He wondered if Eleanor's face would haunt him for the rest of his life. She had looked so terrified, tied to that chair. He tried again.

"Well, then Hans pointed the rifle at Eleanor and I thought he was goin' to shoot her, there and then. So I grabbed the rifle and I tried to get him to drop it. But he was too much for me. The floor's so greasy in the old woolshed still. I think I tripped and the next thing, he hit me with the butt of the rifle. Here and here."

He touched his left ear and his shoulder.

"Then when I fell onto the floor, he belted me in the ribs. Just before I passed out I saw Hilda and I heard her scream. Then two shots."

377

The constable wrote it all down. No one spoke for a few minutes and then Oisin said,

"What happened after that? Next thing I woke up, I'm here. In Brisbane. Is Hilda alright?" He suddenly remembered Hilda.

"You owe your life to Hilda, mate. Don't know how she did it but she got back to the phone and then somehow drove up to the gates and unlocked those bloody padlocks and waited there for me and the rest is history. I got hold of the ambulance and they got you and Hilda out of there. She was in shock but she's OK. She's in the Kilgoolga Hospital."

The sergeant paused.

"I should have known, mate. If I'd thought about it, I'd have taken the guns away from Hans. I should have checked on him. Why the hell didn't I?"

"It was no one's fault, Sergeant. He just got worse the last month. If there's anyone to blame, it's us. Hilda and I should have let you know but we didn't think it was that serious. No one ever thinks these things till it's too late," said Oisin, sadly.

"He's right, Serge. You did your best."

The constable smiled reassuringly.

"What happened after that?" she asked the sergeant.

He brightened up a bit and after a moment or two he said to Oisin,

"Well, I can't remember all the finer details but you and Hilda were in quite a mess, Oisin. But you were a different matter altogether, mate. We had to get you to Brissie."

Oisin heard Hilda's scream in his head again and her face at the door. He wondered how anyone could ever get over that. It was painful having to talk about it but he knew the police were only doing their job. It must have been hard on the young sergeant too. He would never have seen anything like that before. Oisin wondered how he was managing to cope.

378

"How is Hilda now, though? Hans was her brother after all. They'd lived together all their lives, hadn't they?"

"Yeah. Funny arrangement. Hilda's a battler, mate. She'll be fine. Has a message I'm to give to you."

"To me?"

"Yeah. Tell Oisin that 'he's got a job if he wants it, at Wiesental'. Don't know whether you'd want to see that bloody place again though mate, after all you've gone through!"

Oisin thought of Hilda and her kindness to him. She was a funny wee woman sometimes but her heart was in the right place. It must have been hell for her, living with a brother like Hans and everyone in the district, wondering.

"I'd like to see Hilda again. You're right, she's a battler." He remembered her belting the brown snake to death with her shovel. *Aye, Hilda would survive*, he thought.

"There's just one thing that puzzles me, mate about the whole bloody mess," said the sergeant. He was serious.

"What?"

"You know that Hans Seefeldt kept Wiesental bolted down like Fort Knox. No one could get in. Those two iron gates at the top with the padlocks? That was the only way into the homestead. Now, Eleanor Bradshaw, to my knowledge had no way of getting into Wiesental station. When I got there, it was Hilda who had unlocked the gates for me so Eleanor must have locked them after her, right? So how did she get in? Her Citroën was at the homestead but the gates were locked. How did she get keys to the place?"

Oisin reddened slightly although the two police officers wouldn't have noticed because of the bandages. He had an awful moment of indecision. If he told the sergeant, would that make him culpable? Then if he kept quiet about it, would that mean he didn't disclose the whole story and thus he could be guilty of something? The sergeant was friendly enough but he was still a cop. He hesitated.

379

"She asked me to get a set made for her, Sergeant," he said. "I had no idea what would happen. I'm sorry."

"Thought it must have been something like that, Oisin. Don't worry, mate. We all knew about Eleanor Bradshaw. When she made up her mind about something, there was no stopping her. She always got what she wanted. You weren't to know."

He got up to leave. The policewoman slid off the side of the bed and asked Oisin to read and sign what she had written. That was the end of the matter as far as the police were concerned.

"Before we go, mate, do you want to see a photo of my little girl?"

The sergeant opened his wallet and handed Oisin a photo of his daughter. She had bright eyes and curly hair. She must have been about two years of age. The policewoman peered over Oisin's shoulder to get a better view.

"Oh, Serge," she cooed. "She's lovely. Not a bit like you!"

"She'd better be!" said the sergeant, good naturedly. Then he laughed. "I mean, she's lovely, you're right. She's all mine too. That's what it's all about, isn't it, Oisin? Life." He paused. "Hans was a poor old bugger, you know. Just think how different it might have been for him if he'd only had someone to love."

"You're getting soppy again, Serge. Come on, and let this man have some rest. Thought I could drive to the station and you could walk back. You need to run those old feet of yours in a bit more on our footpaths! It's the tried and tested cure for you country blokes!"

"That's enough out of you, young Constable! What was I saying to you about a transfer to Kilgoolga?"

They were still laughing as they left the ward.

They moved Oisin to another ward and it was better there. They gave him a crutch and he started to walk. The few paces became more paces and then more until he could walk up and down the ward. Steps were the next challenge.

"I can walk! Look, I can walk!" he said to Doctor O'Neill when she came along on her rounds. He felt he had turned a corner.

"Told you so!"

He still had the bandages over his left eye.

"Give it time," the doctor said. "We'll get it sorted."

He began to believe that she might just be right. His spirits lifted just a little bit more every day.

Frankie called in to see him nearly every afternoon. He came alone without Claire. She was back at the Kilgoolga High School teaching. Oisin wanted to ask his brother about Claire but he feared the answer. It was better not to know, he reasoned. He couldn't bear the thought that he might have lost Claire to Frankie. It was better not to ask. Frankie was cheerful and they talked.

"Ye don't call me 'Frog' anymore," Oisin said to his brother one day.

"That's because ye don't look like a frog anymore," Frankie replied. "Ye are nearly as handsome as me these days!"

"Smart arse!"

And they laughed then. He couldn't remember when he had last laughed with his brother.

"Ye were always so good at everything ye did," Oisin said to Frankie the next day.

"Some things," Frankie answered and he looked thoughtful, even sad. "Other things, well... "

"What things?"

"I wasn't much of a priest, Oisin. Guess I wasn't much of a brother to ye either."

"Same could be said for me."

"Ye are cleverer than me."

"How come? I couldn't pass exams... not like ye!"

"There's more to life than exams, Oisin. I stand by what I said, ye are cleverer than me... and braver!"

"Don't see how?"

"Just believe it."

They talked of home, of Ballybeg and Oisin asked about their mother.

"She's frail now," Frankie replied. "But still fighting the good fight as always. She misses ye."

"Aye."

"Been tough on her since Da passed away."

"She had Mick."

He hadn't meant to say it. That was a secret only known to him and no one else knew anything about it.

"That she did, Oisin. That she did."

And Frankie looked directly into Oisin's one eye and then Oisin knew. Frankie had known all along that their mother loved Mick, her husband's brother. They didn't say another word about it but it was out in the open at last. Oisin was free of it. His big brother knew. It suddenly felt good.

"It's good to talk to ye," he said then.

"Aye, that it is! Who would have thought it?"

"I was just yer kid brother before. A bit of a nuisance!"

"I'm not denyin' that!" and Frankie laughed.

Then they talked of what he should do next when he got out of the hospital. Frankie asked if he wanted to go home, to Ireland.

"I don't know," was all Oisin could think to say.

"Well, I'll be headin' that way soon," replied Frankie. "Think about it?"

Then Oisin wondered if Frankie would be taking Claire back with him and the thought of them together troubled him but he didn't say a word. He didn't want to know anything about Claire and Frankie being together, not now that Frankie and he were becoming friends at long last and for the very first time. But he thought of Claire a lot. More than he could ever have imagined possible.

"I'll think about it," he said to Frankie. "About comin' home, that is. When I'm out of here and a bit better. I haven't seen much of the country. Might be good to see a bit more than two cities and a lot of land in between."

"Sure, there's a lot of country! Well, think about it... "

Then one day they talked of Eleanor Bradshaw. She was someone who wouldn't go away.

"What should I have done, Frankie? When I saw Eleanor tied up, that is!"

"Don't think there's an answer there. Sometimes we just do what we have to do and then figure it out later. Ye did what ye had to do, it seems to me. It was a brave thing to do."

"I wish I could have saved her."

"She knew what she was doing. Knew all the time. Don't dwell on it, Oisin. Some things we don't know the answers to. Guess that's one of them."

"I thought she knew everything! She made everyone think she did!"

"Well, that's something you've learned now, isn't it? None of us know it all, even Eleanor Bradshaw was mortal. Though she certainly was interesting, that's for sure!"

"I can't argue with that," said Oisin. He suddenly felt relieved. Relieved it was all over at last.

"Claire tells me Eleanor has a son," continued Frankie. "Arrived out of the blue from England. A posh boy. Did ye know about him?"

Eleanor having a son was a surprise. He really knew nothing about her. She had never mentioned anything about her personal life. She had only ever talked about everyone else's life. Her own life was somehow above others. At least, that's the impression she liked to give.

"No. I didn't know that."

Frankie grinned.

"Kilgoolga folk think the posh boy's just there for his mother's money. 'Typical Pom', that's the words they use. They're probably right. It's been my experience that a lot of relatives turn up for the funeral and what they can get after it. One of the deadly sins, ye know. Anyhow, not our problem, is it? The Kellys never had any! Money doesn't mean much to mc anyhow. Yc can only usc it for so much. Only sleep in one bed and wear one set of clothes, isn't that right? The poverty vow was the easiest one of the lot for me to keep."And Frankie laughed.

"Think ye have a point there, Frankie. It's all a bit crazy, isn't it? Eleanor was obsessed with property too. Don't know why. That part of her life never made much sense to me. There's an old lad out there, in Kilgoolga, called Charlie George. Think ye may have met him? Anyhow, Charlie has hardly a penny to his name but the cheeriest man around. Been thinkin' of Charlie lately. I like him."

"Ye seem to have made a lot of friends in Kilgoolga, Oisin. From what I gather, ye have quite a fan club out there. Does that surprise ye?"

"Ye are jokin'! Didn't think I'd made much of an impression. I thought that everyone just thought I was some sort of Irish drifter an' I wouldn't be around long. Then they'd all be able to get back to their own lives."

"Another thing ye are wrong about then, isn't it, brother?"

Frankie got up to leave.

"Oh, nearly forgot," he said, "Claire's brother Harry is going to visit ye. He's been posted to Northern Command here in Brisbane... "

"Ye seem to be seein' a lot of Claire these days... "

384

There, he'd said it. Claire's name was out in the open. If there was anything going on between Claire and Frankie at least he might find out. Just being able to say her name to Frankie was a start.

Frankie grinned.

"Aye. She's a grand lass. One of the best."

The day Doctor O'Neill and the eye surgeon took the bandages off Oisin's left eye was to be a day he would never forget because that was the day that his life changed forever. He began to heal. Walking became easier and once the bandages were removed from his left side, the walking became easier even though he still had the plaster on his left shoulder. Apart from the colourful black and blue bruises along his side, he was otherwise unhurt. The bruises would heal. The memories of that day would take longer. Sometimes he woke in the night and it all came back to him and he saw Eleanor's face once again.

So the day the doctors came to take the bandages from Oisin's left eye was for him anticipation mixed with a horrible feeling of dread. He had accepted the loss of hearing in his left ear with a brave philosophical shrug of the shoulders but his eyesight was something else entirely. His Uncle Mick had worn a black eyepatch over his eye all Oisin's life. Mick had lost his sight after a pub brawl. It looked like history was repeating itself again and in some cruel fashion, too. The irony of it all disturbed him. He had seen nothing but black behind his left eye and it had become almost normal for him. If, when the bandages were gone, it was still black, he wondered whether he had the strength or

385

the courage to go on. *Sometimes*, he thought, *if I could only just shut both my eyes, it would be all over.*

Doctor O'Neill would have none of this talk. They drew the curtains around his bed and slowly and carefully, the bandages were taken away.

"See if you can open your eye now, Oisin. Just a little bit."

It felt strange without the bandages. Part of him wanted to open the eye; the other part hesitated for the fear went through him. His left eye was suddenly not part of his body. It was an alien thing. He felt he was looking down on himself from above.

"Take it easy and when you are ready, just open that eye of yours." Doctor O'Neill encouraged him and she hoped with every hope that she had within her, that when this young Irishman opened his eye, he could see for she had become fond of Oisin and all the medical team had done their very best.

"It's still black," he said.

"You haven't opened your eye yet, not properly. Of course, it's still black."

Then Oisin's mind told his eye to open. He gripped the sides of the chair harder with both hands as if that action would make it happen and it would be alright. Then he slowly, cautiously and without feeling any pain at all, opened his left eye. And the first person he saw with both eyes was the kind face of Doctor O'Neill.

"I can see! I can see! It's fuzzy but I can see you out of my left eye, Doctor... I can see!"

Then Doctor O'Neill and the eye surgeon examined his eye and the eye surgeon said, 'Well done, young man, your eye is saved' but Oisin knew that a miracle had happened in his life and it was the doctors and nurses who had performed that miracle and they were the ones who should be thanked. He could see and he could see them out of both his eyes.

386

"Thank you everyone," he whispered.

"I told you you'd make it, didn't I? Just rest now. I'll be round later and you can see me properly then!"

And Doctor O'Neill gave him another of her devilish winks but she looked pleased.

And on that same day, he received a visitor. He had expected it to be Frankie for his brother arrived every afternoon without fail. This visitor came alone and he was able to see her with both his eyes. She brought grapes and a bottle of the fizzy lemonade that he liked and placed them both on the table beside his bed. Then she brought a chair and positioned the chair on the right side of his bed. Her blue tee shirt was tight and it showed off her figure and when she sat beside him, he caught a whiff of her perfume. It was intoxicating for him.

"Claire?"

He had expected that when she came to see him next, Frankie would be with her.

"Where's Frankie?"

She smiled then.

"At the duty free," she said.

"Duty free?"

"Yes. He's booked his flight home to Ireland. Didn't he tell you?"

"No."

Frankie's leaving was a surprise. He had thought that his brother would have told him. He decided that it was best not to say anything more about Frankie. He thought it would be easier that way so he asked about Kilgoolga and what had been happening.

"Hilda's still in the hospital," Claire told him. "She asked about you. She wants to know whether you're coming back."

He frowned. It wasn't something he wanted to talk about.

"Who is lookin' after the animals then... at Wiesental?"

He remembered the calf that he had rescued that morning before the horror of the rest of the day and then the three goats that Hilda loved.

"Tony and Geoff have been great. I know, they're my brothers but all credit to them! Everyone's helping. The boys took the goats to Kinleven and the dogs too. The chooks are OK. Someone looks in every day. Now that the top gate is open, it's easy."

Claire hesitated a few seconds and then continued,

"Kilgoolga folk look after their own, you know, Oisin. Everyone likes Hilda. Everyone wants to help, even Joseph Bradshaw. He's not so bad."

"I know. Will Hilda be OK though? Must have been dreadful for her."

"She'll be fine, Oisin. Hilda won't give up."

"No."

Hilda wouldn't give up. She would manage. Somehow. The bush bred them tough. Hilda was one of the tough ones.

Claire poured a glass of the fizzy lemonade and handed it to him, without asking. He sipped the sweet liquid. It was cool and refreshing.

"They've been buried, you know," Claire said. "Eleanor and Hans."

"Where?"

"In the Kilgoolga Cemetery. Hundreds turned up for Eleanor's. The shops shut for the day. They had the wake at the Commercial. It was heaving."

"She would have liked that." Oisin smiled, remembering.

"Yes. I know you liked her."

"It was a strange thing. But yes, I did, like her, that is. She was different."

"Well, she's at peace now, Oisin. Time to let it go."

They were both silent. Then Oisin said,

"What happened to Hans?"

"He's at rest, too Oisin, same as Eleanor, I guess. They're in the cemetery but not together. The Lutherans did it all. Just a few people turned up for the funeral but I didn't go. Think Kilgoolga just wants to put an end to it now and we can get on with our lives again."

Oisin thought of Hans then. Hans had always been lonely. He was one of the many lonely people who don't know how to cope with the existential aloneness of life. It was all very sad.

Claire frowned slightly.

"No one wants to talk about it. Everyone thinks you're a hero though."

"Me?"

"Yes, you."

He noticed that she seemed different somehow. Not so prim. He wondered if it had something to do with Frankie.

One of the young nurses came over to the bed. She had a blood pressure monitor in her hand.

"Time for your check up," she said to Oisin and to Claire, "Do you mind?"

Claire moved away and the nurse drew the curtains around the bed. When the nurse had finished, she said to Oisin,

"Your girlfriend can come in now."

"She's not my girlfriend."

The nurse looked surprised.

"Oh," she said. "Thought she was..."

When Claire came back they didn't speak to each other. There was an uneasy feeling between them now.

"Glad to see you have the bandages off your eye. You look a lot better."

"I can see out of both eyes now. Aye, I feel better."

"Has Harry been in to see you?" she asked. She wasn't sure what else to say.

"No. How's he gettin' on?"

She looked cross.

"I asked him to look in and see you. He can be so annoying sometimes although Dad might have been right about the Army. Harry seems to be getting on OK. Still hate the thought of it, you know but things might be changing. Public opinion is more against the war now. People want our boys home. There's an election coming up, if Whitlam gets in, he'll bring them home and end conscription too and then there won't be any chance of Harry going to Vietnam. I'm still marching," she said.

"Aye. Think I would be joinin' ye... if I could." He smiled. It might have been good to have a cause and carry a banner. He wished he had her convictions against the war. But then if Claire had Frankie, she wouldn't be bothered with him. Frankie might march. She wouldn't need him.

His body was healing but he felt sad. He wanted to ask her about Frankie. The thought of Claire and Frankie made him feel miserable. He had to know. At least he'd be able to see her face with both his eyes now.

"Are ye and Frankie... well, ye know?" he asked in his clumsy attempt to get to the truth.

"What do you mean?"

"Ye know! Are ye and Frankie together, sort of thing... ?"

He hadn't expected her to react the way she did. She frowned.

"Frankie and me? Oh, really! I thought you said you were clever when we first met?"

"Well?"

"Do you really want to know why Frankie came to Australia?"

"To see me."

"Well, that to, I suppose but didn't he tell you?"

390

"Tell me what?"

"Frankie's got himself involved with a married woman. Back in Dublin. She teaches at the same school. He's been trying to get over her. That's why he came out here. He took a year off."

"I don't believe ye."

How could this be? Frankie's life was perfect. Always had been. The thought of Frankie in love with a married woman just didn't seem right somehow. Not Frankie but then there was a lot of things that had happened lately that he wouldn't have expected. Maybe Frankie was just another one of those things.

"Well, it's true. He thought he'd get over her if he went away but it hasn't worked. He's going back to ask her to marry him," continued Claire. She sounded a bit like a teacher lecturing one of her pupils.

"What? Ye can't get a divorce in Ireland."

Claire shrugged.

"Oh well," she said. "Live with her then. He loves her."

"There's another thing," she said after a minute or two. "We've got a few things in common, Frankie and me."

"What?"

"Well, we both have difficult siblings. I've got Harry and Frankie's got you."

Claire's brown eyes twinkled. Then she was serious.

"I thought of you in Sydney," she said. "In Hyde Park. When I came back to Kilgoolga, I still thought of you but you were always with Eleanor Bradshaw."

"I know," he said. "Eleanor took over somehow."

"Everyone in Kilgoolga knew that about her. You couldn't help it."

He didn't answer. He didn't want to talk about Eleanor Bradshaw. He wanted to know about Claire and Frankie. He had thought of her a lot too but then Frankie had come between them. Suddenly he remembered Louis.

"What's happened to Louis Bercault?" he asked to change the subject and he remembered what it had been like to see Eleanor and Louis together. It had always seemed an unlikely arrangement but then, you never know.

Claire shrugged.

"That's a surprise too. Louis's got the shop on the market. He's leaving. The women will miss him!"

"Will ye?"

"Don't be daft!"

They looked at each other and laughed. It was getting easier between them.

"Are you going back to Ireland? Frankie thinks you will," she asked him then.

Oisin thought of Ireland. For a brief moment he was back in Ballybeg and he could almost smell the rain. He looked at Claire. She was trying to be prim. Trying so very, very hard to be prim. It's just that it wasn't working and he saw that a tiny tear had rolled down her cheek. It rolled down her cheek and landed on the top of his hand. It was a tiny droplet amongst the black hairs on his hand. It felt wet and warm. Then he took Claire's small hand in his and with the index finger of his right hand, he wiped another tear that had threatened to roll down her cheek to join the other one. He squeezed her hand ever so gently and then he placed the palm of his hand onto her the side of her face where the tears were.

"Now, what do ye think?"

Her cheek felt wet and warm against his hand.

"Well, now," he murmured. "Don't ye think I've all I want in Kilgoolga... that's if... ye'll have me, that is?"

Now he could feel tears welling up behind his eyes too. He felt the slight nod of her head against his hand and he smiled. It felt as if he had come home.

"Well now," he said, "Isn't that just the grandest thing?"

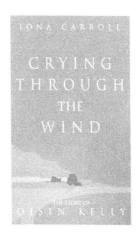

When Bernard Kelly brought Annie Smith home to the West of Ireland there was much speculation followed by a good deal of discussion in the small community of Ballybeg in which he lived. For it seemed to all that Bernard, aged thirty-two was set for a life of bachelorhood, destined to live out his days with his elder brother, Mick.

This is the tale of Oisin Kelly, beginning with his mother, Annie as she struggles to come to terms with her love for two brothers in a small West of Ireland community in the 1950's. Married to Bernard, she is attracted to his brother, the mysterious and much misunderstood Mick. Annie's strong Catholic faith engenders a deep sense of guilt, at the same time it helps her to cope.

The story moves forwards, sometimes gently, sometimes turbulently all the time combining pathos with humour. Although *Crying Through the Wind* is very much Annie's book, the stage is set for Oisin who has a quest of his own.
ISBN: 978-1-909411-30-2

Some other titles from Mauve Square Publishing:

For children:
THE SHADOW OF THE TWO PRINCES by Wendy Leighton-Porter

For Young Adults:
GOLDEN JAGUAR OF THE SUN by Oliver Eade

For Adults:
BOMBER BOYS by Simon Leighton-Porter

Lightning Source UK Ltd.
Milton Keynes UK
UKOW06f1227211015

261090UK00010B/134/P